MW00397215

The Empirion Project

The Enpirion Project

Book 1:
Exordium

L. Bossi

This book is dedicated to my parents and my soulsister.
My three eternal champions in a very difficult world.

Contents

Part 2

Part 3

Part One

A New Life Begins

There's very little that I can recall from the time after I was rescued, other than darkness. I'm unsure if I was even awake or coherent for much of it...or if my mind had simply performed a small kindness by removing it from my waking thoughts. I do remember Nephael though. Not so much him, I should say, but his eyes. Piercing blue, nearly as rare as my green. But it wasn't the color even that I recall, but the kindness I saw in them. I met that gaze briefly when I was rescued; bound, bleeding, dying. And I recall it from my time in medical isolation. Kindness was never something I had been shown, empathy unheard of. I was simply Enpirion, an aberration even among a group of created monstrosities in the ENForcer division, treated with contempt and disdain while at the same time feared and avoided. But those eyes were different. They surely knew what I was and yet there was nothing in them but compassion.

His voice is the other memory that lingers from that time, for the same reason really.

"Stay with me," was what he whispered to me when I was found. Stay with me. Three simple words that, from anyone else, probably wouldn't have meant overly much. But when he said them, there was genuine concern and grief, for someone he didn't even know. Stay with me. Don't die.

I was poorly treated in the capital's medical unit. But that wasn't so surprising...I was never treated well or given much attention by that group. I had been there too often, caused too many problems, probably been too surly with the staff. I couldn't make out the words, only a garbled cacophony of anger through the glass as he arrived and rebuked the healers in charge of me. I was transferred not long after that to a different unit with a different group of healers. In a completely different outpost, though I wouldn't find that out for some time and I had no memory of being transferred. I'm still quite sure that, had it not been for his intervention, I would not have survived the initial days and weeks after my rescue.

Months later, I returned to a world that was both the same and yet ultimately unfamiliar. The ENF unit was the same in name only. Now under Nephael's control, it was no longer a group of individual, specially trained weapons, but a cohesive unit of newly trained, elite soldiers, in uniform, no longer located at the capital, but at the Belanistra Watch. And yet, despite a chance to start over, for me personally, nothing had changed. If anything, things seemed to be worse. Not only had I completely lost my confidence, far scarier were the huge gaps in my memory, extending back long before my capture and subsequent torture, especially concerning my early years. I was now one of three original ENF soldiers remaining and my reputation had not only followed me, but seemed to have been enhanced through speculation and hearsay. I was still feared and avoided. Friendless and alone.

"Mind if I join you?"

I jumped slightly, startled at the presence that had so skillfully snuck up on me. Annoyance at myself quickly seeping in because there had probably been zero skill involved in that artful appearance. I'd been sitting in The Watch's main hall, curled up on a plush chair, vaguely staring at some spot in the middle of nowhere beyond the grand, curved glass wall, the book in my lap forgotten. Probably feeling sorry for myself. I wasn't even sure how I'd started out the day. That was normally where things started lately. Me wallowing in depression and self pity, migrating to my favorite chair and losing myself to some ill-defined point on the horizon. Despite my reinstatement with the ENForcer division, I was still out of commission when it came to actually doing anything. My superiors didn't trust my mental stability, not after what had happened, especially in combination with my background history. So I was free to spend my days alone with my own thoughts, confined to The Watch. But that wasn't the cause of my current mental state. I couldn't really put my current problem into words, the cause of the listlessness, the depression that drove me to this chair day after day.

Nephael simply stared at me, a slight smile pulling at the corner of his mouth as I vacantly stared right back at him, trying to process what he had just asked me. I guess he assumed he wasn't going to get a response (he probably wasn't; he rarely did) because he pulled up a chair across from me and sprawled across it, instantly comfortable despite my obviously uncomfortable air. He studied me for what seemed like an eternity. Those blue eyes had a way of looking at you like they could see inside, turn out all your secrets, but without actually being intrusive. Which I suppose doesn't really make any sense, but that's just how it was with him.

"Where do you go when you stare out that window?" He asked it quietly, that half smile still pulling at his lips. From anyone else it would seem like mockery. How many times had he asked me this in the past few weeks and never received an answer? It was like this was some sort of game we were playing. Except that I didn't understand the rules or the purpose. For some reason today, I actually opened my mouth to respond before hesitating and stopping myself. The half smile quirked up slightly further, but he didn't say anything, merely made himself more comfortable. He adjusted his glasses, propped his feet upon the small etched glass table separating us and pulled a small book out of his officer's jacket. I went back to staring out the window.

This happened more days than not. Same routine. Nephael would try to talk to me, I'd never respond, he would sit there and read. I think with anyone else this would have annoyed me, but for some reason, with him, it had become a part of my day. I don't think I was any more comfortable now than when this had started, yet, deep down, I also felt like I'd miss it if it ended. It was as close as I ever came to trust or friendship and it was kind of nice to have someone around who didn't seem to mind my presence. Even if I couldn't figure out why he was doing it. At first I thought it must have been some sort of order from his superiors, but I threw that out pretty quickly. It didn't make sense. For one thing, none of the higher ups cared enough about my well-being to even take notice of how I was acting or feeling. For another, what purpose would it serve, having my commanding officer befriend me. And I could only assume that was what he was trying to do. He was wasting an awful lot of time with the attempt. I wasn't worth befriending.

I must have audibly sighed because I caught Nephael's change of expression in my peripheral vision. His eyes shifted from the book, an eyebrow slid up. The smile was gone though.

"You ok?"

I raised my head from my arms and stared at him, blinking. I must have looked profoundly stupid to anyone observing the situation.

"I...what?" I finally managed to incoherently stutter. It was a simple question, but that might have been the first time I'd ever been asked it. It also might have been the first time that Nephael had really said anything, outside of his opening questions, during our daily...whatever these were.

"Are you ok?" He repeated, leaning forward slightly in the chair, the book suddenly forgotten on his knee. I narrowed my eyes and pressed myself farther back into the chair, trying to assess the question, the motive. Why was he asking, why did he care? There seemed to be nothing but genuine concern in his eyes. That same look. From before. "Something seems different today," he continued, his voice dropping to a murmur.

I couldn't deny that I desperately wanted someone to talk to. Someone whose shoulder I could break down on, sob out everything that had happened. But I had never had that, never would. Trust led to betrayal and pain. Friendship was something other people had. My walls were cracked enough without someone else adding to it. I unfolded myself from the chair and stood up, intending to leave before this went any further. Nephael's hand snaked out and caught my wrist, not tightly, just enough to stop me in my tracks. He released me just as quickly, possibly from the look of horror that crossed my face at being grabbed.

"I'm sorry, Piri," he said quietly. "Please don't leave. I didn't mean to upset you." Piri. Only he called me that. It was a nickname I had apparently acquired when I woke up in the healing unit. I didn't know why I had never set him straight.

And then it actually hit me what he had said. And he'd meant it. It shouldn't have had the effect on me that it did. Maybe it was just one of those days where the cracks were a little bigger, the walls a little thinner than usual, but it struck a nerve and I couldn't help the single tear that managed to get past. I quickly scrubbed the back of my hand across my face, angry at myself for letting any of what I'd bottled up inside show. It felt like people were starting to stare and I could see one or two of the other ENForcers, looking smart and together in their new uniforms, watching me from across the room. I needed to get out of there. I began looking around for an escape, panic starting to creep in, clouding any rationality that should have existed. Nephael stood; calmly, placidly, still watching me. How did he always manage to seem so tranquil, even when he was worried? Internal calm was not something I normally experienced or understood.

"Let's go somewhere more private, get away from the crowds," he suggested, gesturing for me to follow as he headed off in the general direction of his office. He didn't even look back, just assumed I was following. And I did; I couldn't explain why.

I quickened my steps, hurried to catch up, arms wrapped around myself, struggling to hold it together. It wasn't a long journey and, thankfully, no one bothered us on the way. I'd been to his office once or twice, but always grudgingly and I'd never properly looked at it as I'd spent most of my time planning ways to leave. Now, in an effort to concentrate on anything but myself, I started to look around. It was quite a bit cozier than I'd expected, especially compared to the sterile atmosphere of my previous officer. Besides the expected wooden desk and filing cabinets, there was a kitchenette, a plush couch, bookshelves. A colorful area rug with fringed edges took up the floor space directly in front of the couch. It looked like one of the woven rugs from Bridgeport. Plants were scattered about in colorful pots. Framed artwork dotted the walls; landscapes done in watercolor, a charcoal of The Morring Marketplace in Bridgeport. An artist myself, I couldn't help lingering slightly longer on these. The outward facing wall was solid glass, as only our Seri artisans can craft it, giving view to the spectacular panorama of the outside valley and the Kaerthwyst Mountains surrounding it, which The Watch was built into. I stared, once again simply lost in the horizon.

I must have stood there for several minutes observing in silence, Nephael not saying a word, simply watching me. And then, "Make yourself comfortable," he said, pulling up a chair to sit across from me as I slowly lowered myself onto the couch. The brief moment of peace, of escape from myself, had passed and I could feel everything pressing down once more, threatening to overwhelm me.

"Talk to me, Piri," he said gently. "I'm - concerned. I'm not asking because I have to or I've been told to. This has nothing to do with being your officer. I'm genuinely concerned and I want to help, if I can. Like I said before, something just seems more off than usual today. So please, tell me what's wrong."

Those eyes were staring at me again, boring into me. A wall cracked. And I couldn't stop it. I buried my face in my hands and began to talk, garbled words between wracking sobs, everything spilling out from the capture to the imprisonment, the torture, the deaths of my fellow ENForcers, recovery and awakening in this new place. Alone. Always alone. I don't know how long I went on. I don't know when it ended. I only remember, through it all, being mortified and angry with myself, furious for opening myself up to a stranger, desperately trying to resurrect the internal wall, but it was too late at that point. To his credit, Nephael didn't say anything or press me. He just let me get it out of my system, listening intently. I think he actually brought me a cup of mint tea at one point. And I must have finally cried myself into oblivion because the next thing I knew, I was waking up on the couch, covered with a blanket. Evening sunlight was streaming in through the window.

I slowly pushed myself up to a sitting position, cradling my head in my hands. It ached horribly. My entire face was puffy and sore. I was thinking that maybe I could slip out unnoticed, while Nephael's back was to me in the kitchen, save myself at least a bit of what remained of my pride, when he turned and came back into the main area. He knelt down in front of me, smiling, a new cup of tea throwing off steam in his left hand.

"Feeling any better? Anything I can get you?"

I could only mutely shake my head. He pursed his lips slightly.

"Hmm, well. Here, take this." He pushed a warm, damp cloth into my hand. I did my best not to react as he brushed my fingers in the transfer, despite the shiver it sent up my spine.

"What is this?" I asked.

"Exactly what it looks like," Nephael said with a smile, pushing the tea into my other hand. "A damp cloth. I thought you might want to wipe your face."

I actually felt my face grow hot and hoped to the gods above that I hadn't gone red to match it. I looked down at the tea, glaring into its yellowy-green surface. The burning shame I was feeling only intensified as the silence dragged out. I finally looked up and met Nephael's eyes. He was watching me, calmly, that smile still on his face, though it looked a little sad.

"Why are you doing this?" I whispered, my voice cracking slightly with the strain of trying to remain in control.

The smile quickly turned into a frown as he leaned backwards, dropping himself to the ground, arms around his knees. "I didn't realize I needed a reason to be your friend." He folded his legs under and rested his chin on his hand in thought, never out of eye contact. "Do you need me to come up with a reason? I can if you need me to."

I did need a reason. Trust wasn't something I came by easily, if at all. In my experience, there was always a motive to people interacting with me. No one did anything for me out the kindness of their heart. My silence apparently spoke volumes because Nephael levered himself up onto the couch beside me, arms resting on his long legs as he stared out the window. My skin began to crawl at his proximity.

"I'm not good at putting these sorts of things into words, but I can try." He paused in thought, brows knitting together. "I can only try to imagine what circumstance has done to you. But I do know you're hurt and alone. My heart breaks every time I see you sitting in that chair. No one should have to live in isolation, afraid of the world around them. I just - wanted to talk to you, understand you. Try to show you that not everyone is out to get you.

"I spent months watching over you, after your...extraction. I'd be lying if I said I wasn't feeling a little over-protective. I wanted to know the person I'd helped to save. And when you woke up… You're interesting, intelligent, skilled. I don't have many friends and I'm sorely picky about the ones that I do; I choose them carefully. And, well, I wanted - want - to be yours."

He stopped, continued to stare out the window. I was actually touched. No one had ever said anything even remotely like that to me before.

"…Thanks, I guess," I barely managed to get out. He turned to look at me.

"I know that you can't just drop a hundred plus years of distrust. I know that it's not that easy. But you must get tired of the constant internal battle, of always fighting."

The sadness had crept back into his voice and I looked away, nodding almost imperceptibly. He had no idea how tired I was, exhausted. But could I really take the risk? He seemed so - authentic, so different from anyone else I'd ever known. He'd spent weeks trying to approach me, which I still didn't understand. I was still searching for a motive and coming up empty. I had hit rock bottom; there was nothing anyone could possibly want from me. Maybe what he said was true, maybe not. But I did realize that I couldn't continue like this. I took a sip of the tea. Mint again. How had he figured out that was what I normally drank?

Halfway through the cup, I sat it down and stood up. He looked up at me expectantly as I stood there, rather awkwardly. It was an odd feeling; I almost didn't want to leave, but I also wanted to be alone, to think. "I - I need to go," I finally said.

"If you feel you need to," he said. "But please don't push me away. Let me help you, even if it's something as simple as you talking."

I looked away. "I don't like talking about my problems. My life is private. I like to keep it that way."

He nodded. "I understand. But you know I'm here if you change your mind," he said quietly.

"…Thanks. I'll - think about that."

"I'll take that," he said, smile returning, as I let myself out of his office.

The door to my quarters slid silently back into the wall as I removed my hand from the Sourcepad. Moving moodily inside, I stared around at the barren living area. Other than a few scant possessions, it looked the same now as when I'd first been given it. It wasn't home, just a place where I slept and sometimes not even that. It was just a place I could hole up in without being bothered.

I moved to the bathroom, splashed water on my face and stared at myself in the mirror. I ran a hand through my hair as I summoned my wings, something I hadn't really done since I'd been here at The Watch. I was still slightly uncomfortable in my own skin since my capture.

I heaved a sigh as I looked at my reflection. Nothing about me was normal compared to the rest of the Seri. Green eyes, reddish hair. Several inches shorter than, well, everyone. The ruffled feathers of my wings looked blindingly white even with the lights off. It was bad enough that I had the reputation I did without standing out physically as well. At one point I had come to terms with that, but it seemed like all the old sore spots had come crawling back to the surface, making me feel more isolated than ever.

I turned away in disgust, letting go of the Source. My wings vanished, the energy dissolving, leaving only a faint blueish afterimage. The ragged scar running down my left shoulder blade, the only physical remnant of what had happened months before, twinged slightly and I winced. Another lasting reminder that I didn't want. I paused in the doorway and glanced back at the mirror one more time, trying to see whatever it was that Nephael saw. Try as I might, I couldn't.

I fell backwards onto the bed, staring up at the ceiling in annoyance. A storm was raging inside me after my encounter in his office, conflicting emotions surging against one another. I couldn't help smiling slightly in amusement. He'd managed to get under my skin and, for the first time since I'd awoken here at The Watch, I was feeling something other than listless and despondent.

Rolling over, I fished a sketchpad off the nightstand and flipped it open, staring at the blank page for a moment. The book was empty, untouched since I'd been here. I shook my head slightly, grabbed a pencil. It wasn't long before I had a rough drawing of his face etched out on the page. I stared at it, trying to figure out what sort of strange black magic he'd worked on me today. Eventually, I tossed the sketch aside and curled up, closing my eyes. I still wasn't sure about Nephael, but I'd decided that, at the very least, I wouldn't actively push him away. What did I have to lose at this point.

A Touch of Freedom

"Go away."

I buried my face farther into my arms, hugging my knees to my chest. The sound of the boots shifted slightly on the marble, but didn't leave. I didn't know who it was and I really didn't care. How many weeks had it been, the same routine, trapped in this place? I'd briefly had some hope after my breakdown that maybe something, anything, would change, but nothing had. I still spent day after day, confined to The Watch, gazing miserably at the outside world from the chair I had laid claim to in the Grand Hall while Nephael, I don't know, kept me company. I guess that's what you would call it. To be fair, we didn't sit there in pure silence anymore. Some days, yes. Others we talked. Since that day in his office, I'd kept clear of anything personal, but we'd somehow found common ground on any number of other topics to chat about. Today, though, I couldn't take being inside and I'd wandered off, not exploring, just meandering with no set destination in mind, looking for some new place where I could avoid the world. I just wanted to be left alone in the isolated spot I had chosen to curl up in.

My visitor thumped down beside me, choosing to ignore my words.

"You've picked a beautiful spot to be depressed."

Nephael. Of course it was. No one else would go out of their way concerning me. And he certainly had gone out of his way to find me, sequestered as I was on an outside ledge, off one of the lesser-used walking trails. A stone plinth against my back rose up into a towering winged statue. The ledge, which dropped off into the mountain face, looked out over the front valley of The Watch, surrounded by the great peaks of the range, outlined brilliantly against a crystal blue sky.

I sighed and lifted my head, scrubbing a hand across my face, trying to erase the tear streaks. Nephael wasn't paying me the least bit of attention. He had one leg pulled to his chest, the other slung over the ledge, gazing out into the distance. I suddenly wished I'd thought to bring my sketchpad with me.

"Bad day," he finally said. It wasn't a question. He tilted his head slightly, eyeing me. "I got a little worried when you broke routine, weren't in your normal spot."

I scowled, suddenly annoyed. "Sorry, I didn't realize I had a schedule to adhere to," I spat out, a little more venomously than intended.

Totally unfazed, he just shook his head. "I didn't mean it like that. I was just concerned that something had happened. I wanted to make sure you were ok. And, to be honest, I was disappointed you weren't there because I'm not having a great day either. Misery loves company, after all."

I dropped my legs over the side and leaned back. "Is that supposed to be a joke?"

"Not really, no," he said seriously, shrugging. "I wanted to get away too. And here we are."

"Of all the more enjoyable, pleasant people you could have chosen, you decided to come find me..."

He was quiet for a moment before breaking into somewhat bitter-sounding laughter. "Piri, after all these weeks, do you honestly still believe there's some ulterior motive behind this? I like you, I like hanging out with you. Contrary to whatever you might think, I genuinely enjoy your company. And maybe I'm a little more like you than you seem to think I am. So yes, of all the people I could have probably sat down with, I actively sought out you instead. I didn't want 'pleasant' company, as you put it. I wanted real company. And I was kind of hoping that maybe you wanted some too." He paused, once more staring out at the horizon. "I can leave if you want me to," he said quietly, suddenly somber.

As I looked at him, I found that, despite my prickliness, I really didn't want him to go. I'd gotten so used to his company that there always seemed to be a little void when it wasn't there, regardless of how I was feeling. I shook my head.

"I - no. I'm, I'm glad you're here," I said, looking away. "I like having you around." I felt embarrassed saying it. It sounded silly hearing it out loud. I'd never been good with words. But it was enough apparently. Nephael smiled.

"Thanks. I like having you around too."

Neither of us said anything else for a while, content to just sit in silence and stare off at the mountains. There was always a lot of silence when we were together, but his seemed different today, strained. I glanced sideways at him after a while, wondering what he was thinking about, possibly for the first time ever. Nephael always seemed so placid that it really never occurred to me that, under the surface, he was a normal person who could have bad days, just like anyone else.

"So," I finally ventured, "what happened?"

"Mmm?"

I leaned forward, arms resting on my knees. "What happened today? You seem upset."

"Oh." Nephael was quiet for a moment, then, "There was a Council meeting. We had a bit of a disagreement, that's all."

A 'disagreement' didn't seem like the sort of thing that would generally upset someone like him. It bothered me to see him visibly

16

out of sorts, for him anyway.

"Can I ask what it was about?"

Nephael turned his head and looked at me for the first time since he'd sat down. Intently, eyes boring into me. I regretted asking the question. Council meetings were none of my business. I looked away. The silence stretched almost to the point of discomfort. I was surprised when he finally answered and it wasn't the response I was expecting.

"You, actually."

"Me?" I said with a frown. "I - I don't understand." Instant panic started to well up in my chest. Bad things happened when there were meetings about me.

It must have shown in my face. Nephael reached out a hand, but caught himself and pulled back. He'd learned by now that I didn't like to be touched.

"Don't worry. It's, well, it's not fine, but nothing is going to happen either. Sorry. It was just a discussion about how you're doing and what to do with you in regards to the ENF."

That did nothing to allay my fear. My entire existence had been other people deciding the worth of my life.

"Certain Council members want you, ah, removed," he carefully went on. "Thankfully, due to the nature of the ENF, we have a bit of autonomy. When it comes to the big decisions, very few people have the power to check my decisions regarding it, if I choose to flex my power. You fall under my jurisdiction. I made that very clear."

"What- what happens if I'm 'removed'?" The word was like acid on my tongue. I didn't like the way he'd said it. I'd been threatened with 'removal' before. The last time I'd heard that phrase, it had been in the permanent sense of the word.

"Let's not talk about it. It's not going to happen." He forced a smile.

I wasn't any less terrified, but I was deeply grateful, so much so that it was almost a physical pain in my chest. I'd never had someone on my side like that before, someone who actually stood up for me, cared about my well-being.

"On a different note, I do have some good news for you."

I looked up. His mood seemed to have lightened a bit, the smile no longer forced.

"You're no longer confined to The Watch."

My heart leapt.

"I had to make a bit of a compromise to smooth things over," he continued, "so you'll need to have me with you if you want to go anywhere. The Council doesn't feel comfortable letting you go out alone. I'll apologize up front if you get sick of having me around, but I felt that was a better situation than you being stuck here all the time. I didn't want to rock the boat any further at the meeting today by trying to push things."

I could have hugged him. I'd been granted a measure of freedom and I didn't care if it required supervision. Nephael was the only person I genuinely didn't mind having around, a thought that surprised me when I gave it some consideration. I reached out and quickly squeezed his hand. His eyes widened, shocked at my action. It was all I could think to do, the only way I could convey how I was feeling.

Sketching in the Field

I winged my way over miniature rooftops and tiny people scurrying around like ants, going about their daily business; farmers tending to their fields, a smith at his forge, children dashing back and forth in what I could only assume was a game of tag. It never failed to amaze me how primitive the human villages seemed. The big cities were a major step up, but still so far behind the way the Seri lived. Our control over the Source gave us quite the technological advantage among the races.

I spun in a slow circle, scanning for my newest favorite drawing location. A small hillock crowned with an ancient, twisted tree rose out of the sea of yellow flowers. I folded my wings, dropping like a stone out of the blue. Reveling in the feeling of free-fall, I let myself get relatively close to the ground before flaring both my wings and the Source to stop myself, something only an overSourcer could do. The first time I'd done it in front of Nephael, I'd thought he was going to have a heart attack. Thinking of Nephael brought a slight twinge of guilt. I was out and about alone. I'd gotten quite exceptional at sneaking off by myself. While Nephael was excellent company, there were too many days when he was busy. I'd taken matters into my own hands and, so far, he hadn't said anything.

My feet hit the ground and I landed in a crouch, letting my body absorb the Source-softened impact, my wings scattering golden petals even as their energy dispersed. Readjusting my leather messenger bag and straightening my ruffled clothing, I hiked the short distance from my landing spot up to the tree on the hill. I couldn't help the small sigh of satisfaction that escaped my lips as I settled myself at its base, the heaviness I'd woken up with today lifting ever so slightly. It was the perfect day for an escape. Crystal blue sky with the occasional white, puffy cloud. An ever so slight breeze to keep the day riding at the perfect temperature. I pulled my sketchbook from my bag, pencils, kneaded rubber. A Source-forged blade appeared in my hand and I set to sharpening the pencil.

The breeze drifted through the wheat fields, rustling the tops slightly; the villagers and farmers moved in a steady rhythm, going about their daily lives, normal lives. Something I'd never known, I thought, with a slight twinge of jealousy. I could hear laughter in the air, probably coming from the tavern on the edge of town. If anyone had noticed me sitting here over the past week or two, they seemed not to care and they certainly never bothered to come see who I was or what I wanted. Which was just fine by me.

I kept scanning the area, looking for that one moment, that unique event that would pique my interest. And there it was, along the road, away from the others. A young woman suddenly laughed, throwing her head back in delight, sharing in some quip, something an elderly man sitting atop a hay cart had just said to her. That was the scene I had been looking for. I could never put into words what I looked for when the need to draw from life would hit, when I'd get that itch in my fingers. There was always just something that clicked when I would see it, something that made me suddenly want to immortalize whatever had caught my attention. Pencil to paper. Mark upon mark. Rough at first, then more refined. The soft lead etching its existence onto the toned parchment. And just like that, I was lost in my own world. Nothing else mattered but the scratch of my pencil on the paper, capturing that moment before me.

I had no idea how long I'd sat there against the tree, putting the world before me onto my paper. I was oblivious to everything except my art. Until a soft curse issued from the tree above me as a leaf drifted down and settled on the page in front of me, swiftly followed by a rather large spider, bringing my pencil to a grinding halt.

I recoiled and quickly flipped my book, throwing it off into the grass. Then I froze, not even daring to look up. I didn't need to. I knew the voice. How long had Nephael been sitting in the tree above me? *Why* had he been sitting in the tree above me? I think he knew the game was up and there was no point in trying to pretend he wasn't there because he dropped down beside me with a thump. I couldn't help noticing that he was wearing casual clothing for once, not so different from my own. I don't know why that struck me as odd. Maybe because I only ever saw him in uniform and it never occurred to me that he had a life outside of work. Nephael folded himself up next to me, leaving maybe a foot of space. Close, way closer than I was comfortable with and I was sure he knew it. He leaned in even farther, studying the drawing. It took me a minute to realize that was what he was looking at, as I was doing my level best not to hyperventilate. He was practically on top of me, though he certainly didn't seem to notice or care.

"That's…incredible," he whispered. "I had no idea you were so good. I've seen you sketching before, but I've never actually seen your work."

I could actually feel my face go red. I'd never been good with compliments. I'd never known how to take them or react to them, which normally resulted in me getting angry and defensive. And I'd never really understood why anyone would give them to me in the first place. I mumbled a sort of thanks as he continued staring at the picture. The silence was beginning to leave me unsettled.

"Why were you spying on me?" I finally blurted out, regretting my bluntness as soon as the words left my mouth. Nephael was either unruffled by the question or chose to ignore my harshness. I couldn't figure it out; he obviously wasn't angry with me or he'd have said so right off the bat. And there were any number of reasons for him to have been pissed. I had left without permission and supervision, I was within hailing distance of a human village, I was pretty sure I was supposed to have been meeting one of the healers. But he honestly didn't seem to care. I could have left it go and just talked to him. Like a normal person.

"I wasn't," he chuckled, "spying, per say. And last I checked, I'm technically supposed to be here. Yes, yes, I know you've been sneaking off." He waived a dismissive hand as I started to protest. "But this morning I saw you leave and, well, I thought I'd tag along. You looked..." Nephael trailed off and a slight frown creased his face. More silence. I was starting to become super aware of how close he was to me. Suddenly, "Can I see some of your other work?"

I'm not sure what made me just hand over my sketchbook. The minute it left my fingers, I started to panic inside. I had just handed him my sketchbook. My *sketchbook*. In my entire life, I had never let anyone touch that book. Never let another person touch *any* of my sketchbooks. They were my life, my escape. The fact that he was flipping through the pages so gently, almost with reverence, did nothing to allay what I was feeling. Especially when he hit the several pages of sketches I had done of him, pausing for far longer than he had on any other page. Facial studies, hand studies, sitting, standing, reviewing paperwork. Being out of commission, there wasn't much else to do during ENF meetings and I had to at least pretend I was paying attention (even if everyone knew I wasn't). And I'd have been lying if I said he didn't have great features for drawing. And he was the closest I'd ever come to a friend of sorts. That didn't make it any less mortifying.

He studied the sketches, smoothing the page slightly as he gently traced his own profile with the tip of his finger. "You hardly ever draw me with my glasses on," he finally observed. What a weird thing to notice.

"They're unnecessary. You look better without them." I closed my eyes and leaned back against the tree, hoping against hope that it would suddenly crack down the middle, open up and swallow me. What in the hell had made me say that?

It started out as a snort before turning into full throated laughter. I opened my eyes, frowning. Nephael

25

had closed the sketchbook and was laughing fit to burst. I didn't know what he thought was so funny. I still wanted to curl up and die, but the sight was so ridiculous that I couldn't help starting to smile. He handed back the sketchbook and I quickly stashed it in my bag, shoving my supplies in after it. Getting to his feet, he wiped his eyes, still weakly laughing.

"It's getting late," he finally managed to gasp out.

Late? I looked up at the sun, far lower on the horizon than I had expected. I - we'd - been out here most of the day. He held out a hand and I tentatively took it, something I never would have done a few months ago, and he hauled me to my feet.

"We should probably be getting back. But there's something I want to show you first. Come on." Without waiting for a response, he launched himself into the air, wings materializing, unfolding, leaving a sparking blue trail that quickly vanished in the rush of my own takeoff.

It took me a few moments to realize that we were indeed heading back towards The Watch. I had been blindly following Nephael without paying any attention to where we were actually going; he had seemed so determined in his course that I had simply followed. Now, as I realized the trajectory, I hesitated, slowing my flight slightly and dropping back. He must have sensed my unwillingness to continue because he was suddenly just above me, close enough to touch if I had reached up. The proximity unnerved me. Flying so close felt like an invasion of my space. Nephael was good at that; invading my personal space, setting me on edge, pushing my limits. I knew he did it on purpose, though for what reason I had no idea.

"We're not going back yet, just stay with me." Could he read my mind as well? With no hesitation, he pushed ahead again, assuming I would, once again, simply follow.

And I did for some reason. Something about him always made me more compliant.

As The Watch came into view, his course changed, veering to the east, into the mountains. Curious. I wasn't sure where he could possibly be headed. Then again, exploring the area directly around the complex wasn't something I had really done. Higher, farther in we went, until suddenly we dropped onto a flat area on the top of a peak. The view was undeniably spectacular, with sunset on one end and, presumably, sunrise from the other, but it was the scene before me that held my attention. We were standing among what was left of an old Seri ruin. One of the old stone spheres sat nestled against an inexplicable and ancient cherry tree, that was itself nestled up against an outcropping of stone. A small fountain, still running, gurgled quietly nearby. Several crumbling pillars dotted the outskirts of a central area once presumably paved in stone. Broken pavers could be seen here and there, showing through the waving grasses and mountain flowers. I sucked in my breath and held it, taking in the somewhat other-worldly scene.

"I discovered this place one day while I was exploring," he whispered. "I don't think anyone else knows about it. I like to come here when I need to think. I thought you might like it as a quiet place when you need to get away or want a secluded spot to draw. As long as you don't mind me sometimes being here too." He said it almost shyly, running a hand through his hair.

I didn't know what to say. He had shared something almost sacred with me, his sanctuary. More than that, he had given me a sanctuary as well.

Reva's Transfer

The sun was barely up over the mountains when I alighted on the training field. No one else was around, The Watch silent in the early morning hours. It was the first time I'd come here.

I breathed in deeply and closed my eyes, savoring the crisp air, the silence. I reached out to the Source, stretched my wings. It had been too long. With barely a thought, a Source-forged glaive was in my hand. Eyes still closed, I could feel the coolness of the weapon against my palm.

Time passed in a blur as I moved through my stances, the only sounds the whistle of steel as my blade cut the air and the wind as it moved around my dancing form. When I felt myself begin to tire, I pulled on the Source, pushing my limits, fighting past my fatigue. Falling into the feeling, I lost myself.

It was some time before I became aware that I was no longer alone. I finally opened my eyes as I pulled up my weapon, suddenly on guard. Scanning the area, I relaxed slightly as I spied Nephael sitting perched up on the hillside. I had no idea how long he had been there watching me. He stood and moved towards me as it became apparent that I wasn't going to continue.

"Impressive," he said with a smile as he crossed the threshold of the field. I stayed silent. "Follow me up to the balcony." He nodded in the direction of one of the outlying buildings. "The field will be occupied soon and there's something I want to show you."

I stood next to Neph on the balcony overlooking the training grounds. Quite a few Seri soldiers were now out on the field, along with a handful of the significantly more skillful ENF. The mid morning sun had crested the mountains, but the field, nestled into its high, enclosed mountain valley, was still blissfully cool. Oblivious to the beautiful morning, I found myself keenly watching a single individual on the field. I probably would have been watching her even if Neph hadn't specifically pointed her out. Dark skinned with a shockingly pink streak somehow dyed through her black hair, she moved with a grace and precision that were honed to near perfection, far and away outshining the most skilled there. She was almost a little too fast, a little too on mark. Leaning forward, arms resting on the white, stone balustrade, my eyes narrowed as I watched her.

"She's naturally overSourcing," I said, curiosity peaking. "Who is she?"

Neph glanced sideways at me, a devious smile spreading across his face. "She's your new apprentice."

I was really only half listening, despite having asked the question, my attention so focused on the girl below me. It took a moment to register the response and I was sure I'd heard incorrectly.

"I'm sorry, what?" I turned, the scene below no longer holding the same appeal. Neph had to be joking. Surely.

"You heard me," he said. "Her name is Trevanys, goes by Reva. She's the newest and, for the moment, final new recruit. Out of Marchaven in the south. She's a natural overSourcer. Nowhere near your abilities, but far and away beyond anyone else in the ENF. I want her practicing with the best and, last time I checked, that would be you. She'll be your partner on patrols and you'll be honing her Sourcing skills."

He turned away from the field and began walking back towards the main building. "She'll be joining us shortly in my office. She seemed, how did she put it…," he tapped his chin, "'stoked' to meet you. So I suggest we migrate. Cup of tea while we wait?"

I held back, mortified by what Neph had just thrown at me and how casually he had done it. "Y-you can't just walk away after that," I spluttered. "I can't train someone! And what do you mean stoked to meet me?" I paused, something else he had said suddenly vying for attention. "Wait, did you say patrols?"

Neph stopped, hands clasped behind his back. He rocked back slightly on his heels. "Did I?"

I stalked after him, incensed over his little game, and grabbed his sleeve briefly before quickly letting go, suddenly feeling embarrassed. "You're putting me back in commission?" I ventured hesitantly.

Neph threw an arm around my shoulders, ignoring my flinch, and began to steer me back into the complex. "It's honestly been too long. I'd be lying if I said everyone agreed with my decision, but, last time I checked, they're not in charge of the unit. I see no reason why you shouldn't be brought back on and I've promised the Council that you'll be sticking to patrols, until we see how things go. That seemed to mollify them. And, considering there isn't anything else going on, that's not really a big deal. No one is running anything other than patrols at the moment, including us. If something more pressing crops up, we'll cross that bridge when we come to it."

We passed through the Malthys, a building used primarily for general soldier

30

operations and meetings, coming out onto a stone bridge over a stunning waterfall which swept down the side of the mountain, crossed several times by archways. It was one of a handful of falls that had been worked right into The Watch's architecture. The main hall itself was cut through by a mountain stream, topped by a glass floor, cresting into another set of falls as it exited the building, all eventually merging into the Belanistra River at the base of the mountain. Shimmering rainbows crisscrossed the vista, caught in the spray. Stopping halfway across the bridge, I leaned against the marble rail, staring out across the valley. I ran my hands through my hair. Neph, finally realizing that he'd lost me, backtracked to the midpoint, leaning on the rail right next to me, watching me from the corner of his eye. After what seemed an interminable silence, I finally sighed and slid down the rail, pulling my knees up to my chest.

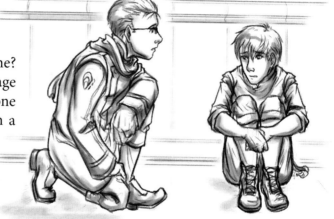

"Neph, how can you possibly think that I can train someone? I can barely manage myself, let alone someone else. Maybe once upon a time, but I'm not who I used to be…and even back then, I wouldn't have entrusted me with any sort of responsibility towards someone else. You can't trust me not to panic now and screw things up. My memory is unreliable, I can't seem to Source quite the way I used to. And…well, you know how people feel about me. What makes you think this will be any different?" I asked, looking up.

Neph crouched down. "First of all, the only real difference is that you've lost your confidence in yourself. Yes, you've got some holes in your memory, but that honestly may be for the best at the moment. Considering the traumatic events you suffered, I certainly can't hold either of those against you."

"*Traumatic events?*" I interrupted angrily. "You have no idea what I went through."

"No," he said quietly, "I don't. I only know what little you've told me and what I've learned from the reports. I also know what I saw there the day I found you. But I do think it's time to come back and realize that you're just as skilled and competent as you've always been. What happened wasn't your fault and you need to start moving on and living life. And you've got a real chance for a new life here. The ENF isn't what it used to be and The Watch isn't Skycrest. Second, I think this will be different because Reva is not your average person. I've met her, talked to her. I can only ask you to trust me, as I'm trusting you."

We didn't have long to wait back in Nephael's office. He had barely gotten water boiling for tea when exuberant knocking shook the door. I was standing at the window, staring out at the distant mountains when the sound broke the silence. I flinched, hunched my shoulders. Why was he doing this to me…

Neph gave the Sourcepad on the desk a brief flick and the door slid smoothly open to reveal Reva, eyes wide and sparkling with excitement, still slightly flushed from the training field. She walked inside, coming smartly to attention, a broad grin on her face. "Sir!"

Neph couldn't help but smile as he waved her to sit down. "Please, Reva, this isn't the capital. We're quite a bit more relaxed here. Formalities are only observed during ceremonies. If at all," he said, throwing a look over the top of his glasses in my direction. I scowled back.

"Sir, I -"

"Just Nephael is fine."

32

"Sorry, Nephael, sir," Reva bubbled, "I'm just, well, a little excited, I guess. It's not every day you get to work with a legend right out of your childhood stories."

That finally got me to turn around. I could feel my face getting tight. "I'm sorry...a what?"

Reva sat herself down, suddenly looking self-conscious. "Well, I mean, I grew up hearing about what you could do, your ability to overSource like no one else in recorded history. I used to beg my father to tell me about your involvement in the Ashtaran Uprising..." She trailed off at what I could only assume was the sudden stricken look on my face.

"That isn't funny. Those battles were massacres." I shuddered and closed my eyes.

"I wasn't trying to be funny," Reva said, serious now. "You were my idol growing up, regardless of the actual circumstances. You were fast, powerful, skilled. Everything I wanted to be as a soldier. When I was recommended for the new ENF, you have no idea; it was my dream come true. When I found out that I would be working with you, training with you, have the chance to actually get to know you. I used to fantasize about that sort of thing." She looked towards Nephael, almost pleadingly, as I turned my back again, leaned against the window. "I know that probably sounds a little...weird. But I don't mean it to be. I have the chance to learn from the best. That's really all I'm trying to say." She clenched her hands in her lap. Heavy silence hung in the air for several moments.

Reva finally sighed and stood, running a hand through her ponytail. Moving towards me, she stopped and crossed her arms. From his chair behind the desk, Neph twirled a pen, silently watching. Reva took a deep breath, steadying herself.

"Look," she began, "Now that I've given you a horrible first impression, let me start over." She held out her hand

33

as I slowly turned. I stared down at her hand, uncomfortable, before tentatively reaching out. All shyness aside, she grabbed my fingers and shook. Neph coughed slightly, hiding a snort of laughter, at the desperate look I threw him. "I'm Trevanys. You can call me Reva, everyone does. It's a pleasure to meet you, Enpirion, and I'm sincerely looking forward to working with you."

I didn't say anything so she plowed on. "Here's the deal. I've heard all the horror stories and gossip and rumors. That sort of nonsense doesn't confine itself to Skycrest, unfortunately. From everything I've heard, you'd think you were some sort of military created monster sporting horns, fangs and claws. Fact is though, you don't. And I never thought you did. Stories and rumors are just that. I like to judge someone for myself, get to know them before I draw any conclusions. I know this is kind of a rocky start and I know you probably didn't want to get shackled with some green recruit, but I think you might be surprised at what I can do." She stopped to take a breath.

"I'm already impressed by what you can do," I murmured, taking her by surprise. "I was watching you practice this morning."

"Oh, thanks," she said, going slightly red, thrown off balance by the unexpected compliment. There was a brutal honesty about her that I couldn't help but like, even if it did make me slightly nervous.

"And...it's just Piri."

Reva blinked, once again thrown off by the sudden shift. "Sorry?"

"Piri. You can just call me Piri," I said, looking down at the floor and moodily scuffing a foot across the marble. "Only strangers call me by my full name here."

Neph smiled and stood, snapping the pen back down onto the polished wooden desktop. "And by that, he means everyone except me. So I'd consider it something of a good introduction that you've been granted permission to use that."

Reva flashed an uncertain grin as Neph ushered us out of his office, pointing to the mountain of paperwork on his desk. The door slid shut, leaving us staring at each other in awkward silence.

Finally, heaving an exasperated sigh, Reva reached out and grabbed my hand.

"Come on," she said, all cheerful enthusiasm, "let's go grab something to drink. I've been waiting entirely too long to pick your brain."

The minute she'd grabbed my hand, I'd frozen, tried to pull back, but she hadn't let go.

"Do you always act so familiar with strangers?" I weakly asked, trying to extricate myself.

She looked down at my feeble attempt to dislodge her grasp on my fingers, a mischievous grin creeping across her face.

"Pretty sure you just gave me permission when you pawned off your nickname on me."

I glanced up in incomprehension, having given up on trying to get free.

"Only strangers…? Yeah, no bells?" She frowned. "Seriously, this is what happens when someone touches you? I mean, I know Nephael said you had a thing about that, but I didn't think you'd have an actual visceral reaction." She let go of my hand. "Sorry."

"It's - it's fine," I said quietly, rubbing my hand

and staring at the floor. "It's an old problem."

Reva pursed her lips, looking me over. "Well, maybe we can work on it together. People tell me I'm a little too physical, so maybe we can even each other out."

She laughed, instantly back to what I could only assume was her normal, jovial self. I really couldn't help but like her. And, regardless, Neph wasn't giving me much choice in the matter.

"So," I hesitantly began. Reva arched a sculpted eyebrow. "You wanted to talk to me…." I scrubbed a hand through my hair. "There's - there's a tea house just off the Grand Hall. We could go there. I guess."

"Tea," she said with another laugh. "Sure, why not. You know, from all the stories, I was expecting someone a little more, I don't know, brash. Arrogant." She tilted her head to the side and smiled. "Awkward and shy were definitely not even on my list. It's cute. And far more likable."

I felt myself flush slightly and turned away, feeling even more uncomfortable than before.

Reva heaved an exaggerated sigh. "Gods above, let's go find that tea place before I do any more damage to you." Without thinking, she reached back out and grabbed my arm, dragging me off in the direction of the Grand Hall.

Training

Reva was what I could term my first true assignment back in commission with the ENF and it was unlike any 'mission' I'd ever been given. While the first week or so of sessions simply ended after practice, it wasn't long before she began tagging along after me, doing her best to, I assume, make me comfortable being around her. If I wandered off for a drink or a snack, I would suddenly find her joining me at my table or find her sliding into a chair across from me in the Grand Hall. I couldn't help but be reminded of the games Neph used to play with me when he'd first been trying to get me to talk. It wasn't long before Reva had nearly glued herself to my side and training her became something of a morning to evening routine, whether we were in official practice sessions or not. When we weren't physically training, she was eagerly prying me for knowledge on my skills, how I Sourced, the extent of my powers. She steered away from personal questions, letting me keep to my privacy, but she was always more than keen to discuss her own past in her usual bubbly and energetic way, day after day.

She Sourced like no one else I'd ever been around, manipulating the energy far beyond any other member of the ENF. And she learned almost frighteningly quickly, harnessing skills that few others could manage. A shriek of delight had escaped her lips the day she'd finally managed to Source-forge multiple weaponry, something few could do and even fewer do well.

Despite my early apprehension, I found myself looking forward to seeing her every day and, much like Neph, having her around didn't bother me. There was no judgment on her part, only an open willingness to learn and an honest desire to be my friend. Reva had forcefully shoved herself into my life and, a rarity on my part, I allowed and actually enjoyed it.

Sitting on the grass along the edge of the practice field, back against a stone wall, electric Source fire crackled across my fingers as

I played with the energy in the lazy heat of the afternoon. A stone's throw away, Reva was practicing shielding herself, trying to form the nearly invisible barrier of energy I'd shown her earlier. It wasn't an easy skill and, so far, she'd only managed it briefly, which was still impressive. There had only been a handful of original ENF soldiers who had been able to do it properly.

I felt a slight shift in energy on the edge of my awareness and glanced up. There was an ever so subtle shimmer in the air in front of her. Her eyes were squeezed shut, face twisted in intense concentration.

With a flick of my finger, an electric crackle of energy shot off, knocking into her shield. With a startled jump and a shriek, her eyes flew open and she lost her hold on the shield. I couldn't help grinning at the look that crossed her face as she glared at me with only the sort of moral outrage that she was able to conjure.

"You're trying too hard," I said with a smile.

"I - what?"

"You're holding on to the energy like it's some poor sod you're trying to strangle. A shield needs to be effortless, something you can call at a moment's notice. Don't fight it." I held out my hand. "Here." She moved towards me, took it. I closed my eyes and took a deep breath as her fingers latched on, slightly uneasy with not just her touch but with what I was about to do. But it was just Reva. It would be fine.

Opening my eyes again, I looked up at her. "I want you to listen to the energy, feel how it moves and flows. It's not just a tool; it's a living thing."

She frowned, loosing her grip slightly. "You know sharing energy isn't -"

38

"Exactly approved of. This is - sort of different. Anyway, how fast do you want to learn the technique? Just concentrate before I change my mind."

She didn't say anything, only looked down her nose in slight disapproval, but she didn't pull away either. She'd been trained and raised in normal Seri society, lived by the norms of societal rules. I'd never known anything but the original ENF growing up, where rules and regulations were barely even considered guidelines. Breaking a minor taboo wasn't something I was going to concern myself over, even if this was on the fringes of it. It was the fastest way to teach her to shield and I knew she'd be able to feel what I was doing. My field was too strong for a Sourcer of her ability not too. With no effort, I reached out to the Source, created a bubble around us, at the same time twining the energy into hers. Gasping slightly, she let go, staring around as if she could actually see what I'd done. Her surprise was short lived though and her eyes had lit up with excitement. Reaching down, she latched back on to my hand.

"Do it again."

The second time, she closed her eyes, nose scrunching up as she concentrated. After I'd released the bubble, she let go and simply stared at me for a while. I was starting to get mildly uncomfortable when she suddenly dropped down beside me, leaning back against the wall.

"I get it. And I think I can do it. Like you say. But," she paused.

"But?"

She hesitated, her voice slightly anxious when she answered. "Well, not like you. What you just did, the way you did it. That didn't feel normal." Reva paused again, then, "You don't Source like the rest of us, do you? I've never felt anything like that. It's like you aren't, well, Sourcing. It's just an inherent part of you."

"The Source is an inherent part of all of us," I said uneasily, briefly wondering if I should have shown her. I hadn't realized she'd be able to sense it in quite that manner. She was a lot stronger than I'd thought.

"That's not what I mean and I think you know that. The rest of us use the Source, are trained how to control what flows through us. You don't. Didn't just then. It's like, like it's just there for you. Part of you." She stopped, unable to explain what she meant. She didn't need to. It wasn't like I didn't know.

"I wish I channeled it like you do, could feel the Source like that," she said somewhat petulantly.

I couldn't help my short, bitter laugh. "No, you don't. Being so different only brings trouble. Having access to that sort of power…" I trailed off, my head starting to hurt, the fuzziness of lost memories just beyond my reach creeping in.

Her fingers reached out, twined through mine. I looked over uneasily, but didn't pull away. She was staring out across the field, eyes glazed slightly as she watched other troops at practice, a rare unhappy expression on her face. She squeezed my hand slightly.

"I know you don't like to, but you know if you ever need to talk…," she trailed off. "I hope you know that I'm someone you can trust."

I nodded slightly. I actually did trust her, despite our rather short acquaintanceship. Neph had been right that first day on the bridge. Reva *was* different somehow, more genuine. She never made any pretense, always forthright about what she thought, whether I agreed or not and I respected and liked her for it.

Arafel

"Who was that you were with earlier? I've never seen him around before." Neph had joined me where I'd been sitting all afternoon, perched on a rocky outcrop overlooking one of The Watch's gardens. I'd spent the morning working with Reva; running stances, honing her Sourcing, answering a thousand questions… she'd mentally exhausted me. My sketchbook sat forgotten in my lap as I lay on my back, enjoying the warmth coming off the sun-baked stone. I'd been half asleep when Neph had found me. He looked up from his book at my question.

"Who, Arafel?"

"Yes? Maybe? I wouldn't be asking if I knew his name. Whoever you were talking to down in the garden earlier."

"Mmm, yeah. He's an old friend, known each other since we were kids." He paused, seeming ever so slightly uncomfortable. "He just arrived at The Watch for an extended stay. Finally got tired of Skycrest, I dare say. He knows quite a few people here, so it seemed a logical choice for a change of scenery. That and all the ruins around here."

I cracked open one eye. "Ruins?"

"Araf is a researcher and historian. He takes quite an interest in the old civilization, probably knows more than just about anyone else concerning the original Seri."

"Oh?" I said, my curiosity suddenly peaked. I loved history. "Could I meet him?"

Neph hesitated.

"Afraid to introduce me to your old friend?" I asked, only half

41

joking.

"What? No!" Neph said, looking mortified, having taken that a lot more seriously than I'd expected. "It's exactly the other way around actually. It's not you that worries me. It's, well, Arafel." He chewed his lip in uncharacteristic agitation. "Araf can be quick to judge and I'm a little worried about his preconceived notions concerning you. He's, uh, already expressed some concern over our friendship."

"Ah." My heart sank. Yet another person who believed all the rumors about my history, feared me without ever knowing me. The worst part was that a lot of those stories were true, if somewhat embellished. I had been trained as one of the Seri Empire's greatest weapons, a tool used without restraint during the Ashtaran Uprising and the subsequent Seri military expansion. I'd committed all sorts of atrocities in the name of war. The fact that I'd been forced into all of it, been brutally manipulated by my own people, seemed to be a conveniently glossed over part of the story.

Neph seemed to know what I was thinking. He shrugged helplessly. "I can introduce you and see how things go. Just - well, try not to judge him too harshly if things don't go well."

"Why? Because he's your friend?" I asked, annoyed and angry, pushing myself up onto my elbows. I felt badly, taking my sudden change in mood out on Neph when it certainly wasn't his fault.

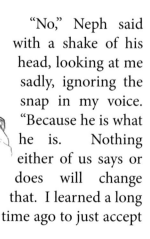

"No," Neph said with a shake of his head, looking at me sadly, ignoring the snap in my voice. "Because he is what he is. Nothing either of us says or does will change that. I learned a long time ago to just accept

Arafel and all his quirks. That's why our friendship works. I would hope that once he gets to know you, he'll change his own mind. Besides, if it wasn't for him, who knows where we'd all be right now."

I frowned. "What do you mean?"

"It's his research that exposed the corruption of the military government, one of the major factors that brought the Empire down. It also exposed and put an end to the original ENForcer division." He paused. "I'd also probably still be in prison if it wasn't for him."

My mouth dropped open. He'd never talked about his involvement in the restructuring that had taken place and I had spent the majority of it in medical isolation, so, even well over a year later, my grasp of what had actually happened was still somewhat sketchy. No one seemed to want to talk about it.

"I used to be a bit of a problem causer," Neph said with a laugh at the look on my face. He pushed his glasses up the bridge of his nose. "The night I got caught breaking into the Library's vault, getting into the confidential files, well, that was apparently the final straw for my superiors."

I almost couldn't believe it. Neph was practically the embodiment of calm and rationality in my mind. I wanted to know more, but Neph was done, I could tell just by his change in body language as he went silent, eyes glazing slightly. He roughly shook his head.

"It's over, though. The past is the past. I'll introduce you to Araf and we'll see how things go."

"I know you're isolated out here at The Watch, but surely you've heard what's been happening in the human cities? Especially where their territory borders Seri land."

I glanced up from my sketchpad at Arafel. The man was somewhat odd looking, even for a Seri scholar. His mid-length open robes were threaded with intricate patterns in gold and silver threads, old civilization in design, and he kept his long hair pulled back in a ponytail, tightly clasped with a delicate Old Seri stick barrette that looked original. Arafel sort of looked like he'd stepped out of an obscure history book on the ancient Seri court. He was currently gazing intently at Neph, who was sporting an expression of forced patience.

It was a beautiful day and I'd quickly gotten down to sketching when Arafel had gone out of his way to pretend I wasn't there, simply assuming that my inclusion in breakfast had been nothing more than Neph forced to babysit his problematic soldier. After several failed attempts at convincing him otherwise, Neph had simply given up. I was doing my best to ignore the suspicious glances being periodically thrown my way.

The Belayn Terrace was relatively quiet and empty, unusual on such a nice day. I sat at the table, munching on an apple and drawing while Neph and Arafel had talked the morning away. Little of the conversation had interested me, as it was mostly them catching up, but something about the way Arafel had asked this newest question made me tune back in.

"I've heard rumors of some things, but very little that I'd term concrete. The ENF certainly hasn't been called into play, so whatever's been happening hasn't filtered this far out yet. Why?"

Arafel leaned back, shaking his head. "It's weird, Nephael. There's been some seriously strange stuff going on. I wouldn't be surprised if the Ruling Council calls you to look into it at some point. Sooner rather than later, I'm guessing."

Neph crossed his arms, looking

slightly irritated. "Care to elaborate a bit? Maybe stop stringing me along?"

"It's been so long, Nephael," Arafel said with a laugh. "I have to make up for lost time." He raised his hands in supplication as Neph's brows started to draw together. "Fine, fine, calm down. There's been a whole host of things taking place. Disappearances, attacks, strange markings left at equally strange ritual sites. There's some sort of new religion among the humans that appears to be behind all of it. More like a cult, if you ask me. And it seems to be targeting non-humans, the Seri more than anyone else."

A creeping feeling was moving its way up my neck.

"Last month, two Seri went missing near Brakon's Landing, which, by the way, seems to be the epicenter of it all," Arafel continued.

"Brakon's Landing," Neph said with a derisive snort. "People vanishing from the streets isn't exactly news. That city is a cesspool, even by human standards."

"Can't say I disagree with you," Arafel said, leaning forward to rest his chin in his hand, "if it weren't for the fact that so many other things seem to be happening along with it. And not just in Brakon's Landing. An Ellundara girl turned up dead outside of Kallin's Fist, inside some sort of weird runic circle. The soldier that found her said her throat had been slit. A Seri farmer on the border near Port Odarin claimed he saw groups of hooded figures conducting some sort of ritual. Next day, a Seri boy was discovered missing. Last I heard, he hadn't been found."

"You know this could all just be coincidence..."

"Nephael, do you really think it's a coincidence? None of this sounds the least bit familiar?"

It sounded incredibly familiar. My hand was shaking as I stared at the half finished sketch on my page. Neph glanced my way.

"I think maybe we should continue this discussion at another time," he said quietly, standing up, putting a hand on my shoulder. Arafel was staring at me like I was on a short fuse and about to explode.

"Is he, uh, safe...?" Arafel ventured, pushing his chair back slightly.

Neph threw him a slightly dirty look as he knelt down next to me. I leaned over, hands gripping my head, as I squeezed my eyes shut, trying to block out the sudden flashes of memory. The robed figures. The rituals. The knife.

"Hey. It's ok."

I opened my eyes, looked at Neph. He took my hand, gently untangling my fingers from my hair, and squeezed it.

"It's in the past."

I nodded, shakily coming to my feet, suddenly wanting to leave. Neph rose with me, nodding understanding without me saying a word. I gave Arafel a brief nod, mumbled a "Nice to meet you," and let Neph lead me back to my quarters.

Nightmares

A thin sliver of flickering torchlight seeping through a slim crack between the door and wall was all that illuminated the all-pervading darkness. Bone-chilling cold against bare skin. The metallic smell of blood thick in the air. Guttural screams from down the hall, beyond the door, past my small cell. A loud crack split the air and the screams came to a sudden end.

I cringed back against the rough stone, feeling sharp edges scratching, digging in my back. Steel cut into my wrists and ankles, chains clanking as I shifted. My fingers, encased in metal restraints, numb and lifeless. Heavy footsteps echoed down the hall. The scritch-scratch of a knife being dragged across the stone wall. Closer.

I slammed awake, heart pounding, breath catching in my chest. I was nearly out of bed before I realized that it was just a nightmare. I leaned back, trying to calm myself. The scar on my back throbbed, like the knife was still there, ripping through my flesh. I could hear the chanting, see the masked and hooded faces swimming before me, feel the ropes biting into me, tearing at my skin. Beads of sweat were running down my forehead, my face. The sensations began to fade, receding back into the world of my dreams. I curled up, breathing heavily as I tried to push away the afterimages in my head. The nightmares weren't unusual, but they had been more vivid this time, more like re-living things. I turned over and stared at the ceiling.

A faint glow on the horizon heralded the coming dawn. There was still time before the sun crested the mountains, time enough. The pre-dawn air was chill on my bare chest as I pushed out with the Source and destabilized the large window, climbed onto the sill and launched myself into the darkness. My wings spread open, cradling me, catching me. They flared ever so briefly as I use the Source to drive myself into a vertical climb up to the very tip of The Watch, then struck off into the neighboring peaks, my feet finally touching down on soft grass. It was still dark up here. Dark and silent but for the gentle gurgling of the small fountain next to the cherry tree. That inexplicable cherry tree that I loved so much. I nestled myself between its roots, pulling my bare feet underneath me, wings dissolving into the chill air. I vaguely regretted not throwing on a shirt as the cold air brushed my skin. The sun would be rising soon, a beautiful sunrise to hopefully dispel the darkness and burn away the nightmares of the past.

My back was still hurting and I shifted position slightly, trying to stretch the muscles, relieve some of the tension. It was weird how after all this time, I could still feel it, especially on my bad days, like it was responding to my mental state. Like it was some sort of perverse mood indicator. I reached back, pushing my fingers into the top bit of the scar, trying to massage the pain away as the sun began to rise. I didn't know why it was still there. No one could figure out why it wouldn't really heal or why it was still causing me pain. And like all things with me, eventually people stopped trying to figure it out. It was too strange, didn't follow the norm. So they pretended it didn't exist. I'd learned to stop asking about it. The healers would get that glazed look that spoke more volumes than they ever could have managed to put into words. They didn't care and they were done with it. They had closed that book and moved on and couldn't understand why I wouldn't do the same. It didn't matter that it was an unresolved problem, that it caused me pain. It was over. So I stopped searching for an answer as well, bottled it up inside and filed it away behind yet another wall.

Gentle, yet persistent, shaking finally roused me from a dreamless sleep. I cracked open my eyes, bringing the world into focus. Neph was crouched beside me, hand on my shoulder. He looked worried. For a brief moment, I wasn't sure where I was or why he would be there.

I scrubbed a hand across my face. A slight twinge in my back brought things back quickly enough and I shivered slightly in the morning air.

I tipped my head to the side. "Hey."

"Yeah, hey. I've been looking for you for well over an hour. You missed practice with Reva. We scoured The Watch before I thought to come here. Are you alright?"

I closed my eyes again, vaguely wishing that I could just sink back into the void and escape for a while longer, but that wasn't going to happen. Answering would just be easier. "I'm…better. I think. I'll be fine."

Still down on one knee, Neph just stared back, eyes slightly narrowed, brows furrowed as he scrutinized me. "Something you want to talk about?"

49

I shook my head slightly and tried to meet his gaze. "It was just… nightmares. That's all. What Arafel said yesterday, it just brought things back, I guess. I just keep reliving that time - I can't -" I broke off, head dropping, a shudder convulsing my body. Maybe if I could actually remember everything that had happened, I could deal with it. But the nightmares were all I had, the fuzzy memories, the constant underlying terror and anxiety. Neph put a hand on my knee and gave a squeeze. I barely noticed, too caught up in my own mind.

"Why don't we go back, get you cleaned up, grab some brunch with Reva. There's a buffet set up on the Belayn…," he trailed off hopefully. I didn't say anything.

Finally, "Yeah. Sure. That sounds nice." I forced a smile. I knew Neph wouldn't let me out of it, would never just leave me here like this. And maybe it would be a good distraction. Something normal.

"Don't sound so excited," Neph said with a laugh. "Come on then. I know none of that helps to eliminate the problem, but, if nothing else, it might help to take your mind off it temporarily." He unfolded himself and walked to the edge of the precipice, turned to look back, waiting for me. I slowly rose, brushing grass and leaves from my bare calves as I joined him. There was a moment of hesitation and then Neph suddenly leaned in, grabbing me in a quick, awkward hug.

"You really worry me when things like this happen."

I felt myself instantly stiffen, breath catching in my throat. The contact didn't last long, was probably briefer than it felt. Letting go, he jerked his head in the direction of The Watch before taking off.

"Piri, no offense meant, but you look awful," Reva said, leaning

50

forward onto the table and pointing a slice of apple in my general direction.

"How am I not supposed to take offense at that," I said, blearily looking up from where I'd been pushing fruit in a circle around my plate.

"Because it's not a critique, it's just a fact. If those dark circles under your eyes get any more pronounced, they're gonna take over your face." She snapped off a bite of the apple with an audible crunch.

I leaned back and rubbed at my eyes, trying hard to stifle a yawn. She wasn't wrong. I hadn't slept well in days. Not that there was anything I could do about it. Until the dreams calmed down, things weren't going to improve. I tilted my head back and stared into the cloudless sky. Snapping fingers suddenly brought me back.

"Have you heard anything I just said?"

I stared at her, somewhat guiltily. "I - no."

Rolling her eyes, Reva pushed herself up from the table, reaching out to pull me along with her. "I was saying that you need to relax, loosen up. You're always so stressed. It's no wonder you don't sleep."

"It's not like it's a choice," I grumbled, following in her wake as she moved off.

As we passed out of the Terrace and into one of the gardens, Reva began animatedly chatting about…something. I wasn't especially paying attention, too tired to really focus on idle chatter. Owing to the beautiful day, the grounds seemed to have more people than usual milling about. I had no idea where we were going, but I wished we'd get there. I couldn't help but notice how groups of Seri grew hushed as we passed. Conversations stopped, some people even began to edge away. It wasn't as bad as Skycrest had been, where the hostility was open and verbal, but it was still disheartening.

"Don't worry about them," Reva said, suddenly interrupting her own chatter. "You're getting that look you get. They don't know you.

Who cares what they think." She stopped and glared. "Want me to go pummel someone for you? How about that guy who's staring at us over there?" She punched a fist into her hand, flashing her teeth in what I'm sure she thought was a menacing grimace, but was so ridiculous that I couldn't help but start laughing.

The tension in the courtyard broke as Reva began laughing as well. Seri smiled and resumed their conversations, moving about their business.

"See? All good now." She grabbed my hand and dragged me towards the edge of the ground where a small waterfall gurgled into a pool. Forcefully sitting me down, she dropped beside me.

I stared at the waterfall, the pool. Looked around at the fish flicking their way past the lily pads. This was very pretty. I had no idea why we were here. I stared back at Reva. "Uh, ok. What is this?"

"This," she said, waving her hand with a flourish and grinning, "is where I'm going to teach you how to relax."

Gods, she was serious. Reva was looking at me expectantly,

waiting for some sort of reaction.

A sharp whistle sounded from behind us. "Piri, Reva." I raised my eyes to the heavens above and thanked the gods. Saved.

"I'm glad I found you. I need you two to go prepare," Neph said, striding quickly across the courtyard towards us. Looking up from the report in his hand, he stopped, one eyebrow raised at the two of us sitting crossed-legged on the edge of the pool. "Starting this evening, I want you two on night patrols. Make sure to check the roster for your rotations. Some of the regular sentries have been reporting oddities and I want keener eyes out there for the next few weeks."

He paused, the eyebrow arching slightly higher.

"Forgive the interruption on this, uh, meditation session you seem to be enjoying, but I'd recommend getting some sleep before you head out this evening. If you pass any other ENF, let them know to drop by my office, if you would."

Quickly gaining my feet, I mouthed a silent 'Thank you'. A brief smile twitched at the corner of his mouth. Waving a hurried goodbye, I sped off, leaving Reva protesting behind me.

A Face from the Past

Only a thin crescent moon and the blanket of stars lit the night as Reva and I winged our way back towards The Watch. I'd volunteered us for the second half of the late night patrol this week, knowing that we could venture out a lot farther under the cover of darkness. Not because I thought it would benefit the patrol in any way, simply because I wanted to explore and stretch my wings. I'm sure Neph had guessed the reason, but he hadn't said anything about it. Reva had been hesitant when I'd deviated from our set course. She'd tried, albeit halfheartedly, to argue against it before finally shrugging her shoulders, flashing her trademark toothy grin and banking after me. We'd moved out over human territory, leisurely soaring over towns and villages, all quiet and dark in the early morning hours.

It was on our return trip, on the very edge of the human-Seri border that I noticed Reva had slowed and fallen behind, coming almost to a full stop mid-air as she used the Source to keep herself aloft. I circled back, wondering what she could possibly be looking at. We were out over empty country, mostly forest and rugged terrain as the land began to shift into the mountains.

I scanned the area as I came level with her, but didn't see anything unusual. I raised a questioning eyebrow.

Reva shook her head slightly and pointed below, towards a small clearing in the trees.

"This is gonna sound crazy, but I could have sworn I saw a light down there..."

I took a harder look, but the forest remained as dark as ever.

"What, like torchlight?"

"No. I don't know," she said, somewhat doubtfully. "I don't think so though. It was more like a flash of, well, purple. Or maybe blue. But it did sort of look like fire from up here, just in the wrong color."

"Uh huh. Purple fire."

She threw me an annoyed look. "Yes, purple fire. I'm telling you, it looked purple from up here!"

"Ok, ok," I said with a grin, "Purple fire it is. I've seen weirder. The area could be Veil. Or starting to shift to it. I don't feel anything though."

"Veil?" Reva asked, confusion written across her face as she stared blankly at me.

I frowned. "You've never seen a Veil zone? Where the Source and the Dark clash?"

She shook her head. "No, that isn't a, uh, 'thing' down in the South. I've never even heard of it."

"Huh," I mused, glancing back down at the forest below. "Sometimes the energy of the underground leaks through. It can get a bit ugly. Weird creatures, temporal anomalies. Nature goes a little crazy. I've seen several permanent ones, but they're normally pretty fleeting phenomena. Couple of days at most. The Source tends to reassert itself after a while and close the rift."

My voice trailed off as a sudden spark of Reva's 'purple fire' briefly lit the trees. It certainly didn't look human, but I couldn't sense any disturbance in the Source that would have indicated Veil. I was suddenly on my guard.

Reva and I cautiously circled lower, trying to pinpoint the exact location of the spark. Landing quietly in the clearing, we stalked over to what seemed to be a blackened circle in the earth. The ground was twisted in on itself, as though a small whirlpool had opened up and snarled the soil and plants into a blackened mess. Spatters of what could only be fresh blood dotted the immediate vicinity and what appeared to be marks of some sort had been crudely scratched into the dirt around the circle, but had been hastily scuffed into oblivion. I reached out with the toe of my boot and turned over what seemed to be part of a hand and forearm, the skin mangled and torn. I had no idea what this was. Judging by Reva's face, she was just as confused and repulsed. The rest of the clearing appeared to be undisturbed and the surrounding forest quiet, though some sixth sense told me that we were being watched.

My skin began to crawl as we scanned the dark forest around us. In the old days, even alone, I wouldn't have so much as flinched at a situation like this, probably would have recklessly gone off into the trees, searching around for an explanation, but those days were over.

"I think we should go," I said quietly. "Remember it, note the location. This," I glanced around uneasily, "isn't safe."

With a brief nod of agreement, Reva took off. I took one last look at the surrounding trees. I could have sworn I'd seen movement, but things were once again still.

It was early morning when we touched down at The Watch. Seeming slightly unsettled, Reva wandered off to file our report. Still pondering what we'd seen, intent on discussing it with Neph later, I found myself back at my quarters without realizing it. I paused in the doorway, suddenly torn by more mundane matters. To sleep or not to sleep. As restless as I was, somehow I didn't think napping was going to happen. Grabbing a book, I headed back out.

The flash of an officer's uniform caught my half-closed eye. I'd been dozing off in the shade, reclining on a bench in one of The Watch's numerous gardens, my book lying half open across my chest. The garden had been built to incorporate pre-existing Seri ruins.

Carved stone walls with intricate bas-reliefs dotted the area, some crumbling, others untouched after tens of thousands of years. An old fountain gurgled quietly in the center, surrounded by greenery and flowers. The bench I was lying across was bookended by the ruins of wide stone columns with ornately carved bases.

I could see Neph crossing the garden from my half open eyes. As far as I could tell, he hadn't noticed me. I was about to raise my hand, call out, when I caught sight of another figure striding towards him on an intercept course. A man I'd thought, hoped, I'd never see again. One that I'd thought had been left back at Skycrest.

"What in the hell do you think you're doing, Nephael?"

Suddenly very much awake, I rolled sideways off the bench, ducking behind one of the ruined pillars, slamming my back against the stone, just in time to keep Sendaryn from seeing me. What was he doing at The Watch? I leaned slightly to the side and peered around the thick column. He had caught up to Neph, who was glaring at him with open distaste.

"Excuse me?"

"What are you playing at, with this Enpirion thing?" Sendaryn demanded, his voice rising.

"Just because I have to talk to you at Council meetings doesn't mean I have to give you the time of day outside of them," Neph said icily. He turned his back and began to move away, only to have Sendaryn move forward and cut him off.

"No, Nephael. I want an answer this time. Why are you protecting it?"

"*It*?" Neph said, an edge of anger creeping into his voice. "We're talking about a person."

"No, we aren't," Sendaryn sneered. "How many times do I have to bring it up to the Council before it gets through your thick skull? Enpirion isn't a person. He's a weapon; a manufactured tool of the Empire that -"

"I'm not discussing this," Neph said, cutting him off. "You've made your views incredibly clear on any number of occasions and, frankly, I'm starting to lose my patience."

"I don't give a damn about your patience," Sendaryn bellowed, drawing the attention of more than a few other Seri in the area. "I'm tired of seeing you allow that, that *creature* to walk around here as though it's like any other Seri. Acting like it's your friend." He paused. "You should have let it die back in Skycrest."

Neph's arm snaked out with lightning speed and grabbed Sendaryn's collar, slamming him backwards into one of the columns. I sucked in a sharp breath, shocked. I'd never seen Neph angry before, never seen him lose his temper.

"I warned you back at Skycrest to leave him alone," Neph said, leaning in until he was only a few inches from Sendaryn, voice flat

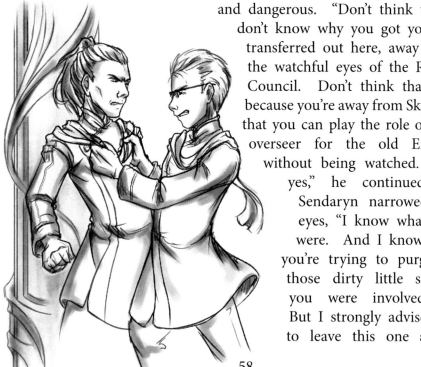

and dangerous. "Don't think that I don't know why you got yourself transferred out here, away from the watchful eyes of the Ruling Council. Don't think that just because you're away from Skycrest that you can play the role of Seri overseer for the old Empire without being watched. Oh yes," he continued, as Sendaryn narrowed his eyes, "I know what you were. And I know how you're trying to purge all those dirty little secrets you were involved in. But I strongly advise you to leave this one alone.

Enpirion is no longer your concern."

"That's where you're wrong," Sendaryn said quietly.

"The Empire is dead," Neph snapped. "It's over."

Sendaryn smiled, a leering grin that made me shudder. Neph roughly shoved him away in disgust. Around the garden, Seri were awkwardly trying to pretend that they weren't paying rapt attention to the scene.

"Don't cross me, Sendaryn. Enjoy your power on the Small Council, but remember that the ENF belongs to me now, every soldier on that squad."

Squaring his shoulders, Sendaryn straightened his uniform, brushing himself down. He glanced around, suddenly seeming to become aware of the small crowd. I sank to the ground and closed my eyes, feeling ill, no longer wanting to listen, hoping it was over. Several minutes passed before the clip of boots on paving stones reached my ears, moving towards where I was hidden. Neph crouched down beside me.

"Are you alright?"

"How did you know I was here," I whispered.

"Call it a sixth sense," Neph said with a twitch of a smile.

"Why is Sendaryn here at The Watch? How long has he been here?"

"Quite a while, actually. He got himself transferred not long after I moved you here, believe it or not. Frankly, I'm surprised this is the first you've seen him. He managed to pull enough strings back in Skycrest to get onto The Watch's Small Council, a decision I couldn't agree with less. Try not to let it worry you. He's dangerous, but I also think he's intelligent enough to understand that he doesn't want me as an enemy."

I opened my eyes, staring hard at Neph as he fell silent. I'd never seen him look so deadly serious, his blue eyes hard and cold as he held my gaze. Abruptly rising, he reached out a hand and pulled me to my feet. He was still intently staring at me, making me more than a little jittery. The sensation was unnerving and served as a reminder that there was something else there behind his normally placid exterior. As I started to fidget, he softened and sighed. Bending down, he grabbed up my book from where it had fallen to the ground in my flight.

"I have to go," he said quietly, running a finger across the gilt page edges. Disappointment coursed through my system as he handed the book to me and began to walk away. He stopped suddenly, turning back. "I…have to go into Bridgeport tomorrow. On business. I was thinking you might want to come, maybe take in The Morring. Get away from The Watch for a while."

My spirits instantly lifted. I hadn't been to Bridgeport in what felt like an eternity, not since I used to sneak off to visit it during my years with the original ENF. My face must have lit up because Neph smiled and nodded.

"I'll see you tomorrow, early."

The Morring Market

When Neph had said early, I hadn't been anticipating a knock on my door at very nearly the crack of dawn. He seemed distracted and out of sorts when I'd groggily let him in. Feeling like I'd be on the raw end of his temper if I dawdled, I spent precious little time throwing myself together and grabbing my bag.

We arrived on the outskirts of the city in the early morning, touching down near the main gate. Bridgeport was bustling, even at such an early hour. The city rarely slept. Leaving me to enjoy myself for a few hours, Neph set off to meet his contact. I couldn't help being more than a little curious as I watched him walk away, quickly losing sight of him in the crowd. I could feel a surge of anxiety, being left alone in such a crowded area, but I took a deep breath and plunged into the throng, determined to enjoy myself and not let the overwhelming amount of strangers get to me.

Bridgeport had always been a favorite destination of mine to slip away to in the old days. As far as human cities went, it was unique. A port city hugging the coast line, its streets started at the base of the high, rocky precipice, winding upwards to the urban sprawl that sat at the top. Wide streets and large, curving stairs, well-worn with use, connected the various levels. Colored banners and pendants fluttered in the ocean breezes.

I breathed in deeply as I wended my way down the neatly cobbled streets, heading towards the center of town and the start of The Morring. Bridgeport's massive open-air market was known far and wide, among all the varying races. It catered in anything and everything, from the mundane to the exotic, local to the foreign. Most of it legal, some of it not. The market ran the length and breadth of the massive stone bridge that arched out over the ocean to connect the main city to the tall peninsular island where the ruling body held sway. Brightly colored stalls were packed end to end and all manner of people thronged the bridge, members of every race trading. While Bridgeport was a human city, it boasted a fairly large foreign population, some of it permanent, others transient, coming and going as the trade winds shifted. Khazda made up the majority of the non-human population. Standing a few heads shorter than the humans, broad-shouldered and naturally gifted in metal and wood working, they were a jovial race, always happy and willing to ply their wares for good coin. A fair number of Seri were scattered throughout as well, and even some of the forest-dwellers, the Ellundara, their luminescent markings dimmed in the broad light of day. All living together.

Unlike the other human cities and settlements where the Seri weren't particularly welcome, a recent thaw in relations from the pure hatred of previous generations, Bridgeport was distinctly lacking in cultural borders. Even during the height of the Seri Empire, when relations among the races had been at an all-time low, the city had always been an open haven. Ignoring trade bans, flaunting the restrictions on Seri-human communication, it had always stood free. Bridgeport and its citizens had only ever been concerned with trade and commerce. Money spoke volumes and carried far more weight than war or politics.

Intrigued by a young painter, I lingered at an artist's booth, watching her create the market scene before her in delicate watercolor. I was so caught up in her work that it took me a moment to register the commotion that had started several stalls down. As it grew louder, both patrons and sellers began to stop their activities to watch the strangely clad figure now shouting in the middle of the causeway. A large crowd was forming around him as he continued his tirade.

Curiosity drew me closer. The man was wildly gesticulating and screaming in some language I couldn't make out, wearing

62

heavily decorated, hooded robes that hid most of his face. It all looked vaguely familiar. A nagging feeling was needling at my mind, something I should have been able to remember, but couldn't quite latch on to. Those robes. The scene was making me distinctly edgy.

Having garnered the crowd's attention, the man switched to the common tongue and began painting a pretty picture of the coming end, how the world would be enveloped in darkness. Several people began to laugh and move away, assuming him to be just another religious fanatic.

Two of Bridgeport's City Watch began to roughly elbow their way through the crowds, eager to shut down the spectacle. The man began to scream and struggle as they grabbed him by the arms and started to forcefully drag him, still thrashing, off through the marketplace. A second man in identical robes suddenly shouldered his way through, pushing aside angry Bridgeporters as he grabbed at the guards, screaming in his foreign language. Onlookers muttered, shaking their heads. I felt my eyes widen slightly as I sensed the sudden flow of energy towards the man, brought in by whatever he was shouting. It ended just as quickly as several more guards rushed to the scene and felled the man with a blow to the head, dropping him unconscious. Both men were dragged away.

"What was that about?"

The unexpected voice in my ear made me jump. I spun around and nearly crashed into Neph standing behind me, intently watching the robed men being dragged away, his brows drawn together, a look of unease that mirrored my own. I shook my head slightly. "I don't know. It didn't last long though. The guards seemed pretty eager to get him off the street." I paused, hesitant. "That one, the second one. He started to summon - " I stopped again. It sounded crazy even to me.

Neph frowned. "Started to summon what? I didn't feel anything."

"Because he wasn't pulling on the Source."

Frown deepening, Neph stared off again in the direction the guards had taken. "I think - no, never mind. Let's just continue on."

I pulled a wry face. "You think it was one of those cultists that Arafel was talking about. Yes, I do pay attention sometimes. Is that what we're actually doing here today, what you were meeting about?"

Lowering his voice, he gently prodded me back into the crowds. "Not here. I don't want to discuss it. Let's just, just enjoy the market." His voice was strained.

We began to wander the bridge, but the atmosphere of The Morring had been ruined by the disturbance. I looked around at the thinning crowds, many of them talking in hushed whispers and casting paranoid glances. City guards had begun to thread their way through the stalls, positioning themselves around the perimeter of the bridge, growing in number. I pulled Neph off to the side of a stall.

"Maybe we should go back. The market's not quite as inviting as it was earlier."

Neph sighed as we turned around, heading back towards the city gate.

"I'm sorry. I genuinely wanted you to have a nice day away from The Watch."

I shrugged. "It's not your fault." I couldn't keep the slight tinge of disappointment out of my voice though.

Neph suddenly began to root through his bag, pulling out a small ornately carved, hinged box.

"Here," he said, holding it out to me. "Maybe this will help."

"What's this?" I flipped the latch and pushed back the lid. It was a brush and ink set, a beautiful one. I looked back up.

"I found it at a street vendor's booth on the way to meet my contact earlier." He shrugged awkwardly. "I thought you would like it."

I stopped walking. "This...Neph, this is expensive," I said weakly. "I can't - you shouldn't." No one had ever given me anything before, let alone something so costly. I snapped the lid shut and held it out, averting his gaze. I felt his fingers wrap around mine as he slowly pushed it back towards me.

"It's a gift."

I reopened the box and removed the delicate brush, staring at the carved jade stem. The engraved ink stone sat nestled on a silk cushion.

"Tell you what," Neph said, resting a hand on my shoulder, "if it makes you feel better about accepting it, you can pay me back with a piece of art for my office. Sound good?"

"But my art isn't worth anything. There are plenty of better artists..."

"Gods, Piri," he laughed, "You're always so hard on yourself. I don't even know what to do with you sometimes. Just accept it and say thank you."

"Thank you," I forced out, feeling horribly guilty.

"See," Neph said with a grin. "Easy. Don't make me feel bad about buying you something."

I felt my face start to flush as I carefully put the brush back and

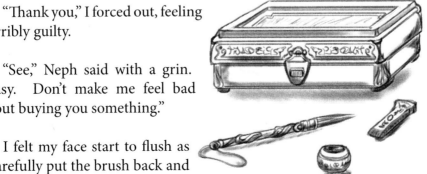

closed the box, stashing it safely in my bag. I knew he was making light of the situation, trying to put me at ease, but it was only making things worse. "I've just - no one's ever given me anything before. It doesn't feel right, getting something for no reason." I don't know why I felt the need to try to explain how I was feeling. I think Neph probably understood it better than I did, but I needed to verbalize it. I didn't want him making light of it.

Sobering suddenly, Neph looked me over, the smile still there but no longer happy or amused.

"Please don't look at me like that," I muttered angrily. "I don't want your pity."

"I'm sorry, I didn't mean -"

I was angry at myself and even angrier that I was directing it at Neph when he had simply been trying to do something nice for me. I scrubbed a hand through my hair and leaned up against the wall. I took a deep breath. "I'm sorry."

"It's ok," he said quietly.

"It's not ok," I said as I closed my eyes, pressing my forehead to the cool stone. "I - I really appreciate the gift. I do. And I'm sorry for taking my own insecurities out on you. It's just that," I paused. He stayed quiet, waiting. "I don't know how to deal with you doing nice things for me sometimes. It's not something I'm used to dealing with. I've never had anyone -"

"Stop," Neph said. He pulled me away from the wall and steered me back down the street. "I understand and you don't need to explain or apologize. I guess I'm sorry too, for what it's worth. I didn't realize it would upset you and I certainly didn't mean to make you uncomfortable. I hope you'll keep the gift though." The smile returned. "I still want a piece of art for my office."

Neph's Quarters

"You do realize that what I told you stays here, between us. Yes?" I glanced around the nearly empty tea room.

After several days of prodding, Reva had finally managed to break me down and I'd related what had happened in The Morring. Neph had been incredibly keen on our return to get every detail that I could remember, especially concerning my ability to sense energy other than the Source. Apprehensive and more than a little vexed over his obvious excitement, I'd skirted the issue as much as possible, until, frustration setting in, he'd finally let it drop. I wasn't sure why I'd explained it in detail to Reva; maybe because I'd already let her see how I Source. I don't know. It was an odd lapse in judgment on my part.

The Seri all knew and understood that more existed out there than just the Source, but most couldn't feel anything else, let alone use it. That energy made us what we were; it was the core of our very being. The mere fact that conflicting energies existed had spurred more than its fair share of conflict in our past, leaving a trail of bloody devastation strewn across the history books of every single race that happened to be caught up in it. During the last war, one I had been intimately involved in, the Seri had executed their own on mere suspicion of sympathizing with the other side, let alone having some sort of connection to the enemy's life force. While things had thawed since the end of the Uprising and the complete restructuring of the Seri governing body, you certainly couldn't do away with thousands of years of cultural stigma overnight. Even my original ENF handlers hadn't known the full extent of what I could do.

Leaning back in her chair, Reva looked me over, but she seemed less than interested in what I'd told her, more intent on the ink set, her long fingers turning it this way and that. "Of course it stays between us; you know I'd never tell anyone else anything you talk to me about. I'm still not sure why you wouldn't tell Nephael though.

I mean, do I really need to explain my reasoning behind that?"

I shrugged. "He's my commanding officer."

"Hmmm, yeah. And there's no conflict of interest there," she said with a grin, running a finger over the lid of the box.

I didn't say anything, didn't really know how to respond. I was still mildly upset about the gift and the way Reva was staring at me wasn't helping.

"Anyway," she continued, "you shouldn't get yourself so off kilter about this. Friends do nice things for each other. Not - not normally *this* nice... He obviously thinks a lot of you. I say take advantage of it; a next step in your friendship you might say." Opening the lid, she pulled out the brush pen, turning it over in her fingers.

I frowned in incomprehension, watching her. "What are you talking about?"

Reva rolled her eyes, replacing the pen and pushing the box back across the table. "Did you ever think about doing things off-hours, rather than the weird chaperon friendship you two have? You know he's not enforcing that policy anymore,

regardless of what the Council seems to think about it, yet he always acquiesces to going along with you everywhere." She pushed her chair back and stood up. "Stop being on-duty friends. We're off rotation for a week. Use it, yeah?"

I trailed after her as she wended her way towards the Grand Hall, a little perturbed that she wasn't focusing on what I thought was the important issue here, namely Bridgeport.

"Aren't you the least little bit curious about what happened on the bridge? The meeting Neph had that he refuses to tell me about?"

Reva tilted her head slightly. "Of course, but there's really no use in conjecture, is there? I'm sure that when it becomes an actual issue, we'll be quick to know what's going on. I'll grant you, the whole thing is odd, but every city has its nuts and troublemakers, especially the human cities. As for the energy thing…," she trailed off. "I don't know. We just have to be patient, I guess. Try not to dwell on it to the point of insanity. I know how you get."

Punching me lightly on the shoulder, she said goodbye and parted ways. I crossed my arms, glowering as she walked away.

Standing outside the door to Neph's quarters, I hesitated. Readjusting my leather bag, I frowned down at the floor, wondering if I should be bothering him off duty, if he'd be put off, think it weird that I'd figured out where in the complex he lived. A few months ago, I never would have risked it, but now… Maybe Reva had been right the other day. Trying to quiet my jangling nerves, I raised my hand and tentatively knocked. Anxious as I was, it felt like hours before I heard a shout from inside to come in, though it couldn't have been more than a few seconds. The door slid open as I pressed my hand to the Sourcepad.

I stood in the doorway and simply stared. Neph's living quarters were, well, spacious. To say the least. I couldn't help but gawk at the massive main living area, the full kitchen, a Source-powered fireplace, not to mention separate rooms for bed and bath. It had never occurred to me that there were different sorts of living areas in the cities. I don't know why. Maybe because I'd never had my own rooms before The Watch. Maybe because, even here, I was holed up in a small, one room situation. But this...this was an actual living space, a permanent home. Custom-crafted furniture, beautiful art adorning the walls. The ceiling, I couldn't help but notice, was part of the living rock of the mountain, rough and natural. There were bookshelves filled with all manner of volumes and artifacts. Just like his office, plants were scattered across the area, living vines creeping their way up the corners and around the shelves. The curved window stretching the entire length of the kitchen provided a breathtaking panorama of the mountains.

Neph sat at an ornately carved round table, scattered with papers and books, chin resting on his hand, simply watching me standing there as I took the place in.

"You're allowed to come in you know," he said with a grin. "You don't need to just stand in the doorway."

Wondering how long I'd been gawking, I quickly stepped inside, hearing the door slide softly shut behind me. More than ever, I was beginning to regret intruding on his privacy, but, now that I was inside, I was trapped. I could feel myself starting to panic, a sensation that was suddenly backed

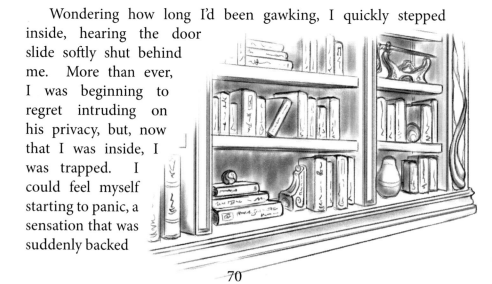

by annoyance and anger at myself. It was just Neph.

Pen tip coming to rest on the document before him, Neph gestured towards the chair across from him. "Come sit down."

I shook my head, moving back half a step. "I shouldn't. I'm sorry, I shouldn't have bothered you."

"It's no bother at all. I'll admit, you were the last person I expected when I heard the knock, but that doesn't mean I'm not happy to see you. What's up?"

"I just -" I stared down at the wooden floor, eyes roving over the colorfully woven area rugs. My fingers involuntarily fussed with the clasps on my bag. "I was going to take a book up to the ruins, read, maybe do some sketching. I was wondering if you wanted to, well, join me."

His face fell slightly and he looked down at the mess on the table in front of him. With a sigh, he shook his head. "I wish I could, honestly. But there's a lot I need to go through here today, reports, matters from the Council." He trailed off, looking with open distaste at the mound of paperwork.

With a nod, I took a step back towards the door, nervously running my fingers through my hair. "Hold on," he said, half rising from his chair. "I don't know if you've actually looked outside. It looks like it's going to rain anyway and gods know I could probably use some company while I'm working. It gets awfully quiet. Why not stay? Make yourself comfortable. Go raid the kitchen for something, get into the books, I don't care."

My head jerked up at the suggestion, my mind a sudden blank. I stared out the kitchen window, heart sinking at the roiling black clouds that were, sure enough, massing on the horizon. I slowly dragged my eyes back to Neph. Stay? I looked around again, a sudden longing ache in my chest. This place was comfortable, welcoming, but it wasn't mine.

"I shouldn't," I whispered. "I don't want to intrude."

"Don't be ridiculous," Neph said, moving to the kitchen and putting on a kettle, the matter resolved as far as he was concerned. "If you were intruding, I wouldn't have made the offer. I'd have told you to get out." He laughed. I smiled slightly, but didn't move, still undecided. It wasn't until he finally turned around and pointed at the couch, "Piri, seriously, sit," that I left my shoes at the door and moved towards the curved couch that dominated the main area, hesitantly curling myself up in the corner of it. I sank into the plush cushions, eyes roving down the intricately carved wood, tracing the detailed spirals and curls, the ornate vines and plant-life that curled across it. Where on earth had he gotten furniture like this? It looked Seri in design, old Seri, but it was obviously custom done and newer.

"Bridgeport," he said from across the room, as if reading my mind. "Amazing, some of the artisans they've got there. All the furniture in here was done by them, bed included." He nodded towards the other room. "I'm hoping there's no cause to move again for quite a while. Transporting it all is a nightmare." He stared around thoughtfully. "Worth it though." He brought a cup of my favorite mint tea over. I sank further into the cushions as I held it while he went back to work at the table.

I simply watched Neph working for a while, head bent over the reports, pen flashing back and forth as he made notes, finger occasionally reaching up to push his glasses back up the bridge of his nose. Those glasses, such a weird quirk. He didn't need them. They were nothing more than a fashion accessory. I'd worked that out months back when he'd left them sitting around one day and, picking them up, had only taken a moment to realize the lens were simple glass. Something about him wearing them had bothered me for weeks after that. But now... I tilted my head slightly. Now I was so used to seeing them, I actually preferred them on.

Neph's pen paused, his gaze briefly flicked up, meeting mine, and he smiled warmly before resuming whatever he was working on. I felt myself flush slightly, caught staring, but my embarrassment didn't last long for some reason and I continued to watch him work. The apartment was quiet but for the sound of Neph's pen. I was amazed at how relaxed I felt, knees pulled up, wedged back into the soft cushions, slowly sipping at the warm mug in my hands. Even back in my own quarters, away from everyone, I was never what you could call comfortable. I was used to silence, but I couldn't say I'd ever liked it; it was never peaceful. Silence, for me, was always a lonely affair, filled with the turbulence inside my own head. I realized though, sitting there, that with Neph it was different. He never seemed to care whether I was talkative or, more often than not, silent. There was never any awkwardness to it, only a peaceful sort of stillness that helped calm the internal chaos.

The day spent in Neph's apartment seemed to have broken through a wall in our friendship, on my end at least. I don't think it would have bothered him in the least if I'd shown up at his door a month prior. On days off, I found myself, more and more frequently, holed up in his living room, sprawled across the sofa. Book or sketchpad in hand, a cup of tea or coffee on the floor next to me, I'd while away the hours while Neph worked at the table, often going for extended lengths in pure silence with only the sound of paper or pencil to fill the void. Those quiet times came to mean everything to me as the days and weeks came and went. So much of my time was now devoted to training with Reva or going on ever widening and farther reaching patrols, that my free time was reduced to a precious commodity. The 'alone' time spent in Neph's company was a vital part of my sanity.

Despite the continually busy schedule, I found myself becoming bored with the routine of it all. Rumors and gossip flew thick around The Watch concerning strange happenings in other cities. Everything from mysterious meetings to disappearances, strange markings on the ground. Some of the stories were wild and overblown, others just odd enough to be plausible. It was hard to tell what was real and what wasn't, though the officers and guild leaders were distinctly on edge and getting more so. Yet, out and about on our constant surveillance, despite all the reports from the extended territories, in our small corner of the Seri world, everything remained quiet.

Piri's Sketchbook: Excerpts

Part Two

Realization

Soaked to the bone and exhausted, I trudged down the hallway, heading towards my quarters and leaving small puddles in my wake. Swiping a limp hand across the Sourcepad, I moodily let myself into the room, peeling off my uniform as I went. The weather had been particularly miserable for the past week, treacherous flying conditions pushing even the best of us to our limits. Despite the driving rain and harsh winds, we'd done our best to go about business as usual.

I leaned my forehead against the glass of the bathroom mirror, hands fumbling to untangle the scarf from around my collar, and squeezed my eyes shut. It felt as though an iron band was slowly constricting around my head, the pressure nearly unbearable. The stress and boredom of the past few weeks had been slowly eating away at me.

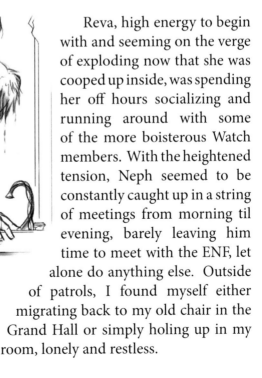

Reva, high energy to begin with and seeming on the verge of exploding now that she was cooped up inside, was spending her off hours socializing and running around with some of the more boisterous Watch members. With the heightened tension, Neph seemed to be constantly caught up in a string of meetings from morning til evening, barely leaving him time to meet with the ENF, let alone do anything else. Outside of patrols, I found myself either migrating back to my old chair in the Grand Hall or simply holing up in my room, lonely and restless.

Finally managing to get out of my wet clothing and attain a state of semi-dryness, I threw on loose sleepwear and curled up on the bed with a sigh, unconsciously rubbing at my shoulder as my scar began to ache.

I knew from the moment that I awoke that the day was a loss, both physically and mentally. The old knife wound ached abysmally, twinges of electric pain occasionally streaking across my back and shoulders. But it was the mental turmoil, the fragmented memories and cracked walls, that had me done in before I had even begun. I lay in bed, eyes open, listlessly staring at the bare wall, not really seeing it as broken memories slipped in and out of reach. I didn't want to move. I didn't want to do anything. I just wanted to shut myself away, try to escape from myself. I was more than content to let the darkness slide in.

Neph would want me to move. To get up. Try.

The thought suddenly cut across the fog. I closed my eyes with a grimace and buried my face in the pillow, trying, unsuccessfully, to shut out the one voice of reason that could make me attempt the day. Cursing inwardly, I dragged myself out of bed, got dressed.

With everyone trapped inside due to the season's perpetual storms and all-round miserable weather, the halls and common areas had a terribly claustrophobic feel as I wandered The Watch, unable to focus or settle. I went out of my way to avoid running into anyone I might know. Somehow, without realizing it, the morning had passed and I was standing back at my quarters, head resting against the door, eyes closed. I took several deep breaths before I let myself in, feeling overwhelmed, for no reason I could identify; on the verge of tears as my mind simply sank to a distant, dark point.

Curling up on my bed, barely aware of the world around me, I let myself slip away.

Returning to consciousness was a slow process, but I could hear my name, feel a hand on my shoulder. I cracked my eyes and glimpsed blue. Blue and gold. Neph was sitting beside where I lay curled on my bed, officer's uniform in stark contrast to the white sheets. He murmured something I didn't quite make out. I stared for a moment, focusing on the gold stripe on his coat, my mind briefly dwelling on the fact that he'd come into my personal quarters to look for me, something that seemed incredibly out of place despite my frequency in his own apartment.

My fingers involuntarily clenched at the small blanket I'd been clutching when I fell asleep and I buried my face in it as I fully woke up and reality crashed back in. Sleep had blissfully taken away the pain, all the emotions that I didn't want to feel anymore fading into oblivion for a short time. I could feel myself starting to shake as I fought to keep from falling apart, trying to hide it from my friend sitting next to me. I didn't know why I cared if Neph saw the tears. He'd certainly seen them before.

His hand was still lightly resting on my shoulder, but I felt the fingers briefly tighten as I hid away. He didn't say anything, didn't ask any questions. Just sat there, silently watching me.

I was briefly surprised when his hand moved to my head, fingers twining through my hair, lightly moving back and forth. My entire body tensed, but he didn't stop. I began to feel myself relax at the sensation and closed my eyes. For the first time, Neph's touch, which I'd finally become used to and accepted in our friendship, sent something different coursing through my system, caused an aching tightness in my chest. It wasn't a sensation that I could put words to just then because it wasn't something I'd ever felt before. I just knew that I didn't want him to stop.

Curling into a ball, I let myself sink into the sensation, the darkness beginning to retreat for the first time that day. It could have been minutes or only a few brief seconds that I lay there, drifting in a sea of tranquility, before it all came crashing down as my internal defenses suddenly kicked in. Terror coursed through my system and I curled into an even tighter ball as my mind tried to rationalize what I was feeling, contain it, push it away.

Almost as if he sensed the sudden turmoil within me, Neph's fingers stopped, withdrew. "It's been a while since you had a swing like this," he whispered. "Come on. Get up, come get a drink with me."

I shook my head slightly. I could still feel where his hand had been in my hair. Intense disappointment that it was gone. Fear and guilt underlying the disappointment. There was a brief silence, then, "It wasn't a request. I'm not leaving you here like this. We can find some place quiet to sit where no one will bother us. Come on."

I slowly uncurled and sat up, pushing myself slightly farther away on the bed. Neph reached out and lightly wiped a tear off my cheek. I shivered slightly, found myself averting his gaze, uncomfortably aware of how close he was. Turning away, I slid off the other side of the bed. Clutching my forehead, I staggered towards the door, Neph silently following in my wake. I wasn't sure which was worse; how I'd been feeling all morning or what I was feeling now. At least the darkness and turmoil, so effectively pushed away, had been familiar territory. This…

"Piri?" Neph's hand came down on my shoulder and I jumped, spinning around to face him. He sounded hesitant, his face twisted in concern.

"I, sorry, I'm fine," I stammered, pulling away. I sucked in a deep breath, trying to regain control. Forcing a smile, I backed away and slid out the door. "I just - " Further words were cut off as I turned and slammed into Reva. Winded and gasping for air, I leaned back against the wall in the hall. Through the fog of trying to catch my breath, I couldn't help but feel somewhat relieved. Reva's appearance broke the tension and awkwardness of being alone.

Reva was laughing and apologizing at the same time, trying to haul me upright. Something about practice. I only caught that one word, but I latched on to it, glad for the chance to get away. Letting her drag me down the hall, I chanced a glance back over my shoulder to see Neph frowning after us.

Avoidance

Things had gotten progressively worse. And I didn't know what to do.

I put my sketchbook aside, page still blank, and hugged my knees to my chest. I'd spent the entire week avoiding Neph, making good use of the clearing weather to be outdoors and doing everything in my power to be anywhere that he wasn't.

My entire life had been spent suffering from loneliness, living on my own solitary island, but this was different. This was a physical pain, an aching loneliness, a craving for something I'd never known. I think it had been itching at me for a while, but that day, lying on my bed with Neph's hand in my hair...that had been the turning point, emotionally. A threshold had been crossed while I'd been vulnerable and now, no matter how hard I tried, I couldn't seem to rebuild that wall.

I was terrified of losing my best friend and I was well aware that my current strategy of avoidance wasn't going to help matters. But being around him was eating me up inside. I needed to control things, to force it back into the recesses of my mind. Telling him was absolutely out of the question. After all this time, I still wasn't entirely sure how or why he was my friend, what he truly saw in me. Unlike at the beginning though, I didn't care anymore; I just went with it and was grateful for it. Deep down, I think I just assumed he was a little odder than I really knew. But this was something else entirely and I couldn't even entertain the notion that we could be anything more than friends. Neph was everything that I wasn't. And what did I know about relationships. Nothing. Less than nothing. And I was quite a bit beyond the normal age for learning that sort of thing. Interpersonal matters of any sort certainly weren't my forte. I was so absorbed in my own thoughts that I nearly jumped out of my skin when Neph dropped himself onto the ground beside me.

"So," he said, not looking at me.

I buried my head between my knees. Neph heaved an exasperated sigh.

"Look, I gave you a week off my sensors. You've been acting strange - stranger than usual - for weeks, and I figured that everyone needs space and alone time. But I'm also your officer and I can't let it go any longer than this. You aren't shirking your duties, but there's no question you're going out of your way to avoid me." He fell silent, staring out at the mountains.

I looked up at him, seeing him simply as my friend for the first time in several weeks. I missed him, horribly. And I could see the pain and anger clearly written across his face as he glared at the horizon, burning a hole through the mountains.

"I'm sorry," I whispered. "I've just been...dealing with some things."

"Regarding me, apparently," he said with more than a trace of anger. I flinched. "I thought we were past this, that we were -"

"Friends," I finished, cutting him off. "We are."

"Then what the hell is going on, Piri?"

"Nothing," I said, getting to my feet, trying to keep my voice light. I reached out a hand. "It's taken care of. I really am sorry, I mean that. I just needed to work through something." My voice caught slightly and I forced a smile. Neph looked at me oddly, but took my hand and let me pull him to his feet.

"You're a terrible liar, you know that," he said quietly.

"Thanks. Forgive me?"

"I'm still angry," he said, frowning.

I grabbed my bag and sketchpad from the grass, taking a deep breath as I straightened up, steadying myself. I could do this. I just needed to bury it all, seal it away, like I did with everything else. His friendship had become too integral to my life to risk losing it.

"Let's grab some lunch. I would feel better being berated over food."

I was rewarded with a twitch of a smile.

"You know there's an ENF meeting in an hour and I need to meet with the Council briefly beforehand," he said. "Are you really not going to tell me what's going on?"

Ah, right. I'd nearly forgotten. No, that was a lie. I'd completely forgotten that a special meeting had been called, having been far too caught up in my own problems to really care overly much. Lunch would have been far more enjoyable.

Looking at Neph, I felt a slight twinge. I pushed it away, not without effort. "I told you, it's taken care of. But - I do have something for you." Change the subject. I fished around in my bag, pulling out an ink drawing, protected between two thin pieces of bound wood. I ran a thumb over the wood, feeling the bump of the grain against my skin. It was Neph's ruins and cherry tree, rendered in perfect detail using the ink set he'd given me, done one early morning when I'd needed to get away. I'd been carrying it around for nearly two weeks, afraid to give it to him.

Neph stared at the package quizzically as I handed it over. He drew in a sharp breath as he gently flipped it open and stared at the drawing inside.

"This -"

"I owed you a piece of art. For your office," I said, somewhat embarrassed, scuffing the ground with one foot. "I thought - I thought I should do a picture that meant something."

"It's beautiful," Neph breathed, still staring, almost mesmerized, at the ink drawing. He finally looked up. "Thank you."

I turned away and started off towards the main complex, feeling my face start to flush.

"Come on, let's at least grab a drink before you have to go."

The ENF Responds

Sitting myself down next to Reva, I took a sip of tea and glanced around the conference room at the other members of the ENF. The entire group was gathered, curiosity written across every face. We'd certainly been called together on short notice, the word having just gone out that morning, and everyone was very much aware that this wasn't a normal meeting. Murmurs ran around the room as they conjectured amongst themselves. Reva softly poked my leg to get my attention.

"Nephael tell you anything about this?"

I shook my head. I'd kept quiet about how I'd been feeling lately and I didn't want to initiate the inevitable questions by telling her that I hadn't really seen much of him over the past few weeks. Reva seemed to have developed a sixth sense concerning my emotional state and had a way of dragging information out of me. I was sure she'd eventually figure out that something was going on, but I had no intention of telling her and making it easy. My lack of time with Neph though meant that I knew as much as anyone else going into this meeting, though I certainly had my suspicions. Anyone here who didn't have some inkling had to have spent the last few months under a rock. The whispering came to a sudden halt as the door slid open and Neph entered the room, followed by Evari. She was one of the few members of the Small Council that I saw Neph interact with outside of meetings, someone he seemed to treat more as a friend than simply a colleague. I'd had little interaction with her, but she always seemed to be calm and smiling. Today though, her features were drawn and serious.

Neph swiped a hand across a Sourcepad on the wall and the lights died as a projection flickered to life, tracing across the wall; a detailed map of the northern half of the continent. Several human cities were clearly marked, along with a handful of other locations. I glanced sideways at Reva who was frowning at the map.

Brakon's Landing, circled in red. Kallin's Fist, Port Odarin. Bridgeport and Warriors Mark. I recognized a spot in the middle of nowhere, marking the location of Reva's 'purple fire'. Whispers erupted around the room as ENF soldiers began pointing out places they recognized, odd happenings from reports they had made or read about.

"All right, settle down," Neph said, raising his voice above the din. Instant silence. All eyes were now riveted on him. "You've probably all figured out why we're here. There have been plenty of rumors going around for quite some time now concerning some rather odd happenings and I know that quite a few of you have witnessed things first hand. I'm not here to discuss the details or talk about which gossip is real. You all have access to the patrol reports if you want to read more about it and I suggest you all do. The fact of the matter is that this isn't all hearsay and it's becoming a rising problem. The Ruling Council out of Skycrest called an emergency session a day ago and has decided to pursue the matter. It was determined that, rather than drafting out of the regular military, the ENF would be brought in to gather information on this issue."

Wrenna, one of the few surviving members of the original squad, punched a hand into the air.

"Yes?"

"Sir, forgive my interruption, but general recon isn't normally our thing. Why us?"

Evari stepped forward. "Because the ENF are faster, stronger and better Sourcers. You all have the ability to summon multiple forms

of weaponry and are better able to protect yourselves should the need arise. And, unlike a typical soldier, you're used to thinking on your feet without the need for officers, orders or armor."

Several soldiers smirked as they glanced around the room at each other.

"We hope your skill set won't be needed," Neph continued. "Our goal is information, not confrontation. But right now, we have no idea what we're going to be interacting with. On top of that, several of the cities have become incredibly dangerous to anyone who isn't human. Anti-Seri sentiment is especially on the rise. And I don't mean the normal leftover animosity from the Seri Empire. This is something new and it's growing in strength. There's more fueling this than we're currently aware of and the Ruling Council is sure it's somehow connected to everything else."

Evari pointed to several locations on the map. "We'll be sending you in teams to what we consider to be the central conflict areas. Nephael and I will be accompanying the teams being sent to the two most dangerous cities. All teams are to go disguised so that you blend in as much as possible, and, thankfully, unlike the other races, we look human enough to pass. Our contacts in each city will help you with blending into the culture. Unless your life is threatened, you are not to reveal that you are Seri, for your own safety. Your goal is to gather as much information as possible on this new human religion that seems to be at the center of every report: its practices, what it preaches, local involvement, how it may be tied to the rising Seri antagonism. Anything that may be relevant. Within the next few days, you will each receive information detailing your assigned team, destination and further instruction. Any questions?"

No one said anything though several people looked uneasy. Evari surveyed the room.

"No one?"

One of the newer ENF shook his head. "I'm sure we all have a thousand questions," he said, "but we'll wait until we've received further instruction, since it may answer a lot of them."

Others nodded their agreement. Evari turned to Neph.

"I like your crew, Nephael. I'd have been stuck for hours with my squad," she said with a laugh.

"Everyone is dismissed," he said, smiling. "If you do have any questions, at any point, please don't hesitate to direct them to either Evari or myself."

I lingered in the room as the others left, wanting to catch Neph on the way out. I was curious, I admit, for more information, but it was more than that. I'd missed him and simply wanted to talk, our run-in earlier having been far too brief. Reva hung back with me, hoping, I'm sure, to catch whatever I managed to get out of him. As the last of the ENF filed out, Farryn, one of my least favorite people and the only other original ENF member outside of Wrenna, threw me a disgusted look.

"Can't just wait like the rest of us," he said under his breath. "Must be nice to be the officer's favorite."

"Sit down, Farryn," Neph said with a trace of annoyance. "I'm glad you three stayed, regardless of the reason. You'll be accompanying me on this mission and I want to make it very clear that while our team is in Brakon's Landing I won't tolerate any insolence or arguments. I know that you two," he pointedly looked between Farryn and me, "have a bit of

93

a history. Right now, as far as this situation is concerned, I don't care. Leave your baggage at home. Brakon's Landing is considered dangerous at the best of times and we have reason to believe that it's at the heart of this strange movement. You three are my most powerful overSourcers and, two of you at least, have more experience than the rest of the force combined."

Reva tentatively raised a hand. "Sir, no offense, but aren't I going to, uh, stand out a bit? I'm way taller than the average human female, dark skinned…. I'm not exactly inconspicuous in a city like that."

"Oh, that shouldn't be a problem," Neph said with a wry grin. "We'll be staying with a contact at one of the temples. Ildra's followers hail from all corners. Passing you off as one of her priestesses won't be an issue. Though you're going to have to eliminate the pink while we're there."

Reva's hand involuntarily clutched at her hair, horror written across her face.

Farryn frowned. "Ildra? High Priestess of Eph? You can't be serious."

"Yes. To both of those." Neph began leafing through a binder. "She's an old friend and has graciously agreed to help us. She has her own reasons for wanting intelligence on the city's governance and is more than happy to assist us in any operation that will garner her information. Reva will be assisting her in those matters while you and Piri will be tracking the cultists."

Reva wandered to the front and began inspecting the map. "That's a bit of a fast jump, isn't it? A few minutes ago it was a religion, now it's a cult?"

Neph shrugged. "Let's just call it what it is. We've seen something disturbingly familiar before."

I hunched my shoulders and closed my eyes, trying to push aside a sudden wash of memories: the chanting, the blood…the sounds of my fellow ENForcers dying.

"Enpirion?"

I looked up. Neph never used my full name.

"I need to ask you a serious question. Taking everything you've been through into consideration. Can you handle working on this?"

Farryn rolled his eyes and I felt a flash of anger.

"I'll be fine," I snapped, a little too quickly.

"Don't answer so lightly," he said quietly after a brief pause.

I crossed my arms, narrowed my eyes. "I'm not." My scar twinged. "I can do my job just fine without that interfering."

Neph nodded slowly. Out of my peripheral vision, I could see Reva looking at me questioningly and I knew I'd be fielding unwanted questions later.

Arrival

It was early evening, long shadows stretching across the landscape as Nephael dropped from the overcast sky to land softly along the tree-line ahead of us. I quickly followed, Farryn and Reva dropping down behind me. Drawing his hood up over his blond hair, he pulled up the round, woven straw hat resting on his back and dropped it on top, gesturing for the rest of us to do the same.

"From here on out, we stay undercover," he said, pulling his glasses off and stowing them in his pack. "There's a tavern about two miles up the road where we'll stay the night. If we head out early morning tomorrow, we should arrive at Brakon's Landing before noon. Keep your mouth shut and, unless you feel that your life is in immediate danger, do not reveal that you're Seri. We have no idea what we might run into in this city. The cultists could very well be the least of our worries. I know you're tired of hearing it, but I cannot stress how deeply the anti-nonhuman sentiment runs in this place. The governors and city council are most likely wrapped up in all of this. There's always going to be a certain amount of risk, but let's try to keep things to a minimum if we can. Understood?"

Not waiting for a response, he set off down the hard-packed dirt road, robes flaring out behind him as his long strides took him quickly in the direction of the tavern. I looked down at my similar dress style. My robes, much like the other two, were a simpler, less ornate version of what Neph was wearing. We all appeared to be followers of Eph, the temple to which we were heading. We'd been briefed on the general tenets of the faith before leaving The Watch, but only enough to pass ourselves off.

96

Considering it was one of the largest of the human faiths, I supposed I should have known more about it, but religion, especially human religion, was never something I'd paid much attention to. The Seri hadn't really had an organized religion in ages. Post-meeting, back in his quarters, Neph had spent at least an hour animatedly chattering to me about the human religious culture. I'd sat there bemusedly staring at him, genuinely interested but not really taking any of it in, just enjoying listening to his enthusiasm.

Reva punched me on the arm.

"Ow, what?"

"Are you going to stand there staring off into space or are you coming?"

"I wasn't staring off into space," I said with a scowl.

"Yeah, uh huh. Because I only called your name three times. Let's go before we lose those two."

Rubbing my arm, I fell into step behind her as she started down the road.

Night had closed in by the time we came in sight of our destination. The tavern's roadside lanterns blazed a path through the darkness, a welcome sight after our long walk in what, for all intents and purposes, was now hostile territory. I glanced up at a wooden sign bearing the name 'The Baron's Arms' as we crossed through the entrance into the main common area. Neph wandered off, leaving the three of us loitering near the door. The room was fairly empty, with only a handful of travelers scattered around, some resting before the blazing fireplace, others drinking at the few time-worn tables. A handful glanced over, nodding greetings as their eyes slid over our robes. Neph had sidled up to the bar and was holding a brief discussion with what I assumed was the proprietor. His normal broad smile on his face, he raised his hands, gesturing back towards the door. I briefly caught something about sleeping in the stable and heaved an inward sigh of relief at the look of horror that crossed the man's face at the suggestion. Several minutes later, Neph returned and led us down a hallway towards a room with one bed and several sleeping rolls stacked in the corner. Moving inside, he closed the door behind us.

"It's certainly not home, but it's free for the night. Let's get some sleep; we're up early tomorrow."

The Temple District

The trek into Brakon's Landing was surprisingly uneventful and we crossed through the scrutiny of the city's gate guards with barely a passing glance. We'd entered the city from one of the slightly more upscale districts, but that didn't detract from the posters and signs plastered across the buildings, all of them seeming to proclaim the superiority of the human population and calling for the removal of anyone who wasn't. They were all stamped with the seal of the governing body, along with a runic symbol that none of us recognized. It didn't really take a genius to connect it to why we were there though. Keeping our heads down, we wound our way through the city, making for Temple Way.

The buildings of the temple district rose up suddenly above the chaos on the streets below. Towering structures hugged each other and crowded the narrow lane, vibrantly garish colors splashed across their outer faces. Every religion from the smallest to the largest sported representation, all vying for the attention of the passing crowds. All manner of the various religious hierarchy stood outside their doors, proselytizing to the streets as they tried to lure in pedestrians. Mixed in with the religious crowd were vendors of every flavor, hawking everything from street food to charms, making the already cramped causeway seem downright claustrophobic.

Neph set a determined path straight down the center of the Way, heading towards the largest and most impressive of the buildings. The street dead-ended

99

into a large open square backed by a fortified stone and wood, tiered pyramid-like structure with several outbuildings; a complex that dwarfed everything else surrounding it. Dressed as followers of Eph, we moved with ease through the crowds who readily parted to allow us passage.

"Stop gawking," Farryn muttered harshly under his breath, giving Reva a slight push in the small of her back. Throwing a dirty look over her shoulder, she quickened her steps.

I scowled, glancing out from under my hood and round straw-woven hat. "Leave her alone. It's hard not to gawk at this place. It's ridiculous." I found myself convulsively clutching at the sleeves of my robe, walking with hunched shoulders as we progressed further into the packed street.

"What's wrong with you?" Farryn asked. "Why are you so fidgety?"

"It's nothing. I'm fine," I said, making a conscious effort to drop my hands. It took more effort than I was willing to give it. "The crowds are just making me nervous, that's all."

Farryn screwed up his face in a skeptical sneer. "Really? Seriously? The almighty ENForcer, scared of crowds? Since when?"

I cast him a baleful look, opening my mouth to form a retort.

"Enough," Neph snapped from in front of us, stopping and turning. He lowered his voice. "We're nearly there. Keep quiet while I speak to Ildra. As I said before, she's expecting us, as are several of her inner circle, but the rest of the temple's followers, for obvious reasons, haven't been told who we are or why we're here. For now, don't speak to anyone. As far as I'm concerned, you've all taken a vow of silence for the moment." He threw a significant look Farryn's way before turning on his heel and setting off once more, the three of us falling into solemn step behind him.

Temple Way's rough cobbles were packed with more than just the pious and its usual array of visitors. Beggars huddled in the narrow

100

alleyways. Their rough, tattered clothing barely clung to their thin frames as they stared vacantly at wooden bowls before them in the hope of coin. We couldn't help but notice the large number of poor in these packed streets, a far cry from the Landing's Upper Circle where the rich and powerful dwelt. The marble towers and gilt statues were visible over the plethora of temple buildings, sitting upon the higher, walled off ground across the city. I tried and failed to repress a shudder of revulsion as my eyes drifted towards the Upper Circle. Brakon's Landing was offensive to me on just about every level, from its massive divide between the rich and poor to its corrupt culture and xenophobic attitude. It had fast become a template for many of the larger human cities, spurred on by the last hundred or so years of fairly intense Seri-human animosity. It had simply evolved from hatred of the Seri to hatred, apparently, of any foreigner: human and non-human alike. Several of the smaller temples had been boarded up; broken windows and scrawled graffiti loudly proclaimed their hostility towards the foreigners who had once been there.

As we neared our destination, Temple Way widened into a large open square, every bit as crowded as the street had been, but boasting several large wooden platforms bearing angrily shouting city magistrates. A handful of bonfires kept the massive crowds at bay, and it was only when Reva gasped aloud, her hand rising to convulsively grasp at her chest, that I realized I was looking at the remains of burned bodies, listening to proclamations concerning the sins of the foreign, how their blasphemy would corrupt the city and its people and how they would be punished for their crimes. The officials had worked the crowd into a frenzy. I hadn't even realized that I'd come to halt until Reva ran into me, causing me to stumble forward. The scene was horrific and I was having a hard time wrapping my mind around the fact that this was supposed to be a civilized human city we were standing in.

Expression blank, all calm determination, Neph beckoned us to go around the outskirts of the spectacle, the only sign of concern his quickened pace. The gates to the temple were quickly unbarred as we arrived, the monks not even waiting for us to knock. They quickly ushered the four of us inside, heaving the heavy, wooden doors closed once more and slamming the bar down, securely locking the mayhem outside. The two identical looking sentries both wore matching expressions of concern as the sounds from beyond the wall gained in intensity. One shook his head.

"This is a bad time to be in the city, my friend," he said, reaching out to grasp Neph's forearm in greeting. "Ildra has been awaiting your arrival. Please proceed inside." With a brief nod, both guards made their way back up the carved stoned stairs to their position on the wall, weapons at the ready.

Ildra was waiting inside the main temple. She came striding across the hall, looking small beneath the vaulted structure, her long robes flowing out behind her lithe form in her haste. Relief was clearly written across her sharp features as she grasped Neph's hands in greeting.

"Welcome to our beautiful city." Ildra grimaced, waving us farther into the complex. She led us down a short hallway to a small dining area, the table laid out with fresh fruits and a ceramic beaker of cold tea. "Things have recently begun to get a bit out of hand, if you hadn't noticed."

"Ildra, please tell me that wasn't -"

"Oh, Nephael, that was exactly what you think." Ildra slumped down in a chair. "A group of Ellundara. They were caught yesterday, trying to flee the city. One of the children supposedly stole some odd or end from the market as they passed through. I certainly have my doubts concerning the veracity of the story, but it no longer matters. They were tried, convicted and publicly executed this morning, as a family. You happened to catch the tail end of the spectacle. The magistrates were sending a message. Not just to the city, I think, but to the temple as well. Our influence here isn't what it used to be and it's failing ever more quickly. This city has never been - well..." She hesitated and shook her head before continuing. "We can't keep the peace like we used to. Eph's presence alone used to be enough."

Neph sat himself across from her. Ildra motioned for the rest of us to sit and help ourselves to the brunch before turning back to him.

"I'm at the end of my rope, Nephael. I screwed up and let things go too far before attempting to step in. I never expected the situation to degrade so quickly. I thought this new group was merely a passing phase, another fanatic sect that would burn itself out as quickly as it began."

Neph held up a hand. "New group. You're talking about the cult?"

"Cult. Yes, that is the word for them, isn't it? They call themselves the Brotherhood. I've never seen a group sweep through a city and garner followers so quickly. They've seeped into every aspect of life here, it seems, and I'm not entirely sure for what purpose. I've heard rumor that it's been happening in cities all across the continent, though perhaps not so violently as what's taken place here. They keep to the background, but there's no question they're pulling the political strings and are behind this current upheaval. Their mark is on all the posters and a number of city officials are sporting it as well. Not all members have been taken in; some of them are good men, but most of the City Watch seems to have been swayed by it.

"Listen, I know your primary concern here is your own race, though Eph knows the Seri haven't been stupid enough to make a home here, but you should be aware that you aren't this group's only target. They may be making a grand show of whipping up Seri hatred, here and elsewhere, but they're also targeting the Ellundara. Quite a few of them seem to have gone missing in mysterious circumstances since the Brotherhood moved in. And while they're pushing the Khazda out, they seem far more interested in the forest children. The only other Source-connected race."

She leaned back, taking a sip of tea, leaving Neph frowning in silence while the three of us exchanged uneasy glances. That had been an odd connection for her to make, but she wasn't wrong. In all of our reports, at least the ones I had seen, all of the abductions and disappearances had revolved around our two races.

The Ritual

Sitting on the ground, back against the wall, I gazed out from under the shadow of the woven hat, furtively watching the two oddly robed and masked figures traversing the market square. They weren't even trying to keep a low profile as they moved between the stalls, their faces hidden beneath the odd, beak-like masks that protruded from their raised hoods. Close beside me, Farryn sat hunched over, a rough collection bowl cupped between his hands, seemingly unaware of his surroundings but for the ever-so-slight tenseness in his form, giving away that he was watching the cult members just as closely as I was. It was the opportunity we'd been waiting for, after nearly a week spent in the market, sitting in this same location with our wooden bowls, surrounded by other monks from the temple. It had been a severe test of my patience, to say the least. Ildra had warned us that it could take time, that the Brotherhood were sometimes publicly absent for long stretches. I supposed I should have just been grateful that it had only been a week. At least our long wait seemed to finally be paying off.

The cultists were moving between the market stalls, lingering at some booths, passing others by entirely. I narrowed my eyes, following their movements. There didn't seem to be any rhyme or reason as to which sellers they stopped to talk to. Some greeted them, others shied away. Several of Eph's monks purposely moved among the stalls, never directly tailing the cult members, but making sure they were somehow always in the same vicinity of the stall owners they approached. Patrons began to move away from the cultists, casting nervous looks in the direction of the monks. Interesting. Despite how thoroughly the Brotherhood seemed to have integrated themselves into the culture, and how perfectly they seemed to fit into the Landing's xenophobic attitudes, the locals still seemed apprehensive about being around the actual Brotherhood members. I continued to watch the monks as the day wore on, curious at the silent power they seemed to wield. I wanted to ask Neph about it. The faith obviously had more influence in the city than I'd realized and I frowned as it suddenly occurred to me that their influence may have been the fine balancing act that was, until recently, keeping the city from descending into complete chaos.

Shadows were beginning to lengthen as the cultists finally began to move away from the crowded stalls. Farryn nudged me in the side, rougher than was necessary. Ignoring the provocation, I stood, Farryn rising at nearly the same time. We pulled off the woven hats and drew up the concealing hoods of our robes. The monks on either side of our location inconspicuously gathered the bowls and stowed them beneath their robes as the two of us began to move away, wending our light-footed way through the throng.

Following the two hooded figures wasn't particularly difficult; they made no attempt to hide themselves as they crossed the city, only picking up speed as darkness began to fall. As we passed into seedier areas of the city, the cobbles beneath our feet began to look worn and cracked, the buildings the same. Dilapidated residences sported boarded up windows, while broken glass and garbage littered the streets. Beggars huddled in the shadows. Farryn and I kept our distance, keeping the cultists just in sight as they wound ever deeper into the poorer areas of the city. Torches were flaring into existence as we finally reached the outskirts of the district and we nearly missed them turning into the large archway of the ancient storm tunnels in the darkness. Ducking in after them, well and truly hidden now in the tunnels, we hastily followed, largely by sound, as they twisted and turned through the labyrinth of passages. Lit only by the occasional wall sconce, the light of the flickering torches cast dancing shadows across the passage's ancient stones.

It seemed an eternity that we tracked back and forth through the underground tunnels, until finally the two figures before us seemed to suddenly vanish. Slowing our progress, we approached the area warily, breasting a ledge with crumbling stairs curving downward against the stone wall of a giant circular room. Gazing upwards, the night sky was barely visible through heavy metal grating. Below, lit by flicking candles, the room was filled with members of the Brotherhood, sitting facing an area where a man in more ornate robes stood.

"What is this place?" Farryn whispered, barely audible from inches away.

"It looks like an old, dried up cistern," I said, gazing around at the crumbling stone, vines trailing down from the lip far above our heads, small plants growing from the walls. "It's ancient. It can't have been used for ages…"

Perched in the shadows of the ledge, we fell silent again, squinting down at the scene below. Several stone archways could just be seen, leading off in various directions. Grooves in the stone indicated that at some point there had been doors or seals, but they were long gone, leaving only black tunnels. The crowd seemed to be growing restless as they sat in silence, all eyes on the man standing before them.

The candles were suddenly extinguished, plunging the room and all its followers into obscurity. Feeling incredibly vulnerable, the two of us huddled together, waiting, eyes straining against the absolute darkness. Just when the silence began to grow oppressive, a low dirge-like chant started from the front of the crowd, slowly gaining in intensity as more and more members joined in. I blinked, rubbing at my eyes as I stared at the low, blue-violet glow that had sprung from the floor and seemed to be growing in intensity, matching the pitch of the chant. Reva's 'purple fire'… It began as one dim light, then others flared to life in a circle, surrounding their leader. Farryn leaned forward slightly, straining to see through the gloom.

"What in the hell are they chanting…," I whispered, unnerved, a creeping familiarity hovering on the edge of my thoughts. Shivering, I drew back slightly, a twinge of pain running through my scar. I didn't like this. The group that had captured me, tortured me... This ritual was far too similar to images that

<inline_image description="Pencil illustration of two figures, one with short hair and a jacket and a younger one in front, watching a dim candlelit scene below with stone archways and hanging vines." />

haunted my dreams.

Farryn shook his head as he continued to listen to the strange chant, apparently unaware of or simply intent on ignoring my rising discomfort. The chanting had reached a fever pitch. The Brotherhood stood, raising their arms, their hooded figures eerily framed by the glowing lights emanating from the floor.

The leader in the circle dropped his arms and the incantation ceased, once again leaving a deafening silence in its wake. The man beckoned with a jerking motion, speaking into the darkness. Two figures emerged from the black recesses of the room, dragging a limp form between them. The body was dropped unceremoniously before the cult head. It shifted slightly, the blood-stained face turning outward, glazed eyes rolling. A young woman, clad in merchant clothing. Ellundara. Her race's pale luminescent markings shone vaguely on her dark skin, through the blood coating her face. Farryn jerked forward, but I grabbed him, forcefully pulling him farther back into the black passage behind us. With a withering glance, Farryn wrenched his arm from my grip. We stared at each other heatedly for a moment before our attention was dragged back to the ceremony.

The incantation began once more and the lights on the floor (symbols, I could now see, though couldn't make out what they were) flashed brighter. The man grabbed his victim by the hair, dragging her partially upright. She struggled feebly, but it was short lived as, with a malicious smile, he withdrew a long blade from beneath his robes and, with no hesitation, ran it across her throat. Blood spattered the dirty stone floor. I swallowed hard against the rising bile in my throat at the gruesome

scene. The body was dropped in a heap in the center of the now pulsing symbols as the unintelligible chant continued. Moving out of the ring, the leader raised his arms, bloody knife held high, screeching the final word of the summons.

The Dark vortex appeared suddenly, swallowing the sacrifice. It writhed in the runic circle, as though struggling to be free of its confines. I clamped a hand to my mouth to stifle an audible gasp, recognizing a miniature version of a much more powerful phenomenon that could be seen in full force in the Depths of the Wild Dark. The vortex crackled with power, spinning ever faster as the misty form of a creature began to coalesce in its center, rising before the congregation. It remained insubstantial, wavering in its form. Words issued from the apparition, in the same bizarre language, and everyone fell to their knees, prostrating themselves before it. The misty form turned, confronting the cult leader. Its voice seemed to rise in anger as it shook the tenuous form serving as its head. It began to fade. The vortex wavered and vanished, the runes extinguished and the room was plunged back into darkness.

Candles began to flicker to life as members of the cult moved around the room, striking matches. The ceremony, whatever its purpose, was over. Incredibly disconcerted, Farryn and I began to slowly back away from the ledge, retreating back into the dark passages leading to the Brakon's Landing sewer system. Exchanging worried glances, we turned on our heels, doing our level best to remain quiet, and slunk off down the passageway.

It wasn't long before we were hopelessly lost in the old tunnel system, leaving both of us frustrated and tempers wearing thin. The cracked and crumbling ruins looked the same no matter which way we turned and neither of us was entirely sure we were even still within the boundaries of the city. The plethora of side passages was far greater than we'd realized. In our haste to keep up with the cultists on the way in, we'd made any number of twists and turns through the old passages. Farryn stopped and angrily kicked a chunk of broken mortar, sending it skidding down the passage.

"This cursed place is impossible to navigate," he said in a rising fury. "We're completely lost."

"Keep your voice down," I snapped in a frustrated whisper through gritted teeth. Both of our voices echoed slightly in the dead air.

"Keep your own mouth shut and don't tell me what do," Farryn shot back, rounding on me. My hand snapped out like a whip, clamping over his mouth.

"Shut up," I hissed. A look of pure outrage twisted Farryn's face, though it died quickly as he realized that I was no longer paying him the least bit of attention. Back down the passageway, where we had come from, I'd heard something. Faint. Distant. Getting closer. Slowly removing my hand, I gestured that we should move on. Farryn cocked his head as we both caught the briefest noise, what sounded like footsteps, moving in our direction. He nodded his understanding. I glared back at him from hooded eyes. With rising urgency in our steps, we began to quickly move down the tunnel.

Through sheer luck, we somehow managed to wend our way back into the main storm tunnels, the stonework slowly shifting from crumbling limestone to the newer brick-faced passages. A slight

110

breeze, barely detectable in the still air, was now directing our footsteps. The sounds of pursuit were beginning to gain in intensity and we put on a burst of speed, trying desperately to make the exit and escape without a confrontation. Rounding a final passage, we emerged into a large chamber, its rounded ceiling ending in a wide, open archway. I breathed a sigh of relief. Farryn and I rushed towards it, only to come to a skidding halt as five hooded men moved from the darkness to bar the exit. Others filed out of the passageway behind us. I glanced around; we were outnumbered at least six to one against an assortment of clubs and blades. I couldn't help smirking. Poor odds for them. One of the men in the archway stepped forward, a short sword glittering in his hand.

"Well, well, what have we here? Two of Ildra's brethren out for an evening stroll in the tunnels? So tell me gentlemen, what brings you to such a pleasant location at this time of night?" His voiced dripped menace. Neither of us said anything. Farryn turned, putting his back against mine, facing the opposing group.

"Nothing to say? Vows of silence is it? Somehow I don't think so. And somehow I don't think you're part of Ildra's ilk either." He raised an arm. We both stiffened, prepared to manifest weapons at the first sign of attack.

"I intend to take no chances."

The snap of crossbows came from the darkness, followed by a brief hiss of air. The first bolt struck my leg and I gasped, vision blacking as I dropped to my knees. My connection to the Source had vanished, blocked. Beside me, Farryn was on the floor, clutching at his chest. I began to panic as I reached out and found nothing. I'd felt this before. The cult from before, chained in the darkness…

I struggled to get back on my feet, still reaching out desperately for the Source, but my body felt numb and unresponsive, in shock. Through the fog in my head, I could hear the man laughing. Reaching down with fumbling fingers, I grasped at the bolt in my calf. I tugged with all my strength, gritting my teeth as I felt skin tear, the barbed edges of the bolt ripping free.

"Oh well, isn't this a nice surprise. I never actually expected two Seri to -" the voice cut off as I lunged forward, Source suddenly flaring in my system, a blade springing to life in my grip. Steel crashed as the man threw his own blade up to block the lunge, parrying away several near hits. But the bolt had done its job. I stumbled back as a wave of intense vertigo made the world spin. The man laughed again as his group moved in.

"I want them alive."

Farryn was on his feet, swaying slightly, fists raised, ready for a fight despite looking disoriented and in pain. The group rushed in, clubs raised. In our weakened state, there was little we could do to resist. Swinging my blade in an arc, I caught one man across the chest, jumping to avoid a low swing from another. Farryn was ducking and dodging, making a good show of keeping them at bay, unable to yet summon a blade. Snapping his leg out, he managed to catch one man in the chest, sending him flying back into the wall. But the fight was short lived as more cult members joined the group. Two more darts hissed through the air, both finding their mark. Farryn let out a pained cry as a club smashed between his shoulder blades, dropping him to the floor. A crack to the head left him unconscious. Furiously trying to maintain my feet through the pounding clubs and Source-deprivation shock, I desperately lashed out and felt my fist connect with a resounding crunch in the face of the man directly in front of me. But there were too many. A hard swipe from a club caught me on the temple and I felt my knees buckle. I hit the floor hard, unfocused eyes staring at a blade inches from my face, resting on blood-spattered stones.

I was only vaguely aware of a commotion at the entrance, of searing pain as hands ripped the second dart from my leg, of the Brotherhood suddenly fleeing and leaving us where we lay. They melted into the shadows, gone as quickly as they had appeared. The thump of steel-toed boots echoed off the walls, mingled with angry shouts.

"What's going on down here?"

"Sir, there…on the floor."

"Hell's teeth, those robes…those are two of Ildra's monks."

"Are they still alive…?"

Rough hands turned me over.

"Yeah…bad shape though. Blood everywhere."

"What should we do with them? You know the captain gave orders not to mess with -"

"Orders or no, we can't leave them, not two of hers. At the very least, Ildra will have my job; the worst, my head. And you can be guaranteed she'll find out. That woman has her fingers and spies in everything this city does. I'd sooner make an enemy of those hooded freaks than cross her, even now. You two, and you, grab them and drag them back to her temple. She can sort them out from there."

"Sir."

"We can get the captain on the way to the temple. He'll want to know what's happened. And let him deal with Ildra when we get there."

Hands grabbed my arms, hauled me up. One eye was swelling shut, the other seeing nothing but a red haze from the blood dripping down my face. Darkness was starting to creep in as the guards of the City Watch began to drag us from the tunnels.

Interludes: Injuries

"How can you possibly be so calm?" Ildra asked in an agitated voice. "Aren't you the least bit worried?"

Soft candlelight lit the small, sparsely decorated room that served as Ildra's private study. The flickering shadows danced across the stone walls, throwing the intricate carvings on the wall into stark relief. Nephael, seated on one side of the old and pitted wooden table, took a sip of his tea and looked up from the report he'd been reading. He shrugged noncommittally.

"I can only assume they're following a lead. I've got complete faith in their ability to handle themselves. The current state of the city certainly concerns me and I don't like the idea of them being out there and not knowing what's going on, but there's always going to be an element of risk in these sorts of matters."

Ildra pursed her lips in a tight frown and stared down her nose at him from her seat across the table, but didn't say anything. Nephael stared at the wavering reflection in his teacup in silence.

The truth of the matter was that he was well beyond the point of mere worry. Midnight had long since come and gone. The group of monks that Piri and Farryn had been with had returned at sunset, reporting their departure to pursue the spotted targets. But that had been the only indication of what they could possibly be doing.

He forced himself to continue reading Reva's report on the happenings at the city council meetings over the past week. Ildra always had her priestesses in attendance to keep up with the current political landscape. Reva's notes were disturbing, to say the least, and only cemented in his mind that the upper social circle of the city were not just in a city-wide race war, but were also funding or supporting the cult they were here to investigate. If nothing else, they certainly weren't discouraging their activities, going so far as to hand down orders that members were to be left to their own devices and not to be interfered with.

And then there were the rallies in the square which had become an almost daily occurrence as the city and its people sought to purge both non-humans and foreigners alike from its borders. Not that many seemed to be left at this point. According to Ildra, people had been fleeing Brakon's Landing in droves for well over a month now. The outer district housing the small non-human population, mostly made up of Ellundara with a small mix of Khazda and Ashtarans, had been the first to empty. Though, oddly, despite leaving, the Ashtarans, citizens of the Upper Dark, seemed to be exempt from the push. The few families that remained in the district were the ones with nowhere to go, born and raised in the city and more afraid to leave than they were to stay. Unfortunately, things had begun to turn violent as the magistrates began to drive the crowds into a furor. Neph had seen more than his fair share of burnings and lynchings over the past week, all in the name of justice and purity. It absolutely sickened him, more so because there was nothing he could do about it. Every time his Seri ventured out for the day, a heavy feeling settled in the pit of his stomach.

His thoughts were interrupted by heavy pounding on the main gates. The sound of a mailed fist slamming on the ancient wood reverberated through the complex. It was followed by the harsh cry of, "Open up, City Watch!"

Ildra briefly made eye contact with him, her heavy gaze conveying more than words ever could have, before tearing off like a shot, heading for the gates. With a sinking feeling, Neph rose and followed.

The gates had already been thrown wide by the sentry monks when they arrived and the guard captain was arguing furiously with them as they stood barring his way. Upon seeing Ildra stalking towards him, the captain shoved past to confront her. His pompous air deflated slightly as she drew herself up before him in silent fury.

"What is the meaning of this? How dare you -" she began, but he cut her off, gesturing behind him.

"We have a delivery. My men found something that belongs to you," he said with a sneer.

His soldiers moved forward, dragging the beaten and bloody bodies and dropping them at her feet; Farryn lay still, Piri seemed barely on the verge of consciousness. Neph knelt down beside them, breath catching in his throat. Awakened and drawn by the commotion, several members of the order had drifted from the temple and were hovering around the doorways. Seeing the prone figures, they now rushed in to help. The captain stepped forward.

"Not so fast. I have some questions."

Ildra's face flushed crimson with fury as he reached out and grabbed her arm. "Get your filthy hands off me," she shrilled, ripping her arm from his grip. "These men need help and you certainly don't seem to have done anything to improve their situation. What exactly have you done to them?"

"This isn't our doing," he snorted. "And you should be thanking me for even bringing them back here. My men interrupted a fight in the storm tunnels; found them in this condition. I want to know what your acolytes were doing messing with the Brotherhood of Radiant Darkness. You know perfectly well that we aren't -"

Ildra gave a short, harsh laugh, interrupting him. "Is that their full title? They're nothing but thugs in hoods. And I have no obligation to answer your questions. You have no authority within my temple, captain." Gesturing to the small crowd behind her, "Get them inside and treat their wounds, if you please." Her face was now a mask of composure and politeness. "I thank you, captain, for saving the lives of my charges and bringing them home." Despite her words, her tone was anything but polite as she turned her back and snapped her fingers. The sentries moved in, unceremoniously pushing the city guards out and closing the gates with a resounding crash.

"This isn't over, Ildra," the captain shouted back as they left.

"I'm sure it isn't," she muttered, stalking back into the temple.

Ildra entered the healing room to find Nephael and Reva worriedly hovering over a crowd of priestesses. They had stripped both Farryn and Piri down and were cleaning and dressing their wounds.

"How are they?" she asked, moving up beside Neph and putting a hand on his shoulder. He dragged his gaze away from the prone figures on the healing room beds.

"A lot of the damage is superficial; it looks a lot worse than it is. Not to trivialize it. They've suffered severe beatings and some of the wounds are more serious than others. They've both got deep puncture wounds in their legs that I can't for the life of me figure out. The skin is torn, like it was some sort of barbed weapon." He shook his head, looking exhausted and haggard.

"I don't understand how this could happen," Reva said, joining them. "Those two are more than a match for anyone."

"I suppose we'll find out when they wake up," he said, his eyes flicking to Piri, who groaned slightly and shifted. Neph's face tightened and a pained look flashed briefly in his eyes.

"We'll make them as comfortable as possible and do what we can," Ildra said. "I know we're not your healers, but we are fairly adept at our own practices." She tried to smile comfortingly.

"Thank you, Ildra. My apologies that we seem to have brought extra trouble to your people, especially after all your help and hospitality."

She waved a hand dismissively. "Never you mind. While I'm quite sure that we'll be receiving some unwanted city visitors tomorrow, you just worry about these two and let me handle whatever situation arises. It won't be the first time I've had a clash with either the city council or the guards since the Brotherhood moved in."

Reva wandered throughout the darkened temple complex, unable to get back to sleep. Dawn wouldn't be far off at this point. She sighed heavily as her footsteps took her back in the direction of the healing chamber, thinking perhaps she would take one last quick look in. As she passed down the corridor, her light footsteps silent on the polished wooden boards, some inner sense made her slow. She crept to the doorway and peered in, somehow unsurprised by the sight that greeted her eyes. She leaned against the door frame, silently staring into the moonlit room as she watched Nephael next to Piri's bed. Both Piri and Farryn, having regained consciousness earlier,

119

had been given sleeping draughts for the night to allow them rest. As she watched, Nephael reached out a tentative hand, fingers lightly touching the livid bruise on Piri's forehead, trailing down his blackened cheek, running across the split lip. He hesitated then pushed a stray lock of hair off his face and leaned over, lips gently touching his forehead. Even from a distance, Reva could see him trembling slightly. A sadness rushed through her as she watched the rather intimate scene.

"Sir?" she whispered from the doorway. Neph jumped, hastily drawing back. Even in the dim light, she could see him flush. He quickly stood, averting her gaze. Reva entered the small room and stood looking down at Piri's sleeping form. Even asleep he retained the slightly melancholy expression he always wore.

"You should tell him, you know," she said quietly. He didn't say anything. Reva reached a hand out, rested it on his arm. He looked away.

"I can't tell him," he finally said, voice heavy. "I'm too afraid of how he would react. He's my best friend; I don't want to lose that."

"I don't think you would. I don't think you'd get the reaction you're afraid of. He's not the same person he used to be; you've changed him quite a bit, you know. Brought out some side that I don't think even he knew existed. And you can't go on like this, you know you can't."

Neph sighed and sat back down, head in his hands. Reva knelt down, placing her hands on his knees. "I've seen how he looks at you when he thinks that no one is paying attention," she said. "Or how he reacts when you touch him. He's good at hiding it, but the reaction is there. I think he's in love with you and just doesn't know it yet. But he'll never take that first step, even if he does. You know he won't. Your fear is nothing compared to his. You need to tell him." She stood back up. "Forgive me if I'm overstepping my bounds, but I thought you should know. Piri is sort of like family." She squeezed his shoulder briefly and left the room.

Assault on the Temple

I awoke the next day in much better shape than Farryn, which I couldn't help but take a slightly guilty pleasure in. My face still looked somewhat worse for wear, but, owing to my natural overSourcing ability, I healed a lot faster than the average person. Farryn still looked pretty rough and was walking with a slight limp.

After the events of the previous evening, which we spent half the morning relating in graphic detail to Neph, the day was disturbingly uneventful. I didn't know what I was expecting, but certainly not such a quiet, normal day. There were no visits from the City Watch, no magistrates patrolling the area. No rallies in the square outside, which was particularly strange considering there hadn't been a day without since our arrival. It was like a calm before the storm and, as the day wore on, I began to feel increasingly unsettled. And it wasn't just me. Neph seemed withdrawn and quiet, while Farryn restlessly paced the temple's hallways. Even the other members of the temple seemed to be feeling the strain, jumping at shadows and casting furtive glances towards the outer city as they moved about their duties.

In the late afternoon, Ildra returned from a day spent observing city meetings, Reva in tow. None of what they had to convey was good but it also wasn't any different from what had been taking place all week: members of the Brotherhood in attendance, new resolutions and proposals on pushing out foreigners, petty squabbling and in-fighting among the councilors. Reva made mention of a new adviser at the baron's right hand, but Ildra was quick to shrug it off as normal turnover, commenting that the man had been in the Brotherhood's pocket for weeks. We were all looking for something out of the ordinary, expecting it. Yet nothing seemed to be happening.

Eventually, Neph and Ildra migrated to more private quarters, leaving the three of us to our own devices. Farryn moved off to the outer wall with the sentries, still unable to sit still. Reva briefly fussed over my outward appearance before demanding an in-depth account of what had taken place. So, for the second time, I related the story.

"I don't understand," she said with a frown as I finished.

"Don't understand what?"

"You said they shot you with a crossbow bolt that cut you off from the Source."

"Yeah?"

"So I don't understand and stop acting like it's not a big deal."

I leaned back resignedly and shrugged. "What do you want me to say? I know what it was and I know what it did. That's about the extent of my knowledge on it. They took the bolts with them when they fled. I'd love to discuss whatever black magic is behind it, but I can't. I'd love to tell you it's somehow tied to the Dark - the ceremony sure as hell was - but I never saw anything in that realm that would allow a standard surface weapon to do that sort of thing."

What I didn't tell her was that I'd felt something like it before. The group that had captured me had used something similar, just far less effective, to control the imprisoned ENF agents. We hadn't been cut off from the energy, but our control over it had been severely limited, like whatever they'd done had closed the tap off, narrowed it to a drip. I'd never known how they'd accomplished it or even how it was implemented, but it was a feeling I could never forget. It was one memory that had vividly imprinted itself and gone nowhere. The technique had certainly come a long way in a relatively short amount of time.

"*Ildra!*"

Reva and I both jumped slightly at the bellow that erupted from outside, beyond the gate.

"Well, there it is," I said, heaving myself up. "Took them longer than I expected."

"Yeah," Reva snorted. "They took their time to plan things out. Do you think we should go out there? I feel like you and Farryn showing your faces might not be overly helpful. The Brotherhood knows there are two Seri in the city. So I'm sure, at this point, the City Watch does as well."

I shrugged. "Farryn's already out there."

"True."

Before we could even make it out the door, Neph was pushing us back inside.

"There's nothing to see. He's gone. And I'd prefer that none of you leave the building at the moment. Farryn's already been ordered back in."

I ground my heels in, craning my neck, trying to see around him. "What do you mean 'he's gone'? Who was it? He only just arrived."

Neph reached out and pulled the double doors shut, blocking our path. "It was the captain of the Watch. He was delivering Ildra an ultimatum. Ordering her to submit to arrest and giving her two hours to consider her reply."

"Oh, I'm sure Ildra took *that* well," Reva said, reseating herself. "I assume she's not going to need those two hours."

"No. I'm not even sure if she read the entire paper before hurling it back in his face and telling him that he had her answer. I doubt we've seen the end of this today."

As the evening wore on with nothing but a heightened sense of tension, I could feel myself beginning to tire. Despite my ability to heal quickly, the previous day's beating wasn't something I could just shrug off. Farryn had wandered off to our room an hour previous and I finally gave in and followed suit.

I hadn't been asleep for long when the sound of shouting broke through and woke me again. Reaching out in the darkness, I fumbled blindly for the light, only to smother a curse as my hand hit the lantern and it came back to me that Source-powered lamps weren't a thing here.

The voices were growing louder. I could hear Farryn fumbling around nearby, probably also looking for a light, obviously about as successfully. With a snort of annoyance, I summoned my wings, flaring the energy through them until the room was illuminated with a dull blue glow, enough to see by. Quickly pulling ourselves together, we rushed from the room, heading towards the sound of the commotion which was steadily growing louder the closer we got to the main entrance. I dropped my wings as we burst into the large chamber. Monks and priestesses were gathered around the room, all silent, all looking concerned as they stared out through the open doors to the outside courtyard. The tension in the room was palpable. I tugged Farryn's sleeve and pointed to where Neph and Reva were standing near the door.

The cacophony of sound coming from beyond the complex wall grew to deafening levels. Angry voices; screaming and cursing, merging together from what I could only guess was a massive crowd. I cast Neph a questioning glance as we stood staring up at Ildra's form where she stood along the wall top, her stiff silhouette all that was visible in the blaze of firelight. I could barely make out her enraged shrieks.

"What's going on?" I had to shout to be heard above the mob.

"They know we're here," Reva said, leaning in close.

I shook my head. "I know things are bad here, but surely there's no way that a handful of Seri in a temple caused all this. It sounds like half the city is out there."

It's not just us," Neph said. "I think we were just the excuse to rile up the crowd. The guards are out there demanding our heads and Ildra's arrest." He grimaced. "While that isn't a good turn of events, I'm finding the crowd itself a bit more worrisome. They're demanding the expulsion of the temple from the city. And, judging by their tone, I'm guessing they don't intend to let anyone leave peacefully."

"I don't understand," Farryn said, pushing his way in. "I thought you said this faith was one of the humans' largest."

"It is. It's also one of the most influential and Ildra has been one of the few powerful voices speaking out against everything that's been going on here. Eph's followers have blatantly opposed the crackdowns, going out of their way to help non-humans. Pushing them out would eradicate the last major block."

"The cult is recruiting followers," I said. "You saw as well as I did how the monks were policing the market the other day. With them out of the way, there's no one to stop the spread here. And no one to care if people go missing."

We fell silent as the crowd began chanting. I felt my blood run cold as I listened to the foreign sounding language, the same they'd spoken at the ritual. The only word I understood was 'Seri' and I was sure I didn't want to know the rest.

"How could they possibly know we're here," Farryn said weakly.

"Oh, come off it, Farryn," I said, anger suddenly rising. "We were caught out in the tunnels. The cult knows we're Seri and we were dressed from the temple. It doesn't take a genius to put it together. We know the Brotherhood is working with the local government or they're part of it. Either one amounts to the same thing and it means, because of us, the temple's got trouble." A flaming object sailed over the wall, sending embers skidding across the stones as it crashed into the courtyard.

Members of the temple rushed about, trying to beat out the sparks as another fiery object slammed into one of the outbuildings. Leaning out over the wall, Ildra began frantically screaming at the Watch officers. Sudden silence descended. In the eerie stillness, Neph pulled us farther back into the complex.

"Sir?"

We all turned as one of the higher monks approached, reaching out to grab Neph's sleeve with both hands, eyes wide, his whole body shaking.

"Please, we have a problem. Inside." He looked back over his shoulder. "They're in the temple. Brother Emmeric is dead, several of the sisters ran…" He trailed off helplessly, fingers clutching Neph's robes. "Please."

"Who -" Farryn started.

"Who do you think?" I interrupted with a snarl.

The monk began to move backwards, trying to drag Neph with him towards the darkened hallways. Gently prying the man's fingers loose from his sleeve, Neph pointed back towards the courtyard.

"Reva, Farryn. Stay with Ildra and don't let anything happen to her. Do what you need to do. Piri, come with me."

Without question, they moved outside, heading towards the wall.

We followed the monk in silence, moving quickly through the winding corridors, deeper into the temple. I realized the place was bigger than I'd originally thought as we descended a stair into an underground passage. At the bottom, Neph halted.

"How big is this place?" he asked the monk.

The man shook his head slightly. "Not very, not down here. There are a handful of storage rooms at the end of this hallway, used for food and supplies. Several of us were working down here when they showed up."

"Showed up from where?" I asked with a frown. "Is there an outside entrance?"

"Yes, but it's not how they got in. We have an emergency exit, in one of the rooms. I don't know how they got in." His voice trembled as he gazed down the passage. The end was shrouded in darkness, where its torches had been extinguished. We began to move slowly forward, the monk lagging behind, trying to keep our bodies between him and whatever might be hiding in the shadows.

A hooded figure, barely lighter than the surrounding darkness caught my attention. Reaching out, I halted the other two. The shadow moved again, something coming up in front of it.

A crossbow.

I didn't think, simply reacted. Source-forging a bow, I snapped off an arrow faster than the eye could follow, dropping the figure in its tracks. The weapon clattered to the floor. I turned to see the monk crouched against the wall, trembling fingers covering his eyes. Neph was simply staring at me in baffled silence, mouth hanging slightly open.

"What?"

"How did you do that?"

"Do what?" I said, confused, turning to throw a glance over my shoulder back down the hallway.

"Shoot him. Without physical arrows. You Source-forged an arrow. Kept it corporeal until impact. No one can do that."

I looked back with a shrug, nonplussed. "I don't know. I've always been able to do it, I guess."

Further talk was interrupted by another figure that appeared out of the darkness, grabbed the crossbow from the floor and vanished back into the gloom. Twin swords were suddenly in Neph's hands. He motioned for the monk to go back upstairs and the man fled with no second bidding. With a nod towards me, we advanced down the wide hall, side by side. Releasing one of his swords, Neph grabbed a torch from a sconce on the wall.

"So, there's a way out of here," I whispered as we moved along.

"I have a bad feeling we're going to need it," Neph said, glancing upwards as the sound of shouting briefly reached our ears. "But first we need to clear this place out. The last thing we need is a group of crazies in our way if the temple needs to evacuate. Keep an eye peeled for the other one."

"He's trapped down here," I said with a shrug. "I'm more concerned with how the hell they managed to get in here in the first place."

Neph stopped and pointed through an open doorway. In the flickering torchlight, the chalked circle on the ground was clear, its outer edges surrounded with symbols scratched into the stones, its inner dimensions crisscrossed in lines and crude marks.

"A portal? I've never seen them used on the surface." I stared at the floor, intensely curious as my mind reeled back to my travels in the underground, odd things I had seen down there, strange uses of energy. Disrupting the temporal plane could be dangerous.

"Your guess is as good as mine, but I'd venture to say you're probably right," Neph said. "I don't know what else it could be or how else they'd have managed to get in here. Someone had to have drawn it from this side though. Someone must have -"

I jumped back, narrowly avoiding the swinging torch, as Neph cut off and whipped around, sword rising swiftly to crash against the oncoming blade. The cultist gasped at the shock of the impact, staggering backwards. Neph didn't hesitate as he whipped his sword around, felling the man without a word. He pushed the body lightly with the toe of his boot.

"Sorry. I didn't get you with the flame did I?"

I reached out and plucked it from his hand, relighting the extinguished torches before cramming it into an empty bracket.

"No, but maybe we try to avoid adding any more marks to my face," I said as I reached down and snatched up the crossbow. "I've got more than enough collateral damage from yesterday." I popped the bolt out, turning it over in my hand before tossing it away with a snort of annoyance. A regular bolt, nothing special. "Anything on the bodies?"

"Couple more crossbow rounds, knife apiece. Nothing I'd call incredibly unusual," Neph said, rising from where he'd been rummaging around the corpses. He held up one of the knives, grimacing as he turned it about in the firelight. The deeply etched symbols winding about the handle looked to be stained in rust-colored blood. "Solid bone, if I had to take a guess."

"Yeah, cause that's not weird," I muttered.

I looked around the now brightly lit passage. The monk's description had been accurate. The passage dead-ended in a storage room, with two smaller rooms off to either side, including the one with the portal circle. I moved towards it, Source-forged a blade and began scratching through the markings. We didn't need the thing opening back up. The other two rooms seemed empty enough, except for the body of what I could only assume was the aforementioned Brother Emmeric. Neph joined me out in the hallway and we slowly headed back towards the stairs.

"I don't get it. Did we miss something? You don't think some of them made it upstairs ahead of us?"

Neph shook his head. "I think they miscalculated, weren't expecting anyone to be down here this late at night." He stopped suddenly, head cocked. "Do you smell smoke?"

BOOM

Dust rained down on our heads, the walls vibrating. The sound came again, louder, stronger, as though something had forcefully slammed into the building above us. The sounds of pounding feet and terrified screams suddenly punctuated the stillness. Without a word, Neph and I dove into separate rooms and began frantically searching the walls, shoving shelving aside, pushing crates out of the way, trying to find the passage out. It was well hidden at the end of the storage room. Shoving aside a set of wooden shelves, I ripped away the covering over the wall and manhandled open the heavy door to reveal the dark, slightly damp passageway leading out of the temple, its stale air spilling into the room. I repressed a shudder as I stared into the claustrophobic darkness, the storage room light barely illuminating the slight downslope of the passage.

The commotion coming down the hall tore my gaze away. Neph strode in, quickly followed by Farryn and Reva dragging a struggling Ildra between them. She looked wild; screaming, thrashing and trying to break away from them. Blood ran down her face from a graze on her forehead. The denizens of the temple, a mishmash of followers, guards, and caretakers streamed in behind, some with minor injuries, others with obvious burns. A crackling above and sudden shift in temperature sent all of our faces tilting back. The thick flooring above us creaked and groaned and a snake of flame briefly appeared, licking at the underside of the floor through a gap. Unceremoniously throwing Ildra over his shoulder, Farryn pushed past me into the tunnel, as Reva began to herd the rest in after him, disappearing midway through along with Neph as they helped the burned and wounded.

As the last of the followers entered the room, I slammed the door shut, throwing the bar and locking us inside. I didn't know if anyone was planning on pursuing through the fire, but I wasn't taking chances. The heat was worsening, the liquid flames now visible as they crawled across the ceiling. The fire seemed to be spreading too fast, almost unnaturally so. Hurrying the last person into the tunnel, I rushed in after.

Shoving terrified temple members ahead of me, the last of the group, we raced through the earthen tunnel, trying to gain the other

132

side. I tried not to contemplate when this passage had last been used, last been maintained. Water dripped from the roof and roots curled out from the earthen sides. The shoring quaked as the explosive heat of the fire, the collapse of part of the temple, shook the passage. I could feel the searing heat behind me, glimpsed small roots starting to curl. Chancing a glance backwards, I nearly stumbled to a halt at the sight of the dark figure standing there, engulfed in flames; the head of the Brotherhood, staring back at me from the entrance.

"Tell Ildra that her time here is over. Yours soon enough."

With a leering grin, he held out his fingers, traced a runic form in the air. The air seemed to explode outward, rocking the foundation, even as he somehow vanished in a sheet of purple fire. I snapped up an instinctual barrier born out of sheer panic, saving us from the brunt of the spell as it slammed against us. The barrier shattered, the shockwave blasting those of us at the back off our feet. Scrambling upright in the flickering darkness, I grabbed the nearest body and hauled it up. I could hear people screaming as they rushed blindly forward in the darkness. The tunnel shuddered and cracked. Heaving myself forward, breath ragged, I could see the exit ladder not far ahead, vaguely illuminated from the open hatch above it, could see reaching arms desperately hauling people up. And then I heard the roof begin to collapse in behind. I didn't dare look back, only threw out a prayer to any god that might be listening and ran. I'd barely realized the last person was scrambling up the ladder, that we'd somehow made it, when arms reached down and grabbed me, physically hauling me out of the ground even as the tunnel collapsed in with a resounding boom of earth and water.

Return to The Watch

Screaming profanities and curses, Ildra threw herself into the river, desperately trying to claw her way back towards the burning temple, even as Reva and Farryn dove in after her, dragging her back to the shore. The several dozen inhabitants of the temple huddled together on the bank, staring back across the water. With a muffled boom, the upper level of the tiered structure collapsed inward. Wild cheering could be heard over the sounds of the crackling flames.

Neph and I stood side by side, the exit to the collapsed tunnel at our backs, watching in silence. Smoke billowed into the night sky, obscuring the stars, the haze reflecting the orange glow, the water a shimmer of fire. A pang of guilt twisted my stomach and I looked away.

"This is our fault." I hadn't meant to say it aloud.

Neph's hand briefly squeezed my shoulder. "No. Maybe." He reached up, pinching the bridge of his nose as he squeezed his eyes shut. "We were the catalyst for it."

I winced as part of the outer wall fell in, sending ash and embers drifting across the water.

"I hope it was worth it."

Neph was silent for a moment. "You don't think it was." It wasn't a question.

"No," I spat out, not really caring, "I don't. All we have are more questions and," I angrily waved my hand at the inferno, "this." I turned my back on the water, staring at the crowd behind me, some tending to the injured, others trying to raise morale amongst themselves as their home burned. Ildra was moving amongst her followers, trying to remain the pillar of strength even as she briskly dragged a hand across her cheek, brushing away soot-stained tears.

"Sir?"

With a sigh, Neph turned as Reva approached. "Get everyone up. They'll figure out soon enough that we weren't caught in the blaze and I don't know what the mindset of that city is. The least we can do is get these people to the closest shelter and it's not long to dawn."

"You don't think they'll come after us," Reva asked, horrified. "They've driven the temple out of the city, surely they wouldn't kill them. They're innocent people!"

I heard Farryn mutter something about how that hadn't seemed to matter thirty minutes previous.

Neph shook his head, gazing back across the water. "Eph's followers helped keep order in the city; they were a threat that's been evicted. I don't intend to find out how far the city is willing to go. Reva, get Ildra and tell her that we need to leave. Farryn, Piri - help the wounded. Let's move."

"What exactly are we supposed to do with all these people?" Farryn crossed his arms, leaning back against the wall. With a scowl, he dragged the toe of his boot through the dirt on the floor, stirring up a small cloud that merely blended with the soot and filth that clung to his stained robes.

I wearily cast a glance around the inn's crowded common room. It looked quite a bit different from when we'd first stopped for the night on our way here, its primary patrons now consisting of an entire temple's worth of exhausted and scared humans. Neph and Ildra sat at a table in the corner

135

where they'd sequestered themselves for nearly three quarters of an hour. Reva, having done her best to help the injured, was now across the room and periodically prowling the back hallways while Farryn and I kept a wary eye on the front.

"Seriously," he continued, "we can't take them back to The Watch. And they sure as hell aren't going to be welcome back in Brakon's Landing."

"Would you shut your mouth," I snarled, pushing away from the wall and moving off into the room. "These people have enough problems at the moment without adding you into the mix."

I was only a few feet away, my back to Farryn, when I heard him say, "Mayhem and destruction. Just like the old days. You must be enjoying yourself in all this."

I twisted around in a fury, but before I could utter a retort, a rough hand clamped down on my shoulder. "*Enough.*" Physically turning me around, Neph gave me a firm shove towards the back of the room. "Reva could use some help in a quick flyover. Report to me when you get back. Go."

In the early dawn twilight, Reva and I winged our way over Brakon's Landing. Even from our height, the smoldering remains of the temple cut a brilliant scar across the religious district. The crowd seemed to have dispersed once the entertainment had come to an end and there didn't seem to be any indication of pursuit, which I honestly found a little disquieting considering the earlier violence. Everything seemed to have started and ended entirely too quickly.

"So what was that about back there?"

I glanced to the side to see Reva frowning at me. It was the first she'd spoken since we'd departed the inn. I didn't say anything.

"Nothing, really? Nephael practically manhandled you out of the common room. I thought for sure you were going to start a fight. What did Farryn say to you?"

Banking slightly, I altered my course back out over the city, scanning the roads outside of town. "It's nothing. Farryn and I just have a history, that's all. He's not my favorite person, if you hadn't noticed."

"How could I fail to notice," she said with a short laugh. "But it seems like more than general dislike between you two."

"Yeah, well…" I trailed off. I didn't really want to discuss it. It hadn't really been what he'd said to me, so much as the implication of what he'd said. Or the fact that he'd said anything at all. Farryn had been a thorn in my side as far back as I could recall; physically bullying me through my childhood and moving on to verbal harassment as we'd gotten older. I'd spent an inordinate amount of my free time learning how to avoid him.

"Go ahead and be that way. You know I'll get it out of you at some point."

I heaved an inward sigh. She would. At some point I couldn't identify, Reva had mutated; no longer leaving my personal life alone, she'd somehow managed to entangle herself in it and I'd just let it happen. Some twisted part of me seemed to enjoy the challenge of it.

She altered our course, heading back towards the inn. "Let's go back. There's nothing to see."

"This isn't your fight, Nephael. I appreciate your concern and misplaced guilt, but it's not your duty to take care of us."

Reva and I stopped cold at the sound of raised voices as we entered the inn. The atmosphere of the crowded common room was strained and awkward. Eph's followers seemed to be doing their best to ignore what sounded like a borderline fight erupting between Ildra and Neph in the back corner. Farryn was across the room, leaning up against the wall near the fireplace, arms crossed, pointedly not looking in their direction.

"This is, at the very least, partially our fault -"

"Don't be ridiculous," Ildra cut in. "Things were going to come to a head one way or another. Your presence only made it happen a little sooner than I expected."

"A little sooner than expected," Neph blustered, standing up. "Ildra, they burned the temple to the ground...they tried to kill you, all of you!" He waved a hand, angrily sweeping his arm around, encompassing the room. "If you think I'm just going to fly off and leave you here in this state -"

Ildra stood, defiantly leaning forward. "That is exactly what you are going to do. Eph survives, Nephael. We've been surviving for a thousand years. And what exactly do you think that you and three other Seri can do to help us?" She held up a hand, forestalling Neph's protest. "No. That is, and will remain, my final answer. I thank you, my friend, but no. We will pilgrimage to another temple, as we used to do, and what will be, will be. Go home. Tell your superiors of what you witnessed here and take care of your own people. I think, perhaps, that you have bigger problems than we do."

"At least let me see you off safely," Neph said, lowering his voice and retaking his seat.

Nodding her head, Ildra acquiesced. "You may see us off, but no more. I'll send word when we reach our destination, wherever that may be."

Shadowcats

I glanced up from my sketchpad as Reva moodily plopped down on the grass beside me. When she didn't say anything, I resumed my drawing, happy that her arrival hadn't disturbed my model.

I'd nearly finished, had finished enough at least, when the creature shifted position from where she'd been lying in a pool of dappled sunlight. Moving several feet, she stretched lazily before putting her back to me, the tail of puffed shadow twitching slightly. Staring at the cat, Reva finally broke her silence.

"What is that thing anyway? I've seen one or two around The Watch. Or maybe it's the same one. I can't really tell."

I leaned back against the tree behind me, flipping the cover of my pad closed. "Shadowcat. Not sure if someone keeps her or if she wandered in. She's from the Veil."

The creature turned its head to stare at us, glittering golden eyes catching the sun. As if she could sense me talking about her and was deciding to join the discussion, she suddenly rose and slunk her way towards us. Reva recoiled slightly at her approach, but I held out my hand with a smile.

"Are you sure it's safe?"

I scratched the top of her head and around her ears as she pushed into my hand, issuing a low, rumbling purr. "Of course she's safe. She's no different than any other domestic pet. Well, sort of."

"You said it was from the Veil," Reva pointed out, eyeing the shadowcat somewhat warily. "I mean, I haven't seen a Veil zone yet, but you didn't make them sound like the safest of places." She paused. "Does it have a name?"

"Verna. Neph told me," I said, running my fingers through the silky blackish-blue fur, my fingers slowing slightly on her somewhat thicker silvery stripes. The tip of her tail, which was more like smoke than fur, writhed and curled as she lay down beside me.

Reva lay back in the grass, her interest in my furry companion suddenly at an end. She pursed her lips, staring up at the cloudless sky in irritation. I knew the source of her mood. It had been several weeks since our venture to Brakon's Landing and it was as though nothing had happened, like we'd been thrown back into limbo. Our normal routine had resumed shortly upon our return and, other than a flurry of initial, lengthy reports and interviews by the Small Council, we'd been completely cut off from information about the situation.

The other ENForcers had come back with stories not that dissimilar to our own as far as the Brotherhood was concerned, though ours had certainly taken the award in the category of excitement and violence. As a group, we'd been asked by the Council to be discreet with our experiences and to avoid discussing matters with anyone, including amongst ourselves. Needless to say, it hadn't taken long for each team's story to circulate like wildfire through a place as small as The Watch.

"What could the Ruling Council possibly be debating," Reva suddenly burst out angrily, startling both myself and Verna. The shadowcat hissed, arching her back in annoyance at the disturbance. "It's been weeks. Weeks of nothing. What was the point if they're not going to do anything?"

"And what would you have them do?" I asked, wearily closing my eyes. I was as annoyed at the inactivity as she was, but I also understood why they seemed to be balking when it came to taking any sort of action. "Until the Brotherhood directly moves against us, here on our own territory, we're stuck. We don't need another war with the humans on our hands, not when we've only just recently gained such a cautious peace. Though I'm not sure why they haven't at least issued a warning to everyone about the danger." I shrugged.

Sitting up, Reva heaved a frustrated sigh. "Hasn't Nephael told you anything?"

I pulled my knees up, hugging them to my chest, watching as Verna moved off to a new pool of sunlight. "I haven't seen much of him since we got back," I said quietly. "He's been busy." I felt a twinge in my chest as I stared unhappily at the lounging shadowcat. Drawing in a deep breath, I pushed it away. "It wouldn't matter anyway. I'm sure he's under orders not to discuss things. And, unlike the rest of us, he takes that seriously."

"Oh, I'm sure if he'd make an exception for anyone, it'd be you."

I looked up sharply. "What exactly is that supposed to mean?"

She didn't say anything, just stared at me with an inscrutable expression. Finally, "Huh, you're serious. Anyway, we've got patrol soon." And without another word, she stood and walked off, pausing briefly to pet Verna on the way.

Bad Memories

Late afternoon sunlight slanted down through the skylights slitted into the roof over the terrace. While still cool, it was the first beautiful day of the newly dawning spring and most of The Watch seemed to have been drawn outside to enjoy it. I hovered around one of the doorways, steeling myself to go out there by myself. With my past history, I'd generally avoided social situations on general principle as one could only take so much when it came to open fear and whispering. But while I'd never been comfortable in crowds, since being captured there were times now when, for no particular reason, I found myself panicking around them, feeling trapped. There'd been times when it felt so overwhelming that I nearly lost the ability to function; shaking, my heart racing, feeling like a vice was closing around my chest. These episodes had grown increasingly rare in the past six months, but that underlying anxiety seemed to always be lying in wait.

Despite having been at The Watch for nearly a year and a half now, other than my secluded chair next to the Grandview, I'd done my best to avoid being out in the general public, spending my alone time in secluded locations away from anyone not actively seeking me out. When I was in the more populated areas, even with Neph or Reva by my side, I still felt keenly out of place. Terrified that my hated life at Skycrest would begin to repeat itself and just as fearful that I would be caught in one of my episodes. But today I felt a little better, a little stronger, thanks in large part to Neph's confidence in me. Putting me back in active service had done wonders and having such a close companion helped on untold levels. I smiled inwardly; it was a strange feeling for me to have grown so close to another person, to come to rely on them being there as an integral part of my day. If it hadn't been for him, I would still be sequestered in my chair or my room, alone, and never dreaming that maybe I could do something as normal as get myself a drink, sit on the terrace and sketch the mountains.

Taking a deep breath, my heart pounding slightly as I worked up my courage to go alone into the crowd, I walked out, hesitant at first, but becoming more confidant as I gained ground, heading towards a table along the balcony. I looked around as I walked, but no one seemed to be bothering about me. The general chatter was more concerned with the escalating activities of the Brotherhood, something I swore the public had more insight on than we did, and the situational warning and human-territory travel ban that had finally been issued by the Ruling Council in Skycrest.

Realizing I'd been holding my breath, I let it out slowly as I sat down. If this had been back at Skycrest, I'd have been the center of attention, none of it good. I couldn't help being slightly relieved that circumstance seemed to have made me irrelevant as social discussion. Maybe Neph had been right after all; things were different here and time changed things. Pulling my sketchbook from my bag, I got to work laying out my drawing.

Wrapped up in my own world, it was quite a while before the conversation at the table behind me began to intrude on my consciousness. My pencil jerked to a halt, hovering over the paper as I listened in, catching snatches here and there. I recognized several of the voices; healers from the capital, probably visiting. Men and women who had spent years dealing with me, putting me back together, and eventually coming to loathe my presence as much as I had loathed theirs. And the stories I was catching, spoken just loud enough that it was obvious I was meant to hear them, were very much at my expense. I could feel my face start to flush with anger as one of them erupted into raucous laughter. The Skycrest healers had spent the better part of a century being a constant source of torment and humiliation, built upon my sometimes weekly encounters with them. I had been angry and reckless and

they had been tired of putting up with me. The relationship had been a sour one from my late childhood on as they had been commanded to deal with me regardless of the situation. My moods had gotten progressively worse as I'd aged and I was forced into more horrific and compromising situations. But they had also known that, as dangerous as I had been trained to be, I was also passive and terrified of my superiors. Confronting them, in any sense, over how I was treated, was something I would never had dreamed of, had been specifically trained not to do. And they'd known it. They had seen me at my most vulnerable and knew that, as long as they kept me alive, nothing else mattered because I was simply a tool that had to be kept functional. While others had reacted with open fear and revulsion, the healers had taken to simply making my life emotionally miserable. My mere existence had always seemed to be an affront to them and a waste of their time; time that they could have been spending on more worthwhile patients.

"Is it really true," the conversation turned more serious, "about the things they used to have him do?"

"I heard he wiped out an entire division by himself during the Uprisings -"

" - more blood on his hands than the rest of the original ENF combined -"

" - murdered an entire Ashtaran village -"

" - everyone -"

The voices were Watch healers now, curious, questioning. Great, just great. I bowed my head, running my fingers through my hair. The fact that what they were saying was all steeped in truth just made everything worse. I'd hoped to escape my past in this place and it had predictably followed me. I shoved my sketchbook back into my bag and stood, doing my best to remain in control, but I could feel the mental shift as fuzzy memories came flooding back in and the ever-present undercurrent of post-capture anxiety began to rear its ugly head.

145

"Hey, Enpirion! Need some help?"

I turned slowly, trying to master my breathing, trying not to let them see how bothered I was. A familiar healer from the capital, Embarric, was staring me down, a leer plastered across his face. As a child I'd been terrified of the man and the adult me wasn't really any less afraid. He'd taken a lot of pleasure in causing me pain, both physically and mentally. The others had fallen silent. The Watch healers looked uneasy as he stood and moved slowly towards me. Pushing my chair in, I started to back up, eyes riveted on his face.

"What, no hello for an old friend? It's been so long," he sneered. "When did we last see each other? Hmm?" He took a step forward. "I have to admit, I was rather disappointed when they took you away from me."

"Leave him alone, Embarric," I heard a Watch healer softly say.

"He's not going to do anything," Embarric said with a snort of laughter. He continued to move forward, the look on his face becoming uglier as he inched closer. If the terrace hadn't been roofed over, if there hadn't been so many people, too many tables, I'd have attempted to take off. I just needed to get back to the main complex.

Conversation in the immediate vicinity had died, talk of the Brotherhood fading as attention shifted to the two of us. I felt my hands curl into fists as I inched backwards, eyes riveted on the man in front of me. My heart was racing and it was taking an awful lot of focus to control my breathing. I felt a spark of hatred towards myself that Embarric could still elicit terror in me. I continued to back up as he slowly moved forward. I could feel him pulling on the Source, vaguely see the tell-tale threads of energy around his fingertips.

"Embarric!" One of the Watch healers stood.

Embarric jerked forward and I scrambled backwards, slamming into one of the wrought chairs. I felt my ankle twist and a sharp stab of pain rip through my leg as I twisted and fell, hitting the ground hard. Embarric had halted, staring down at me, his grin somehow even wider. Ignoring the pain, I scrambled to my feet and limped

146

quickly away, followed by the derisive laughter of the Skycresters and the stares of onlookers, several of whom had risen and were looking angrily towards the capital's table.

I ducked around a corner, back against the wall, breathing heavily and clutching at my chest. I was having trouble focusing as a band of tightness began to squeeze at my temples. Sinking to the floor, my right leg throbbing, I clutched my head in my shaking hands, burying my face between my knees.

"Piri?"

Reva's voice, concerned. I heard her crouch down in front of me, her hands coming to rest on my head. I flinched.

"Don't -" I gasped out, feeling like my breathing would stop if I completed the sentence. Her hand didn't move, but her long fingers curled slightly through my hair.

"It's ok," she said in a soft voice. "What you're feeling, you can fight it. You're strong. Stronger than what you're feeling right now. Come on." She stood, her other hand latching onto my own and lifting it with her. "Let's go somewhere quiet. I'll help you." Without much thought, I let her drag me to my feet. My head was swimming and I only vaguely registered Reva slowly leading me to my favorite chair then temporarily vanishing before returning with a glass of cool water, which she pressed into my trembling hands.

"I heard part of what went on out there, on the terrace," she said, an undercurrent of anger audible in her voice.

I didn't say anything. My body was starting to calm down, leaving me exhausted and upset. I sipped at the water as Reva jabbered animatedly beside me, trying to create a diversion. It was a combination of righteous anger on my behalf and graphic, vicious descriptions of what she'd like to do to the Skycrest healers. I was grateful for her distraction and I couldn't help starting to laugh as her talk of inflicted brutalities became more and more outlandish. Reva flashed a toothy grin.

"Feeling better?"

I nodded slightly, one knee drawn up to my chest, pain coursing through the other leg, glass still cupped between my shaking fingers. "Yeah," I whispered, "a little better, I guess."

"Better than twenty minutes ago, that's for sure. Geez, Piri. Scared the hell out of me back there. You looked like you were going to pass out."

"Sorry," I muttered, feeling suddenly embarrassed. Reva shook her head and leaned in, looking me over.

"Don't apologize. There's no reason to. You're practically family, like my big brother. I wasn't going to just leave you there."

Brother? She'd said it so casually, but the term stunned me. The look on her face was sincere, earnest. She'd meant it.

"Who was that guy anyway?"

I leaned my head back and closed my eyes. "A healer from Skycrest."

"Some healer," she snorted. "What exactly was he planning on doing, especially there in the middle of everyone? I could feel him pulling on the Source from across the room."

"Embarric was good at causing pain," I said quietly. "He especially took pleasure in it when it came to me. And there was never any trace of what he did since he used the same skills to torment that he did to heal. He was a memorable staple of my childhood." I took a sip of water. The shakiness was starting to calm, but exhaustion and anger were taking its place. I opened my eyes to see Reva simply staring at me. Her hand inched forward, coming to rest lightly on my knee.

"Why didn't you fight back? Today, I mean. He doesn't have any power or control here."

"I can't," I said, looking away.

She frowned. "Why? I don't understand. You could crush that guy."

"No, you don't understand. I was conditioned to never raise a hand against the Seri. When I say I can't, I can't."

"I'm sorry, I - "

I cut her off. "You don't need to say anything or be sorry. It is what it is and nothing can be done to change it."

"Still," she said.

I shrugged. With a sigh, Reva stood and reached out a hand.

"Well, come on," she said. "Now that you're somewhat calmed down, let's get you back to Nephael's. I have to go on patrol soon and you're still looking a bit peaky. Not gonna leave you out here like this and his place is closer than yours."

When I didn't make a move, she plucked the glass from my fingers and heaved me to my feet. Without really caring, I let her lead me off toward Neph's quarters.

The Confession

Back in Neph's apartment, I sat at the table, staring moodily at him as he wended his way through a backlog of reports. A cup of tea sat forgotten. I'd been sitting there silently. The incident with Embarric, several hours later, had left me feeling bitter and brought up a whole host of issues from the past.

"Why do people hate me?" My voice sounded muffled, face nearly buried in my arms as we sat there, only my eyes glaring over my skin. The question sounded trite and childish even as I asked it. Even though the way I had been treated by the general population had been a constant source of emotional upset in my book, talking about it wasn't something I'd ever done. Why would I? It would never have changed anything.

"They don't hate you." Neph said it so offhandedly, taking a sip from his coffee. He didn't even look up from the report he was reading. I narrowed my eyes, scowling at him, taking offense at his total lack of reaction. He knew me and he knew I didn't talk about things like this lightly. It bothered me that he didn't seem to be taking me seriously.

"Then why do they still avoid me, talk about me behind my back? I thought maybe I'd left it behind at Skycrest, but I didn't. It's just not as obvious here. People are still afraid of me, still avoid me." My voice was getting louder, higher, as it was always wont to do when I was upset. "What have I ever done to any of them to deserve the way I'm treated? I go out of my way to be inoffensive. I barely talk. I keep to myself. When I've tried to be friendly, I'm pushed away. Like I'm some sort of contagious disease. And I sure as hell can't change my past, as much as I'd like to." It wasn't really The Watch so much that I was angry about, but the run-in with the Skycresters had brought back a lot of bitterness. My voice cracked slightly and I lowered my eyes, burrowing farther into my crossed arms. Silence. I heard the sound of the coffee cup gently hit the table, the papers rustle as they were laid down.

"They don't hate you. At least not here; I can't really speak for the capital. People here just don't know you or understand you." Neph's voice was low, somewhat melancholy as he finally responded. "You're just an anomaly in their world. You aren't something that fits into their preconceived notions of what people are supposed to be, how they're supposed to act and think. And so they're unsure of you; they judge and they don't make the effort to understand. You're a creature that doesn't fit into their universe and they don't know how to deal with that. So they push you away, even if it's not intentional. And, let's face it, whether you realize it or not, you're a little intimidating, especially given the stories surrounding you. You can be a bit…harsh…sometimes. You don't come across as an easily approachable person."

I raised my head from my arms, pushed back from the table, angrily getting to my feet and nearly falling over again as pain shot through my side. "So that makes it ok?"

"I didn't say that - "

"I'm not stupid. I hear what people say about me when they think I'm not paying attention. The stories they pass around don't fall on deaf ears; they make it back to me. I'm not blind either. I see how people keep their distance, their change in body language when I'm around. Just because it's not as obvious here as it was at Skycrest, doesn't mean it's any different. I might be something they don't understand. Maybe I *am* an anomaly, but that doesn't mean I have to be so openly despised," I said, voice rising as I grabbed the cup off the table. I stared into it, realized it was empty and slammed it back down. The mug shattered.

I jerked my hand away from the shards and moved across the

room, trying to keep as much weight as possible off my leg and reseated myself on the couch. "I can count on one hand the people who gave me a chance and didn't condemn me for what I used to be." I looked down, rubbed a thumb across my open palm, not even caring as small droplets of blood rose to the surface where the ceramic had cut me. "I'm always the outcast. I've always been the outcast," I whispered, the tears finally starting to creep their way down my face. Neph seated himself next to me, one hand pressing a towel against my palm, the other hand gently wiping tears from my cheek. Even as upset as I was, a part of me registered that kindness and intimacy.

"What happened to bring this up?" he asked in a low voice. I mutely shook my head. I didn't really want to discuss what had happened on the terrace. "You wouldn't tell me when you got here, you won't tell me now. You show up looking sick and injured with no explanation. I'm going to call Reva back and ask *her* if you continue on refusing to fill me in."

"Please don't."

Neph leaned back, frustration written across his face. "Then tell me what happened. Did it have something to do with the group from Skycrest?"

I looked up. He knew they were here? Of course he did. I put my head back down and mumbled the story, now embarrassed and ashamed over what had happened, sure that I was somehow at fault. But when I chanced a glance back up, Neph's eyes had hardened to ice and the anger written there was not what I was expecting.

"I'll be having a little chat with our visitors, make no mistake," he said quietly. "That sort of behavior may fly at Skycrest, but it is absolutely not tolerated here."

I felt a rush of gratitude as he leaned back, closed off, thinking.

Suddenly, "You should really go see one of the Healers about your leg. Hand too."

I shook my head. I had no intention of going to the healing unit, not after what had happened, when several of them had been there and done nothing to stop it. Besides, the injuries were superficial. I didn't know why he was so concerned.

He sighed. "Well, if you're not going to get it checked, you're not going back to your room either. No, don't give me that look. You're having a hell of a time even walking and you're obviously still incredibly upset. And, honestly, it's your mental state that concerns me more than the leg," he said, glancing over to the remnants of the mug on the table. He reached out and took my hand, which was still bleeding slightly. The tight sensation ripped through my chest as he gripped my fingers and I felt my breathing quicken. I gritted my teeth, trying to push it away. Why did this always seem to happen when I was feeling vulnerable? Neph didn't seem to notice as he glanced out the window at the darkened sky, a vast blanket of stars now stretching across the heavens. "I'll sleep on the couch. You can take the bed."

"What, no!" I yelped, pulling my hand free. "I couldn't, it wouldn't - I'll be fine going back."

Neph frowned and gave me an odd look. "What's wrong with you? Don't be ridiculous. Your room isn't even close to here. Let me find you something to sleep in."

He moved off towards the bedroom. I was shaking all over now and it had nothing to do with the day's earlier events. I hugged my arms around my chest, willing it to stop. I didn't understand this, thought I had gotten it under control. I spent most of my free time hanging out in Neph's quarters; talking, drawing, reading. I shouldn't be feeling like this all of a sudden. I'd spent too long and worked too hard to kill what I was feeling. A matched sleeping shirt and pants suddenly landed in my lap causing me to jump.

"If you want to go get changed, I'll help you to the bed. Are you alright?" Neph was staring at me in some concern. I jumped up,

153

nearly falling over as I put weight on my ankle. He grabbed me, wrapping an arm around my waist as he hoisted me towards the bathroom. At the door, he let me go. "Be careful. Call me when you're done."

"A-are you sure this is ok?" I muttered, now clothed in Neph's slightly too large sleepwear, being helped as I limped shakily to his bed. He frowned.

"Of course it is, stop asking. I'd rather you not be alone. I'm perfectly fine sleeping on the couch, ok? Stop being weird; it's not a big deal." Neph gently lowered me onto the bed. I was starting to feel acutely uncomfortable, my heart pounding from him being so close. I flinched slightly as he helped me slide my leg up under the sheets. His closeness was increasingly starting to bother me and I could feel my face starting to flush again.

"I really do wish you'd go see the healers about that," he sighed, staring at my leg, now a shapeless bump in the covers. I could feel my face tighten at the thought and looked away.

"I'll be fine by tomorrow. I heal fast enough without them. You know that," I said, an acerbic edge to my voice. He nodded slightly, looking somewhat unconvinced, but didn't push it.

"How's your hand?" He reached out and took my fingers again, running a thumb up my palm. The bleeding had stopped; it was only a shallow scratch. "That looks fine. I'll leave the door open a bit. If you need anything, I'll be right out here, ok?" He was looking at me intently, those blue eyes boring a hole through me.

I nodded, relieved when he finally turned away and left the room, pulling the sliding door mostly closed behind him. My heart was still pounding, a lump in my throat. These feelings still weren't something I knew how to deal with and, despite my best efforts, they hadn't gone away. I looked down at what I was wearing, my hand coming up to grasp the fabric near the collar. Without thinking, I pulled the collar up to my nose. It smelled like him. I held the fabric there, eyes closed. For some reason, that smell was safety and comfort and something I couldn't quite identify. I could feel myself starting to shake again and I quickly curled up, back to the door, face buried in the pillows.

Where am I? I slowly sat up. There was no fear or panic in the thought, only confusion. In the darkness, eyes wide, I sought for something familiar. A few seconds lapsed before it came back to me that I was in Neph's bed. I couldn't help but notice that it was far more comfortable than my own, much like everything in his apartment. I slipped out of bed, restless, testing my weight on my leg. The Source had done its job in the few hours I'd been asleep. It still hurt, but it was bearable and I could walk without much of a problem. I moved silently around the room, not really having any purpose or intent. Hesitantly, I moved to the door and silently peered out at Neph, curled up on the couch with a light blanket, blond hair catching the merest glint of the crescent moon's light as it filtered through the window. Leaning my head up against the door frame, I watched his sleeping form, trying hard to ignore the ache in my chest. I needed to build the walls again, couldn't let this go any further in my head, couldn't delude myself that there could ever be anything more.

As I turned away, my eyes were suddenly drawn to the bedside table, to a small framed picture resting on it. It was the ink drawing I had done for him, what seemed something of an eternity ago. I had vaguely wondered at one point what had become of it, never having seen it again. It had never occurred to me that he would have kept it here, in the bedroom.

I crawled back into bed, feeling miserable.

The smell of coffee and bacon woke me, midmorning, and I found myself crawling from the bed and slipping into the living room without any conscious thought, drawn simply by the aroma. I could barely remember the last time I'd had it; it had been ages ago, at a market stall in The Morring. It certainly wasn't part of the Seri culture and generally had to be obtained, for a high price, in Bridgeport. Neph smiled as I drifted into the room, beckoning towards the table where he'd laid out a spread of early seasonal fruit and two mugs of fresh coffee.

"Morning," he said. "How's the leg feeling? I notice you made it here without a limp. Must be the smell of good food. Amazing healing properties." He flashed a grin as I grabbed a piece, closing my eyes as I took a bite, savoring the smoky flavor.

"Where -"

"Bridgeport, of course," he said, snapping a crisp piece in half. "Been keeping it frozen. Thought I'd pull it out, special occasion and all. I don't generally have guests for breakfast and certainly not such a welcome one."

"Welcome, right..." I pulled a wry face as I sat down. "Sorry about last night. And the mug."

Neph shrugged. "Don't apologize. It was just a mug. Easy enough to replace. Let's not worry about it. I'm just happy you're feeling better."

Was I feeling better? I certainly wasn't upset anymore, but there was still an undercurrent of emotion running through my system, unrelated to the previous day's events. As I sat facing him, I let my eyes roam around, soaking in the morning sunlight, the colors, Neph himself, watching me with his quirky half-smile. A part of me was genuinely happy sitting there, enjoying breakfast with him. But it all seemed bittersweet, like I was staring through a window at a life I wanted and could never have.

I reached out for my coffee, savoring the aroma. It was Neph's fault I drank the stuff. It was Neph's fault I did a lot of things I'd never done, never would have done.

"Thanks," I said. He arched an eyebrow. "For, for everything. I'm not sure I've ever properly thanked you. I owe you a lot, you know. I probably wouldn't be here if it wasn't for you." I stared down into my mug, feeling embarrassed.

Neph reached out, a smile playing the corner of his mouth, and briefly squeezed my hand.

"Can…I talk to you?"

I glanced up from where I was curled up on the couch. Still ensconced in Neph's sleepwear, I was immersed in a history book I'd found on his desk. My discomfort from the night before had passed with breakfast and, somehow, I was still here, had been here all day, unable to bring myself to leave the comfort and safety I associated with this place. Neph had given me an odd, little smile when it had become apparent that I had no plans to change, let alone go back to my own room. At some point the sun had begun to set on what had been a cool, drizzly early spring day and the soft Source lamps had flickered into life.

Neph was in the kitchen, back to me, staring out the window at the sunset. Or possibly watching me in the reflection; it was hard to tell. I put the book aside and straightened up, eyeing him closely. Something about the question, the way he'd asked it, made me nervous and I was suddenly afraid I'd overstayed my welcome.

He stayed facing the window, head down now, shoulders slightly hunched, like he was wrestling with what he'd just asked. I stayed silent, waiting. This wasn't like him. With a deep breath, he straightened, mind apparently made up. Crossing the room, he sat beside me, facing me. The intensity and seriousness in his expression made me quail slightly and I felt myself draw back from him. One hand reached out and caught my own, gently but firmly hanging on, keeping me from pulling away.

"I need to tell you something," he said quietly. Once again he fell silent. His thumb began, almost absentmindedly, rubbing my palm as he simply stared at me. I glanced down quickly, eyes widening slightly as my heart started to pound, fear and anticipation carving a pit in my stomach at the sensation. For as simple as it was, it was an intimacy he'd never shown before.

"Piri," he took a deep breath and the struggle was visible in his face. "I've been fighting with myself over this for months. And...I've decided that I need to tell you something. I don't - I don't know how it's going to end or how you're going to react, but I can't keep it secret anymore and I can only hope that it doesn't ruin what we have. Because what we have means everything to me. But, but I want this to be more." He paused before finally whispering, "I love you. I have for a while now."

I didn't say anything. I couldn't say anything, couldn't move. I was frozen in place, his hand still clutching mine. One part of me was registering shock and disbelief; what he was saying couldn't possibly be true. I still didn't think enough of myself to ever believe someone could love me. That other part that I didn't quite understand, had been fighting with for months, awoke at his words. And then, just as shocking to my senses and with no warning, he leaned in and kissed me.

In that brief instant, I thought my heart, pounding so fiercely, might actually stop. I could feel my breathing quicken, my hands start to shake. Neph had his free hand against my head, fingers running through my hair. His lips lingered for a moment before he slowly pulled back. A shudder ran through my body as I rigidly sat there staring at him, numb with shock. And yet a part of me had

wanted desperately to respond.

"Please say something," Neph finally said, a note of pleading in his voice. "Is there even a possibility that you might share my feelings?" I couldn't speak, but I found my head nodding without conscious thought, even as my mind was frantically trying to stop me. His fingers curled through my hair again and I looked down, suddenly unable to meet his eyes. I felt him lean in, his forehead resting against mine.

"You're my best friend, Piri. I couldn't imagine my life without you at this point. I don't want to do anything to push you away or make you uncomfortable. We can take things slowly. As slowly as you want."

I still didn't understand how I really felt, was still in complete shock…and the entire situation terrified me. I didn't know what it meant to love someone or how that would change things. But I did know that Neph was the only person I had ever grown close to, the only person who had ever managed to get inside my walls and, just as he had said, I couldn't imagine my life without him. Gods knew I'd thought about it, but it was a fantasy, nothing more.

I pulled back. Neph didn't make any move to stop me, just leaned back slightly, watching me. I suddenly felt like I had the first time he'd said he wanted to be my friend: disbelieving, wanting to know why, afraid of some possible motive that I couldn't see, and utterly conflicted. He seemed to know, could read it in my face.

"My reasons haven't changed," he whispered. "They're the same now as they were back then, just more so. You may still not think you're worth it, but I do."

I hung my head. "How could you possibly love someone like me? You have no idea some of the things I've done, been forced to do. Being friends with me is…something, I guess. You don't want to get any closer." I could feel tears forming as I said it, was intending to stand and leave before my body refused, but Neph didn't give me a chance. He reached out and pulled me close, burying his head in my shoulder as his arms wrapped around me.

"It's too late for that. I don't care about your past history. All I care about is the person you are right now, here in front of me. That's who I fell in love with, who I want to be with."

"But I've never - never been with -" I stopped, the internal struggle threatening to spill over. "I don't know how. I don't know anything…" I looked away, flushed, embarrassed.

"I have no expectations," he said. "We can figure it out together."

The Weeks After

The next few weeks were a strange transition for me, comprised of awkwardness and discomfort on a different scale from anything I'd ever experienced before. Neph, it turned out, was surprisingly physically affectionate, once he'd been given the go-ahead to actually touch me. I didn't know why I found that to be such a shock; he'd always been more physical than I'd been comfortable with. It was only little things; his hand in my hair, a finger brushing my cheek, a kiss on the forehead. But that was all it took. The first few times he made contact, my initial reaction was to tense up, recoil. It wasn't that I didn't like it. To the contrary, I craved the sensation of his touch. But allowing Neph to touch me, in any sense other than friendship, was a completely different level of trust that I wasn't even vaguely familiar with. There was a barrier, a difficult mental wall that I had to work past. My body was the one thing in the world that was truly mine, that I had learned to be in total control of and I had spent every waking moment since that realization protecting it. It was one thing for me to do it damage or put it at risk, quite another to allow someone else. I'd spent too many years with other people using me and abusing my body and powers. Too many decades suffering the hated touch of my handlers. I didn't want anyone touching me, didn't want to open myself up. So the idea of intimacy easily ranked at the top of my list for violation of my property. I would have never let anyone else do what Neph was doing, but even with him it wasn't easy. In fact, it was the most difficult thing I'd ever been faced with. Anything beyond minor physical intimacy was out of the question and Neph knew it. Accepted it.

The kiss on the couch had caught me off guard and I'd had no idea how to react, so I'd simply frozen. In subsequent days and weeks, I'd learned to relax a bit, though it hadn't been easy. Only someone as patient and understanding as Neph would have been willing to put up with me. And knowing that was a great help in beginning to overcome the physical barrier. This was someone who had proven time and again that he cared for me, respected and understood my boundaries. He knew my limitations and, while he would always push them, he never broke them, always knew when to stop. And, probably most important to me, short of that first stolen kiss, he'd asked my permission before doing it again.

I found myself spending more and more time in Neph's quarters, no longer migrating back to my own rooms if it got too late. His bed could have held four people, let alone someone as small as me, and I'd readily claimed the right side, as he generally slept on the left. The first time he'd sidled up next to me to sleep, I'd thought I was going to hyperventilate. But it never went beyond cuddling and sleep, and I came to love the simple closeness of being next to him, the feel of another person beside me. I think Neph was elated the first time I worked up enough courage on my own to curl up against his left side, arm across his chest. I'd fallen asleep draped across him, never having believed that I could feel comfortable and safe against another person.

In public, no one would have known our relationship had so drastically changed. The last thing I wanted was to draw more attention to myself, and our friendship had already been well over the boundaries of a subordinate and officer. Neph had simply shrugged his shoulders when I'd brought it up, a bemused smile tugging at the corner of his mouth. He'd gone along with it though, playing pure professionalism in public. I think he treated it almost like a game, coming to revel in his private time with me, when he could drop the act. For what it was worth, I began to revel in it as well.

Reva, through some sixth sense I could never begin to explain, seemed to know that something had changed almost instantaneously and had her suspicions confirmed when she'd burst into Neph's office, report in hand, anxious to relay some odd thing she'd seen on patrol. We'd been sitting on the couch together, his arm around my shoulders as I leaned against him, only talking, but it had been more than enough for her. Flushing and grinning fit to burst, she had backed out of the office, profusely apologizing. Suddenly apprehensive, I'd left not long after, mind a blank as I wandered haphazardly towards the practice field.

"*Well?!*"

I nearly died of fright as Reva's leering face appeared over the wall next to me. Taking several halting steps backwards, I stared up at her, one hand clutching at my chest. She leaned farther over the edge, her face lit up with anticipation. Of what, I had no idea.

"What the hell, Reva! Are you trying to kill me?"

Vaulting the ledge, she slid down next to me, laughing, and punched me on the arm.

"How did you ever develop a reputation for being a terrifying monster...you're such a kitten."

I wasn't sure if that was an insult or a compliment, so I settled on glaring at the shrubbery as I rubbed my arm. Hooking her arm through mine, she pulled me along beside her.

"So I want to hear all about it," she said, the leering grin returning.

"What are you talking about?"

"Oh, come on. Don't be dense! You and Nephael. I knew something had to have changed. You've been, well, different… calmer, stronger somehow. Happier, I think. Didn't occur to me what had caused it. Gods, Piri, come on! I've been waiting months for this and I know you sure as hell didn't initiate it. So, he finally cornered you and have his way or what?"

I felt my face flush and ground to a halt, pulling out of her grip. Reva rolled her eyes as I tried to splutter a response.

"I'm joking, Piri, get a grip. Honestly, I'm kind of proud of you for even letting him touch you like he does. I was shocked when I saw you sitting with him earlier." She eyed me critically before a smile split her face and she broke into a series of incredibly unReva-like giggles. "Come on, let's go back to your place. Whatever you were doing can wait. I want the story."

I spent the rest of the evening fielding questions and trying to explain how, no, unlike her apparently, I'd had no idea he'd felt that way about me. She finally grabbed me in a bone-crushing hug, told me I was stupid, and left me mentally exhausted. I spent the next several hours lying on my bed, staring at the ceiling, as I ran my entire friendship with Neph through my head, right back to the day I'd first broken down in his office, trying to pick things apart.

The Warning

The aroma of coffee permeating the room woke me from a blissfully dreamless sleep. Opening my eyes, vaguely annoyed, I lay in drowsy confusion at the darkness that greeted me. Beyond the window lay a blanket of stars, the night sky not holding even a hint of the coming dawn. A faint glow shown from beyond the closed bedroom door. Stifling a yawn, I slid back the door.

Neph was sitting hunched over, body stiff and tense with his elbows on the table, fingers gripping his hair. Fully clothed, though he'd obviously dressed in a hurry. I paused in the doorway, frowning as I eyed him. It couldn't have been more obvious that something was wrong. I rubbed a hand across my sleep-crusted eyes. It was entirely too early to have the day ruined.

Grabbing a cup of coffee from the kitchen, I sat down at the table. He didn't move or say anything, only continued to stare at the papers in front of him. Beside the binder, his officer's communicator pulsed with a faint glow. Reaching out a finger, I slowly pulled the file he'd been reading towards me, turning it around. I began scanning the first page and found myself flipping through a series of reports, only taking the time to glance over key words and phrases. I didn't need to read it all. The incidents were all more or less the same, a series of abductions, murders and weird occurrences, and all concerning the Brotherhood, as per usual.

Neph still hadn't said anything. Hadn't even acknowledged my presence or the fact that I'd stolen his report. I flipped the folder closed and pushed it aside, briefly glancing at the communicator again. It couldn't have gone off that recently, not for coffee to have been brewed and a new report to be sitting at his disposal. And there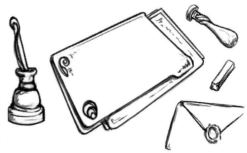

was obviously something else. What time had he gotten up?

I took a sip from my mug, wondering how much I was going to need to get through the day. Reaching out, I gently touched his arm. "What's wrong? That binder is awful, but no more so than the usual. What happened?"

He finally looked up, blinking slowly, dark circles giving his eyes a haunted look. "Embalyn's Cross was attacked."

Embalyn's Cross. I frowned, wracking my brain, trying to pinpoint the location on a mental map. Medium size Seri city, close to the human border. "Define attacked."

Neph leaned back, pinching the bridge of his nose as he squeezed his eyes shut. "Maybe attacked isn't the right word. I don't know what else to call it. Two guards were found, butchered at a ritual site set up around the city's Source Spring."

"Ok. In Embalyn's Cross..." I stifled a yawn. "I don't mean to sound callous, but while that's pretty horrible, it doesn't seem like the sort of thing to drag you out of bed at whatever gods awful hour this is. So what's the catch?"

"You're right," he replied, idly flipping open the report binder and blindly leafing through the pages. "It's not their deaths that roused the entire Conclave, not just the officers. It's what the Brotherhood did with their deaths. They somehow shut down the Spring. Only for an hour or so, but they still shut it down. No one even knows how they infiltrated the city without being detected, let alone made it to the Sanctum."

I stared at him, eyes wide, struck dumb with disbelief. "That's... not possible." No Spring meant no power. No Seri city had ever experienced a blackout. The Source was harnessed to control everything; the lights, doors, plumbing, communication. A city would be crippled without it. And how did you even block a natural, integral part of the world? "Did - did anything else happen?"

Neph shook his head, staring down at the table, voice flat and

166

emotionless. "Did anything else need to?"

No. It didn't. The Brotherhood had sent as clear a message as they could. They had found a way to disable our cities, a way to block the Source on a large scale. If it had only been a test, it had certainly been an effective one. I couldn't help but feel a streak of anger towards the Ruling Council though.

"This could have been avoided you know, could have been stopped before it ever got to this point. The Council has had warning for months. How many people have to go missing, wind up dead, before they do something? If they had bothered to care, they could have taken care of this with the original group, back when I was taken captive." I couldn't keep the acid out of my voice.

Neph was still fooling with the report, now unhappily picking at a corner of the binder. "I'm not going to disagree with you, but the politics have become…complicated. The Empire wouldn't have given a second thought to wiping out the Brotherhood and the consequences be damned. The Restructuring changed all that. But now things have swung from one extreme to another. The Ruling Council has become paralyzed when it comes to taking action. They're trying to repair generations worth of animosity, war and subjugation with a neighbor that may have a much shorter life span, but seems to have a much longer memory.

"But this - this is different. An outside force has now directly attacked us. The Conclave has been summoned to Skycrest. Everyone. The Guild leaders and officers, all of the representatives, ambassadors. I'll be leaving later this morning."

"You know this is going to get worse," I whispered. "They let it go too long."

Reaching out, Neph twined his fingers through mine. "I know. I wish I didn't agree with you, but I do. Hopefully I won't be gone long and maybe something will finally be decided. Try not to cause any trouble while I'm gone." He forced a smile.

It was on the third day of Neph's absence that the warning blared over the emergency speaker system, something I hadn't heard used since my childhood when the Ashtaran Uprising had been raging. Three chimes split the morning, stopping activity, heads swiveling towards the sound in alarm and confusion. Dropping out of the sky, just off a late night patrol, Reva and I listened in rapt silence as the voice of the High Magister filled The Watch, knowing that the same was being heard by every Seri in every city.

"The Ruling Council requests your attention."

A pause followed, leaving a tangible void.

"As many of you are aware, a threat has been building over the past several months. There are Seri who have vanished and are presumed dead while others have been brutally murdered. All of their losses have been keenly felt."

Out of my peripheral vision, I saw Reva roll her eyes. "Like they care," she muttered.

"Three days ago, the border city of Embalyn's Cross experienced an unprecedented occurrence: a complete shutdown of its Spring, a direct result of a radical human sect known as the Brotherhood of Radiant Darkness. For reasons yet unknown, they have chosen to directly target our race. Due to the extreme escalation of events, the Council has determined, in an effort to

168

safeguard our people, that new measures will be instituted in all Seri-occupied territory."

"Yeah, reasons yet unknown…like after even half of what we've done over the centuries, anyone needs a reason to hate us," I said to no one in particular. Losing interest, I turned to Reva. "Let's get some lunch."

Only half listening to the continuing announcement, I wended my way onto the Belayn Terrace, Reva following at my heels. The brunch buffet was nearly deserted and I grabbed a plate, munching my way down the tables. Reva gaped at my apparent unconcern. The message continued to blare in the background, reiterating the travel ban and detailing a distinct uptick in military activity, enhanced patrols and new guard routes. It went on for quite a while. I didn't particularly care. Neph would give us our instructions when he got back, if the Council even bothered with our unit. Most of what they were discussing dealt with the everyday soldiers. And while it was a relief to finally hear the Council doing something, it was all defensive measures, meant to make the general populace feel more secure. None of it would do anything to actually stop the problem and I could only hope they were planning something else covertly. Though, considering the ENF was technically supposed to be their covert unit, I could only assume they weren't.

"Seems kind of pointless, doesn't it?" Reva sat down and put her feet up on a chair. "I mean, great along the border to fortify the cities, but what's the point in a place like this that's nestled in the mountains? The Watch is a fair flight from the border. Pretty serious haul for an earth-bound race. And we're nowhere near the farthest out."

169

I pulled a face as I sat down across from her. "I'd like to hope we're too far out. But let's be honest, we've seen signs of them doing... whatever it is they do...a lot further into our territory than you'd expect. Remember your purple fire and whatever bizarre ritual we stumbled on? I mean, yeah we'd been flying over human territory, but we weren't at that point."

"Huh, yeah. I guess not." Reaching over, she snagged a slice of apple from my plate. "What do you think they're doing anyway? I mean, it doesn't take a genius to see that they've been practicing at something, and getting better at it, for the past year."

"Longer than that. They were trying to somehow control the Source, I think, back when-" I stopped, images flashing across my mind as unwanted, lost memories pushed through. I squeezed my eyes shut, hunching over as I tried to push away the flashes of memory.

"Piri?"

It's fine. Nothing." I straightened up, pushing away from the table. "It was a long night. I'm gonna grab a nap."

Laying claim to what was left on the plate and dragging it across the table, Reva waved me off.

Return From the Conclave

I was lying in bed reading, having woken up far earlier than usual, plagued by dreams, and unable to get back to sleep. With only a single Source light on its lowest setting throwing a dim glow next to me, I flipped a page in a small, worn history of the human religions. It was something I'd snagged from Neph's bookshelves not long after our return from Brakon's Landing. I'd been reading it piecemeal, mostly on nights like these.

A small chime sounded in soft tones from across the room. Six bells. So it was finally dawn. Yawning, I turned another page, feeling my eyes droop slightly.

The hesitant knock on my door several minutes later, as I was just beginning to nod off again, took me by surprise. Without thinking, I fumbled at the bedside table, knocking against the Sourcepad and opening the door.

"Can I come in?"

Suddenly awake, more than a little confused, I stared at Neph outlined in the doorframe. "Yeah, of course." I sat up as he entered. He seemed distracted, clothing disheveled. I patted what little space there was on my bed and he squeezed in next to me. Leaning back, he folded his hands over his stomach, glaring up at the ceiling like he'd suddenly developed a personal vendetta against it. He was still in his uniform, had to have just returned from Skycrest and, for whatever reason, had come here first.

"Neph?"

Turning on his side, he draped an arm over my chest, closing his eyes as he rested his head on my shoulder. After a few minutes of silence, he finally cracked one eye. "How do you stand it? This bed is really small."

"No kidding," I said with a laugh. "Are you going to tell me what's wrong or just complain about my standard issue bed?"

He sighed, closing his eye again. "Just - frustrated. The whole Council is so incredibly frustrating. The entire Conclave wants action. They're justifiably concerned, upset, and want something done, but without the Council's ok, all of our hands are tied: the Guilds, the Officers, everyone. And they're doing nothing. Pretty words yesterday, small actions meant to pacify the worries of the public. I don't know why I ever expected something to be done." He gave an angry snort and fell silent again.

Frowning at the dark circles under his eyes, I brushed a piece of stray hair off his forehead. "Have you been awake all night?"

"Mmmm."

"Let's go back to your place. Get changed, go to bed."

"I - no." He didn't move, gave no indication that he had any intention of moving. "Too much to do today. One hour. Just - please - just give me an hour." His voice trailed off. I realized he was already asleep.

I gave him two hours, not feeling the least bit guilty at the reproachful look he gave me over it. Despite his claim of crushing amounts of work, he loitered in my small quarters long enough for me to realize that he apparently had no intention of leaving without my company. I grabbed my sketching materials and trailed him back to his apartment.

A mountain of paperwork was stacked on the table when we arrived. I couldn't help gaping slightly. He'd only been gone a few days. Dragging a hand across his face, I heard him mutter, "Evari, damn her," as he sat down, pulling the top binder off the stack. I couldn't help feeling sorry for him. So much of his job seemed to revolve around paperwork and organization that he never wanted to deal with.

Morning sunlight lanced through the window. I scrubbed a hand across my eyes, squinting in the brightness. Throwing on a pot of coffee, I settled myself in for the day, glad I happened to be off-duty.

The sun had only just set for the evening when exhaustion finally claimed Neph. I was honestly a little surprised that he'd lasted as long as he had. He'd barely moved from the table all day, distractedly picking at a plate of food I'd sat next to him in the late morning. I wasn't entirely sure how much work he'd actually accomplished or if he was stuck in his own mind, stewing over the meeting. The anger and frustration were clearly written on his face. But I could finally see his head starting to nod as he fought to stay awake. More than happy to turn in early, I extracted him from the heap of papers, gently pushing him towards the bedroom.

The Attack

A shudder ran through The Watch. My eyes snapped open. The room was surprisingly well lit and it took me a moment to realize that it was the moonlight streaming through the glass, that it was still dark, very dark, out. Beside me, Neph had thrown off the covers and vaulted from the bed. He was already half dressed as I slowly sat up. I realized I was sweating, my heart racing. Something was wrong,

more so than whatever had rocked the complex and jolted the two of us awake. I glanced around the bedroom, trying to put a finger on what was causing my sudden panic.

"Neph…"

He turned towards me, already in full uniform, somehow looking completely put together and awake despite the circumstances. I could feel his questioning gaze, waiting.

"Neph. The power is out."

There was a heavy silence as he stared at me.

"The power - what?"

I swung my legs over the side of the bed, stood up, my back to him. I was beginning to shake. This was wrong. Wrong on so many levels. This couldn't possibly be happening, not here.

"Can't you feel it? The power is down," I said, trying to keep my voice from cracking. "There's an - an absence. A void." I closed my eyes, took a deep breath, needing to steady myself.

Neph didn't say anything, but I could hear him trying to turn on the lights. "This isn't possible..." he said, his voice trailing off

He ran out of the room. I followed behind, still in my sleepwear, bare feet cold on the hard wood floor. I reached for the Source, flared my wings, pushed harder till they emitted a faint blueish glow, enough to light the room ever so slightly, enough to see by. Neph stood at the entrance to the apartment, a hand on the pad that opened the door, his head resting against the wall. I walked up, put a hand on his shoulder and gently pushed him away as I placed my hand where his had been and electrified the pad. Temporary, but enough for the door to silently slide open. If we had been trapped, so was everyone else. Reva was the only other person here, that I knew of, who could overSource strongly enough to force her way out of her quarters. I could only hope there were others.

Dressed in full uniform and alert, I wandered the seemingly deserted corridors, Neph at my side. As we passed through the main hall, a movement outside caught my eye. Something darker than the darkness. I moved up to the Grandview window, pressed my face against it, squinting, trying to see what had grabbed my attention. There, at the base of the mountain, near the main river entrance. There was movement. And then suddenly my field of focus expanded and I realized that I hadn't been looking at the big picture. There wasn't just something moving, there were a hundred somethings moving. It looked like a small army camped on our doorstep. And with the Source powering the complex down, it was only a matter of time before they managed to break their way in. I stumbled backwards, turned, began racing towards the rooms of the other ENForcers, screaming back over my shoulder at Neph as he

175

raced to catch me. We had to somehow wake The Watch. A feeling of dread that I couldn't explain was coursing through my system. The Seri military was the most highly trained and formidable in Aetrelys; there was no rationality behind my fear. But something was very wrong with all of this. We needed to evacuate, of that I was certain.

My mind raced as I sped towards Reva's door, Neph hard on my heels. How were the two of us going to open every door in this place? Without the Source coursing through the architecture, very few Seri were strong enough to morph even small portions of the glass, so that escape route was gone. Breaking through the doors or getting them open was the only option. The Watch, like every Seri city, sat on a Source spring. Naturally occurring locations where the energy was powerful at the surface; a visible, surging, liquid energy that could be harnessed. What was the shuddering we had felt;

an explosion of some sort, the Source shutting down? Just like at Embalyn's Cross, they had found a way to block our spring at its origin. And where had the small army of what I could only assume was the Brotherhood come from?

Reva's door was closed when I arrived, but a note had been stuck to the door.

Waking the others. Will send to main hall. - R

Short and to the point. I couldn't help smiling slightly as I read it; there was something very Reva about leaving a neatly written note in the middle of an emergency.

Seeing the note, Neph peeled away, heading back towards the main common area. I took off for the residential sectors, intent on getting as many people as possible out before it was too late.

Reva and I had been periodically crossing paths as we zigzagged back and forth across the complex, overriding the system and opening doors. Soldiers followed in our wake, rousing the population, moving them to the main hall. Most that we passed were still in their night clothes, soldiers and officers included. A handful of us were in full uniform, mostly the ENF it seemed. I guess Neph had succeeded in drilling us on proper attire even at the worst of times. We had worked our way through about seventy-five percent of the rooms when the main gate was finally breached. The explosion could be heard throughout The Watch, the vibration creeping through the soles of our boots as we continued our mad rush. At one of our crossing points, Reva grabbed my arm and we pulled together, both of us breathing raggedly.

"You have to go back to the main hall," Reva finally managed to gasp. "Orders from...Nephael. Get them...get them out. Only you're," she stopped to catch her breath again, "only you're strong enough to morph the Grandview."

My eyes widened. Morph the main window. Three massive stories that curved around the mountainside. It hadn't even occurred to me how we were going to evacuate everyone once they were gathered, though now it seemed obvious, if slightly insane. With a jerk of my head, I turned and moved back towards the gathering point, trying not to think about the kind of energy I was going to have to pull in short order. I could hear fighting in the distance as Seri soldiers fought to hold the lower levels, keep the intruders at bay until we could clear the place. Unfortunately, from the sound of it, things didn't appear to be going well. I put on a burst of speed, trying not to contemplate what might be happening.

I burst into the hall, slamming into a wall of people. The area was nearly at capacity, with Neph and several other officers standing on a table near the window, trying to keep order. Soldiers surrounded the perimeter, division officers wending their way through the throng. I was never going to get through this. With a burst of energy, I pushed above the heads of the crowd, gliding across the room and alighting next to Neph on the table.

"I'm ready to drop the Grandview. We need to go. Now."

Neph nodded slowly. "More than you know. We've got bigger problems than we thought. I'll explain later. We're going to take everyone to Emyr's Crest. It's closest."

I nodded, not particularly caring where we went as long as it was away from here, though I couldn't help but briefly wonder what a small Seri city like Emyr's Crest was going to do with the entire population of The Watch.

Stepping forward, Merrant, head of the Small Council, raised his voice above the panicked din.

"Be ready to fly when Enpirion drops the window. Please try to remain calm and stay with your group." Silence fell as expectant, fearful faces all turned to watch me. In the quiet, the battle on the lower levels could be heard much more clearly. And much closer. How close was Reva to getting everyone out?

I felt a hand on my shoulder. "Are you sure you can do this?" Neph asked, his voice shaking slightly, the worry audible. I gave his hand a brief squeeze, eyeing the window, unable to keep my nerves from showing.

My voice shook slightly. "I don't have much of a choice."

Taking a deep breath, I turned to face the glass. Closed my eyes. Reached out to the Source. The window was monolithic and I was going to pay for that kind of overSourcing. My wings flared, I could feel the energy coding slowly creeping across my skin, glowing softly in the darkness. I pushed outward, extending my influence across the window. Higher and wider, taking it all in. And then I twisted. The only way I could possibly describe how I manipulate the energy, change what's around me. I could feel the glass shift, change, and then suddenly it was nothing but energy. I could feel the strain, holding the window in this flux state. I gritted my teeth. I could vaguely make out Neph shouting something, the rush of bodies moving past me. And then the screaming started. I nearly lost my hold on the window. I strengthened my grip on the Source, pushing it further before turning and opening my eyes. The world was in hyper-sharp focus, a slight blueish tinge on the edges of my vision. I was starting to push things too far. It was one thing to overSource in a burst, another to hold that sort of energy for extended periods.

The front runners from the invading force had broken through, which meant that the opposing Seri force was dead. And prisoners apparently weren't on their to-do list. Stragglers and soldiers near the back of the room were cut down without mercy. The ENForcers who had been manning the perimeter rushed in, putting themselves between this strange force and the civilians. With a sickening feeling, I watched as one of the invaders leveled a crossbow and put a bolt through a soldier's leg. His wings vanished, his weapon dissolved. And just as quickly, he was dead, a sword point appearing between his shoulder blades.

In my peripheral vision, I caught sight of Reva tearing in from a back entrance, Farryn close on her heels, waving her arms, a few civilians in her wake.

179

That was it, the last of them. She turned to ward off an attack, twin swords streaking into existence as the intruders moved to intercept her, cutting down several of those with her. Blood spattered the marble floors and sculptures, stained the walls. Fallen bodies draped across furniture. I could see one of the invaders level a crossbow at Farryn's back as he reached down to sweep up a child. With a massive surge, I threw up a barrier between the Seri and the outsiders, the power of the shockwave knocking both parties to the floor. The bolt, a moment before meant to take down a fellow ENF, clattered to the marble.

"Get out," I screamed. "I'll hold them back."

Reva ran up and grabbed my outstretched arm. "Piri, you can't -"

I shook myself free, wincing at the burning sensation that was slowly creeping up my spine. "No," I gasped, "get out. Now. I can't... can't hold this much longer."

Reva hesitated only a moment before she took off, the remaining Seri following her. When the last person was out, I spread my wings and launched myself backwards. I had to get out of firing range before I let everything go, but I could feel myself losing control. I'd pushed the glass beyond the point of no return. With the last of my strength, I thrust the barrier farther backwards into the attackers, just as I lost control of the window and it reverted, bulging slightly for only an instant before it exploded, shards ripping through the invading force. On the verge of losing consciousness, I felt arms wrap themselves around my chest, dragging me up into the sky.

The Meeting

"How many are dead…officially?"

"Forty-two civilians. Two hundred and thirteen soldiers. And there are five missing, presumed dead."

Momentary silence fell across the room as everyone took in the numbers. No army could outmatch the Seri military, even when taken by surprise. Not in weapons or hand-to-hand combat. Even a small group was a deadly force to be reckoned with. And yet they had been defeated. Not just defeated but brutally taken 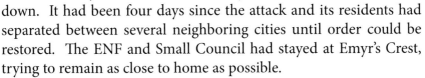 down. It had been four days since the attack and its residents had separated between several neighboring cities until order could be restored. The ENF and Small Council had stayed at Emyr's Crest, trying to remain as close to home as possible.

With The Watch down, communication was reliant on physical messengers and it had taken some time to get organized. Reva and Farryn, having given their version of events earlier, stood stationed at the door while the Small Council discussed the incident. Reva shifted her weight slightly. They had been standing there for what felt like hours while the Council sat around the large circular table, going over the details of the attack again and again. It wasn't until a Runner showed up with the final death count that there had even been a break in the bickering.

"So tell me, Nephael, how is it that an entire damn army somehow managed to get past your so-called elite patrols?"

Neph's brows knitted together, an uncharacteristic snarl curling his lips as he stood up, his hands slamming down on the table.

"Don't you dare point fingers at me, Sendaryn. The regular divisions patrol the area as well. And it's not like we were expecting an attack on one of our most remote outposts. The ENForcers didn't see them and neither did your crew, so maybe you should go berate your Watch officers before getting on my case. And if it hadn't been for my 'elites', there would have been a massacre."

"Oh, I'm sorry," Sendaryn shot back acidly, "you don't consider two hundred and sixty Seri to be a massacre?"

Nephael leaned across the table, eye to eye with Sendaryn, his voice dangerously low. "Compared to what it could have been? I think we got off lucky. If it hadn't been for Enpirion and Trevanys, there might not have been a Watch community left to talk about."

"Oh yes, your precious Enpirion, savior of the day. Lucky he was in your room that night."

Neph's eyes narrowed to slits. "And what exactly is *that* supposed to mean? My personal life is none of -"

"*Enough.*" Merrant's raised voice cut in. "I believe our messenger has more information to relay, if we would allow him a moment to get in a word or two," he said, his voice dropping back to its normally tranquil level.

All eyes turned back to the Runner as he held out a small box, several of the Council looking openly relieved at the interruption. "Sir, I was also told to give you this. The division that returned from The Watch said they pulled it from one of the bodies. They said they scoured the area but it was the only one they could find, so the attackers probably took the rest when they left. And I…I ran into Enpirion." He said the name hesitantly, eyeing Sendaryn nervously. "Outside. I've been told to tell you 'don't touch it.' Which also happens to coincide with what the scouts told me."

Tuning into the discussion, Reva nudged Farryn, whispering out of the corner of her mouth. "Did he just say he ran into Piri?" Farryn only frowned in response. "He shouldn't be out of bed. What's he doing wandering around do you suppose?"

Farryn shrugged ever so slightly. "It's Enpirion. He does what he pleases." He looked uncomfortable as he said it. He'd been distinctly quiet since the attack.

Neph crossed the room and took the box from the Runner, opening the lid to gaze quizzically at the object resting inside. "It looks like a crossbow bolt. Odd markings though, weird tip. I - Oh…" His eyes suddenly widened, realizing what the object was as he tilted the box slightly so that it rolled around inside.

Sendaryn moved around the table and snatched the box from his fingers. "I'm tired of hearing that name. Like that degenerate's opinion is worth anything." Nephael curled his lip, but kept silent as Sendaryn began to reach for the object.

Unable to stand listening anymore from where I'd been eavesdropping outside the room, I slammed the door open, snapping it back into the wall with the kind of Source push that only I could manage. Reva heaved a sigh and looked towards the ceiling as I strode angrily into the room.

"It cuts off the Source," I spat out, reaching out and snapping the lid shut, nearly taking Sendaryn's fingertips with it. "It's the same weapon that was used on us back in Brakon's Landing. I'm sorry that my 'opinion' isn't worth anything. And apparently my report on the matter falls into that same category since it's seemingly gone missing or you'd have known that already. I wonder how that could possibly have happened. I suppose it's a good thing I decided to invite myself in. Like I said before, don't touch it."

"How do you know that it cuts off the Source?" Sendaryn demanded, ignoring the jibe about the report, heat rising in his face.

"I thought I was fairly clear when I said it's the same thing I was hit with in Brakon's Landing. Or maybe it was because I watched them shoot a soldier during the attack and I saw the after-effect," I shot back. "That was right before they shoved a sword through his neck. *Sir.*" We stared each other down, eyes locked. Neph winced slightly at my insolence, but didn't say anything.

"And is there some reason you decided to withhold that information from the Council?" Sendaryn's voice was deadly quiet.

My fists clenched, one hand unconsciously rising slightly. Sendaryn blanched and backed up a step.

"Because last time I checked, not only was I not invited to attend today, but I've just spent the past several days recovering from a severe overSource. Oh, that saved The Watch," I snarled, my voice rising in anger. "I'll be fine though, thanks for asking." I glared daggers at Sendaryn whose face was slowly turning an unnatural shade of red, a vein in his forehead starting to throb. Neph pinched the bridge of his nose and leaned back in his seat. Before more could be said, Merrant rose from his seat at the head of the table.

"Everyone relax, please. Obviously there is information we're missing here, an oversight that we need to remedy, though understandable, I think, in light of this unprecedented and tragic event. Tempers are running high and none of us are thinking clearly. It is time that we took a step back and handled this properly. You can all go. Sendaryn, I will discuss the missing report with you at a later time." He aimed a pointed look in Sendaryn's direction, narrowing his eyes. "Nephael, Enpirion, please stay."

I slumped down in a chair as the rest of the Council filed from the room, followed by Reva and Farryn. Before she closed the door behind her, Reva shot me a look. The kind of look that only she could give. There was an entire speech berating my behavior crammed into that two second glare. I sighed and closed my eyes, leaning my throbbing head back. I should have just left it alone, stayed in bed. Should have let that ass, Sendaryn, find out for himself what the bolt did. Neph had known and made no move to stop him taking it. It would have served him right. I was intent on continuing vengeful thoughts of what could happen to Sendaryn when I felt cool fingers slide across my cheek. I opened my eyes a slit.

"Why are you out of bed? You look awful," Neph whispered. "No offense." His lips quirked upwards in a brief smile, but I could tell that, underneath his legitimate concern, he wasn't happy with me.

"Gentlemen, if you please."

Merrant reseated himself, beckoning for us to join him. Neph's fingers lingered for another moment, his eyes clearly saying, 'We are going to talk later.' I stood and followed him, feeling sick to my stomach. Neph and I never fought and the mere thought of a disagreement upset me. I knew I deserved whatever he might say. I'd been completely out of line, but I couldn't help being slightly resentful. Outside of Neph and Reva, as per usual, no one cared that I'd spent several days feeling like I was going to die. Forget that I had blacked out, mid-air, making sure that the citizens of The Watch had made it to safety. I was still sick and would be for days. The Council hadn't even bothered to look at my report...or it somehow hadn't actually made it to them. Which was more than likely the case and definitely

Sendaryn's fault, the more I thought about it. My accusation earlier had been out of anger, but I had probably been correct. Sendaryn was a problem and always had been. The man had wanted to let me die after I'd been captured and tortured. He'd lobbied to have me removed from the ENForcers. I was absolutely sure that it was his doing that my report had gone missing and unread.

"Enpirion?" I jerked back to the present with a start. Merrant and Neph were both staring at me. Neph looked more than a little concerned.

"I - sorry, Sir," I mumbled. "I'm still recovering." It wasn't a lie and sounded a lot better than 'I'm sitting here ruminating on how bitter and angry I am at the system'. Merrant flashed an amused grin, like he knew exactly what I was actually thinking.

"I understand. I intend to keep this as short as possible so that you can return to your quarters. As there has been some oversight in procuring your account of the events in question, I would like to hear the story, right here and now, especially concerning this rather interesting weapon, which I believe you have some first-hand experience with. I will have someone look into the whereabouts of the formal report, which I am fairly certain must exist," he said with a knowing smile. He leaned back, spreading his hands. "So, let's begin."

Merrant's short meeting was anything but. At the two hour mark, he finally dismissed us. By that time, I was beginning to fade due to legitimate health reasons, rather than made up ones. Neph steered me towards his own borrowed quarters, rather than mine, apparently unwilling to leave me by myself.

Stumbling through the doorway, my battered energy reserves

finally gave out and it was only Neph's quick reflexes that kept me from falling as the door slid shut. We'd walked back in silence and it continued as he guided me towards the bedroom. I was still dreading what he was going to say about the meeting and was more than a little surprised when he leaned in, his lips suddenly locked against mine. With some difficulty, I finally managed to pull back, head swimming.

"Neph, I'm going to pass out if you don't stop. Seriously," I managed to gasp out, feebly extracting myself and collapsing onto the bed. Dropping onto the other side of the bed, Neph started to laugh uncontrollably. I struggled to lever myself up on my elbows and stared at him. He'd obviously lost his mind.

"Gods, I'm sorry," he said, finally calming down, wiping tears off his face. "I just…you have no idea how much I was hoping you would actually hit Sendaryn." He held up his hands defensively and bit his lip as my mouth dropped open. "I'm glad you didn't. For future reference, please don't. But the look on his face. I almost wish you hadn't stopped him from touching that bolt." He fell silent for a few moments, sobering, then continued. "Don't get me wrong, I'm incredibly annoyed over your behavior. Your actions reflect on the entire group, not just yourself. And you're well aware that the ENF has a lot of prejudice to overcome. And yet…I was angry when it happened, but now I just can't be. Only because of who it was."

I lay back, staring at the ceiling. Neph's reaction had actually made me feel even worse. No lecture, nothing to assuage my guilt. I'd been in the wrong and he knew it. Turning on my side, I curled up.

"I'm sorry," I finally said, closing my eyes, unable to share Neph's mood. "I'm just…I'm angry. Angrier than usual today. But I shouldn't have interrupted the Council and acted like that. And Sendaryn always makes it worse. Just seeing him makes me furious."

We lay in silence. Neph eventually pushed himself up, leaning back against the headboard. "I hate that man," he muttered, uncharacteristic bitterness lacing his voice. "I don't understand why he's been allowed to remain in a position of power. He has entirely too much influence. Mark my words, one of these days, he's going to be trouble." He reached over and brushed a stray bit of hair from my forehead before curling up next to me. "Apology accepted," he said softly. "Though I'm sure it won't be the last time. It never is," he added with a slight smile.

Going Back to the Dark

It was nearly noon when I wandered out of the bedroom, yawning, still clad in my borrowed sleepwear. It was the first time since the attack that I'd felt like myself again. I was still scrubbing the sleep from my eyes as I meandered across the room towards where Neph sat at the table, chin resting in his hands as he gazed out the window. A familiar scene. I should have recognized that something was wrong, but my brain hadn't quite caught up to my body yet.

Grabbing a mug of coffee (where Neph had acquired coffee here in Emyr's Crest was beyond me), I joined him. It was only then, sitting there across from him that I realized something was off. He didn't say anything. Didn't even raise his eyes to look at me. I reached out hesitantly, touched his arm. I felt sick to my stomach. This seemed to be how bad news always started.

"Neph?"

Silence for a moment, then he sighed and ran his hands through his hair. He stared at me for a moment before shaking his head.

"They're sending you to the Depths; you and Farryn."

One sentence. It was all he needed. I felt my blood run cold.

"When?" I asked in a mortified whisper.

"Soon," he said, just as quietly. "We're returning to The Watch tomorrow. The Grandview is closed off until the damage can be repaired, but the Ruling Council wants life back to normal as soon as possible. As if," he finished with a derisive snort.

"So they've repaired things...?"

"I wouldn't say repaired, but at least the power is back on. It

189

came on while a cleanup crew was there the other day."

While a cleanup crew... Surely not. "Neph, it's been over a week."

"Nine days, to be exact," he said quietly. "The Spring core was surrounded with the remains of some sort of ritual. Not so different from the one at Embalyn's Cross, just a lot more...complicated. And grisly. We still don't know what they did or how they did it. The markings at the site have all faded. The Spring sprang back to life when the last one died. And one of the scouts found another shard of stone, the same as the tip of the crossbow bolt. Seems sloppy to leave those behind. Maybe they were trying to send another message. They want us to be afraid."

I closed my eyes. Nine days. They had disabled the Spring for nine days.

"We weren't the only city you know," Neph continued. "Two others, neither near the border, were attacked in the same manner in the nights following The Watch."

"You know it was the Brotherhood. The markings on their clothing were the same. And the weapons. But, gods Neph, there was an entire army of them. Where the hell did they come from? How did they transport an army that large without us seeing?"

"I - only have a theory."

He fell silent, staring at the table. I took a sip of my coffee, not really tasting it, just needing something to do as I tried to process what he'd just said, trying to see the connection to his initial statement, thinking I did but really not wanting to acknowledge it.

"Neph - I'm missing something. Why the Depths?"

Neph leaned back, unhappiness written across his face.

"You aren't missing anything. You saw one of the rituals first hand. Think about what you saw, the vortex you described. Everything that went with it."

He was right and my heart sank as I let myself put two and two together.

"Portals controlled by the Dark."

"We know there's a definite connection," he went on, "but we don't know what it is. This is no different than our trip to Brakon's Landing. We need information. We're desperate for it now."

"Yes, and Brakon's Landing, which is paradise compared to the Depths, turned out incredibly well," I said sarcastically.

Moody silence fell. Neither of us looked at the other, both lost in our own thoughts. I tried to calm the wash of fear that was flooding my system at the thought of being sent into the Depths, the epicenter of the Wild Dark, as the region was colloquially known...a world far below the ground and governed by an entirely different sort of race, a different energy. One completely at odds with the surface world. I'd never been entirely sure if it was even technically part of our reality or if it was some realm that merely bordered ours. The Seri had spent over a hundred years in a war with the denizens of the Upper Dark, but the creatures of the Depths were another matter entirely. It wasn't a place I enjoyed, by any stretch of the word.

"I'm sorry."

I looked up. Neph was still staring at the table. His hand reached out and grabbed mine, squeezing tightly. I think he was trying to stop his own hands from trembling, more than comfort me.

"I tried to convince the Council to send someone else, but -"

He stopped, voice cracking slightly. I could hear the fear there, mirroring my own.

"There is no one else," I said quietly. He looked up, eyes finally locking on to mine. "No one else has been there and managed to come back."

"Making it back once doesn't prove -"

"It wasn't just once," I said with a shake of my head.

"Your file…" His voice trailed off with an almost pleading whine.

"I told you, Neph, there are things I had to do that you don't know about. No one does. I wasn't there just once or twice." I stopped, squeezed my eyes shut. I really didn't want to think about it. The Depths were horrible, the creatures terrifying. I'd barely made it out alive the last time they'd sent me down there. I'd been far more reckless back then and hadn't especially cared if I'd lived or died at that point. I'd been almost numb to the fear and pain. Things had changed.

"I don't want you to go," he said, his voice barely even a whisper. "What if you don't come back?"

Heaving a resigned sigh, I stood up. I didn't want to talk about this, didn't want to think about what was coming. I needed food. On the way to the kitchen, I leaned over and kissed the side of his head.

"I always somehow manage to come back. It's what I do."

The Night Before

Reva stared at me from across the table, eyes hollow. She wasn't really looking at me, but was lost in her own troubled thoughts. We'd only been back at The Watch for a few short days and it was all I was going to be allowed to enjoy. Farryn and I were set to leave the following morning. I'd resigned myself to going, knowing there was no way out of it. Wallowing in fear wouldn't help me down there. I needed to do what I'd been trained to do, what I'd trained myself to do...close myself off, lock my mind, make sure my walls were impenetrable. It was a lot harder than it used to be.

We'd been sitting here on the Belayn for several hours, neither of us speaking much. There wasn't much to say. My feet were propped up on the table, my sketchbook resting against my knees. The page was still blank, my pencil tapping against my leg.

"Piri?"

I looked up.

"I don't know much about the Depths. I just know enough to be afraid. And I'm scared I'm going to lose you." Her voice shook. It was the first she'd spoken about me going. Giving myself a mental shake, I dropped my feet, pushing my sketchbook onto the table. Reaching out, I awkwardly took her hand, trying to force a smile.

"Would you believe me if I said it's not as bad as everyone thinks?"

"No," she snapped. "I wouldn't."

I sighed. "What do you want me to say, Reva? There's nothing I can do." Suddenly wanting to be alone, I stood, stuffing my supplies into my bag. "I have to go pack," I said resignedly.

Rising swiftly, she grabbed me in a crushing hug. Releasing me just as suddenly, she pushed me to arm's length, fingers tightly grasping my forearms, giving me a hard stare.

"You better come back."

"Piri..."

I didn't respond. I could just tell from the sound of that whisper that it was probably going to ruin what was left of my night. So I stayed silent, concentrating instead on the steady beat of Neph's heart, the gentle rise and fall of my head on his chest. I knew it couldn't last...he could sense I was awake and whatever he wanted to ask, he probably wasn't going to let me off the hook, not when I was leaving in the morning. But I didn't want to talk. All I wanted was to hold on to this moment of peaceful oblivion. I squeezed my eyes shut, turning the darkness into something more complete, and in that darkness, I felt gentle fingers brush my face, tracing patterns on my features: a thumb running across my brow, down my cheek, the corner of my mouth.

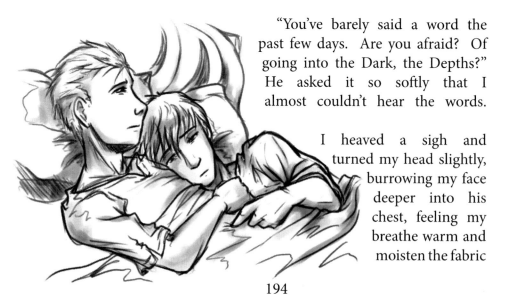

"You've barely said a word the past few days. Are you afraid? Of going into the Dark, the Depths?" He asked it so softly that I almost couldn't hear the words.

I heaved a sigh and turned my head slightly, burrowing my face deeper into his chest, feeling my breathe warm and moisten the fabric of his shirt. The Wild Dark. Of course I was afraid. Deep down, behind those solid walls, I was petrified. Only a fool wasn't. It was a question asked by someone who had never been there, would, most likely, never have to go there. That vortex of ruin, deep beneath the ground. It got into your head, tried to change you, confronted you with everything you feared in yourself. Even the Ashtaran races of the Upper Dark only lived on the very edges of it and avoided going into the Depths. It wasn't just what it did to your mind, it was also the creatures that lived there. Old things...no, ancient ones. Beings at home in the madness, wielding strange powers and controlling powerful forces.

I had spent more time than I cared to think about in those anomalous places, carrying out dangerous missions that no one else could be sent on. Not that any of my experience would necessarily save me. There was no map of the Depths, as it shifted and changed constantly, its preserved ruins and decayed cities ever changing. I had hoped, prayed, that I never had to go back. But down there, somewhere, was, if not an answer, then a clue to the situation that now plagued the Seri, threatened our way of life. The only saving grace was that, this time, I would have company. Farryn might not be my first choice in a traveling companion, but if anyone would have a chance of remaining stable, it was someone as stubborn as him.

Neph's hand moved into my hair, fingers gently moving back and forth. In the old days, I wouldn't have felt any reservations about throwing myself into an assignment like this. I wouldn't have felt anything at all. What did I care where they sent me? There had only ever been me and I had never really considered myself worth enough to care. No one else certainly had. But things had changed. And now I was terrified. Terrified of losing myself, losing what I had gained. Losing Neph. I didn't deserve the warm, kind person pressed against me, lacking in judgment and giving me everything of himself, holding himself back on my account. How long had it been and I still hadn't come to terms with how someone like him could ever love someone like me. But if there was one certainty in my life, it's that I didn't want to lose that. At this point, it would destroy me.

I slid my fingers up under his shirt, pressing them to his skin, wanting to be as close as possible, draw some of his warmth and life into myself before I had to let it go again. Needling at the back of my mind, a tiny voice couldn't help but question why this sort of intimacy was ok, but anything beyond it terrified me.

We simply lay in silence for a while. Neph never pressed me for an answer to his question. I could hear his breathing beginning to slow as sleep crept in. A sudden urgency stole over me as I listened, wishing I could drag the peaceful moment on forever. But there was only now and tomorrow I would be gone.

"I love you," I said quietly, eyes closing. The first time I'd been able to say it out loud. I was leaving. It was important. I could feel myself drifting off, despite how desperately I kept trying to cling to consciousness. His arms curled around me as he burrowed his face in my hair and kissed the top of my head.

"I love you too," he whispered.

Departure

At the crack of dawn, I found myself sequestered together with Farryn in one of the smaller conference rooms, poring over a map showing the known entrances to the Upper Dark. Bayn, a guildmaster and member of the Small Council, had taken charge of prepping us for our journey. Despite being ENF, the entire Council seemed to be taking an active role in the mission.

Farryn tapped his finger on the map, shaking his head as Bayn frowned.

"I'm telling you, this is where we want to enter. It's a whole lot closer," he said. Bayn's lips formed a razor thin line as he crossed his arms.

"My journeymen told me -"

"I know what they told you," Farryn interrupted, "but, like I keep telling you, that cave is closer and I've been through it. I don't really care what your guildsmen say. Just because they know maps and land formations and whatever else it is you physiographers do, doesn't mean they have any clue where we need to go. Unless something major has sealed off *this* point," he jabbed an emphatic finger, "which I doubt, there's an Ashtaran village no more than a half day's journey through there. And the guy running The Dark Line knows me." He paused. "It's an inn," he answered flatly to Bayn's questioning look.

"How do you know he's even still alive or running the place?"

Farryn gave an exasperated snort. "Trust me, he's fine."

I was hunched down in the corner, double and triple checking our travel packs, only half listening to their bickering as I made sure we had what we would need. Which, admittedly, wasn't much. We were traveling light and, more or less, roughing it. Food would be, hopefully, easy to come by in the Upper Dark, so rations were limited to the Depths. I checked my pack's inner pockets for the upteenth time, making sure the meager collection of drawing supplies I'd packed were all accounted for. No matter how many times I went through everything, nothing changed. It was nearly time to leave. Sighing, I stood up, a pack clutched in either hand. It took a few moments for Bayn and Farryn to notice me as I stood there, watching them in annoyed silence.

"Enpirion, you have something to add?" Bayn asked rather crossly.

"Can we go?"

"Yes," Farryn said, grabbing his pack from my outstretched hand and moving quickly towards the door. Bayn threw up his hands in exasperation.

"Fine," Bayn said. "You'll figure it out."

"Yes, we will," Farryn said under his breath.

I followed him out, head down as we walked towards the Grandview Green, ready to head out. A hand dropped onto my shoulder, making me jump slightly, and I whipped around to find Neph had come up behind me.

"Trying to slip off?" he asked quietly. I wrapped my arms around him, leaning in, eyes closed. This was the moment I had been trying to avoid by silently stealing away in the early morning hours. But now that it was here, I was grateful for it.

"I didn't want to wake you," I whispered.

"You didn't want to say goodbye," he said just as softly, his arms curling around me. He buried his face in my neck. We stood in silence for a moment.

"Are you ok?" Neph finally asked.

"No," I said, "but I will be. I'll have to be." The moment was broken and he pulled back, studied me carefully for a moment before brushing a stray wisp of hair off my forehead. With a tight smile Neph leaned in and kissed me, quickly, fleetingly.

"Please be careful," he said, his fingers lingering on my cheek. "And good luck."

The Watch quickly grew smaller before vanishing into the distance as Farryn and I sped across the sky. Farryn was out in the lead, determinedly avoiding speaking to me if at all possible. I could have easily outstripped him, but let him have the lead, content to fly in silence. We had a long day ahead of us before we reached Farryn's entrance to the Upper Dark. I was admittedly curious as to why he'd spent enough time there to have current contacts, but I bit my tongue on asking.

I chanced a quick glance over my shoulder, but The Watch had already faded from sight. I heaved a sigh, banking in a slow turn as I followed Farryn. I should have been enjoying the flight over the countryside; the feeling of the wind rushing through my outstretched primaries, the beautiful day. But I couldn't help the melancholy weighing on me, over what I'd left behind and what I was winging towards.

We were flying fairly low over human-controlled territory at this point and I could actually see peasants stopping their activities, craning necks backwards to stare and point. It wasn't often, I was sure, that they witnessed Seri passing overhead. Honestly, it was making me a little nervous. Announcing our presence to every settlement along our route seemed both unnecessary and dangerous, especially considering the current tensions.

With a quick Source push, I pulled level with Farryn.

"Hey!"

"What?" he called back without looking up.

"Think we could maybe go higher, be a little less conspicuous?" I asked in some annoyance.

"Why? No one is going to bother us. Last I checked, humans can't fly."

"Oh yeah, no, they just have Source-killing crossbow bolts. Did you seriously just ask me why? Especially after what happened to us in Brakon's Landing? Or how about a bit more recently at The Watch? Can we at least *try* to play it safe and not get killed before we even get started?"

Farryn rolled his eyes, but rose higher, wings pumping strongly as he propelled himself through a cloud bank. As I once again pulled level with him, he glared over at me, looking me up and down like I was some new creature he'd never seen before.

"What?" I finally snapped.

He shook his head. "What happened to you? When did you turn into this timid, cautious..." He cut off, let the thought hang. "I'm not sure which is worse, former angry, reckless you or...this."

I glared right back him.

"Sorry I'm such a disappointment. I didn't realize you kept such close tabs on my personality."

He snorted, pulling slightly ahead again. I dropped back even farther, not wanting to be near him. The two of us had never had the best relationship and being stuck with him on this mission was no walk in the park. I just needed to hold my tongue and do my job.

Landing with a soft thump, I stared upward at the massive entrance leading into the mountain. Dark-hued triangular flags, maroon and blue, covered in silvery embroidery and Ashtaran script, were woven among the rocks and vegetation. Several of the largest rocky protrusions were covered in writing. I'd never managed to pick up the Ashtaran language, other than a few words here and there, no matter how hard I'd tried. The complex runic symbols were a chaotic mix representing letters, words and entire phrases and the meanings could vary depending on how you voiced their sing-songy pronunciation. Thank the gods for the common tongue.

Dropping down beside me, Farryn strode right into the cave mouth without a second glance. Doing my best to push my competing anger and annoyance into a mental corner, I said goodbye to the sunlight and followed him in.

Into the Depths

Farryn and I trudged silently through the caverns of the Upper Dark. We'd been surprisingly lucky so far in our travels. The Ashtaran cities might not have been overly welcoming, but Farryn's connections had proven invaluable. I was still having a hard time believing that, after so many years, Farryn would still have had any pull whatsoever, but, against the odds, with Farryn at the helm, taverns had housed and fed us, and with no questions asked. I was developing more than a sneaking suspicion that his Ashtaran connections had nothing to do with old ENF business, as he'd so vehemently argued with the Council several days prior, and were much more recent affairs than anyone knew. I probably didn't want to know and it was saving us a lot of hassle.

Now, several days trek beyond the borders of the last lingering settlement, and several stories below as well, the scenery was beginning to drastically change. The perpetual twilight of the Upper region was slowly darkening the farther we descended, the walls themselves becoming rougher, older. Strange carvings and ancient markings had begun to appear in the living stone, unnerving and warped depictions of some long forgotten civilization.

The passages were widening. At times, we found ourselves passing through caverns so large there was no way to tell where they ended. We were crossing through one of those now, marching around the edges of a bio-luminescent lake, its greenish waters throwing shifting reflections across the otherworldly vegetation and ruins that ran the water's edge. Right around two feet into the water, the light suddenly hit some invisible wall, unable to penetrate the darkness beyond the lake's edge, leaving a black pit in the center of the cavern. Farryn's nerves were starting to fray. I could tell just from his body language. The silence, but for the steady drip, drip of water coming from some monolithic, twisted stalactite, was suffocating. Once we had left Ashtaran territory, Farryn's guidance had been at an end. The Upper Dark wasn't all that dissimilar from the surface, as far as cities and everyday dealings. But he was in strange, unfamiliar lands now, farther than he'd ever gone, relying on me to lead the way.

"Do you know where we're going? Seriously, I mean?" Farryn angrily snorted, flopping down on a moss-covered boulder (I hoped it was moss, anyway). He idly picked up a stone and skipped it across the lake surface. Halting, I followed the stone's path across the water before turning an annoyed look upon him.

"Yes and no," I said quietly. "We're getting closer. I can feel the shift in energy. And that's what I'm following. It's the only way. And please don't do that."

His eyes slid back to the lake surface. The ripples caused by the stone were still imprinted on the surface, as though they had been etched there. The dripping water had ceased, the droplets now hanging frozen in mid-air. "We should keep going."

Farryn abruptly stood, staring in unease at the now immobile scene before him. I pulled my cloak around myself, readjusting my pack and setting off again, open irritation in my movements.

"Strange things happen down here," I said testily as Farryn caught up. "Try not to exacerbate things."

We passed through increasingly stranger caverns, the rock formations twisted and warped, the plant life sporting oddly lurid colors. Strange creatures prowled nearly unseen in the darkness, only their eyes visible as they caught the shimmering light that seemed to always illuminate their path. I never had been able to figure out the source of that radiance, though gods knew I'd spent enough time trying back in the day. The atmosphere grew more and more oppressive the closer we came to the Depths. And then, quite suddenly, we'd arrived. Coming to a halt, we stared grimly at the wall ahead of us. Or what should have been just another cavern wall. As far as we could see, to either side and up into the darkness, was a solid sheet of shifting blue mist, cut through with dancing indigo and the occasional blood red, like a macabre aurora. It shifted between looking solid one moment and gaseous the next, twisting in on itself, constantly undulating.

"Welcome to the Wild Dark," I whispered, shivering slightly.

Farryn moved along the ground before the wall, scuffing back and forth with the toe of his boot. He crouched down, brushed fingertips over something scratched into the stone. I frowned and moved towards him, wondering what he was doing, slightly annoyed that he was disturbing things again.

"Look at this. Runes, markings of some sort," he said, pointing at the ground. "Don't they sort of look like those ones the Brotherhood were using? They go in either direction. But these look, well, recent."

I leaned over his shoulder, staring at the markings, just visible beneath a fine layer of dust. Farryn was right though. They didn't look like they'd been there for long. And I certainly didn't recall them from any previous visits.

I shook my head roughly, trying to clear the creeping feeling that was inching its way into my mind. "It's time. Let's go." I reached out towards Farryn. "Don't go through without -" I never got the sentence completed.

Farryn hesitated for only a moment before plunging through the curtain. I followed swiftly after, panicking slightly, hoping we hadn't been separated. Luck was with us, thankfully, and we both emerged in the same location. Towering cliffs rose up on either side of us. The path forward led straight between them. I reached out and grabbed Farryn's cape, jerking him to a halt as he started to move forward.

Are you nuts?" I snapped. "We're not on the surface anymore. The

laws aren't the same here and nothing plays by the rules you're used to. I've never had that wall drop me in the same place twice. We could easily have wound up in totally different locations. And, unlike me, you'd have been screwed. You can't just rush headlong into things down here."

Farryn wrenched the fabric out of my grip and looked around. "Well, we're fine, right?" he sneered. "We both made it through in the same place, so who cares." He started forward again.

I felt my hands clench into fists, felt the blood rising in my face.

"What the hell is your problem anyway?" I stormed over to a jutting rock and installed myself on the edge of it. "And I don't just mean right now, I mean in general. I've spent most of my life putting up with you, putting up with your jeering and bullying. And I've never understood why. And, in case you haven't noticed, I'm trying to keep you alive down here." I pointed an angry finger down the path carved between the steep rock. "That, down there, is like nothing you've ever experienced before. I've had the unfortunate experience of having been here more times than I'd like to think about. You saw some weirdness on the way to the wall, saw how things were starting to change. And I know how it can get to a person, but there's no excuse for the way you're acting. Whether either of us likes it or not, we're on this mission together and we need to act as a team. I'm going to do my best to lead us into the heart of this gods forsaken place, but I can't do that if you won't listen to me."

Farryn simply stared at me, seemingly surprised by my outburst. Just when I thought his silence had gone on long enough, his eyes shifted to the side, head dropping slightly.

"I -" He paused. "Maybe you're right. Where does that path lead?"

I narrowed my eyes, but I knew it was the closest I would get to an apology. I'd never even gotten that close before and at least he seemed ready to listen.

"We lucked out," I said, pushing myself off the rock, trying to let go of my anger. "The path ends at the Void Plains. It's a lot closer to the City than just about any other place we could have been dropped."

"The City?"

"The ruined City. I don't know what else to say right now. I'll explain more as we get closer. I'm assuming that's where we're headed. I'm sure I'll know soon enough. It's sort of the..." I waved my hand in a vague motion, "epicenter, I guess you could say. But long before we get there, we have other parts of the Dark to cross. The Plains are normally narrow and, as far as I can tell, dead. It's empty space. Just low, rolling hills. I've never encountered anything in them, except..." I hesitated.

Farryn knitted his brows. "Except what?"

"Just - just be on your guard. I've caught glimpses of things in the distance on previous occasions. Large creatures, things I can't explain. They've never been close enough to see properly and I've never run into one up close. But things change. Nothing is ever the same." I frowned slightly, glancing down the path. Not far down the way, it took a sharp turn and cut off our view. "Like that, for instance. The last time I was here, that path was a straight shot through these cliffs."

"Anything else I should know about?"

"Try not to bring out your blades. Weapons aren't much use down here."

"And I'm supposed to defend myself how?" Farryn asked.

I shrugged. "With any luck, you won't need to. And unless we meet something truly physical, like one of the Masters, your weapons won't serve you much good anyway. Try not to provoke anything. We're already strangers to this place and the creatures here will know that and be drawn to it."

"Anything else?"

I shook my head. "I'll tell you more as we go, depending on what we run into. Let's go. Let me take the lead."

Farryn nodded and extended his hand in a sweeping gesture towards the path, beckoning me onward. The gesture severely annoyed me, but I tried not to show it as I set off into the cliffs.

The Cathedral of the Dark

It seemed like we'd been walking forever along this twisting and turning path through the cliff faces. I couldn't remember this way ever having been such a trek. It had been several hours as far as I could tell and there didn't seem to be any end in sight. Just when the path would straighten out and my hopes would begin to rise, we'd once more take a turn and the long haul would continue. As there was no indication of day or night in this place, we could only really guess at how far or long we'd actually traveled.

Just as I was beginning to wonder if we shouldn't take a break for a while, the next turn finally brought a change in the long stretch of blank rock walls, though it wasn't the one I'd been waiting for or expecting. The path dead-ended into another cliff, its flat face only broken by a single arched entrance. Two carved panels traced their way into existence on either side of the arch as we approached, followed by a resounding crack as pillars topped with a beam and ornately carved pediment snapped out of the rock. Though difficult to see, we craned our necks to make out the oddly carved figures on the rock above us.

I'd seen this place only once, a long, long time ago. And there hadn't seemed to be any harm to it. In fact, the place had been a bit awe-inspiring. I nodded my head towards the opening.

"Shall we?" I could tell that Farryn's curiosity had been peaked and it wasn't like we had much of a choice. And after the long walk, which had been in almost complete, stony silence, we could do with something different. I only hoped that there was another tunnel inside that would lead us out. Last I'd been, this path had been both entrance and exit.

Grinding to a halt at the end of the passageway, Farryn's mouth dropped open slightly as he gazed at the view before him. "What is this place?"

His hushed voice, tinged with wonder as he stared in awe, echoed across the massive chamber. He slowly moved out of the arched entrance and down the short flight of shallow, stone steps.

Polished with age, their centers curved inward and worn from the footsteps of some ancient and long forgotten civilization, the three radiating steps deposited us within the cavern. The room was muted hues of grey and blue, interspersed with dancing hints of reds and oranges from the flickering torches positioned around the outer wall. I glanced around, wondering, as before, who kept the torches lit. The sound of our boots echoed dully on the floor stones.

Radiating from the curve of the stairs, the fitted stones arced outward towards a central pool, sunken into the floor and ringed with ornate stonework. A small fountain still bubbled quietly within, sending ripples to the outer edges. High above our heads, arches, carved into the living stone walls, met somewhere in the darkness. Intricately carved pillars encircled the hall, rising up to join them. At the far end of the chamber, just visible from where we stood, was a large shrine. Depressions held the ruined, carved remains of ancient, forgotten gods, not dissimilar from the carvings we had seen on the way into the Depths.

Making random sketches of the architecture, I joined Farryn at the pool. I gazed down at my wavering reflection. Several lotus flowers floated on the rippling water. Pink blossoms lined the edges of the pool. Touches of brilliant color in this odd, stark place, lending an air of illusory peacefulness. Frowning slightly, I looked up, trying to discern where the blossoms had come from. High above our heads, the branches of an ancient, twisted tree could be seen breaking through both the rock and the darkness, its dense boughs hanging above the pool. Strange. That hadn't been there before.

"I just call it the Cathedral," I finally whispered. "I've only seen it once before. It's changed slightly since I was last here. Like everything in the Depths."

Farryn pulled his cloak tighter about himself, shivering slightly as he moved off, exploring the room. I understood his apprehension. A heaviness pervaded the air that seemed as timeworn as the stonework. There was something about this place that seemed to set it apart from the rest of the Wild Dark. It hinted at something older than the ghosts that inhabited this ruined world. How long had this been here, who had used it? And what had happened to them and their world to turn it into the twisted wasteland it was now?

Glowing white eyes began to flicker into existence around the outskirts of the chamber, watching us as I joined Farryn and we wended our way towards the shrine. Farryn had yet to notice our watchers, so intent on investigating the architecture…and I kept quiet and let him look, following close behind. This place, as far as I could remember, was no threat to us. At least as long as we remained no threat to it.

As he neared the pedestal, Farryn finally caught sight of the eyes. Faster than I could blink, a blade was in his hand, knuckles turning white on the grip. I quickly put out my hand, grabbing his arm and forcing him to lower the weapon. The eyes ahead of us began a slow creep to red.

"Put it away," I said in an urgent whisper.

"Are you *insane*?" He looked at me in disbelief, his whole body tense, voice an octave higher than usual.

"You can't hurt them. Put it away. *Now.*" I began to back away.

Closing his eyes and tilting his head skyward, as if praying to the old gods we stood before, Farryn released his sword, letting it dissolve back into thin air. The eyes wavered slightly, the red receding back to white.

I breathed a sigh of relief, trying to calm my shaking hands and frayed nerves. I had no idea what these creatures were entirely capable of and I had no intention of ever finding out. I'd had the same experience the first time I'd been here. It had scared the hell out of me then as well. Most creatures of the Dark attacked your mind. I didn't really want to think about what they could do physically if provoked.

I hadn't even noticed that Farryn had begun to, rather quickly, move back towards the exit, intent on leaving by exactly the same route that we'd come. With one last glance at the myriad of watching eyes, I jogged after him.

We emerged from the rocky passage into a completely different location in the canyon, a new path heading away, straight as a shot. I breathed a sigh of relief even as Farryn rounded on me in a fury. Before he could open his mouth, I raised my hands in a placating gesture.

"Look, before you fly off the handle, I'm sorry. I probably should have told you when I first saw them arrive. I guess I was maybe getting back at you a little bit for earlier. They aren't dangerous, as far as I know. But I'm still sorry."

Farryn glared at me for several moments before he started to unexpectedly laugh. I stared at him in stunned silence.

"I guess I deserved that," he finally said, wiping tears from his eyes. "Up until I had the living daylights scared out of me, that place was actually pretty interesting. So let's just keep going, yeah? See if we can get out of this place."

The Void Plains

The path out of the canyon ended abruptly, the sheer cliffs suddenly giving way to an open expanse of low rolling hills, stretching away to the far horizon. A few gnarled and stunted trees dotted the landscape. The grass, a uniform foot high, had an odd, shimmering blueish-black tinge. It moved slightly in a mysterious breeze that neither of us could feel. I watched uneasily as a large creature, looking like shadow itself, stood and stretched, out and away on one of the hills.

"I thought you said this place wasn't very big."

I jumped at Farryn's voice. Even though it was barely a whisper, it had sounded like thunder splitting the unnatural, dead silence of the Void Plains. As the sound of his voice died out, he moved slightly closer to me, looking unnerved. "It looks like it goes on forever," he said meekly.

"It's an illusion," I said as quietly as I could manage. "It's not as big as it seems. Well, normally."

"There's a normal down here?"

I grinned slightly, though there was really nothing amusing about it, and waved for him to follow as I stepped out.

We'd been trekking across the Plains for nearly an hour in the perpetual silence when the whispering began, soft and insistent and all around us. I halted, reaching out to grab Farryn's arm and bringing him up short beside me. He looked around nervously.

"What's going on?"

I shook my head. "I don't know." I whipped around as the sound of rustling grass caught my attention, but the Plains seemed as dead as ever. I could feel a sense of dread forming as I scanned the fields. The grass had stopped moving, now static and just as lifeless as the rest of the area. But there, back the way we had come, a wall of darkness had formed, moving  towards us, picking up speed as I watched. As the advancing storm-wall bore down, the grass blackened and rotted, the trees crumbling to dust. Red-eyed creatures flickered in and out of existence, leaping and cavorting along the front's edge. I took a step back, my breath catching in my throat, panic rising. The whispering had risen to a sickening shriek.

Continuing to back away, my feet moving when my brain had frozen, I finally turned and fled.

"Run!"

"Are you crazy?" Farryn screeched, tearing after me. "You've got wings, idiot!"

I could feel him grabbing at the Source even before his wings were out and knew instinctively that something was wrong. The air around him burst into shimmering shards as he launched himself skyward.

"Farryn, NO!"

With a massive surge, I caught him six feet into the air, heavily bringing him back to the earth. We slammed into the ground, rolling several feet before I managed to regain my feet and pull him upright, dragging him along as I broke back into a run. Rivulets of blood ran down his exposed skin. The shimmering in the air, like shards of glass, had vanished, but his skin was crisscrossed with shallow cuts where he'd come into contact with it.

Breath ragged, limbs burning, we pounded across the Plains, the storm hard on our heels, the shrill whoops and screams of the shadow creatures all around us. Panic drove me harder and faster, lending speed I wouldn't have thought I had. My thoughts were focused on one thing and one thing only: reach the bridge. I desperately scanned the land ahead of us. Where was it?!

A wind was beginning to rise, whipping at our cloaks and packs.

The ground had begun to tremble beneath our feet, spikes of rocks jutting up through the surface as though the land itself were trying to stop us, forcing us to dodge obstacles now in our mad flight. As I made the mistake of looking back over my shoulder, I felt my foot catch on one of the protrusions, newly  sprung up in my path. Unable to stop myself, I went down with a muffled shout. Farryn, too close behind, slammed into my body, our momentum carrying us forward in a rolling, tangled heap. We slammed up against a boulder, bruised, gasping for air. With a whimper, I squeezed my eyes shut. The storm would be on us in seconds.

Farryn's fingers dug into my shoulder and I opened my eyes. Silence. The Void Plains stretched out behind us, grass waving lightly in the nonexistent breeze, as though nothing had happened. Painfully sitting up, I turned around and heaved a sob of relief. We were perched on the edge of a massive chasm, a gaping abyss. And there was the bridge, spanning its awesome width, connecting the Plains to the City beyond, its ruins just visible across the span.

Standing small in the bridge portal, between the two monolithic stone pillars rising up either side, Farryn gazed out across the expanse. Ornate tracery covered the entranceway. Pennants with faded gold rippled slightly in a light breeze. By all rights, the bridge shouldn't have been able to exist. Nothing supported the weight of the massive causeway as it stretched the abyssal chasm. Several feet ahead, I leaned against the parapet, looking down into the seemingly bottomless depths.

"Please tell me that we can fly across this thing."

I looked up as Farryn approached and shook my head. "We walk."

"You can barely see the other side! This thing has got to be miles across."

I started walking and he fell into step beside me. "It is. And it takes a while. But there's no flying across it. The Source doesn't work on this bridge. I'm not entirely sure the Dark would either."

I was exhausted after the ordeal on the Void Plains and didn't want to argue. Thankfully, he didn't push the issue and we continued to pad along in silence.

After nearly an hour, the end was finally drawing near and we could see the ruined city stretching away in both directions. Farryn's footsteps slowed as he studied it, his face registering both awe and disquiet. The facade looked as though it had been abandoned since the beginning of time. Many of the closely packed buildings soared to astounding heights: twenty, thirty, forty stories. Complex and elegant sculptures and carvings covered the sides, accentuating shattered windows, curving around crumbling pillars. Hints of color, muted with age, shone through the misty darkness and the black tendrils of shadow that curled across every surface. A grid-like system of streets crisscrossed the metropolis, lined with skillfully wrought lampposts that were never lit. It could have been the city of some great civilization. Maybe it had been.

But it was the ruin itself that, more than anything, told you how very wrong this place was. Some structures were missing entire floors, as through the building had shattered in the middle and the top portion, caught in a bubble of suspended time, had forgotten to collapse. Shards of glass and rubble hung in the air, slowly twisting and tumbling to nowhere. Dust clouds hung frozen. One skyscraper leaned far beyond the tipping point, stuck forever in a collapse that would never occur. Every so often, as though time had suddenly caught up in a localized zone, masonry would crack or fall, only to be arrested mid-air.

As we stepped off the bridge, I put out an arm and brought Farryn to a halt.

"Before we go in, there are some things you need to know."

The Ruined City

Our trek through the City had proven surprisingly uneventful thus far and I was starting to get uneasy. I'd glimpsed the occasional shadowy figure staring down from a window, but so far we'd been left alone. Looking around, I shook my head slightly. It was only a matter of time.

It came as no surprise when Farryn ground to a halt, eyes bulging in fear. I pulled up short, waiting, wondering what he was seeing and if I'd have to do something. The darkness around us was filled with pale, wispy figures, glowing eyes watching intently. They'd appeared out of nowhere, silently creeping up as we'd moved through this section of the city. The darkness beyond their immediate location was almost absolute; the writhing, shifting mist just visible on its edges. I closed my eyes, taking a deep breath to steady myself as I realized what was going on. We'd been trudging through this part of the ruins for nearly forty minutes now, a shockingly long time for someone to go without seeing the visions. I had tried to explain this sort of thing before we'd come in, but knowing it and actually experiencing it were two different things.

A soft whimper escaped Farryn's lips as he backed up a step, one hand rising to grasp the fabric of his shirt collar. The misty creatures had moved in closer, as if drawn to his fear. He took a step backward, head jerking from side to side, eyes darting across the ground at something only he could see. His breathing was starting to become erratic. I heaved a sigh and quickly moved towards him. Grasping his face, I jerked his head forward, forcing him to make eye contact.

"Look at me," I whispered fiercely. With real effort, Farryn ripped his gaze away from whatever he was staring at. His eyes were open wide, pupils dilated. "It's not real. Whatever you're seeing, it isn't real."

Farryn tried to jerk his head away, eyes straying, but I kept a death grip on his face, trying to keep him focused.

"Why are they here..." he whimpered. "They're dead. All of them."

He stared hard at me, on the verge of tears. What could possibly unhinge Farryn? I'd never really known what sort of missions the soldier before me had been sent on, but if they'd been even a fraction of what some of mine had been, I could only imagine what was being dragged from his mind.

"I killed them all," he whispered, bringing my attention back to the present.

"Who did you kill?" I asked. "What are you seeing?"

Farryn shook his head, breaking my grip as I relaxed my hand.

"They were just children. There's blood everywhere. The ground is covered with it. But it was so long ago." His voice quavered. "Why are they here, in this place?" He shivered, sinking to his knees, arms wrapped protectively around himself, eyes squeezed tightly shut.

Children. I'd been sent on a mission like that once. An Ashtaran settlement. It was one of the few missions I'd outright lied about following through. Killing an entire village of innocents. A sharp pain flashed through my head as a sudden memory came flooding back, something I'd lost and would have preferred it stay that way. I squeezed my eyes shut briefly, pushing it away. This wasn't the time.

I dropped into a crouch beside Farryn. The eyes in the darkness continued to watch us. There was a cold amusement in their light and a soft hissing sound emanated from their featureless heads, like an echo of laughter caught in some long forgotten place.

"Listen to me, Farryn," I said, putting my hands either side of his face again, trying to force him to focus on me, "what you're seeing, it's just an afterimage, a memory. That's what this place does. I've been seeing -" I paused, not wanting to describe the horrors from my own past, "Look, I've been here before, I know what it does to you. You have to be strong. The Depths try to ruin you, to destroy you from the inside out. It gets into your mind, drives you to insanity. You can't let it. This won't be the last nightmare you see while we're down here. Frankly, I'm surprised it's the first, but that's why they chose you to come with me. Your mind is strong. Anyone else wouldn't have made it this far. Things aren't going to get any easier. This place shifts and changes and those creatures come and go. Sometimes they choose to prey on your past, sometimes your fears, your weaknesses. Other times they're just there, watching. But whatever we encounter, we need to keep going. We need to figure out what's happening." I rose to my feet, dragging him with me. He stumbled as he came up, leaning on me for support for a moment before pulling away. I could see his eyes clearing.

"Thanks, Enpirion."

I glanced sideways at him as we started to move forward again. "It's nothing, don't worry about it."

"No, but I mean, well. Thanks for before too. And, well, I guess, I'm...sorry. I-I should have said it sooner."

The tone of his voice made me once again come to a halt. "What are you talking about? The Plains?" I asked, genuinely puzzled.

Farryn looked uncomfortable. More uncomfortable than the Depths were making him, which I didn't think was possible. "No, I mean back at The Watch. During the attack. If it hadn't been for you, that bolt would have hit me. I know you threw up that barrier." He looked away, running his fingers through his short hair. "And I guess I'm sorry for all the shit I put you through, back in the old ENF. All the stuff I said. You're, well...you're not what I thought you were."

I simply stared in stunned silence, not knowing what to say, how to respond. No one had ever apologized for how they'd treated me and Farryn was the last person I would have ever expected it from. I could feel heat starting to rise in my cheeks.

"It's - it's fine," I muttered, caught completely off-guard and unsure how to react. I shuffled slowly from foot to foot, watching Farryn even as he watched me. I didn't know what to do other than just keep moving. "Come on. Let's keep going." Farryn nodded and followed, looking at least slightly relieved at my response or, really, lack thereof.

Finding a sheltered area to hide, which was surprisingly difficult, we dropped, exhausted, to the ground. If I could have found a way to forego sleep in this place, I would have. We'd been exceptionally lucky so far. The strange zones of the city were unpredictable. Sometimes you could move through and encounter very little, other times you were plagued by the shadowy denizens and their hallucinations. But even at the best of times, I'd encountered more than what we were experiencing. I was actually beginning to feel like it might have been less luck-related and more akin to something keeping everything at bay. A shiver went up my spine at the thought. Regardless, the atmosphere of the City, the emptiness and desolation, was oppressive and took its mental toll, instilling a deep-seated fear that lingered on the edge of your mind.

Curled up in a corner, tight as a spring, Farryn had already slipped into a troubled sleep. Fighting to stay awake, I took the first watch.

Interludes: Events at Home

Neph sat slumped in the plush chair, staring moodily into the shifting bluish Source flames of the fireplace, a mug of coffee cupped between his hands, slowly going cold. It had been over three weeks since Piri and Farryn had left for the Depths and almost as long since the majority of the population of The Watch had returned to life. He would have liked to have called it 'normal life', but it was far from. The entirety of the complex seemed to be operating on a heightened sense of fear. The damage to The Watch had been quickly repaired; the Seri's master craftsmen had worked round the clock, but the mental damage was far harder to overcome. The two hundred and sixty dead had been cremated following a somber ceremony in their honor. Seri from a multitude of cities had flown in, as well as all members of both the Small and Ruling Councils, as they had for the other cities.

Within days of the Ruling Council handing down the decision, Seri cities around the continent had upped their security measures to levels not seen since the start of the Ashtaran Uprising; both airborne and ground patrols were monitoring the cities day and night, the archery battalions were manning the walls and ballista ports. No one was permitted to leave

Seri-controlled territory. The standard army was back to daily training, honing their already advanced skills to the edge of perfection. The capital city of Skycrest, already surrounded by walls, had fortified practically overnight. Perhaps the most significant change though were the gated and heavily guarded primal Source springs whose caverns at the bases of the cities had been closed off for the first time in recorded history. It had been nearly one hundred and fifty years since the start of the Uprisings, which had ushered in an era of Seri military domination that had only just ended. And here they were gearing up for war all over again. But this time, rather than the aggressors, for the first time, they were the hunted and the fear was palpable.

Taking a sip of his coffee, Neph sighed and closed his eyes. The ENF, split into teams, were on extended airborne patrols, monitoring the vast landscapes between the cities, leaving Neph with quite a lot of free time on his hands. He should have been catching up on reports and paperwork, but he just couldn't seem to motivate himself to do it. The stress of outside life was really just background noise in comparison to what was actually bothering him. He'd spent most of his time sequestered here, in front of the fireplace, worrying, sick to his stomach over Piri. They'd had no idea how long the mission would take, but the longer they were down there, the more dangerous the situation would become. Other Seri before him had attempted the Depths and never returned. The only consolation he had was that Piri had been there and back before this, knew what to expect. He hoped, anyway; it was all he had to cling to. And on top of the fear and the worry was the overwhelming loneliness, the emptiness of the place. It was a physical ache in his chest.

A slight trembling caused him to open his eyes. Neph stared into the fire as the vibration increased, causing the room to shudder, before stopping as suddenly as it had started. The small earthquakes didn't even faze him anymore, they were becoming so frequent. They weren't the only strange thing to happen in the past month. There had been a marked upsurge of abnormal creatures wandering close to settled areas, creatures that generally weren't seen outside of Veil anomalies. He'd already heard reports of several encounters from other cities that had ended in injury or death. The Seri couldn't even identify half of what was wandering around out there anymore, as if some crazy farmer had taken it upon himself to start cross-breeding the already bizarre creatures that dotted those zones. And the odd noises, during all hours of the day, strange sounds from the earth that no one could pinpoint or identify. He glared into the coffee, staring it down as if it were to blame for everything that was happening.

A second tremor shook the room, stronger than the one before it, knocking a book off the shelf. Neph leaned his head back and sighed.

Piri, where are you?

The Dark Maelstrom

"Enpirion."

Farryn slowed his steps, pulling his cloak tighter around himself. Several steps ahead, I stopped and turned, looking back questioningly.

"You've...you've been here before," he whispered, coming even with me. "Is it always like this?"

The two of us stood silently for several minutes, staring around into the shifting blackish-purple fog, crumbling stone structures rising from the mist to tower overhead.

"Yes," I finally answered. "It was a long time ago."

I pushed back my hood and gazed upwards, eyes narrowing. "But things are different. They always are. The various zones are the same, but they move around, come and go. These ruins, the landscape...it's all changed from the last time I saw it. And it was different the time before that. The ruined city always seems to exist, and the crumbling mountains in the distance, though both always seem different, in a state of flux. But this time there *is* something new," I pointed upwards, "and we seem to have a guide towards our destination."

Farryn looked up, following my outstretched arm. He'd been blindly stumbling after me, hood pulled low. I don't think it had occurred to him to question where I was heading or how I knew where to go. After countless days in the city's perpetual twilight, the oppressive atmosphere had him completely on edge, his senses dull and foggy. I could see it in his eyes, his movements. I knew that permanent edge of panic that he was fighting to keep at bay, a creeping sensation that seemed to seep into every bone, every muscle, honing every nerve to a razor's edge. Now, his eyes shifting upwards, he gasped as he realized what I had been following.

225

Luminescent blue energy writhed above our heads, hundreds or maybe thousands of feet high, it was impossible to tell in this strange environment. It was like a multi-faceted river coursing through the Depths, but it jerked and twisted, like a beast in agony, trying to escape. It flowed from all directions, all hurtling towards some distant destination.

"Wha-what the hell is that?" he yelped. "It looks like the Source."

I clamped a hand over his mouth, fingers digging roughly into the skin. "Would you be quiet," I hissed, my face inches from Farryn's, eyes darting wildly back and forth. "You're going to draw attention and that is one thing we do *not* want. Those creatures from before? Those are just, I dunno, ghosts, I guess you could say. They're not the masters of this place, not what we need to be concerned about."

Farryn pulled back, looking guilty. "I - sorry," he whispered apologetically. "This place. I just -"

"Forget it," I said. "I know. Let's keep moving. That Source energy is going somewhere. We need to find it."

How long had we been trudging through the city, past crumbling towers frozen in time? Days, weeks? There was no way to tell. When we could go no farther, we would hole up in a ruin and sleep. Upon waking, we would continue moving forward, always following the Source above our heads as it flowed onward. At times I considered throwing caution to the wind and taking to the air, but I knew it would end in disaster. Two creatures using the Source in the Depths…we would stand out like blazing torches in the darkness.

We had been plodding along for hours, down a wide thoroughfare, step after step along the cracked flagstones. It took me several moments to realize that something in our surroundings had changed. The towering, crumbling buildings to either side seemed to be thinning. I blinked, looking around. They weren't just thinning out, they were literally vanishing. I could actually see through some of the walls, like staring at a wavering reflection. The solid structures were slowly dematerializing, looking more like the ghostly creatures that inhabited the city, that even now stared down at us through the broken windows. And a sound was starting to become audible, just on the edge of my hearing. I'd thought my nerves were just jangling from being in the Depths, but the more I focused on the sound, I now realized that it was actually the cause of my heightened nervousness. It was a low thrum, wavering in volume and tempo, electric crackling periodically cutting through. The frequency was enough to set your teeth on edge and it was growing increasingly louder. There was only one thing it could be, a phenomenon I had rarely encountered down here and never in the City. It had to be one of the great, writhing whirlpools of the Dark. But this sound was far beyond anything I had heard before. Whatever we were coming up on sounded exponentially larger than anything I'd ever stumbled upon.

And suddenly, the crumbling metropolis came to an abrupt end. My mouth dropped open in shock as I ground to a stand-still and took in the scene before me. The dark maelstrom was like nothing I had ever seen. It stretched to the horizon, spiraling at a breakneck speed, but unevenly, jerking uncontrollably, halting altogether for brief moments; the unnatural movement was stomach-turning. Electricity crackled across its spirals, casting a pulsing, unnatural light across everything near the rim. Its gaping maw wound down into bottomless darkness. The thrum of its movement vibrated through the ground, producing a high keening noise that was setting my already-frayed nerves even further on edge.

Neither of us moved, both terrified to take another step, unsure where stability ended and the swirling vortex began.

"Do, uh, do our wings work down here?" Farryn asked nervously, eyeing the outer rim.

I glanced sideways at him, eyes going wide. "Are you planning on flying out over that thing? Because I am *not* going out there."

Glowing runes, burning with a cold fire, surrounded its edges. The energy racing across the sky of the Depths coalesced in what I could only assume was the center, forming a crackling cascade as it streaked downward, merging into the whirlpool somewhere out of sight. Vaguely registering a tug on my sleeve, I tore my eyes away. Farryn silently pointed off to our right, at a figure just past the city's border, hunched over in a concentration of the burning script. We warily moved towards it, carefully slinking along the edge of the ruins. The closer we came, the stranger the figure appeared; crumpled over, limbs at odd angles. Wings spread.

"Gods," Farryn whispered, looking sick, staring at the broken and bent feathers, "it's Seri. But..." He shook himself. "We need to see that up close. I'm going to get a look." He sounded a whole lot braver than he could ever possibly be feeling at that moment.

Throwing caution to the wind, knowing we needed to see what was going on, we sprinted across the short stretch. I halted several feet away and began pacing the outside of the circle, a sudden weight settling in the pit of my stomach, coldness beginning to spread through my body. Coming around to the front of the setup, I froze.

Farryn halted just at the edge of the runic circle, careful not to step on it. Grabbing pencil and paper from his pack, he quickly scribbled down a handful of the symbols before turning to the figure. It sat in the center, horribly mounted on a wood frame, butchered, mutilated, its head lolling to the side. As Farryn slowly crept forward, the head suddenly jerked back, eyes rolling, coming to rest on him. The abomination before us was still alive, if anyone could call it that. Farryn put a hand to his mouth, looking ill. He turned and quickly walked to where I stood, still frozen in place, eyes riveted on the scene before us. He grabbed me by the arm, forcefully dragging me back into the shelter of the city's remains before falling to his knees and throwing up. I simply stared back in the direction of the maelstrom in mute horror. Looking farther along the vortex, I could see a myriad of figures, all seemingly Seri and Ellundara, spreading out to the horizon, all within the more concentrated ritualistic circles.

"We have to kill them. We can't just leave them like that," Farryn finally managed to gasp out, dragging the back of his hand across his mouth. His words finally slammed me back to reality. My eyes snapped to Farryn, alarm written across my features as I emphatically shook my head.

"Have you completely lost your mind," I said fearfully. "Whatever is going on out there is way beyond us. And I'm not entirely sure they're still technically alive. I am, however, very sure that if we attempt to interfere, we'll never make it out of here." I swallowed hard, my eyes flickering back towards the whirlpool again. "I don't particularly relish the idea of joining that collection."

"But-"

"Farryn, no! Even if we could do something about a handful of them, that thing is huge. You can't even see the other side. It's a death trap. We need to go. *Now*. This is bad. Really bad." I took a step backward, shaking violently. Farryn nodded mutely in agreement; something in the way I'd said it must have finally thrown up a red flag. Without a word, he reached out, putting a steady hand on my arm, concerned. I flinched but didn't move.

"What's wrong, you look -"

"I don't know. Being that close -" I said, cutting him off, backing away into the ruins, away from the vortex. "It's taking Source energy. I could feel it pulling -" I shuddered. "Those bodies. The marks. They're so familiar, too familiar. I don't know why...," I

229

shook my head violently. "It's old, Farryn. That ritual. I can feel it. Taking the energy -" My voice trailed off and I took a deep breath. "We need to get away from here." I grabbed at a crumbling stone wall, seeking support, feeling as though I was about to pass out.

Grabbing me around the waist, Farryn pushed me forward, moving back the way we'd come. I could only hope beyond hope that we would go undetected.

We struggled back through the ruined city, which seemed to be warping and shifting before our eyes, doing its best to render us hopelessly lost. If it hadn't been for the energy coursing its way across the cavernous roof, there would have been no way to tell which direction we were heading. Black, formless shadows, eyes glowing white, trailed behind us, seeming to swell in number with each turn we made. Farryn still had an arm tightly around me, moving us forward, though, at this point, I think it was more for his peace of mind than as a support aid. The creatures were beginning to surround us, crowding every window and doorway, the broken sidewalks, crumbling streets. Not for the first time, I began to wonder what this wreck of a city and its ghostly inhabitants really were, what they might once have been.

Farryn saw the Master before I did. His reaction was stronger than any words he could have uttered in warning, like an animal that had suddenly become aware that it was being hunted. I could see the whites of his eyes, pupils dilated in fear. He dropped to the ground, clutching his head, a slight whimper escaping his lips. I understood the reaction. I'd had it before. But staying out in the open wasn't an option and, pushing aside my own physical discomfort and weakness, I grabbed him, forcefully dragging his stiffened form into the protective cover of a ruined wall. It wasn't much, but it was better

than nothing.

I could feel the panic trying to cloud my mind, but I closed my eyes, breathing deeply, forcing it back. I'd done this before and I could do it again. I had more practice than most with keeping the darkness at bay.

I was feeling stronger than back at the whirlpool, my energy returning the farther from it that we got, but this situation was something I would have preferred to have avoided. My fingers curled around the shattered and crumbling rock and I slowly poked my head out, just enough to see the creature moving through the inky mist, scattering the dark inhabitants before it.

A massive hulking form, the smooth horns projecting out from the sides of the head. The color of the thing was as vexing as ever to the senses. One uniform texture, a glossy black, but if you looked closer, it writhed like disturbed fog, shifting and moving about under the surface. The eyes, blazing white slits in the otherwise featureless face, stared into the darkness.

I knew this monster. Its name was Merythalis.

I was sure it knew we were there. I ducked back behind the wall, my breath coming faster than I would have liked. Farryn pressed against the stone, head between his knees, fingernails pressed into his scalp so hard that a small trickle of blood was beginning to run down his face. I knew the creature was inside his head. Bad memories from what seemed like another life, ages ago, began to drift back through my own mind, of missions to the Depths, of encountering this monstrosity, others like it. I would have taken any of the other masters of the Dark over this one though. There was something particularly malignant about Merythalis, a malicious cruelness that seemed to exceed its evil brethren.

I reached out and gently put my hand on Farryn's shoulder, hoping that I wasn't shaking as much as I thought I was, trying to stay calm and in control for the both of us as I wracked my brain for some way out. He didn't even look up or make any acknowledgment that I existed.

Sibilant laughter began to seep into the mist, surrounding us, growing in intensity. I crouched down against the wall next to Farryn, hugging my knees to my chest, one arm around his shoulders. Merythalis definitely knew we were here. And it probably remembered me. Creatures that old had long memories.

Flight

I could feel a push on my mind, like tendrils trying to find purchase, creeping around the edges of conscious thought. I closed my eyes, pushed myself behind my walls. The laughter gained in intensity and I felt the Dark recede from my mind even as Farryn stiffened and gave another whimper of fear.

"Visitors to my realm," it hissed. The voice filled the mist, echoing off the buildings, surrounding us. "Delightful. And one of you has been here before, several times if I am not incorrect. If you think I have forgotten you, Little Seri, you are sorely mistaken."

I could hear its form softly slithering over broken cobbles. I grabbed Farryn's head with both hands, jerking his face level with my own and shook him until the fog cleared from his eyes.

"Listen to me," I whispered urgently, fighting down my rising panic as the sound drew closer. "We have to run. We don't stand a chance against this thing, not here on its home turf. If we get separated, follow the Source back the way we came, but…" I looked around fearfully, knowing that if I lost him, he'd never get out. "Do me a favor, don't get separated."

He nodded, mutely stumbling to his feet as several massive, clawed fingers curled around the stonework above us. My breath caught in my throat. Grabbing his arm, I peeled away, dodging fallen arches and pillars as I streaked up the avenue, dragging Farryn along behind me. I chanced a glance back. Merythalis was gone. Not good. Only instinct saved us as I forcefully threw Farryn through the closest doorway, his figure vanishing into the interior darkness as I dived in after him. With a resounding crash, the creature lunged from the murk, claws raking the building as stone cracked and crumbled, the doorway crashing down behind us. Part of the building, in its flux state of ruin, collapsed, dust and rubble freezing in midair on the way down as the environment shifted around us. Farryn no longer needed any urging. He tore up the stairs before us, round and round as we looped upwards towards the roof with Merythalis close on our heels, a trail of destruction behind us.

My breath was coming in ragged gasps as we finally reached the top of the building, Farryn slamming bodily into the rooftop door. The ancient barrier gave way, wood splintering and shattering as we burst through, never slowing. Racing to the edge of the roof, we both launched ourselves out into space, wings snapping out. There wasn't space to gain height. Half flying, half gliding, I grabbed a window ledge, felt my foot slip on smooth marble, launched myself towards another building, pushed off, leaping up and out, moving from one tall building to the next, trying to gain height. I could see Farryn desperately doing the same as Merythalis watched from the rooftop, glowing eyes following our movements. The blank face suddenly split into a leering grin, rows of razor-sharp teeth filling the gaping maw. The creature faded into the darkness, like mist, vanishing.

I clamped on to the remains of some ancient decorative carving, hanging several hundred feet above the ground. The facade before me exploded. I heard Farryn cry out as I fell backwards. Time seemed to stop as I stared into the narrowed, gleaming eyes of Merythalis, larger than life, leaning out, teeth bared, clawed fingers reaching for me. Panic flared, pushing adrenaline and Source energy through my system like a drug. I twisted, pumped my wings as hard as I could, plunged backwards at a speed only an overSourcer could manage. The claws grazed my leg as I shot out of reach, raking through fabric and skin. I ignored the pain, spiraling away, wings pulled tight before springing wide, long feathers flaring on one side to bring me around in a fast, hard curve. I came in fast above Farryn and the two of us streaked off across the city, straining on the Source, our wings streaked with the code of the energy.

"Gods, your leg."

I pulled my leg back before Farryn's reaching hand made contact. "It's nothing, it looks worse than it is. It's shallow." Blood had soaked my shredded pant leg and it was probably slightly worse than I was making out, but I didn't want him, of all people, fussing over it. It would heal quickly enough and the bleeding had nearly stopped.

We were crouched in a broken structure on one of the city's rooftops, exhausted after a good hour of strained flight, covered in scratches and grit. We'd struggled to put as much distance as possible between Merythalis and ourselves. I didn't know how successful we'd been, but we couldn't go any further without a break. The crackling energy of the Source still streamed above us, the only physical indication that we were heading in the right direction. I could feel the change in energy, barely, as we came closer to exiting the city, but I was having trouble focusing. All I wanted to do was stay curled up in the corner of this ruin, hidden in the darkness, and rest. I brushed a thumb across my cheek, trying to clean off some of the sticky dust. Rooting through my pack, searching for my canteen, a loose bit of paper sticking out of one of my sketchpads caught my finger. Curiously, I pulled it out, wondering which page had come loose. An aching pain gripped my chest, breath catching, as I stared down at Neph, the lifelike sketch gazing back up at me. It was a drawing I'd done ages back and hadn't even remembered as being in this pad. A lump formed in my throat as I sat frozen with the picture. I finally leaned my head back and closed my eyes. I would have given anything to be out of this place. To be back home.

"You ok?" Farryn asked from the broken entrance to our shelter, where he'd sat like a coiled spring since we'd landed.

"I'm fine."

A brief pause as he

scrutinized me, glanced down at the drawing clenched between my shaking fingers. And then, "You miss him. You actually love him, don't you?" There was an undercurrent of incredulity to his voice, like he somehow believed me incapable of caring for another person. Though, truth be told, I never would have thought it possible either.

I cast him a withering glance, didn't bother to respond. He was the last person I wanted to discuss that with. I'd spent the entire journey down here trying not to think about Neph, trying to ignore the ache in my chest every time I did. I had never dreamt that there'd come a time when I would be craving physical touch and comfort from another person. Never thought I would miss someone else's company and presence. Being away from him in this horrible place had only driven home how much I actually cared for him, missed him. I hated the Depths, but I'd never wanted out of them so badly as I did now. Never had a reason for wanting out of them as much as I did.

I turned my thoughts elsewhere, to more immediate concerns, trying to distract myself. Pulling out a pencil, I quickly set to roughing out some of what we had seen since coming to the Depths, starting with more generalized ideas for warm up; the entrance wall, the plains, the city. After a handful of quick sketches, I moved on to more specific creatures and events. I put aside a drawing of the maelstrom and began a more detailed piece of the mutilated figures we had witnessed. This had become a ritual for me, a way to calm myself when we stopped. None of the pieces in my stack were refined, something I would do later once we managed to get out of this place, but I had to get things down before my memory betrayed me.

As my pencil scratched across the paper, inserting some finer details, I paused, arrested by the glowing runic symbols that had surrounded the sacrifice (if that's what it had been). A cold chill ran up my spine. Just as back at the actual site, the same feeling of familiarity began to needle at the edge of my mind, some memory that was missing. From before.

"Hey, Farryn," I said in a low voice, stretching out my hand with the drawing clamped tightly in my fingers. He winced as he looked back over his shoulder, eyes falling on the grisly details.

"Thanks for refreshing my memory on that," he said roughly. "Like I needed a reminder."

I shook the paper slightly. "It's not the image I care about right now. Those symbols, the ones that were around the base..."

When I didn't continue, he raised a questioning eyebrow. "What about them?" he finally asked. "I copied a bunch of them down. We've got a record."

"It's not that," I said with a shake of my head. "Did you, I don't know, recognize them? It's not the first time we've seen them. I know. But I mean, from before. Before all of this started? From way before all of this."

He stared for a moment, face oddly blank, then, "No." Another pause. "I don't know."

"And that means what, exactly?"

"It means that I don't know. They do seem oddly familiar, but I don't know why or where I ever would have seen them. I just have this weird feeling like I've seen something similar. A long time ago." He turned back to continue staring apprehensively into the city, leaving me to stare at the drawing.

The sound of falling masonry in the distance caused both of us to jump. Farryn leaned slightly out of the shelter, taking a quick glance around. One of the myriad ghostly figures drifted past causing him to jerk back inside. I rolled to my feet, trying to keep weight off my injured leg.

"We should probably keep moving," I said, shoving my drawings back in my bag. "We won't be safe until we leave the Depths. It can't follow us. I'm hoping it can't follow us beyond the City. I'm pretty sure that it's trapped here." I moved to stand beside him, gazing back towards where I knew the maelstrom churned in the distance. I was more than a little unnerved by how quiet things were. Merythalis was allowing us to leave, I was sure of it. I just couldn't figure out why.

"He -" Farryn began.

"*It.*"

"Fine. IT said it remembered you..."

"Yes."

"Care to elaborate?"

"Not really, no."

Farryn frowned. "Look, that thing was definitely making a beeline for you. If there's something I should know - "

"Exactly. It was after me, not you. Drop it." I could tell he wanted to press the issue. I wasn't interested. "Come on," I said, stepping out. "Let's at least try to make the Void Plains. I want out of here."

The bridge rose up in the distance, spanning the deep chasm and leading back to the Void Plains. Ruined banners, torn and tattered, fluttered from the cracked and crumbling archway, reflecting the devastation on this side. I could almost feel Farryn's confusion as he surveyed our passage out of the City. The bridge was one of those odd things here in the Depths. No matter where you exited the City, there it was, leading you back across to the Plains. There was no rhyme or reason to its inexplicable ability to exist wherever a traveler was. I'd never encountered a time when it wasn't there, spanning the unending chasm that separated the two lands.

Landing at the edge of the ruins, we cautiously looked about. The short, open distance to the bridge was clear, which made me

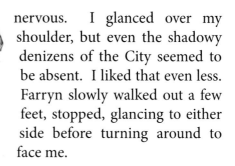

nervous. I glanced over my shoulder, but even the shadowy denizens of the City seemed to be absent. I liked that even less. Farryn slowly walked out a few feet, stopped, glancing to either side before turning around to face me.

"Well, this is unnerving. I don't see any alternative though, so let's get over that thing as fast as possible."

I nodded and moved out after him, the unsettled feeling in the pit of my stomach going nowhere. At the edge of the bridge, Farryn stopped again, craning his neck to look up at the arch.

"Remind me again why we can't just fly across this thing?" he said.

"We've already had this conversation," I said with some annoyance.

"I know. I guess I just -"

"Don't believe me, apparently. Go ahead, try it. Step onto the bridge and try it." I waved a languid hand towards the span ahead of us. "I'd say go step off the edge and try it, but, unlike the maelstrom, I'm very sure of how that one would turn out."

Farryn scowled as he stepped out onto the bridge.

"You don't have to be an ass about it. I was just asking."

Squaring his shoulders, he turned his back on me and started across the bridge. I ran a hand through my hair, vaguely registering how gritty it felt, and glared at the cracked pavers beneath my feet, as if they were somehow at fault.

With a sigh, I fell into step beside him. "Look, I'm sorry, alright? I'm just…on edge. This place is getting to me. And I don't know why we can't fly across, I really don't. There's something, I guess in the chasm, that disrupts the Source. This place is sort of like a barrier between the City and everything else. If you tried to summon your wings right now, anything for that matter, nothing would happen. I'm honestly surprised you didn't try when we crossed the first time," I said with a shrug.

"For what it's worth," he said, glancing at me, "I did believe you. When we first crossed. Which is why I didn't try. You're not the kind of person who says things for effect. Or makes things up. If anything, I've learned that you're almost too honest and blunt for your own good." Farryn frowned slightly and looked around as we neared the midpoint of the expanse. "Have you ever actually told a lie or intentionally wound someone up? I feel like you'd be so eaten up with guilt you'd eventually explode."

I didn't realize he was trying to lighten the mood until I noticed the slight smile curling the corner of his mouth. I relaxed slightly. Something about Farryn had changed. I didn't know if it was being in the Depths or something before, but I was having trouble reconciling the person here with me now to the one who had tormented me throughout my entire late childhood and most of my young adult life.

Behind us, breaking the stillness and silence, came the crack of masonry. We both stopped, whipping around to stare back at the ruins of the City. I sucked in a breath. Merythalis sat perched, larger than life, atop one the broken towers, its body curled around the building. Glowing white eyes silently watching us. It didn't move, made no sign of advancement. A chill shot through me and seemed to solidify my belief. It really was letting us leave. I reached out and grabbed Farryn's sleeve as I began to slowly back away, once again moving towards the far side and the Plains.

"Come on," I whispered.

Homecoming

Winging our way quickly over the open countryside, Farryn and I had been, unsurprisingly, spotted long before our arrival by varying soldiers on patrol. Neph, along with two members of the Small Council and several lesser officers, stood awaiting our return. We were both traveling at breakneck speed and it wasn't long before we were gliding over The Watch and touching down on the large green off to the side of the Grandview's main, tiered hall.

My feet had barely touched the ground before Neph, throwing decorum to the wind, had grabbed me in a bone-crushing embrace, nearly winding me. I closed my eyes, fingers digging into his back. I could hear Farryn being heartily greeted by the other officers. Pulling back, Neph put a hand under my chin, lifting my face, studying me. I knew my eyes looked sunken, my normally pale skin an unhealthy greyish pallor. Farryn shared the same haunted look; it wasn't uncommon after spending so much time in the Depths and would vanish with a few days of rest. I dropped my head back on to Neph's chest.

"Please tell me that debriefing can wait until tomorrow," I whispered.

Neph sighed and shook his head. "I wish it could," he said, "but the Council said that, on no uncertain terms, they wanted the details tonight. Things have been, how do I put it... unsettled since you've been gone. Patrols have been watching your return since yesterday and they're eager for news. The sooner we get started, the sooner you can both rest."

241

It wasn't long before we were standing before several members of the Small Council and a handful of silent, horror-struck officers in one of the smaller conference rooms. Shifting back and forth, we had carefully told the entire story, from entering the Upper Dark to our flight from the Depths, reporting the Depths in almost agonizing detail, reliving every horrific moment. Hours had passed with no interruptions, only the scratching of pens as two officers took detailed notes. Finally finishing our story, Farryn and I lapsed into silence, staring at each other with the same sunken expression. No one said a word.

Evari finally cleared her throat and stood. "We need to get this information to Skycrest. This is..." Her voiced faltered and she ran a trembling hand through her hair.

With a start, I suddenly stood up and dived for my pack. "Wait!" I rummaged through its contents, finally withdrawing my stack of slightly crumpled sketches. I shoved them in her direction, avoiding looking at them. Evari tentatively reached out to take them and began leafing through the pages. She sucked in a sharp breath as she did.

"These are -"

"Drawings," I finished for her, "of the Depths. What we saw. I wasn't able to refine most of them until we were back into the Upper Dark, but I did my best, with Farryn's help, to recall the details. He was able to record some of the symbols on the spot." I paused just for an instant, eyes clouding slightly as I gazed at the symbols on the page Evari was now intently studying. "I'm sorry we weren't able to get more."

Bayn had sidled up to stare over Evari's shoulder at the stack of nearly two hundred sketches. He was turning slightly green around the edges as she flipped her way through them. Her fingers paused on a sketch of the splayed figure, drawn in grisly detail.

"You've both done more than we could have ever asked for," Merrant said in a low voice, rising from his seat at the end of the table. "You have the Council's sincerest thanks, both for your mission and for your willingness to give us this time here today, especially when we know how exhausted you both must be." He looked at each of us in turn. "Please rest and take care of yourselves for the next few days. I will convey this information personally." And with that, the meeting was finally over. Everyone began to drift from the room, lost in their own thoughts.

Farryn was among the last to leave. As he walked out the door, he looked back. "Enpirion?"

I raised my head from where I'd lain it down on the table. "Mmm?"

"I'm - I'm glad that mission was with you. I meant what I said in the Depths. And," he paused, looking first at Neph, then back to me, "take care of yourself. You deserve it." He threw a quick salute to Neph before leaving the room.

A gentle hand came to rest on my shoulder and I looked up. "Come on," Neph said quietly. "Let's get some food, then go home."

I'd hardly eaten anything, only picking at some fruit, despite having barely had anything all day. All I really wanted to do was get back to Neph's quarters and relax. Just the two of us. My feet were dragging as we arrived at his door. I could feel the weight of everything that had happened pressing down, but I didn't really want to think about it. There would be time for that later. Being home had never felt so good, I marveled as we crossed the main room together. Home. It was a nice thought, knowing that I had a place where I actually belonged.

As we entered the bedroom, I collapsed into him, letting his arms support my weight, so relieved to, at long last, be off duty, to be home after the stress and exhaustion of the Depths. A month in that place had felt like years away. Years away from him. And it had made me realize exactly how desperately I had missed him; his touch, his idle conversation, the way he looked at me. I pressed myself in closer, burying my face in his shirt, sliding a hand up under the fabric even as his hands slid up under mine, brushing across my back, one finger tracing a path down the scar on my shoulder blade. I shivered slightly.

"Gods, I missed you," he whispered.

I felt his lips begin to caress my neck, gently, but with an underlying urgency I'd never felt and before I knew what I was doing, the feeling infectious, my fingers were fumbling to undo the top button of his pants. He paused, briefly, breathing heavily on my neck.

"Are you sure?" It was the briefest of whispers and I had to admire the kind of understanding and restraint he'd maintained to this point. I looked up, meeting his eyes, that clear crystalline blue, even in the semi-darkness, and nodded. I wanted to tell him exactly what I'd felt down in the Depths, what it had made me realize, but it wasn't necessary. His desperation for me was as strong as my own. His lips locked onto mine, pulling me in as he pulled off my shirt, undid my pants, his hands as gentle as always, moving slowly, carefully, in perfect rhythm with my actions and emotions. He'd been moving me backwards and I felt the bed bump the back of my legs, let myself be lowered down. I closed my eyes as his lips moved down my chest, simply letting myself fall into the sensation. I gasped slightly as his lips moved around me, took me in, one hand gliding up my thigh. After that, I lost myself in his touch, the feel of him against me, exploring my body as I explored his. And, for the first time in my life, I gave myself over completely.

I opened my eyes to late-morning sunlight. I was alone in bed. At some point, Neph had pulled a blanket over me. I felt…vulnerable lying there, having exposed myself on every level for the first time in my life. But, for once, I was also calm and untroubled, my mind still. I pulled my legs up to my chest, my fingers curling around the blanket as a smile crept across my face. I could hear life in the other room, beyond the closed bedroom doors, could smell fresh coffee brewing. Past those doors was someone who had somehow inserted himself into the void of my life, become my best friend when I wasn't paying attention, accepted me and, despite everything, loved me.

I rolled out of bed, straightened the covers and searched around for my clothes. Neph had pulled out clean clothing, left everything on top of the small dresser in the corner. I quickly bathed and dressed, pausing before the sliding doors that separated me from the main living area. I ran a hand through my hair, suddenly feeling shy as my other hand rested on the door. I'd crossed a final barrier the previous evening, changed things permanently. Trying to shake things off, I threw open the door…and froze. Neph's back was to me, seated at the table, a mug cupped between both hands. Across from him, deep in conversation, was Arafel. A conversation that abruptly halted with my appearance. I took a step backwards, hand clutching the door frame. Neph's head swung around as he heard me and the only thing that stopped my retreat was the smile on his face, the hand he extended towards me. I moved forward slowly, warily eyeing Arafel sitting there across from us. There was no surprise in those eyes at my appearance, so he'd already known I was here, but, unlike Neph, there was no smile gracing his features and he was eyeing me like I was some sort of feral beast, animosity written plainly across his face. I felt fingers curl around my hand as I got closer to the table and I finally broke eye contact, looking down at Neph, unable to help softening a bit as he kissed my hand, the corner of my mouth twitching up slightly as he looked at me with that same light in his eyes from the day before.

"Morning, love. There's fresh coffee in the kitchen; hot water too, if you'd prefer tea," he said. "Grab something, come join us."

I edged towards the kitchen, feeling a bit like a wild animal, skittish and paranoid with Arafel's gaze boring a hole through my back. Pouring a cup of coffee, I watched their reflection in the window as I slowly added cream, narrowing my eyes against the early morning sunlight streaming through the glass. Arafel was standing, shaking his head slightly, leaning in towards Neph and, barely audible, "I didn't want to believe it was true." The reflection walked stiffly towards the door and left, leaving Neph alone at the table twirling his glasses between his fingers and heaving a sigh. The sense of contentment that had pervaded the air upon waking was gone, swept aside by the brief encounter. Frowning bitterly into the drink in my hands, I sat myself across from Neph, settling into the chair that Arafel had vacated. My hands curled around the warm mug. Neph reached across the table and rested his hands over mine.

"Sorry, I wasn't expecting Araf to show up for a visit this morning," he said apologetically.

My eyes flicked up before dropping back to stare at the coffee. "I don't care that he was here, Neph. It's him leaving that bothers me. Especially like that." I leaned back and met his eyes. "It's always the leaving that bothers me with people. He's afraid of me, like so many of the others. I guess I would have hoped that, after all this time, he would have formed a different opinion, considering the situation. He could at least try." Extracting myself, I took a sip from the cup.

"I told you back when you first met him how difficult he can be. And I don't think it's just fear, like you might think…" Neph said, shaking his head slightly. "He is - was - a good friend, but he's always been too fast at judging people and making assumptions. Don't worry about him. One of these days he'll come around. And if he doesn't," Neph shrugged, trying to look nonchalant, though I could tell he was upset, "then he doesn't. It would hurt to lose him, but you're far more important to me." He pushed the mug of coffee off to the side, grabbed my hands again, a genuine smile suddenly creasing his face. "Forget Araf. I have something more important to discuss."

My eyebrow twitched up, curiosity peaked.

"I want you to move in. Here. Permanently."

I felt my breath catch slightly. I didn't know what I'd been expecting, but it hadn't been that. Neph suddenly seemed to grow uncomfortable, almost embarrassed. He pulled off his glasses and began fidgeting with them again.

"I figure, you're generally here most of the time anyway. And, anymore, the place feels empty when you're not. When you were gone… I can't tell you…. And well, after last night -" he trailed off and stared at me, an almost pleading looking on his now slightly red face. I found his embarrassment cute in a way; I seemed to be the only one who could evoke this sort of self-conscious reaction.

I leaned back with a shy smile, hands going back to the cup of coffee, idly spinning it in a circle. "I would love to," I said quietly. And I meant it. This place was home to me. He was home to me. Even if I did have reservations.

"But?" Neph asked, sensing that there was more to the answer than he was being given.

"But, well, up til now, we've been discreet and kept things mostly quiet. This will officially be the end of that. People are bound to talk. And not just because it's me. There are regulations about this sort of thing, especially for officers. I don't want this to affect you…" I looked away, unhappily.

Neph leaned back and grinned. "If that's really what you're worried about, don't be. I gave consideration to the regulations governing officer-subordinate relationships long before I originally told you how I felt. I decided you were more important and no one has bothered to correct me on the matter. And if people want to talk, let them talk. My reputation as an officer is well established and no change in my personal life is going to affect that. Besides, idiots like Sendaryn have been making snide remarks about my relationship with you for some time now. If you think people haven't been conjecturing for quite a while, you couldn't be more wrong. The fact is, I want you here; nothing would make me happier."

I took another sip of coffee, staring into the soft brownish liquid as I tried to hide the fact that I'd gone red. "So…when?

Neph raised an eyebrow. "When? If you have no objections, I was thinking today. How about I make us some breakfast and then we go pack?"

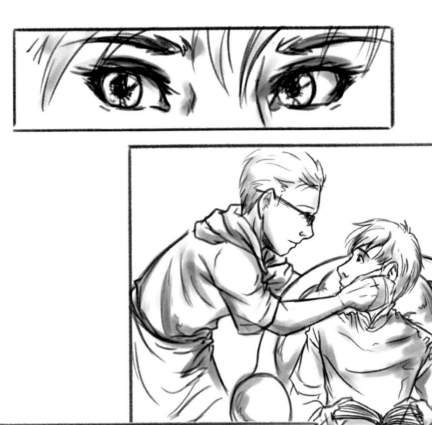

Welcome home...

Piri's Sketchbook: Excerpts

Part Three

Ley Lines

The still night air, unseasonably warm, whistled by as Reva and I winged our way home from a night patrol. We'd crossed paths several times with other soldiers, from The Watch as well as other neighboring cities. My first few patrols after returning from the Depths had been anything but normal. I'd finally been able to give Reva a first-hand introduction to a Veil zone, at the time feeling a little excited myself at seeing one after so long. After coming across the fourth one in a week, I'd been feeling significantly less enthusiastic. The zones weren't just becoming more frequent, they were becoming a lot more dangerous. The creatures, once simply unique and sought after as exotic pets, were now quite a bit larger and abnormally aggressive. Worse yet, they were straying from their home turf and taking up residence on the surface, content in their new environment after the Veil faded away. Increasingly though, the Veil wasn't fading.

I glanced down at one such area in the forest below me, its shifting luminescent mist and odd, twinkling lights setting it apart in the darkness. That one hadn't been there the other day. I sighed, making a mental note of its location. A month ago, that would have raised any number of red flags, but the strangeness was now a daily occurrence. I couldn't say that any of us were getting used to it, but it had certainly become the new normal.

The forest ended and we were crossing open

flatland. I scrubbed a hand across my eyes as I stared at the passing landscape. The earth seemed to be glowing. Beside me, Reva began to slow.

"Am I just really tired or -" She glared in my direction, like whatever was happening was somehow my fault.

Blinking, I rubbed at my eyes again, face screwing up as I slowed and stopped. Wavering lines seemed to be sparking into existence below us, rippling across the countryside.

"What do you think it is?"

I turned my head towards the two soldiers who had winged their way up next to us, a patrol out of a different city.

"They're ley lines," I whispered, a slight shiver running up my spine at the electric tingle of energy now in the air. "Energy paths. But something seems, well, wrong…doesn't it."

The energy, which had been a faint blueish color, had slowly degenerated into an ugly purple, spurts of darkness jerking and writhing across the earth. The bands curved across the land, gaining in intensity before flaring suddenly and abruptly vanishing. The four of us hung in the air, waiting in uneasy silence, but the night remained quiet and the ley lines didn't reappear. With only a nod between us, we broke apart, heading home.

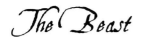

The Beast

Sitting in my chair on the ground floor, next to the Grandview, I frowned over a report detailing some of the insane experiences other members of the ENF had encountered in the past few weeks since Farryn and I had returned from the Depths. Events on the surface had been not-so-slowly degrading. Well into what should have been a glorious Fall, the days, more often than not, had been unusually warm, dark and stormy. A handful of clear days had marked an exception, rather than the typical norm. The periodic tremors were now a daily occurrence and it was always a welcome break when they would occasionally skip a day or two. A melancholy had settled over The Watch as its inhabitants were kept bottled up inside the complex, as much due to warnings from the Ruling Council as the strange weather. From what I gathered, it was much the same in every city.

I kept absentmindedly running my fingers through my hair, leaving it in an unkempt state, small tufts sticking out at odd angles. Reva, who had been pacing back and forth in front of the window, had recently come to a halt next to my chair. I'd been trying to ignore the constant movement she was creating in my peripheral vision.

"Hey, Piri, come look at this thing." Reaching out a hand, Reva began pawing at the air behind her. After several missed attempts, she finally made contact with my shoulder. Not really paying attention, I distractedly pushed her hand away, murmuring incoherently as I turned to the next page of the patrol report.

"Piri!" Reva turned in open irritation and grabbed my arm.

"What is it?" I said with an annoyed sigh, looking up.

"Would you put that thing down for a minute and come look at this? It's seriously starting to freak me out."

Rolling my eyes, I stood and pressed my face up to the glass, gazing out in the direction of her pointing finger, not really caring what new anomaly was out there to be added to the already long list. It only took a second though for my eyes to lock on to what she was talking about. Mouth dropping open, I stared in fascinated horror at the creature that was lurching its way across the open ground of the valley.

"What...is *that*?"

Reva gave me a hard poke. "See! What is that thing? Look at the size of it! It's gotta have wandered over from the Veil, but that thing is weird even by those sorts of standards."

She wasn't wrong about the creature, though I questioned her conclusion about the Veil. Watching it slowly move past familiar landmarks, I guessed the creature was at least twenty feet tall. It walked upright, its overly long front limbs dragging on the ground, giving it an oddly clumsy gait. It was difficult to distinguish any sort of individual features as it appeared to be made of coalesced shadow, though I had no disillusions about what was going on under its outward appearance. Bunched muscles writhed under the misty flesh. My skin began to crawl the longer I looked at it. This creature was far more akin to something you'd find in the Depths than in the Veil.

The strange day certainly wasn't helping to make the creature seem any less odd or intimidating. The low-hung clouds had a strange greenish cast to them, giving the outside world an almost otherworldly appearance. The tension in the air was heavy, like a storm was lingering somewhere just over the horizon and the odd flashes of lighting had certainly seemed to indicate one. Several small quakes had rocked The Watch earlier, rattling both the architecture and the already degrading morale of its inhabitants.

Looking around, I realized that Reva and I were no longer the only Seri peering out the Grandview. Small groups crowded the glass, going up all three stories, all watching the creature wending its slow way across the valley. Quite suddenly, the thing stopped and turned its large head to look directly up at the complex, glowing white orbs shining above its wide muzzle. Its mouth spread wide, revealing row upon row of gleaming, sharp teeth. Even from a distance, the effect was disturbing and several Seri stepped back from the glass with audible gasps of alarm.

A brief tug on my uniform's scarf drew me away from the glass. Wrenna had sidled up and was looking as unhappy as everyone else.

"Is it just me or are those things getting weirder," she whispered, fingers involuntarily picking at the collar of her ENF uniform as she looked from Reva to myself. "They're looking less and less like Veil and -"

"More like the Wild Dark," I finished for her, voice low. I turned back to the window. The creature was continuing to stare up at us, frozen in place. "You think that thing can see us up here?" I asked, unnerved. "It seems awfully intent -" I cut off as, in one swift motion, it swerved in our direction and began sprinting towards the base of the mountain, its speed in complete contradiction to its earlier movements. Screams erupted around the room as it began to scale the lower rocks and was temporarily lost to sight.

The other ENForcers stared at each other in dumbfounded silence for a moment.

"That's, uh, that's a problem," Reva said weakly.

"Can we even hurt that thing?" Wrenna asked hesitantly. "It doesn't seem, well, entirely physical, does it?"

Reaching out a hand and placing it palm down on the glass, I twisted, morphing it just enough for them to pass through.

"Trust me, it's real enough. We can't let that thing gain access to The Watch. Let's go." Wings flaring to life, we launched ourselves skyward.

Archers and lancers peppered the mountainside, weapons at the ready as they tensely held the entrances and terraces of The Watch's sprawling complex. Circling low, weapons not yet in hand, we watched the creature. It had stopped its ascent as soon as it had caught sight of us, gazing upwards in rapt curiosity. Its head wove back and forth in an oddly hypnotic pattern, eyes locked on our circling figures.

Flaring my wings, I slowed to a near stop. We had to get that thing off the mountain. A fight on the rocky slopes wasn't going to end well and would eventually wind up with The Watch defenders involved. I wrinkled my nose, glaring down at the strange beast.

Maybe...

With a fizzle of energy, a bow flared to life in my hands and a Source-forged arrow snapped off at lightning speed. The creature issued a low, threatening hiss as the arrow grazed the side of its head before hitting the cold rock and vanishing with a sharp snap. I fired off a second warning shot, snaking it past the other side of its head. The beast's mouth opened in a snarl, eyes now focused entirely on me. Good. I sank lower and the creature turned, hackles raised. It took a step back down towards the ground.

Releasing the bow, I motioned to either side, back towards the clearing below us. With mute nods, Reva and Wrenna moved off. Continuing to descend, I began to circle back, eyes always on the beast to make sure it was following, but I needn't have worried. It was now steadily descending, intent on only one thing. Landing lightly on the open ground, a short distance from the base of The Watch, I waited for it to finish its decent. Scrabbling down the stonework, the creature paused. It glanced back up towards the outpost. With a scowl, I shot off another arrow, not bothering to miss this time. The streak of energy plunged into its haunch, leaving a bleeding wound as the arrow vanished. With a deafening roar, the beast charged me, covering the distance at an incredible speed.

Reva and Wrenna dropped down on the left and right flanks, weapons poised.

"We're gonna have to take this thing down," Reva shouted. "It's too volatile, too dangerous."

I nodded in agreement. I'd have preferred to drive it off like we had so many of the other strange appearances, but she was right. This one had to go. I watched it carefully as it drew progressively nearer, glaive forming in my ready grip.

Suddenly, it flickered and was gone, leaving empty air where it had been only a moment before. I blinked in shock, staring at the now desolate ground between myself and the mountain.

"Wha -" I had barely formed the word when it shivered back into existence, a large muscular forelimb slamming into my chest, throwing me backwards. With a resounding crack, I slammed into

263

a tree, taking out several branches as I crumpled to the ground, pain coursing through my upper body. Gasping for air, I dragged myself to my knees as the girls dove in, blades flashing. One arm cradling my bruised ribs, I watched the attack, eyes shifting quickly as the creature flickered in and out of existence, dodging the swift blades and swifter reflexes of the two ENF soldiers. Managing to finally score a hit, Reva jumped back as the creature let loose an ear-splitting screech and lunged straight for her. Taking to the air, she and Wrenna hovered just out of reach, gazing down in angry frustration. Muscles rippling beneath skin that seemed more composed of darkness than flesh, the beast moved in tight circles, head tilted upwards, watching them. Struggling to my feet, I leaned back against the tree, ignoring the pain, eyes narrowed as I stared at the angry creature. There was no question that thing was something from the Dark. Or at least something created by it. Stopping it was only going to be possible if we could pin it down, keep it grounded in the physical world of the surface.

Kneeling, ignoring the pain, I placed a hand, palm down, on the ground and reached out to the Source.

The ground began to crackle as electric energy flared across it, circling around me, spiraling up my wings and across my skin. A faint blue glow could be seen surrounding my figure as the sky slowly darkened. Thunder rumbled in the distance and I opened my eyes at the sound. Dropping to the ground nearby, Wrenna screamed at me, "What are you doing?!"

I gritted my teeth. "Something drastic."

The creature stood frozen in curiosity, staring at my electrified form, seemingly transfixed.

Its mouth gaped open, eyes wide, teeth gleaming wetly. I noticed for the first time that it had several sets of eyes, smaller, going back the side of its head. I reached further inside, gathering the energy, bending it to my command.

Beneath my palm, the ground began to grow warm. I could see the coding of the Source now lighting up under my skin. Drawing my focus in, I let it go in a massive surge.

The energy exploded across the ground, a streaking ball of chain lightning moving almost too fast to see. I stumbled backwards, thrown off balance as the energy was forcefully torn from my control. It slammed into the beast, causing it to rear back, a terrifyingly human scream erupting from its thrown back head. Both Reva and Wrenna reeled at the sound. Reva shook her head, face screwed up in a look of horror as the creature crashed to the ground, writhing among the crackling energy that now bound it.

Neither moved in to kill it, both watching the scene play out with mortified fascination. I found myself doing the same as its form began to shift and melt into itself, becoming almost fluid as it jerked about. And then it was simply gone, melting into the ground as the Source swirled about it in a raging vortex before it too sank beneath the earth.

Landing beside me, the three of us stood in stunned silence.

"Gods almighty, Piri," Reva finally breathed, "what the hell did you do to that thing?"

Moving cautiously forward, I edged towards where the beast had been. The ground was blackened. The grass, what was left of it, dead and falling to ash. I tentatively reached out a booted foot and prodded it. My foot sank into what was now some sort of oozing mire. I quickly withdrew, somewhat shaken.

Wrenna knelt down and poked a finger into the sludge. It

bubbled slightly.

"I've *never* seen anything like that. And I'm not talking about the bloody monster. I've seen you use an attack like that before and that is *not* normal. What happened?"

I could only shake my head, at a complete loss.

Thunder rumbled again, closer this time. Much closer. A flash of lightning split the sky as several large drops of rain spattered to the earth. More drops followed.

"Let's get back into The Watch," Reva said, taking to the air. "Someone is going to want to hear about this."

Wrenna gave a short, harsh laugh. "Something tells me that half The Watch just witnessed this. If Nephael and most of the Council don't already know, I'll be shocked."

I nodded in agreement and pushed off, wings beating forcefully. Though short-lived, we'd certainly created a spectacle. Lightning sharp pain lanced through my bruised ribs as we winged our way back up the mountain. Grimacing, I slowed slightly and glanced downward, taking one final look at the burned and oozing earth. I couldn't help the chill that shot up my spine or quiet the nagging worry plaguing my thoughts.

Changes

Neph hitched an eyebrow as we walked into his office, all three of us sopping wet and bedraggled, my arms and face covered in bleeding scratches from my encounter with the tree.

"Hear we had a bit of an incident. I assume it's been taken care of."

Reva nodded slowly, glancing sideways at me. Wrenna looked agitated. We hadn't spoken on the way back, each of us lost in our own thoughts about what we had witnessed. No one was jumping to speak about it.

Neph leaned back and frowned. "Is it dead?"

Everyone looked at me.

"Uhm, well. Yes?"

For a moment, the only sound in the room was the pounding rain on the window.

"I feel like I shouldn't have to ask for an explanation," Neph finally said, an edge creeping into his voice.

I slumped down on the edge of a chair with a sigh.

"You know things are getting weird out there, Neph. I don't really know what happened. I think it's dead. I don't know. It's gone, whatever the case."

"Piri vaporized it," Reva said flatly.

"I didn't vaporize it," I snapped back.

Neph looked at Wrenna. "Anything to add?"

"I don't know either, sir," she said, crossing her arms. "He hit it with the Source and it sort of, well, melted. Took part of the ground with it. I've never seen anything react to the Source like that."

Thunder crashed outside, shaking the room as lightning split the sky. I stared out into the storm, lost in thought, pushing and pulling on the Source, playing with its eddying form. What had gone wrong? I kept replaying the scene in my head, the Source being dragged from my control, ripped away and sucked down into the earth with the creature. Just like the Source river in the Depths. It wasn't a coincidence. It couldn't be.

"Enpirion?"

I started, coming back to the present. Everyone was staring at me. Again. I ran a hand through my damp hair.

"Sorry."

Neph was eyeing me critically, arms crossed. His expression finally softened.

"Something's changed, hasn't it," he said. "What is it?"

I shook my head slightly. "I don't know," I said quietly. "The flow of the Source seems different."

"It's being pulled into the Depths."

"Stronger than before though. It's a disruption now."

Wrenna and Reva were glancing uneasily back and forth between us.

"What exactly does that mean?" Wrenna asked.

I shrugged noncommittally. "Your guess is as good as mine. It's all connected. The Brotherhood, the Depths, the Source. All the odd happenings. But I don't know why or what it's leading to. I only know that I'm starting to feel the change."

I had nearly limped my way back to our quarters when I felt Neph's hand come down on my shoulder. I leaned back against the wall as he turned me around, breathing heavily as pain shot down my side. I closed my eyes, trying to control the spasm.

"Are you alright?"

I opened one eye. "I'll be fine. Anyone that tells you slamming into a tree doesn't hurt after the adrenaline wears off is a liar. Just - just give me a day or two."

He nodded slightly, reaching down to hook a hand about my waist as he helped me navigate the rest of the walk back.

Falling in an ungraceful heap on the couch, I watched Neph wander somewhat aimlessly around the apartment before finally stopping, hands splayed across the kitchen counter, to stare out the window at the raging storm.

"You seem awfully on edge today. What's wrong? Another spring go down?"

He began tapping a finger, somewhat angrily, before filling the kettle and slamming it down on the burner. "Not since the two wild, mountain springs near Shallyn's Peak. Who knows how many of them they've found though. It's not like we've ever kept close track of the smaller ones, unless we decided they could be harnessed." He fell silent.

"What are we going to do?"

He gave a short, barking laugh. "About which catastrophic event? The Brotherhood permanently offing springs or the fact that the Wild Dark is apparently siphoning off our life blood?"

"I'm pretty sure they're one in the same."

Neph walked over and slumped down next to me. "Does it really matter? It's not like we can march an army on either problem. The human governments sent Skycrest a unified ultimatum the other day, in response to the missive the Ruling Council sent them, basically saying that if we moved on the Brotherhood, they would consider it an open act of war. And marching on the Depths, not that I think we could successfully maneuver an army through it regardless, would amount to the same thing. We'd be forced to move everyone through the Upper Dark and it would never happen. And, personally, I don't think we could stop either at this point even if we tried."

Merythalis at The Watch

"What the hell is that?"

It wasn't his exclamation, but the edge in Neph's voice that caught my attention. Coming to a halt, I looked up from the missive I'd been scanning. I realized that Neph had come to a stop several paces behind me and was now staring out the Grandview. And it wasn't just him. Murmurs were beginning to erupt around the common area, people pressing against the glass. Not just on our level either. Looking up, I could see any number of Seri on the open levels above me, all coming to attention as curiosity swept through the crowd. Everyone moving to the window, straining to see...something. I felt like I was having a replay of the previous day, deja vu sweeping over me. The fight with the beast had begun all too suspiciously like this and I wasn't looking forward to a repeat performance. I groaned slightly in annoyance as I joined Neph.

"What now?"

I stared out the window. Neph's question had been an accurate one. What the hell was it? There was no creature, but a ripple on the horizon. It looked like a heat shimmer, stretching across the earth, conforming to the landscape. But it seemed to be faintly glowing with some sort of eldritch light. I moved closer to the glass, peering into the distance at the strange disruption. Unlike the Seri around me, idle curiosity wasn't what I was feeling. After two or so months, we'd all gotten more or less used to seeing strange creatures outside, but this was something else entirely. Unease began to creep up my spine as I stared. I could feel Neph close beside me. Reva moved up on my right side. The shimmering seemed to be moving closer. No, it was *definitely* moving closer. At an alarming rate.

The shockwave hit The Watch within seconds, racing across the distance and slamming into the complex. Glass cracked and screams erupted as people were thrown to the ground. Only a Source push kept me grounded and on my feet. And only the Source reinforced architecture kept the place intact.

The quake seemed to last forever before ending as quickly as it had begun. My mind vaguely registered Reva's fingers crushing my arm, cutting off the circulation. The handful of ENForcers and soldiers in the vicinity were already moving between the civilians, helping the injured, trying to bring order. Neph's hand grabbed my shoulder as the unexpected, second wave hit, stronger than the first, knocking all three of us off our feet. And the sound that came with it blocked out the rest of the world. A high pitched shriek that drowned out everything else, like the earth had begun to scream. Reva, along with many of the others around us, had covered her ears, trying to block out the deafening noise. Children were in tears, clinging to panicked adults. Everyone helpless as the violent quake continued.

Neph's fingers closed around my chin, pulling me around to face him. His lips were moving, but no mere Seri voice could have competed with what surrounded us. I shook my head and he started pointing upwards, through the two open levels above, towards the skylight. I couldn't hear a word, but the message was clear enough. Find out what was going on, if there was any immediate danger to the outpost. I gave a brief nod. My wings snapped out and I shot towards the ceiling, energy coursing through my veins, pushing my vertical surge. As I neared the glass, I extended my field of influence and it destabilized to allow my passage. The cold air hit me in a rush as I burst through. And just as suddenly, everything came to a halt, leaving me hovering above The Watch in eerie silence. Abnormal silence I realized, the longer I held still. No birds, no breeze, nothing. The same unease that had crept in before the shockwave hit began to resurface as I slowly began to turn, scanning the area. I was looking for something, anything. I should have flown out towards the source of the wave, but something held me there at The Watch, some strange feeling at the back of my mind that something was wrong. Not out there, but here. Right now.

And then I saw it.

The dark figure was just standing there, waiting, one ridge away, among some of the old ruins. I didn't know who or what it was, but it radiated menace. This person was a threat, pure and simple. I hesitated for a moment, some small voice in the back of my mind telling me to be cautious, but old instincts were kicking back in, the arrogant confidence of bygone times suddenly slamming into gear.

I dropped out of the sky like a bolt of lightning, hitting the ground hard, a glaive instantly in my left hand. Rising slowly, a smirk crept across my face as I squared off with the figure standing opposite me on the field. It had been a long time since a lone intruder had dared to set foot in my territory. The stranger didn't move, simply stood at ease, watching me. I should have known better than to initiate a fight without knowing what I was up against, but coming head to head with a more powerful opponent was a rarity and that had never stopped me before.

"*Well?*"

My head snapped up at the sibilant hiss that emanated from the figure's mouth. Well? Well, indeed. I drove in, weapon at the ready. A long sword, the blade dark as midnight, snapped into existence in my opponent's hand. Something in my mind threw up a warning, but I ignored it. The clash of steel rang out as our weapons collided, sending sparks flying at the force of the impact. We circled round the plateau, the fight a blur as we moved, equally matched in speed and ferocity. Every move I made was met with precision, the stranger perfectly parrying my attacks. Frustration was beginning to creep in at my inability to dominate the fight. In my peripheral vision, I could see blurred shapes holding position in the air, closer to The Watch, not moving in towards us, simply observing it seemed. There was no question they were ENF, but what was keeping them at bay? Another warning shot through my system and I hesitated slightly. The figure lunged, taking advantage, but my reflexes, at least, were faster. With a surge of energy, I threw myself sideways, narrowly avoiding the deadly point of its sword. And there was my opening.

I morphed the glaive into a short sword, whipping it around and driving it squarely through my opponent's midsection. I was breathing heavily, sweat dripping down my face, despite the chill air. I lifted my head to stare into its eyes. There was surprise in those eyes, but more so in my own as I studied the face before me. Featureless. Only those glowing eyes, which now narrowed. A crack appeared where its mouth should have been, creeping up and revealing sharp teeth. And then I knew what this creature was, as every warning system in my brain started screaming.

Merythalis.

It was impossible. It couldn't possibly have gotten out of the Wild Dark, and yet there it was before me, in human form. I had only a split second to realize that I was in serious trouble before I was cut off from the Source, my weapon dissolving, my wings vanishing. The shock made me gasp, dropped me to my knees, my vision blacking for a split second. Long enough for Merythalis, completely unharmed, to grab me and slam me backwards to the ground, straddling my body as it leaned in, a hissing laugh escaping through its teeth. The fingers lengthened, sharpened, wrapping themselves around my shoulder, beginning to dig in, piercing my skin. A wave of energy shot through my body, tearing through every fiber of my being, emanating from those fingertips. I gritted my teeth, refusing to cry out, but I could feel tears slip down my cheeks, unbidden, as the searing pain coursed through my system.

"I've been waiting some while to meet you again," Merythalis whispered, its face only inches from my own. "I was quite intrigued when you turned up in my domain again after so many long years. Such an opportune moment for a reintroduction. And what a pleasant surprise that you would be the one to greet me here and now, saving me the trouble of hunting you down inside."

The fingers dug in further, ripping through my shoulder. I could feel blood soaking my uniform, staining the ground.

"You are different from the other children of the Source."

I was powerless, paralyzed. A clawed hand grasped my face as it continued.

"I can see the fear in your eyes, but I have no intention of killing you."

The fingers were starting to squeeze. Breathing was getting difficult.

"I'm afraid I don't fully understand how your power works, but I think I am beginning to see. And more than that, I am beginning to understand how useful you could be." The mouth widened to its full length, revealing more teeth. It took a moment through my blurred vision to realize that it was grinning. "Your method of channeling is quite - fascinating. So let us, mmm, turn things back on. See how it truly works. Shall we?" Merythalis removed its claws from my shoulder. Touched my chest.

I screamed. The creature laughed as the sound tore from my

throat. The Source surged back through my system, ripping through every nerve. Energy coding flared across my skin, cracking it open, rivulets of blood soaking into my uniform. My vision began to go red at the edges, black. I could feel the energy building, coalescing where the claws touched my skin. As my vision started to fail, I could make out the look of shock that crossed Merythalis's face, like something had gone wrong. Then everything stopped, just for a second. Silence. Void. And then the energy exploded.

I could hear voices. I couldn't make out the words, but they were there. In the darkness. I pushed towards them, desperately trying to get out of the blackness that enveloped me. My eyes cracked open. And then the pain hit. I gasped as it flooded back into my senses. I stretched out a hand, groping for something, anything. Wanting to feel anything other than that searing fire. A hand latched on to mine. Two hands. Neph's face came into view. His mouth was moving, saying something. I couldn't hear it. It was too much. Blackness took over.

I awoke in The Watch's Salaerium, in one of the medical isolation rooms. Everything hurt; the left side of my body throbbed. A thin undercurrent of panic was on the edge of my consciousness and I could feel my defenses trying to keep it at bay. What had happened?

I heaved myself up in the bed, straining to get myself into a sitting position, gasping slightly, my breath catching at the pain. I was only wearing a pair of thin, cotton pants, leaving my chest exposed, showing the damage that Merythalis had caused. Where it had touched me was an epicenter of black skin that radiated out in Source code patterns, running down my side, up my neck and face. The farther they got from the central area, the lines began to take on a faint blueish tinge. The rest of my body was a series of bruises and purple marks. Small blood spots dotted the sheets where wounds had reopened at some point. A faint noise made me look up. Neph was asleep in a plush chair in the corner. He looked haggard, dark circles under his eyes, like he'd been awake for days and finally couldn't push himself any further. How long had I been unconscious?

"Welcome back," a soft voice said from the doorway. I jerked my head up, instantly wishing I hadn't moved so quickly as the pain intensified, my head splitting. I groaned, collapsing back against the pillows. Round face, dark hair, grey eyes; a healer, judging by his uniform, but one I wasn't familiar with. He moved to the bed, laying a hand on my chest.

"Hold still," he said, "I can deal with that."

I could feel him channeling the Source, but something was different. The pain began to recede, as did my underlying anxiety, leaving me with an almost euphoric feeling of lightness. It took me a moment to realize what was going on.

"You're a Soother," I said, eyeing this new healer with curiosity. They were unusual, frowned upon actually. The ability to manipulate physical sensation and emotion was rare among this group and most Seri considered it an invasion of privacy. Healers who could Soothe generally kept it to themselves. At the moment, I had no complaints.

"Is that a problem?" he asked. I shook my head. "Good, I wasn't expecting it to be." He stilled for a moment, eyeing me critically.

"You know, I've dealt with some strange cases, but I have to admit, that was a new one, whatever you did up there. Consider yourself lucky I was here because I'm not sure that any of the other healers could have managed it." He frowned at the burn mark on my chest, hand still resting on it as he channeled. I could feel the energy shift and change as he worked, different from any other healer I'd ever dealt with. It was a curious sensation.

"You gave that one quite a scare you know," he nodded his head towards Neph. "He nearly went crazy. I almost had to throw him out of here while I was working."

Neph was still asleep in the chair. The healer followed my gaze and smiled slightly.

"You're lucky to have him; he refused to leave your side. I put him out, against his will. Just about an hour ago actually. He'd been awake for almost two solid days. I'd have preferred to get him into a bed; he's going to be rather stiff from sleeping in that chair, but that's his own fault."

I goggled at him, his oddly casual air and cockiness throwing me for a loop.

"So," he continued, looking up and meeting my eyes. "I understand from, uh, let's just call them my colleagues, that you aren't the easiest patient among the Seri. Then again, I've never gotten on particularly well with them either. So, somehow, I don't think you're going to be a problem. Not for me anyway." He grinned broadly. "I'm Larkyn by the way, your new healer. I'd say you can probably consider me something of your own personal healer as no one else was all that forthcoming when I was looking for help earlier. Your reputation seems to travel."

"Great. Nice to know," I murmured, closing my eyes.

"No need to get snarky. Besides, if you're going to be getting yourself into situations like this, you'd rather have me at the helm anyway and not one of the regular incompetents. No offense to them."

I cracked one eye. "How is that not offensive to them? Not that I'm disagreeing with you. But at least they're better than the group at Skycrest."

Larkyn snorted. "Ahh, Skycrest. Don't get me started. There's a reason I left. Didn't know I'd have access to their all-time favorite patient when I came here though."

A spark of anger flared, but died quickly. I didn't have the energy to spare on Skycrest. There was something slightly reassuring though in knowing that I wasn't the only one who apparently had a Capital-related grudge in play. A knock on the door halted the conversation. Pushing a glass of water into my hands as he left my side, Larkyn crossed the room and touched the Sourcepad. Reva nearly knocked him over as she burst in.

"Piri!"

Larkyn grabbed her, keeping her from throwing herself on me.

"You're awake! Gods, I've been worried sick." She extracted herself from Larykn's grasp and settled on the side of the bed, looking me up and down. I saw Neph stir slightly, eyelids flickering before settling back down as Larkyn lightly touched his shoulder. Who was this guy? I'd never seen a healer who could knock someone out with a touch.

"Piri?"

I tried to bring my focus back to Reva. She spat out a vulgar curse in the old language as her eyes roved over my injuries. I nearly choked on my water.

"Are you going to be ok?" she finally asked, gently running her fingers over my chest, looking pained herself as she touched the damage.

"I'll be fine," I said, choking back a laugh as she swore again. "You know how I heal. The Source will take care of it."

"It's not funny." She looked over to Larkyn. He shrugged.

"I can't deny what he's saying, though I'm seeing it in action for the first time. This is far better already than it was yesterday. I can't explain what happened, but I can tell you that anyone else would have been dead. It's quite fascinating, really. I've never met a living Source Spring before. They're incredibly rare."

I pointedly didn't meet Reva's piercing look. Seeming completely unruffled by the heavy silence he'd created, Larkyn merely made himself comfortable on one of the chairs, hands clasped behind his head.

"So, you knew."

"Of course I knew," I muttered.

Reva shifted slightly, glaring at me. "Why didn't you ever tell me that's what it was? You let me close enough to feel the difference, but you never told me?"

A streak of anger flared at her accusatory tone. "For the same reason he," I jerked my head in Larkyn's direction, "doesn't advertise that he's a Soother."

Attention momentarily diverted, she stared incredulously at Larkyn, eyes lit up with intense interest. "You're a Soother?" The sudden shift in her voice was almost miraculous, her innate inquisitiveness temporarily overriding whatever else was currently going through her head.

For the first time since he'd entered the room, the cocky smile faltered. I could tell that Reva was waging an internal war between her curiosity and her misplaced annoyance with me. Unfortunately, I won out, her attention snapping back to me when Larkyn didn't respond. Her mouth thinned into a severe line.

"You should have trusted me enough to tell me," she said rather sullenly.

"Why? What difference would it have made?"

"Does Nephael know?" she demanded.

"Of course not."

Larkyn rose, moving towards the door, pausing in the entryway. "For the record, yes he does. And judging by his complete lack of surprise, I'm going to say he either knew beforehand or had heavy suspicions about it long before I confirmed it. Can't imagine it wasn't in your file. I'll, uh, be back to check on you later." Without another word, he slipped out of the room. Heavy silence hung for several minutes after his departure.

"Piri..."

Suddenly exhausted and cold, I pulled a blanket up over my exposed chest, wanting nothing more than to go to sleep.

"Reva, please don't make a big deal about this." I closed my eyes. "Even I don't know exactly what that means other than knowing that I Source a whole lot differently from anyone else. I just know that it's the reason they took me as a child, why they wanted me. The way I field energy has caused me a lot of problems. Can you blame me for not telling anyone I'm a whole lot stranger than they all think?"

"I - I know. I'm sorry. It's just -" She stood, looking downcast, and started pacing the room, stopping briefly to stare at Neph's sleeping form before abruptly turning back towards me. Her fingers unconsciously reached up to grab her ponytail, agitatedly pulling at it. "This whole thing is just upsetting. For a while there, we thought we might lose you. No one even knows what happened. The Council is going to be all over this when Larkyn releases you. We tried to intervene, you know, but there was some sort of barrier stopping us, like whatever that creature was, it wanted you all to itself."

She paused as Neph shifted slightly, mumbling in his sleep. I followed her gaze, lingering on him. Reseating herself, she grabbed my hand, crushing my fingers in a death grip.

"Piri, what *was* that thing?"

Pulling my hand free, I ran my fingers over my discolored flesh, my mind flashing back to the creature perched on top of me. The leering grin, the glowing orbs. I shuddered, once again feeling those clawed fingers. "Merythalis."

In a sudden blinding panic, I sat bolt upright, grabbing at my head as pain lanced through it.

"Gods, Merythalis! What happened? Where -"

Reva gently pressed me back down. "We don't know. Like I said, no one really knows what happened. The flash of energy was blinding. When we could see again, that creature was gone. There was only you in a ring of destruction. For a minute we thought you were dead." She paused and scrubbed a hand across her eyes. "Gods, Piri, you should have seen it. The shockwave leveled the area. We were kind of hoping you'd be able to tell us what happened."

I squirmed, uneasy. I didn't know what had happened. Nothing made sense and I really didn't like the turn things had taken. Merythalis had come looking for me. Out of the Depths, something I hadn't thought possible. I wasn't self-centered enough to assume that I was the creature's sole reason for coming to the surface, but it had actively sought me out. It had said as much when I'd been trapped beneath it.

"Piri?"

I tried to force a smile. "I don't know, Reva. I'm as lost as you."

Spread Thin

I woke with a startled shout, nearly jumping out of bed before Neph grabbed my arm. The sound of the alarm, screaming over the emergency system, had shattered the early morning stillness, bringing an abrupt end to my disturbed dreams. For a moment, I stared around the room in incomprehension, blearily rubbing at my eyes, expecting the dark corridors of my newest nightmares.

As reality reasserted itself, I looked at Neph, casually reading beside me, ignoring the siren. Lying on the sheets between us, his officer's comm pulsed.

"What's going on?" I had to shout to be heard.

Languidly waving a hand, he continued reading. With a sigh, I leaned back, waiting for the alarm to come to an end. It seemed to be going on for quite a bit longer than was necessary. Neph obviously had no desire to talk until it finished, so all I could do was wait. I rubbed at my slightly aching shoulder, now a week healed and with barely a mark to show for it. Rather like The Watch itself. It had been an unusually quiet week, a fact that, in complete contrast, had put everyone even further on edge. The Councils, not having any clear means of action and at a complete loss, had turned a blind eye to the incident with Merythalis, acting as though it had never taken place. My account had done nothing to clear things up and I'd gone out of my way to avoid mentioning the creature's personal interest in me. Every day brought more worry that something new would take place, something to top the escalating series of bizarre events. And so tensions had continued to rise. Yet nothing transpired. It had been a tense week and the alarm shattering the unnatural calm was almost a relief.

Movement in my peripheral vision caught my attention as I dug in my fingers, trying to massage out the stiffness. I glanced out the window. The darkened, stormy sky was full of activity. Winged shapes. The army.

The shrieking call of the emergency system finally came to an end. If I strained, I could hear the muffled sound of an announcement. Turning to Neph, I raised a questioning eyebrow.

"I turned off the apartment speaker," he said, still not looking up. He hadn't actually turned a single page in all this time and his fingers were clamped down so hard that his knuckles had actually turned white.

Sliding out of bed, I moved to the window, a hand pressed to the glass as I watched the figures receding into the distance. Several flashes of white stood out among the uniforms. Members of the ENF.

Farryn, Reva and I lounged in moody silence in the Grand Hall, draped across one of the long, curved couches that dotted the area. The distant strains of a melancholy violin from some lone musician elsewhere in the hall drifted in to mingle with the quiet gurgle of the fountains. The normal daily chatter of The Watch was muted and apprehension hung thick in the air. With approximately half of the complex's military presence missing, the place felt somewhat deserted.

In the early light of dawn, war had erupted along the Seri-human border when a contingent of human soldiers had unexpectedly marched across the demarcation, laying waste to the first sleeping town they'd come across. It had happened so quickly that there'd been little time to react and the settlement so small that few soldiers had been nearby to help.

No one seemed to be sure if the group had been officially

organized or what the motivation had been. The only clear thing was that, while no one on the other side was taking credit for it, none of them were denying their involvement either. The aggressors had been too well kitted to have been unofficial, yet they'd all worn the mark of the Brotherhood as well, a sign that was more than a little troubling. The cult seemed to have insinuated itself into the general populace and taken root in the fabric of the human culture at a speed far greater than anyone could have predicted. For the first time in our history, our side was weakened and the general opinion seemed to be that we were finally getting what we deserved.

Forces from all the major cities and outposts had flown on short notice to defend the border, leaving everyone in a state of heightened unease. Things had been bad enough with the steadily worsening environmental issues and the strange, aggressive creatures which were now becoming a massive problem in the low-lying settlements and farms, where several people had been killed in attacks. The Brotherhood itself, though strangely silent, had shifted its sights to small, wild Springs after managing to permanently disrupt several smaller Seri cities. Now, with war on the border, our resources were spread thin and morale seemed to be at a record low.

The Dark Mark

Dark mist
swirled around
me as I walked forward, down the cracked pathways, past
the crumbling buildings. I was alone. I must
have become separated from...from -

286

I stopped, disconcerted. Who had been with me? Surely someone had been. I wouldn't come here alone. I hadn't been here alone in ages. I turned around but the way was blocked by a solid, dense wall of mist. This was all wrong. Why was I here?

The sound of something heavy dragging along the ground caused me to jerk back around. In the mist, there, ahead. A giant, dark form was rearing up. I couldn't move. Suddenly felt like I couldn't breathe. It was only a dream. It had to just be a dream. I started to panic as the creature drew closer, seeming to coalesce out of the mist. A long, dark finger reached out, caressed my face. I shuddered at the touch, tried in vain to pull away, dragging in rasping breaths against my constricted lungs. The creature began to smile, the shadowy flesh splitting open as the edges drew back to reveal its sharp teeth. The head closed in, coming to rest mere inches from my face. I could feel my breathing getting shallower, my heart racing in my chest, abject terror coursing through my system.

"If you think you can hide, you're wrong," it whispered. "And if you think our little duel was the end of things, you are sorely mistaken. I've thrice let you leave my domain in the past, despite my curiosity and despite, hmm, past events. But now you've got my attention and I don't lose interest easily." It pulled back slightly and frowned, head titled to one side. "I am, however, growing tired of this little game." Merythalis began to circle, its serpentine body coiling around me. "I won't destroy you." Its voice suddenly held a harsh, cold edge as it leaned back in, close to my ear. "I can make use of you before the end, when you will either submit or die. I have a long memory, Little Seri. And this will be a pleasure for me as you suffer in the process." It snapped off the final word as it grabbed my left arm, digging in those long, claw-like fingers. Where they pierced, darkness started to spread, burning, searing into my skin. Merythalis began to laugh.

I hit the floor hard, legs tangled in the sheets, dragging half the blankets off the bed with me. I struggled to free myself, my left arm thrust away from my body, eyes wide in terror. I could feel the blood pounding in my temples, the metallic taste of adrenaline in my mouth.

I was only vaguely aware of Neph grabbing me, wedging himself between my body and the bed. Could hear his desperate voice on the edge of my senses as he tried to calm me down, restrain me, stop my screaming. But I had lost all rational thought. Every fiber of my being was focused on the black smoke-like mark that was slowly creeping up my arm, scrawling runes crawling as if alive, burning themselves into my living flesh. I could still hear Merythalis's laughter, echoing somewhere in the back of my mind. Rivulets of blood ran down my arm from raw welts, dripping onto my night clothes, the floor. My blood-covered right hand was splayed out, fingers hooked like claws, wrist now solidly held by Neph, the muscles in his arm taut and strained as he struggled to keep me from tearing at my own skin.

The mark stopped its crawl just above my elbow, glowing with a final eerie light before settling into an inky bruise. The symbols continued to creep and crawl. My screams finally dissolved into wracking sobs. The adrenaline that had surged through my system was spent. I was shaking and exhausted, my heart racing, occasionally missing a beat in its speed. Where the design crossed my skin, all sensation of the Source had vanished, leaving oddly numb areas patterned across my arm. But worse than the mark, I could feel the Dark lingering somewhere in my mind as surely as the brand lingered on my arm. As though Merythalis was still there, somehow reaching across the boundary.

Neph was talking. I tried to focus, but it was impossible. I closed my eyes, desperately trying to push away the Darkness I could feel creeping in. It didn't matter; he wasn't talking to me. Someone gently lifted up my marked arm. I could feel someone else wiping the blood from my hand, my arm.

"Enpirion?

Fingers pushed damp hair back from my forehead. A cold cloth was pressed against my face. Neph was still curled around me on the floor, hadn't moved from his position despite the small crowd that seemed to have gathered. He was shaking almost as hard as I was, his breathing harsh on my neck. His fingers were still gripping my wrist, hard enough to bruise. I opened my eyes slightly, closed them quickly, feeling queasy as the mark swam in my vision, the Dark needled my thoughts.

"Enpirion. Can you hear me?"

I finally managed to register Larkyn's voice as he ran a finger over the mark, turned my arm over, probed the energy surrounding the brand, muttering to himself.

"Vharga…it's impossible…"

Neph was trying to explain what had happened as best he could, not that there was much he could say. I could only register a tangle of words and only one really stuck in my mind. Dragging up memories from what seemed like a lifetime ago.

Vharga.

Interludes: Conjecture

"You know those marks?" Neph asked, exhaustion in his voice as he collapsed onto the couch. Larkyn had finally managed to put Piri to sleep, no mean feat through the fear and adrenaline. Several soldiers who had come running at the sounds of screaming had been dismissed back to their patrols. Only Larkyn and Evari remained.

Back out in the living room, Larkyn paced agitatedly, periodically casting worried glances back towards the bedroom. Evari sat down beside Nephael, handing him a cup of hot tea. He accepted it gratefully with shaking fingers. Larkyn finally halted and folded his arms across his chest.

"This isn't good, Nephael. I don't know how to handle this. It's way out of my experience. Anyone's experience. That's… I've only ever read about it. Never thought I'd see it…"

"What is IT?" Neph snapped. "What the hell just happened in there?"

"What happened? I have about as much insight on that as you do. But I'd recognize those symbols anywhere; I'll never forget seeing them. That's Vharga." He hesitated for a moment before plowing on. "It's old, ancient in fact. I don't know where it came from; not sure that anyone does. Not much even seems to be known about it or how it works. Whatever it was or used to be, we've certainly long forgotten it. All I know is that it's a series of marks, runes of a sort. When you know what you're doing, they can be used to manipulate energy, any energy. There didn't seem to be any differentiation from what I read." He looked back towards Piri's sleeping form, just visible in the semi-darkness through the open bedroom door. "Where it's touching his skin, the Source is, well…gone."

No one said anything for a moment, then, "What do you mean by 'gone'?" Evari asked softly.

"Just that," Larkyn said, shrugging his shoulders helplessly. "Gone. It's not there. And there's nothing I can do about it. I'm not sure if anyone living could do anything. I'm probably one of a handful of people who even knows enough to recognize what those marks are."

Neph leaned back and closed his eyes, the cup of tea in his hands forgotten. "So what exactly does that mean?"

"I don't know, Nephael. I honestly don't. I wish I could tell you something, anything, but I can't. I've never come across anything like this. It's completely new territory. All we can do right now is watch and wait. Other than his justifiable mental state, he's perfectly stable at the moment. But you know he's a spring. He's not wired like the rest of us and I have no idea what the purpose of this thing is.

"When he wakes up, we can see if he remembers anything, can give us some indication of what happened. I don't know what else to do right now."

Neph opened his eyes, frowning. He seemed distracted. "What did you say those marks were called again?"

291

"I'm fairly certain they were called Vharga. It was an old word. Something to do with tearing or separation. I don't even know what language it's from," Larkyn said, sounding defeated.

"Huh." Neph shook his head, gazing blankly out the window at the star strewn night. Minutes passed in silence, each absorbed in their own thoughts.

Evari suddenly sat up straight, eyes widening as she clamped a hand on Nephael's wrist. "Those marks!" she exclaimed, "I've seen them before. Recently. They were in the Depths. Or something incredibly similar, at the vortex. Farryn copied a handful of them down." She stood and began to anxiously pace. "Farryn and Enpirion said they were surrounding mutilated bodies, some sort of ritual, surrounding the maelstrom, as far as they could see. How many times did they stress that it was somehow sucking in Source energy? There's no way that's coincidence."

Larkyn stared at her blankly, nonplussed. Neph nodded slowly. "Something tells me we have a bigger problem on our hands than we originally thought," he whispered. He lapsed back into silence, staring thoughtfully at Larkyn who was glancing questioningly between them.

"Larkyn, I'm curious, how exactly do you know about this Vharga if, as you said, it's so 'long forgotten,'" he asked.

Larkyn sighed as he pulled a chair around, straddling it, his arms folded across the backrest, chin resting on them. "Honestly, it was just something I ran across; nothing weird or sinister. I've done a lot of odd research into healing and energy manipulation over the years, trying to find better ways to help the people I deal with. None of it was exactly Council approved. I came across a text on it ages ago. Old, nearly falling apart. I wish it had been more comprehensive, but it was barely a few pages. The researcher managed to cram a lot into those few pages, but nothing concrete. It did detail a number of the symbols. But without knowing how they work, they're just that. Symbols."

Neph frowned in thought. "Evari, you know Arafel. Can you go wake him? It's practically dawn; he'd be up soon anyway and I don't want to waste any time. Don't - don't give him specifics about the situation here. Just explain that we need information on these Vharga. Tell him I want him on it immediately, every available resource he has. Tell him it's urgent. If anyone can dig up information, it'll be him."

Evari raised an eyebrow.

"Don't you think it might help his research if he knows why?" she ventured.

"I - no. Arafel isn't, uh, overly fond of Enpirion. I would prefer -" He dropped off. Not pushing him further, Evari gave a brief nod and left. Neph stood, rubbing a hand across his eyes, muttering to himself. "Vharga. I know I've heard or seen that word somewhere…"

Standing as well, Larkyn pointed towards the bedroom and gave him a slight push on the back. "Go get some sleep; I'm not going anywhere. I'll crash on the couch. Might raid your kitchen if you sleep in. We'll see what Enpirion has to say in a couple hours."

Memories Return

I awoke to the semi-darkness of the early hours of the morning, feeling muddled, foggy. Neph lay beside me, on top of the sheets, still asleep. What had happened? For a moment my mind drew a blank. And then it all came back. I could feel the Dark needling at the edge of my thoughts, the Source dead zone creeping across my left arm. With a groan, I extended my arm, fingers outstretched, staring at the brand crawling across my skin. Raw scratches and torn flesh crisscrossed the area; my own work. Oddly, I felt inexplicably calm and, with a sudden spark of annoyance, realized that Larkyn must have punched down the fear, forcefully put me sleep.

Neph shifted, turning on his stomach and burying his face in the pillow. He looked exhausted. My right wrist was forming livid purple marks, the perfect shape of his fingers where he'd grabbed me. I looked back to the complex script on my arm. Vharga. It was the last thing I could remember hearing. Larkyn had said it. I knew the word. It had triggered something deep in my mind, some fragment of a memory lost. After the trauma of my capture, the months in medical isolation, I'd returned missing more than just memories of my rescue and recovery, more than minor fragments of my imprisonment and torture. I'd lost entire sequences from my past, my training, my childhood. Not that the inability to recall any of that was necessarily a bad thing, but it was still a part of me that I couldn't reach. It had simply been a blank area, covered in fog, causing turmoil within my mind. But now it was coming back, as if that single

294

word had opened a floodgate.

Pieces of my early childhood with the ENForcers began to resurface, vivid memories of being forced into using my already highly developed abilities. Obedience forcefully taught with both physical and mental pain. Of being marked with the symbols that I couldn't resist, a script that deadened my emotions and made me utterly compliant, forced me to follow through with whatever task had been set forth. But always leaving the memories of what I had done, vanishing afterward to leave me with the guilt and horror. Drawn or carved on my neck, across my shoulders and chest. Sometimes a single symbol, other times a complex string of runes. I could remember the feeling as they were activated, as they seared themselves into my flesh, took over my mind. Vharga. An ancient script, made for control.

I'd never known if that dead script had been used on any other ENF or if I had been the only one. I had certainly been the youngest, the hardest to get under control, emotionally unsuited to the killing machine they had turned me into. I'd never been able to discuss it due to one lone rune under my hairline. It had acted as an anchor point of control for everything they did, but it had also kept a reign on my tongue. For the first time in ages, I wondered if it was still there, still active. Not that it would have mattered. Even long after I had learned to fight the Vharga, resist its influence, I had kept my silence. I'd had no one to discuss my situation with, nowhere to run, no one to turn to. My life would have been forfeit had I resisted my handlers; that had been made clear from the beginning and I'd never had reason to doubt their threat. I had always been alone, kept under the firm control of the Seri government. Until my capture. Until Neph had freed me.

Sliding out of bed, careful not to wake Neph, I grabbed a robe, dragging it over myself as I tried to hide my arm, not wanting to see those crawling marks. I silently wandered into the main living area. My head was throbbing. Larkyn was asleep on the couch, one arm curled under his head. I stared at him in a sleep-dazed stupor for a moment before moving to the kitchen, feeling drained.

"How are you feeling?"

I jumped in fright, nearly dropping my glass of water.

Larkyn was sitting up, staring at me intently from above the dark circles lining his eyes.

"Come, sit," he said, gesturing to a spot next to him. "I want to talk."

Head in hands, I told Larkyn as much as I could, my voice a droning monotone. Everything I could immediately recall about my training and the Seri officers' use of the Vharga, as I had understood it. At least, everything that seemed immediately pertinent. There was plenty that I left unsaid, that was painful, unnecessary and unneeded. Not long after I'd started, Neph had wandered out from the bedroom looking worn. He'd quietly joined us as I'd plowed on. Neither spoke or interrupted, though both looked sorely tempted on more than one occasion.

By the time I'd finished, the sun had crested the mountains. I'd stopped the telling with my final mission, the investigation into the missing ENForcers and the cult. The mission that had nearly killed me. Without a word, Neph moved to the kitchen, put on water for coffee. He looked mortified, stunned into silence. I knew that my files had been mostly classified or destroyed, that he was hearing it all for the first time.

Larkyn sat with his head propped in his hand, elbow resting on one knee, looking thoughtfully into the distance.

"You said you learned to fight it," he finally said. "The Vharga," he clarified when I just looked blankly in his direction.

I shook my head. "I can't fight whatever this is doing if that's what you're driving at. This…thing," I cast a disgusted looked at my arm, "is different. Way different. My trainers were inept children in comparison to this monstrosity."

"Hmm…" Larkyn reached out and put a hand on my arm. I could feel him probing, digging deeper and deeper, trying to figure out its purpose. Eventually he pulled away, shaking his head in frustration. "I don't get it," he said. "It's just surface, for the moment anyway. But there's no Source where it touches. Nothing. What does it feel like?"

"Numbness," I said. "It doesn't hurt, not anymore…other than the damage I caused myself. It's just nothingness and -" I hesitated. I didn't want to tell them about what I was feeling, the Darkness dancing on the edge of my consciousness.

Larkyn raised an eyebrow as my silence lengthened. "And?" he prompted.

"I - nothing. It's nothing." I stood, joined Neph in the kitchen. We stood side by side, neither of us saying a word, both staring out the window at the mountains in the distance. He suddenly turned, grabbed me, pulled me close.

"I had no idea," he said, voice harsh against the side of my head. "If I had known back then… I could kill them for what they did to you."

I wrapped my arms around his waist, buried my face in his chest.

"Whatever this thing is, we'll get through it. We'll find a way past it." He pulled back. Taking my wrist, he ran his fingers over the thick bruises he'd left behind. "I didn't mean to hurt you. I didn't know what else to do."

I shook my head, exhausted and overwhelmed. At least the

marks on my wrist would heal.

I can make use of you. Merythalis's words.

I repressed an involuntary shudder.

Damage Done

I paused in the bedroom doorway, surprised to see Arafel sitting at the table, several old volumes stacked in front of him. It was the first I'd seen him back here since I'd moved in, though I knew Neph periodically met him for lunch.

"Oh…hey."

He glanced up at my less-than-enthusiastic greeting, eyes widening slightly as they locked on to my arm. I instantly regretted not throwing on a robe over my night clothes.

"Good morning," he said, rather stiffly, after staring at me just long enough for things to become incredibly awkward. Where was Neph…

There was freshly made coffee in the kitchen. Pouring a mug, I snagged a muffin from the counter and slid into a chair across from Arafel. I could see his whole body tense up. Picking at my muffin, I frowned as I watched him begin to flip through one of the ancient-looking books, doing his level best to ignore me. The more I studied him, the more I had to agree that Neph was right. There was more to Arafel's attitude towards me than I'd originally thought. I just didn't know what it was.

I was just starting to enjoy how uncomfortable my presence was making the man when the door slid open and Neph entered, followed closely by Evari. I was still picking at the muffin as he crossed the room, ruffling my hair as he took a seat, pulling one of the books over and opening it to a marked page.

"How are you feeling?"

I shrugged. "No better, no worse. A little tired. Anxious. What is all of this?"

Neph pursed his lips slightly, looking down at me over the top of his glasses. "How long have you been sitting here?" He eyed my half-eaten muffin. "Long enough." He turned to Arafel. "Did you even say anything?"

Arafel moodily opened another book. "I said 'Good morning.'" Like he was some sort of saint for doing so. I rolled my eyes. "I think a more relevant question would be along the lines of," he pointed an accusing finger in my direction, "what is that thing on his arm? It's obviously why you had me woken up at the crack of dawn the other day, though it's nothing like anything I've found. Not that I've found much. I was able to collect very little before I was told that what I was asking about was classified information and I could either leave the archives or be escorted out. Maybe you'd care to explain why?"

I probably could have explained why, considering what the Seri Empire had done with that knowledge, but I kept my mouth shut. I had no intention of volunteering any information.

Evari was leafing through one of the volumes. "There's not much here. Hardly more than what Larkyn told us. Nothing that even explains where it came from. Is this really all you could find?"

Arafel was staring at my arm again, ignoring Evari.

"Have you told the rest of the Small Council about that?"

Activity ground to a halt as all eyes swiveled to Arafel's stiff figure. Evari and Neph exchanged heavy looks.

"Until we learn a bit more about this, the Council doesn't need to trouble themselves with it," Evari said, a note of underlying steel in her voice. "They have enough on their plate."

There was a moment of awkward silence.

"Arafel, please don't," Neph said almost too quietly to hear.

Their eyes locked. For a brief moment, Arafel's gaze softened and I thought that maybe he would acquiesce. I shifted in my chair and took a sip of coffee.

Arafel's gaze snapped back to me and his eyes narrowed as if he had just remembered that I was there. Pushing back from the table, he stood, snatching a text from Evari's hands and sweeping the table clean of the rest. Arms full, back stiff, he stalked towards the door.

"After all these years and everything we've been though, does our friendship really mean that little to you?" Neph's question froze the room. His voice was low, but there was a coldness there I hadn't heard before.

Arafel stopped and looked over his shoulder. We all looked at Neph.

"You're the one who turned your back on me," Arafel finally snarled. The door slid shut behind him.

"Great." Evari slumped down in Arafel's vacated seat, chin in hand. "There goes our one chance at maybe figuring this out before the Council overreacts. Not to get personal, Nephael, but was there something between you two or does he always act like a jilted lover?"

"No," Neph snapped. "That's just him." He stormed into the kitchen and began rummaging through the cold cabinet. Evari looked at me and raised an eyebrow. I shrugged, nonplussed. There was more to the story, I knew, but I left it alone; Neph had always seemed to go a little off-color the few times I'd asked. Evari peered at Neph, her eyes a bit unfocused, contemplative.

"Hmmm. He's far more open with you than he ever was with me, so if you don't know, that's that, I suppose."

It was a few seconds before what she said penetrated my brain and my coffee paused halfway to my lips. "Excuse me?"

She quickly stood. "Oh, nothing. Nephael, I'm heading out to talk to Merrant, see if I can smooth things over. Hopefully I can get to him before Arafel finds someone else and causes too much damage. Either way, the Council isn't going to be happy."

"Fine." Neph slammed the cabinet shut, grabbed a knife and began angrily attacking an unfortunate piece of fruit.

"So now what," I asked quietly, a bit distractedly as I watched Evari leave the apartment, wondering just exactly what she'd meant with her offhanded comment. I absentmindedly rubbed a hand over the markings on my arm. They crawled slowly beneath my skin, leaving strange numb effects as they went, temporarily depriving anywhere they moved of the Source.

The knife clinked down on the granite counter. Neph hunched his shoulders and stared out the window. "I don't know."

The Change

Ear-shattering thunder split the day as lightning forked across the sky. The Watch shook slightly and it took me a moment to realize it was the third small tremor of the day and not the sudden raging storm that was pounding against the mountain. I glanced out the Grandview, but the blinding rain obscured everything beyond the glass. The storms seemed to be as frequent as the quakes at this point.

Farryn hesitantly waved to me from across the room. Since our time in the Depths, our relationship had thawed quite a bit. We weren't exactly friends, but we definitely seemed to be on friendlier terms and he'd done his best to maintain that. Raising my hand, I moved towards him, snagging a glazed scone off a buffet table along the way. Hesitating, I grabbed a second. My energy levels had been noticeably flagging since the appearance of the mark, leaving me constantly trying to find ways to keep my fatigue at bay. For better or worse, I'd chosen to fill the void with sugar.

In the two weeks since the mark had appeared, life had been surprisingly normal. Or as normal as things could possibly be. When the Council had remained silent on the matter after a week, and Neph seemed less than inclined to discuss the meetings, I'd stopped worrying about it, going about my patrol duties as usual. Though unnerving and strange to look at, the Vharga on my arm didn't actually seem to be doing anything.

Continuing on, munching as I went, I passed one of the large, sculpted fountains, the graceful figure towering over me. Through decorative glass panels in the otherwise marble floor, pure Source energy

303

could be seen, flowing like liquid through the ground, the life-blood of the city. Stepping out across the area, I suddenly felt the mark shift, as if waking up. I paused, glancing down at my arm, anxiety instantly creeping in. Despite the warm temperatures, I had taken to wearing my long-sleeved uniform to cover it, not wanting to draw attention. Pulling back the sleeve slightly, I stared in growing consternation at the writhing runes, now pulsing faintly as they slithered across my skin.

Trapped in the middle of the room, surrounded by visible energy, I stood stalk still. A spark of electricity crackled across the floor. Nearby, several people stopped their conversation to look over, an officer's mug pausing on the way to her lips. I anxiously took another step forward. And I instantly knew that something was wrong. The mark flared, the scrawling characters starting to burn their way up my skin, extending their reach to my upper arm. The energy beneath my feet jerked and twisted, writhing under the glass. Muted cries rang out around the hall as the lights flickered. A rending shriek split the air as the glass panel directly under my foot cracked, the energy smashing upwards against it. An explosive shockwave rippled through the ground and knocked me off my feet. Crackling electricity danced across my skin. I scrambled backwards, breathing heavily, clutching at my arm as burning pain ran through every nerve.

The lights in the hall snapped off, plunging the room into twilight, even as the Source conduit went dark. The mark instantly calmed, leaving me staring in horror at the floor. The hall was deathly silent, all eyes on me. Several nearby soldiers, hesitating briefly, began to move in my direction. Before they could cross the distance, Farryn scurried over, forcefully hauling me back to my feet and pulling me away from the panels. After a moment, the familiar blue light of the Source flared back into existence beneath the shattered glass and the electricity flickered back on.

Dragging me out of the hall, away from the frightened crowd, Farryn finally stopped to look at me, his expression a mixture of confusion and fear. "What did you do?"

I shook my head, numb with shock. I felt weak and shaky, was having trouble focusing. Beneath the fabric of my uniform, I could feel the runes in their slow dance, now stretching across my wrist and upper arm, everywhere it touched devoid of feeling.

With Farryn's arm around my waist, I stumbled back to the apartment, on the verge of overwhelming panic. I could feel the Dark in my mind, on the edge of consciousness, smoldering in the background, but slowly growing in intensity. Reaching the door, I put my hand out to the Sourcepad, only to hastily snatch it back as the device sparked. Taking a deep breath, I hesitantly reached out a shaking finger. Knocking my hand aside, Farryn slammed his own down on the pad. The door, thankfully, slid open. Lurching in, I collapsed on the couch, exhausted.

The sensation of cool fingers brushing across my cheek woke me. I opened my eyes to Neph's concerned features. He looked tired and stressed. Pushing myself up, I scrubbed a hand across my face, still feeling slightly strung out.

The first stars were just beginning to show through the breaking clouds. At some point in the hours I'd been out, the storm had ended. I let Neph pull me to my feet and steer me towards the bedroom, listening as he talked about his day, pointedly avoiding the day's earlier incident. When I asked if the Council had brought it up, all I received was a tense smile and "Don't worry about it." The Neph equivalent of yes, but he was doing his best to keep me distracted.

Putting his fingers inside my collar, he began to unbutton my uniform. Smiling slightly, I leaned into him, forehead resting against his chest as his fingers moved slowly down the coat. My fingers wrapped around his as he began to pull the tunic off. His hand brushed my chest. And I froze. The mark. My fingers clamped down, stopping him. I recoiled, pulling away, not wanting him to know that the mark was spreading. I couldn't explain what had happened earlier and it frankly terrified me. And having him know scared me almost as much. I didn't want anyone knowing. Staring down at the floor, I clutched at the front of my uniform, fingers digging into the fabric.

"It's alright." Neph's hands cupped my face, his lips brushing the top of my bowed head. "If the mark is bothering you, I won't touch it."

Guilt ripped through me. All I could do was bite my lip and nod my head.

Digging out a long-sleeved shirt, I changed in the bathroom.

Confined to The Watch

I stood scowling at the floor, arms tightly crossed, outside of the Small Council's meeting room. Larkyn leaned against the wall beside me, frowning slightly, but otherwise seemingly unruffled by our summons. Larkyn's presence could only mean one thing - this was about the mark. I'd known this would happen eventually, but as the weeks had gone by, I'd just sort of hoped they'd forgotten. I tugged down on the sleeve of my uniform, silently cursing Arafel as I made sure that nothing was showing.

A quake, stronger than usual, shook the building. I put a hand against the wall to steady myself. The power flickered, coinciding with a twinge in my arm as the mark shifted. Larkyn's frown deepened as he turned his head to stare at the sputtering wall lamp.

As quickly as it had begun, the trembling stopped and the Source reasserted itself, evening out the building's power. The lights normalized.

"Well, that's new," Larkyn said softly in tones of mildly peaked interest. I glanced at him, wondering how he possibly managed to get through life so unbothered by the increasing chaos around him.

A quick aftershock dimmed the lights again. I could feel the pull on the Source, its normal pattern wavering as it was once again disrupted. I chanced a peek out the window just in time to see, not surprisingly, the corrupted ley lines just before they vanished back into the earth. Just like the quakes, their appearances were becoming somewhat more frequent. It was like a disease that was slowly spreading through the world.

The door across from us slid open

307

with a soft hiss, drawing my attention back to the situation at hand. A clerk stepped out and gestured for Larkyn to follow her inside. Casting a somewhat dejected look in my direction, he trailed her into the meeting room. The door slid shut.

After nearly half an hour, the door re-opened and Larkyn shuffled out, followed, to my surprise, by Farryn. They both wore slightly guilty, apologetic expressions.

"Enpirion." The clerk beckoned me forward.

Larkyn put a hand on my shoulder, squeezing gently as he passed.

"Sorry, Piri," Farryn whispered. "We tried to play things down as much as we could."

I watched their figures recede down the hall, only vaguely registering that Farryn, for the first time ever, hadn't used my full name.

"Enpirion." There was a cutting edge to the clerk's voice as she once again called for me.

"You've been awfully quiet." Neph surreptitiously slid a square of Bridgeport-acquired chocolate he'd been hoarding across the table, interrupting the tower I'd been moodily forming out of my rice. Pausing construction, I reached out and snagged it off the table. Neph certainly knew my weaknesses when it came to peace offerings.

"It's not so bad," he smiled weakly. "You're still allowed to be on duty around The Watch, at least. And they aren't forcing supervision..."

"Yeah, no, they're just confining me to The Watch because they don't trust me. Oh, and forbidding me from any of the public common areas was a nice touch." I angrily snapped off a piece of the chocolate, glaring across the table. "Why weren't *you* at the meeting?"

"Ah." Neph began shifting the remains of his dinner around his plate, taking up where I'd left off with mine. "The, uh, Council doesn't want me involved in matters directly pertaining to you right now."

I scowled, going back to shaping my rice. "Conflict of interest, I suppose. What's the point of sleeping with a Council member if it doesn't garner me special treatment?"

Neph snorted and began to laugh. I leaned back and pushed my plate away, nowhere near as amused.

"You realize they've basically put me under house arrest, confined me to the apartment," I said quietly. "Practice in the field, patrols and the apartment. That's it. I'm not allowed to go anywhere else. Not allowed to do anything."

Neph's laughter faded. "I know. And I'm afraid they're taking some of their anger at me out on you. No one was happy when they learned, secondhand, that Evari and I had kept it quiet for several days. But what happened in the Grand Hall really put everyone on edge. It's not just the Council. The other residents have been voicing concerns. They're afraid of -" He bit off the end of the sentence, the final 'you'. A look of instant regret crossed his face as I grimaced. "That's not - I didn't mean it like that. You know I don't - "

I popped the rest of the chocolate in my mouth, trying not to get upset. "Whatever, Neph. I know you don't feel that way, but you and I both know that most everyone else does. It's exactly what you said."

He deflated. "Yeah."

There really wasn't anything more to say. I stood up and took my plate into the kitchen, set it down and wound up staring out the window at the heavy sky. Neph's arms wrapped around my waist, his chin nuzzling into the crook of my neck.

"I'm sorry."

"For what?"

"For the action the Council is taking. For not being able to convince them it's unnecessary. I did try. Things got a bit heated and that's why they threw me out. They ought to be trying to help, not pushing you away."

I leaned back against him. "I suppose I should just be grateful that they didn't lock me in a room and throw away the key. That's what would have happened back in Skycrest."

"That doesn't make it right. They shouldn't be treating you any differently from any other person who might be in this situation."

I continued to stare out the window, watching a strange creature skulk across the valley floor. With a dejected sigh, I turned around, placing a hand on Neph's chest. "No one else would ever *be* in this situation, Neph. At least things are better here. And I have you."

Disciplined

The oppressively warm day pressed in, wearing my nerves thin. Despite being in the air, Reva at my side, I felt like I was still stuck indoors and I was dreading having to go back and be cooped up alone all day in the apartment. Again. The past week had been awful.

On our umpteenth circuit of the area, I finally decided that I'd had enough. Wheeling away from The Watch, I climbed above the heavy cloud cover, drinking in the cold, high-altitude air.

"What exactly do you think you're doing?"

Rocketing up through the clouds, Reva leveled out just above me. Rolling over, I met her disapproving gaze.

"I'm taking a detour." I grinned at her. "Gonna join me?"

She frowned. "You know you aren't supposed to leave the area. And we're supposed to be on patrol."

I rolled my eyes. "Oh come on, Reva, I can't take it anymore. I'm going stir-crazy. I'm sick of being cooped up, of not being able to do anything or go anywhere. And how many more times can we circle The Watch? It's not like we're the only ones out running laps. We'll stay up high; no one will even notice us. Besides, I used to do this all the time in the old days." Without waiting for a response, I flipped back over and shot off with a Source-powered burst.

After a hard, sustained push, I finally slowed, spreading my wings wide to drift on an updraft. Reva had to have figured out at this point that I was intent on leaving Seri-territory, but she didn't bring it up. If anything, she seemed as relieved as I was to get away from all the tension and the over-crowded skies. We glided along in silence, eventually passing over into human lands.

"Piri?"

"Mmmm?"

"Have you noticed anything a little, uhm, odd? About the places we've been flying over?"

I opened my eyes. I hadn't been paying the least bit of attention to the land below, more than content to just enjoy the flight. Focusing on the ground for the first time, I began scanning the area, trying to figure out what Reva could be talking about. At first glance, nothing stood out. Slowing to a stop, I took a longer, harder look. We were over a small city, its buildings a close-built jumble, chimneys with gentle wisps of smoke poking randomly out of the chaos. Except for one rather large complex on the outskirts with a bizarrely constructed, spiral-like temple squatting in the center. Even from our height, it looked newly built. I figured it had to be what Reva was referring to, but I wasn't entirely sure why. I think my extended silence finally clued Reva into the fact that, unlike her, I obviously hadn't been taking note of anything.

"See that weird looking temple?" She pointed down in the same general direction I'd been looking.

"Yeeeeeah?"

"There's been one in every city we've passed over. Literally every single one. Even the small towns and villages have had them… smaller versions, but definitely the same thing."

Suddenly intrigued, I dropped a little lower, trying to make out who or what the place was dedicated to. I certainly had my suspicions. Pretty strong suspicions. I was less than surprised when I caught my first glimpse of a heavily embroidered robe on one of the temple's occupants, spelling out exactly who they were from quite a distance.

"Since when does the Brotherhood have an actual network of temples," I mused.

"Network is right. They're everywhere," Reva said. "And it's not just that; check out the actual temple district."

I shifted my focus. The normally crowded, rowdy streets of any human religious center were practically empty, deserted. That was… concerning. I looked back at the Brotherhood's walled compound, my curiosity ratcheting up a further notch.

"Think we could get down there unnoticed?" I glanced at Reva, half expecting her to reject the question out of hand. But a slow grin was crossing her face. I wasn't going to have to argue it out with her. I'd already won.

Dropping softly to the earth, I quickly dismissed my wings and slipped behind a wooden column, barely avoiding a passing member of the Brotherhood. A moment later, Reva joined me, watching the robed figure as he paused at a grotesquely carved idol.

"We're not going to get far dressed like this," she murmured, frowning as she picked at the vibrant scarf on her uniform. "We stand out like a torch in the dark."

"Yeah, no kidding," I said, eyeing the man at the statue. Stepping out, I took several quick strides toward him, clamping a hand across his mouth and an arm around his neck as he tried to turn at my sudden approach. Squeezing down harder, I dragged his struggling form back towards Reva, who was staring at me in open disapproval. Ignoring her, I started to strip the hooded robe off the now-still body.

I paused. "What?"

"I - nothing," she said with a slight shake of her head. "We're going to need another one."

"Yeah, well, go find your own crazy cultist. I'm sure there are probably a million of them scattered around here." Sliding the robe on over my uniform, I donned the hood and began looking for somewhere to stash the unconscious Brother at my feet. I assumed he was unconscious, anyway. I didn't bother to check. Reva disappeared through a darkened archway. I smirked as I heard a muffled thump. She reappeared shortly after wearing an identical robe, the hood drawn low.

The temple wasn't large and it took precious little time for us to wander around the spiral corridor into the main chamber. There were surprisingly few members of the Brotherhood inside. They all seemed to be crawling about outside, doing what, I had no idea. The place was starting to make me nervous. I could feel the energy here without even trying, coalescing somewhere deep beneath the ground. Standing in the massive arched entryway into the main room, we hesitated. A handful of Brothers knelt before a circular,

314

stone altar in the center of the space, their bodies silhouettes in the strange, violet flickering of the torches. I couldn't help but flash back to Reva's purple fire as I stared at them. It seemed like a lifetime ago.

My eyes flicked down to my arm briefly as I felt the mark stir slightly. Trying to ignore the creeping sensation, the pulsing numbness, I took a deep breath and moved farther into the room, doing my best to act like I was supposed to be there. My eyes began to dart across the sinister markings adorning the walls. The Brothers paid us no attention as they knelt at the altar, eyes closed, chanting strange words in low voices.

Reva tugged gently on my sleeve and jerked her head slightly, questioningly, towards the walls. They were covered in unusual, scrawling writing, haphazardly painted in black and red with seemingly no rhyme or reason. The characters grew and shrank as they moved in and around grisly depictions of the great city of the Depths. A giant black, horned figured dominated the tableau. I rubbed my eyes thinking the firelight was playing tricks on me. It took me a moment to realize that the writing was actually moving and crawling around on the wall. The room was eerily quiet but for the figures chanting at the stone plinth and I suddenly realized with growing unease that the fires burning in the wall sconces were silent. Reva and I exchanged troubled looks before moving closer to the Brothers.

The altar they surrounded was carved with what appeared to be similar Vharga to what Farryn and I had witnessed at the maelstrom, but in abundance, carved in varying sizes across the surface of the stone. The center was a shallow basin. Dark liquid glimmered in the firelight. Considering past experience, I could certainly hazard a guess at what it was.

As we watched, the hooded figures spread their arms, palms flat to the stone. The Vharga flashed briefly and I bit my lip as pain shot through my arm. Blue veins of energy began to snake their way across the ground, circling the stone and lighting it up as it began to bleed through, like liquid, spreading through intricate carvings we hadn't been able to see. It carved its way across the surface, a closely woven, complicated pattern, moving in and around the runes. As it merged with the liquid in the pool, the pure liquid blue of the Source rippled and shifted, its light fading to a purple-black and spreading back out through the altar. It was the same as the corrupted ley lines we had all witnessed on so many recent occasions.

The mark twitched again and I felt it crawl another inch up my arm. The corrupted energy roiled. I swore before I could stop myself. Out of the corner of my eye, I saw Reva start to move towards the door. The chanting stopped as the Brotherhood glanced up, turning their heads to look in our direction. Biting my tongue, I retreated, hastily backing out as they began to rise, as the energy spidering across the floor jerked and sparked. Trying to crush my rising panic, knowing this was going to turn into yet another incident if I didn't get out of there, I quickly retraced my steps out of the temple and ducked outside, willing my racing heart to calm itself. I could feel the mark writhing, reacting to the Source and whatever the Brothers had done.

Reva grabbed my shoulder, her fingers clamping down on my shaking body. I was suddenly exhausted.

"Come on. We need to get out of here."

As I summoned my wings, which seemed to take some effort, I heard the distinctive click of a crossbow echo from inside the temple. Not bothering to reply, I launched myself skyward, Reva right beside me. Throwing a quick glance down at the swiftly shrinking temple, I could see a handful of figures watching our retreat, thankfully far out of shooting range.

A small crowd met us as we touched down on the Grandview Green, followed shortly after by the two soldiers who had fallen into formation with us as we'd crossed back over into Seri territory. They both looked smug as several angry-looking officers moved to intercept us, knowing we were in for a severe reprimand, at the least, for violating orders. We were still wearing the Brotherhood's robes, our uniforms hidden beneath their vibrant, arcane symbols. I couldn't help returning the smug look as Neph shouldered his way through and waved everyone off, laying claim and responsibility to us and leaving quite a few officers scowling in his wake.

He eyed us coldly, lips drawn into a thin line. I felt myself wilt as his ice-blue eyes bored holes through us. "My office. *Now.*"

The door slid shut as Neph seated himself behind his desk, his posture exuding tightly controlled fury. Reva and I huddled together in silence. She glared at me, her eyes conveying an entire speech about how she'd told me we shouldn't have left Seri lands and how this was all my fault.

"I don't know what you two thought you were doing in human territory, but I assume by your interesting new uniforms that you've got a good story to back it up." He pointed to the chairs. "*Sit down.*"

Pulling off the intricately embroidered robe, I dropped it over the back and hesitantly lowered myself onto the chair, the desire to flee a whole lot stronger than the idea of sitting there and explaining myself. I couldn't help thinking that this was going to be an awkward night in the apartment. Beside me, Reva was slowly folding her robe. I looked back at Neph.

"Are we in trouble?" It was a dumb question. I wasn't even sure why I asked it. Maybe because I didn't really know what else to say.

Neph leaned back, squinting his eyes shut as he pulled off his glasses and pinched the bridge of his nose. "That depends entirely on what you tell me. I'd suggest you make it good because I'm going to have one hell of an argument with the Council on why I apparently directed you to ignore orders from Skycrest and obtain intel deep inside human territory."

Finally setting aside her disguise, Reva perched herself on the edge of her chair. She looked down at the floor and her voice shook slightly. "To be fair, sir, I think what we learned outweighs our disobedience...even if we learned it purely by accident." She paused and glared at me. I shrugged, helplessly realizing that she obviously had high hopes for that declaration. Looking at Neph, I wasn't so sure.

Neph waited for someone to continue. When Reva didn't speak, I took up the story, detailing our deviation, our flight over quite a few different cities and villages and the one new feature that seemed to unite every place we looked. I finished with our venture into the temple, leaving out the mark's reaction only to have Reva fill it in for me. Neph's eyebrow rose slightly, the only indication on his otherwise stony face that he was both intrigued and more than a little annoyed with my redacted account.

Silence settled on the room like a lead weight. Reva's earlier conclusion about our circumstances was obviously wrong and we both knew it. Staring shame-faced at the floor, she began to pick at the hem of her uniform.

Neph picked up a pen and began to absentmindedly twirl it between his fingers. "Do you really think that Skycrest wasn't aware of everything you just told me?" His voice was calm, cold. We could have used a knife to carve through the room's tension. He leaned forward.

This was one of those dangerous, rhetorical questions and I wanted nothing to do with it. Because, up to that very moment, it had never occurred to me that Skycrest was aware of what we'd just told him, that they had covert agents keeping tabs on the threat against us. The more I ran that through my head, the more uncomfortable I became under Neph's piercing glare. I glanced at Reva. She was still staring at the floor, hunched up, doing her best to disappear into the chair.

"You directly disobeyed orders, not out of some misplaced sense of duty, but out of boredom, if I'm properly reading between the lines. You put yourselves in unnecessary danger in the process. And, while on some level, I appreciate your initiative, this was certainly not the time considering the current situation."

I opened my mouth to reply, thought better and closed it again. After a moment though, I realized that I didn't really care. Anger was bubbling to the surface. Anger at being cooped up, anger at the seeming inaction of the Seri government. "How can you just expect us to sit back and do nothing," I finally exploded. "For months there's been nothing. *We've* been doing nothing, *Skycrest* has been doing nothing. I'm sick and tired of running patrols, of being treated like a run of the mill soldier, of being stuck in here like a prisoner. Just because the Council is content -"

"Do you really think they've been doing nothing," Neph hissed, cutting me off. He slammed the pen down on his desk. Beside me, Reva winced. "The Council has spies all throughout the human realm. They've been doing everything in their power to figure out what's going on, trying to sabotage the Brotherhood's actions, stop them from spreading their poison through the entire human population. The fact that it isn't working is beside the point. Just because you are unaware of this and the ENF has been grounded doesn't mean that nothing is going on."

Reva finally looked up. "But why not us? We're supposed to be their elite squad. If they're not using us, then who?"

Neph gave an exasperated snort. "There are plenty of more subtle units than this one, whether you're aware of them or not. Let's be honest here, the current ENF isn't as different from the original unit as some might like to believe. We're not a covert unit, not really. We're called into play when the Council wants to guarantee that something will be taken care of and they don't particularly care if the outcome causes public outrage. The ENF is their brute squad; used just as much to convey certain messages as to accomplish any particular mission." He leaned forward, all stone and sharp edges.

"The fact of the matter though is that I can't have members of my squad taking matters into their own hands. You especially." He turned his gaze pointedly on me. I felt myself tense. "You were already confined to The Watch. If you thought the Small Council was paranoid before, you've just made things much worse. And you've both put me in a very difficult position."

"What right do they have -"

He held up a hand and I bit off my words. "I am not going to debate this. The discussion is over. You need to understand that if something like this happens again, it's going to be out of my hands. The power to protect my unit only extends so far. Believe me when I say that you do not want the Ruling Council getting involved." He stood up and pointed towards the door. "Hang up your uniforms. You're both suspended from duty for the next two weeks and confined to the complex. Consider yourselves lucky."

The door slid open. We were dismissed. Reva shuffled out, shoulders hunched, head down. Neph pointedly avoided looking at me. Feeling sullen and moody, I stalked out.

The rest of the evening only served to put me in a fouler mood, starting with the Sourcepad at the apartment door. It sparked and flickered as I tried to open the door, hitting me with an electric shock before finally giving in on the third attempt. The same problem greeted me at every turn, from the lights to the stove top. I was on the verge of tears from the pain and frustration when I finally gave up and retreated to the bedroom, curling up with a book and attempting to forget the day and the scrawling, volatile runes that continued to inch ever further up my arm. Every time the mark reacted to the Source, I could feel the Dark stir in the back of my mind. For a while I had been able to ignore it, but as the days went by, it had begun to get stronger, had begun to manifest visually when I closed my eyes and actively sought it out. A dark flame, cold as winter, lurking in the recesses of my mind. No amount of wall building would make it go away. I could feel it there now, mocking me as it gained a firmer foothold.

I realized that I'd read the same paragraph at least four times and still had not a clue what any of the words actually said. Snapping the book shut, I stared somewhat blankly at the wall. It was getting too dark to read anyway and I couldn't bring myself to fight with the lights. My anger had died down, though I was still feeling somewhat resentful.

The soft swish of the door heralded Neph's return. Lights flickered on as he crossed the living room and stopped in the bedroom doorway, his figure a dark outline in the door frame. After a moment's hesitation, he crossed the short distance and turned on a lamp. Leaning over, he kissed me on the forehead.

"Look, I know you're angry, but I'm hoping that's not why you're sitting here in the dark."

"It's not," I said stiffly.

Flopping down next to me, he began to undo his officer's jacket. "You know I can't treat you differently in situations like this," he said softly. "This…us…it's going to cause difficulties. I wish it wouldn't, but it's going to. I just wish you wouldn't do things to make it worse. I do everything in my power to defend you." He stopped and took a deep breath. His hand inched across the space between us, fingers curling through mine. "I don't want to fight."

Leaning my head back, I shrugged, resignedly. "Forget it, Neph. I'm not sorry for what I did, but I know I shouldn't have done it. I'm only sorry that it put you in a bad spot. I'm still not used to having to worry about my actions affecting other people. I'm not mad at you and you have every right to be angry with me. But it's been a bad day and I'm tired." It was somewhat more than that. I felt exhausted, physically and mentally, and suddenly I wanted nothing more than silence.

Neph's eyes flicked briefly towards my arm. I tugged my overlong sleeve farther down, hiding the newly spread Vharga cutting across the back of my hand. "Reva said you reacted to the Source again."

I wasn't sure if that was a question or a statement, but I stiffened up regardless, which was more than enough to confirm things.

"Piri - "

"I don't want to talk about it, Neph. Please just leave it alone," I snapped. "It's fine. *I'm* fine." Which was a lie. I wasn't fine, was anything but. But it was my problem, not his or anyone else's, and I could deal with it alone.

The Mark Spreads

Reva frowned as I joined her on the practice field. In our two weeks off-duty, we'd been forbidden from even visiting the field, let alone practicing, and it had felt like a lifetime. Even this early in the morning, the sun was slowly heating things up, for what was surely going to be another abnormally warm winter's day. Many of the other soldiers scattered around the field had gone bare-chested or sleeveless this morning. Shirtless on the field had never been my thing, especially once I'd acquired the scar on my back, but today I'd gone completely overboard to hide my skin, not wanting anyone to see the mark crawling across my arm, slowly spreading. I shook my head slightly, trying to pull myself together, ignore the malaise the mark was causing. I pulled down on my long sleeves, tugging the new glove on my left hand up slightly as I flexed my Vharga-covered fingers. I could already feel beads of sweat beginning to slide down my forehead, but I didn't care. I tossed a mostly-eaten apple away into a bush on the edge of the field as Reva marched up to meet me, open criticism written all over her face.

"Ok, so you've officially gone crazy," she said, reaching out to pluck at my sleeve.

"Yeah, hi to you too." I pulled my arm away. A slight breeze stirred the air, teasingly, doing absolutely nothing to dispel the weird summer-like weather.

"Piri, you can't be serious. I know you're trying to hide that thing, but, honestly, this is ridiculous. You're going to pass out from heat stroke before we're halfway through sparring."

323

I stepped back and my glaive flared to life between my fingers. My eyes narrowed to slits as I slid into a defensive posture. I was testy and tired and in no mood to be hassled. Reva sighed and summoned her own polearm. She shook her head slightly as we began to circle one another.

"So, what are we working on today?" she asked.

"OverSourcing."

Almost faster than Reva could follow, I struck. Flaring her energy, she threw up her weapon, barely blocking the blow. She staggered backwards under the pressure.

"Gods, Piri, take it easy."

"Don't release the energy," I grunted, jumping back, out of her reach. "Learn to fight with it, not just when you need it, but permanently. You've always been too fast to let it go. Stretch it out, see how long you can run it."

"This is going to be a short lesson if you suddenly think I can overSource like you."

"It's called practice for a reason," I shot back in annoyance. Her wings sprang to life with enough force for me to feel the energy thrown off. Diving back in, we clashed, weapons moving like lightning, questing, seeking openings and opportunities. As we moved across the field, I caught glimpses of other soldiers stopping their drills and practice to watch the bout. Wings shifting in and out as we jumped impossible heights and danced around each other, the two of us wove through the morning, neither of us giving an inch, the sound of steel reverberating through the air.

I wasn't sure how long we'd been going, but I could tell that Reva knew something was wrong. She hesitated slightly as she brought her polearm swinging around. Only her quick reflexes kept her from taking a swipe to the head as she dismissed her weapon, rolling to the side and regaining her feet. Playful boos could be heard from disappointed Seri on the edges of the field. I glared as she circled, not recalling her blade, but watching me intently. I knew my normal grace was missing, my movements not quite as smooth as they should have been. With a spike of panic, I felt my wings flicker slightly, too fast for any normal Seri to catch, shifting from corporeal to Source. Reva stopped moving, her eyes widening. The panic was replaced with a flash of anger and I dropped the point of my blade to the ground, where it sank into the earth.

"What's wrong?"

"You tell me," Reva said, arching an eyebrow. "Are you feeling alright?"

My lips tightened, brows knitting together. "I'm fine."

Reva rolled her eyes and crossed her arms. "You aren't fine and you're a terrible liar. You've been fighting entirely right handed, you're slow to respond. Something is crazy off with your energy. And, no offense, but you look awful."

"Don't be ridiculous," I said, face starting to redden in anger.

"I'm not being ridiculous," she snorted. "I don't know what's going on, but I think we should stop. If you don't want to talk, fine. Go check in with Lark -"

Reva threw up her weapon just in the nick of time as I suddenly came at her, glaive moving almost too fast to follow, determined to prove her wrong. Refusing to admit to myself that she was right. Sparks flew as our blades clashed once more, weapons morphing into short swords as we drew in closer, wings pulled in tight, then flaring out as the dance began again. Cheers erupted around the field. It was taking all of Reva's skill to keep me at bay as I threw everything I had at her. And then it happened. The mark awoke. My wings vanished in the blink of an eye, weapon dissipating. I stumbled and fell to my knees, gasping as pain, knife-sharp, shot through my arm, snaked its way across my chest, my back. Reva rushed to my side grabbing at my body as I started to collapse. She ripped up my sleeve, sucking in a sharp breath at the strange glow now coming from the crawling runes. Other soldiers and ENForcers

on the field were rushing towards us. I barely registered one of them yelling for help as Reva put her arms around me, trying to support my weight as I slowly went limp against her.

"Piri? Piri, *hey!*"

She tapped a hand lightly against my cheek, panic lacing her voice as she screamed for help, but I was barely registering what was going on around me. The only thing I could focus on was the pain as it slowly engulfed my body. I could feel the Source being pulled painfully away. I sucked in a ragged breath, struggling to remain conscious as my vision started to blur. I heard twin thumps next to us, a flurry of voices. I could barely distinguish Farryn's in the mess of sound, Reva's shrill with fear. And then I felt familiar hands lift me off the ground.

Neph. Relief surged through me. My safety net had arrived. It was my last thought before everything went black.

I opened my eyes slowly, squinting slightly against the sunlight streaming in through the window. I had no idea how long I'd been out. My body felt heavy and drained. I stared vacantly, weakly, at the ceiling. Beyond the door I could hear voices. I shifted my attention, feeling exhausted.

"I wish I had something better to tell you, Nephael, but I don't."

Larkyn sounded resigned, defeated. "It's been days and nothing has changed. I keep trying to tell you that and you're not listening."

"But I thought it was only where the mark was…" Neph. He sounded frantic, terrified.

"It was, at first. I told you, I don't understand this thing. And I don't understand how you didn't notice this. Nephael, don't take this wrong, but you two live together, sleep together. I assume more than that. How could you possibly have missed this?" He asked it softly, trying not to sound accusatory.

"Because he hasn't let me touch him in weeks. He's always got long sleeves on, hiding it, hiding how it's affecting him, refusing to talk about it. I should have known. I should have seen it." He slammed a fist against the wall in frustration. "I didn't *want* to see it."

"It's not your fault. But I still have no idea what to do about it."

"Please, you have to do -"

"Nephael, there is *nothing* that I can do," Larkyn said, cutting him off. "It's still acting like a drain, siphoning off his energy. I tried flooding his system yesterday and it was drawn away as quickly as I could give it. It's cutting him off from the Source. I don't know how long he can survive like this. I told you, the mark is killing him."

"Larkyn, please -" Neph's voice cracked. I stopped listening, tried to block out the conversation. I couldn't bear to hear him like that.

'Days,' Larkyn had said. I closed my eyes and focused on the mark, on my body. It felt empty, like a hollowed out shell. Except for the Dark. I could see it clearly now; no longer was it just a vague feeling. The mark's energy stood out like a beacon, an all-consuming black flame burning with an intense, chill light, drawing away all the warmth and energy. In the middle of a vast empty space it hovered, its purple and blue flames flickering and wavering in a nonexistent breeze. In my mind's eye, I moved towards it, at first hesitantly. I'd tried to approach it before, but the stronger it became, the more I'd come to fear it. It was an invasive force in my body. I felt violated, damaged. But something was different this time. The sound of Neph's voice reverberated through my head, pleading with Larkyn, breaking. I continued to inch forward and the closer I got, I could feel rage beginning to build, quenching the fear as it rose, red hot and searing, far more powerful than anything else. Larkyn was right. I couldn't survive what it was doing to me. Down in the core of my being, I knew that for fact and I now seethed with anger over it. I didn't deserve this. I hadn't deserved any of the terrible things I'd been put through, all the years of pain and hardship, torture at the hands of my own people. And now this. I had finally managed something I had never expected, never dreamed was possible. I had managed to find happiness, a new life, come to terms on some level with myself…and now it was going to be cut short, forcibly ripped away. While the person I loved was helplessly forced to watch.

Drawing up short before the flame, which seemed to grow and intensify, bubbling as if laughing and mocking my inner pain, I reached out a hand. My fingers stretched towards the heart of its pulsing core. The cold strengthened. It was so deeply intense that it burned and I could feel the tips of my fingers in the physical world starting to blister slightly. I paused, staring balefully at the flame. What I intended was wrong, forbidden by everything that the Seri were. Our race were creatures of the Source, an energy in direct opposition to everything that was the Dark. The two didn't mix. They corrupted, destroyed. I didn't care. Not now. The fury inside was rising to a crescendo and driving me on. I had been the victim for entirely too long and I wasn't going down without a fight. Not this time. It might still kill me, but I was going to make Merythalis pay. With a snarl, I plunged my fist into the flame, right into the core of the dark energy.

Turning Point

Neph jumped from his chair in alarm as I staggered out of the room, hand clutching at the mark, my bare chest heaving. My breathing felt ragged, strained, like a vice had slowly closed around my chest. Vision unfocused, heavy, fogged. My eyes roved around the room, barely seeing it, barely taking it in. Reaching out to grab me, Neph snapped his hand back as I jerked away, briefly unsure of who he was, what he was doing. I doubled over as pain shot through me, the mark flaring brighter. I felt my eyes light up, briefly glowing with the energy, no different than when I pushed an overSource too far. Raising my head, I tried to clear my mind, focus on Neph, standing there frozen, lost, hands still slightly raised and looking on helplessly. I shook my head, one hand stretching out, grasping. The spell broken, Neph grabbed me, supporting my weight as I collapsed against him.

"Let me get Larkyn..."

"No. I just - I just want to go home," I said weakly. "Please."

Hitching an arm under my legs, Neph hoisted me up, alarm creasing his features as he looked at me, arms shaking. My vision sharpened as the light flashed through them again and I squeezed my eyes shut. Coldness. Darkness. Neph stood uncertainly, holding my limp form. His indecision was palpable as he hugged me to his chest. I kept praying he would just leave, take me with him, get me out of this place. He finally started to move back towards the room when Larkyn appeared, placed a hand on his shoulder, stopping him.

"Take him home," Larkyn said quietly. "I'll come by and check on him." He pushed a small object into Neph's pocket. "If it's an emergency, you can summon me with that and I'll come as quickly as possible. If it makes him more comfortable, being at home, then take him there."

"Larkyn...something happened. Just now. Something's different."

I opened my eyes slightly. The light was gone, the room still out of focus. My head hurt, everything hurt. Looking down at me, Larkyn shook his head.

"I don't know what's going on, Nephael, I really don't. This has gone well beyond my understanding. None of the other healers here will even come near him. They're afraid. Honestly, so am I, but for entirely different reasons. Keep an eye on him, try to make him comfortable. That's all the advice I can give right now. I'll do my best to try to keep him stable. For as long as we might have." He shrugged helplessly. "Who knows, maybe he'll rally. Enpirion's - unique."

A tear streaked Neph's cheek as he looked down at me, cradled in his arms like a child.

A small quake suddenly rocked The Watch, the tremor ending as quickly as it had begun. Thunder rumbled in the distance as the day made one of its quicksilver transformations. Larkyn turned to stare out through the window as roiling black clouds began to form, transfiguring the winter's summer-like day. What little was left of open sky had turned an oddly unsettled greenish hue and the contaminated ley lines wavered in and out in a hazy spider web across the range. On the far horizon, a vortex of cloud descended in a swirling mass.

"Tornadoes," Larkyn said, almost too quietly to be heard. "When have you ever seen a tornado in the mountains..."

Neph remained silent as he stared out at the distant funnel, tightening his grip on my body.

"It's dying, you know." It slipped out, barely audible. I was hardly aware that I'd spoken as my mind drifted out to the energy around me.

Both of them stared at me, but my eyes were now fixed on the distant range.

"You can't see it from here, but it's dying. The land, us, everything," I whispered. "I can feel it."

Neph's eyes met Larkyn's.

"Take him home, Nephael," Larkyn said softly.

I awoke in my own bed, thankfully lucid, with Neph curled up beside me. His eyes were red and puffy. He'd cried himself to sleep. I levered myself up, that small act physically exhausting me. Neph stirred in his sleep and I stopped moving, not wanting to wake him. Sitting there, staring at my partner beside me, feeling on the verge of collapse all over again, I reached out to the Dark. It wasn't like accessing the Source, something that flowed easily, was a natural part of who I was. This was different, was more like a battle of will. It was almost like the energy could sense that I was an intruder who had somehow gained the upper hand and was now trying to keep me away. Wrenching on the energy, I exerted my will, fueled by anger, and felt power course through my system, erasing the exhaustion. I held a hand out in front of my face and watched as Dark energy danced across my fingertips, purple and green-tinged sparks of electricity, so like the Source and yet so vastly different. The flickering light gave the darkened room an eerie glow, somehow completely normal looking against the equally strange storm that raged outside the window.

Neph shifted again and his eyelids flickered. I quickly released the energy, pulling away from my tap into the Dark, feeling the soul-sucking weariness begin to invade my body all over again. I'd eventually have to find a way to tap it permanently without anyone noticing, a constant overSource, for want of a better term.

"Piri?"

Neph's voice sounded numb, heavy with sleep. But he tried to sit up beside me all the same, struggling to wake himself. He stretched out a hand, ran his fingers across my neck.

"Go back to sleep, love." I leaned over and kissed him softly on the cheek before pulling him down beside me. He stared at me for a moment in the semi-darkness, the only sound the heavy drumming of the rain on the glass, our faces only inches apart.

"Please don't leave me." It was the barest whisper, barely audible even as close as we were. I buried my face in his chest as he wrapped an arm around me, pulling me against him.

Larkyn's Office

"No matter how many ways you phrase the question, the answer remains the same. No. I cannot explain it," Larkyn said with more than a hint of irritation as he leaned back in his chair, glaring at the grim crowd surrounding his desk. "As I've stated before, that mark is well beyond my experience and I can't begin to predict what it will do. I can only tell you what I've observed. Which, if I might remind you, I have done on several occasions when asked."

The small office felt unusually claustrophobic, crowded as it was with several members of the Council, many of whom had been aggressively questioning Larkyn for the past quarter hour. Neph stood beside where I sat, hand on my shoulder, worry creasing his features as we faced them. My energy levels were waning as I vacantly stared at the wall, listening to their bickering. I wasn't entirely sure why I'd been required to be present for this debate regarding my wellbeing, a matter that none of them actually seemed to care about in regards to me personally. I felt like they could have done just as well without me.

"It ought to be locked up," Sendaryn hissed, stepping forward.

"You know I'm sitting right here," I mumbled. Neph's fingers clamped down on my shoulder. I wasn't sure if he was warning me to be quiet or if it was an involuntary reflux.

Merrant, arms crossed, looking stiffer and more serious than I'd ever seen him, had been silent during Larkyn's rundown of my collapse, as well as his inability to explain my sudden, inexplicable...well, not recovery, but certainly stabilization. I was fairly certain that Larkyn had his suspicions, judging by the surreptitious looks he'd been throwing me for the past several days but he had, thankfully, kept his mouth shut about it.

"Look at it," Sendaryn continued, throwing out an accusatory finger. "Can you honestly tell me there isn't some deeper connection to what's happening, sitting right there in front of us? You think it -"

"Watch your mouth, Sendaryn." Neph's fingers were starting to hurt. Wincing, I brushed his hand and he loosened his grip.

Sendaryn's face twisted in disgust. "You think - *he* - looks normal? How is it that several days ago he seemed on the verge of death and now suddenly he's not, but looks a whole lot more like he belongs in the Underground?" Referring to me like an actual person seemed to genuinely pain him.

I squirmed uncomfortably. In the eerie light filtering in from outside, my slightly sunken features, dark circles and unhealthily pale skin probably looked even worse than usual. I thought his assessment was a bit harsh, though rather closer to the truth than I would have preferred. I thanked whatever gods might be listening that the mark only lit up when I connected to the Dark.

"Am I the only one here who hasn't gone completely blind to what's happening around here, how everywhere he goes something strange happens? How justifiably afraid people have become?" His voice had gone up several octaves. "He's not Seri anymore. He's as much a part of this -"

"Enough." Merrant finally broke his silence. "Nephael, I want him removed from the force." He held up a hand, silencing Neph's protests, which were only slightly louder than my own. "I do not agree that he needs to be confined any more than he currently is, but I do not want him acting in any capacity outside of a civilian at this point and I would advise that he keeps his distance from the general public. One thing Sendaryn is correct about is Enpirion's effect on those around him, due to his current...condition. Starting now, he's done."

Sendaryn bristled. "That's it? You're just going to let him continue to wander where he pleases, go where he wants, even after everything that's happened? Without even a detail assigned to keep watch? Despite admitting that he's a problem?"

"This is not the place for that dialogue." Merrant gave me a hard stare that sent a chill up my spine before turning his gaze on Neph and finally returning to Sendaryn. "This discussion is over."

Without another word, he swept out of the room, motioning for the other Council members to follow. Harsh looks, that did nothing to boost my confidence, were cast in my direction as the room slowly emptied, finally leaving only myself, Neph and Larkyn.

"You're going to want to watch that one," Larkyn said softly, his narrowed eyes locked on Sendaryn's retreating form. "He's trouble."

Neph nodded distractedly as he made his way out. I rose to follow, grateful to finally get out of there. Desperate for a brief connection to the Dark.

"Oh, Enpirion?"

I glanced back.

"You want to be careful. You're treading in dangerous waters."

My eyes widened in horror as I stared at his placid face, but he gave no further indication of what he might mean by that statement. Waving a dismissive hand, he motioned me out.

In The Garden

Ducking my head around the wall of a hidden folly in one of the more remote gardens, I quickly took a furtive glance around the area, making sure I was well and truly alone. I had already wasted more than enough time making my roundabout way here. The only living thing besides myself seemed to be The Watch's lone shadowcat, which was slinking across the stone pathway, stalking some soon to be unfortunate creature that I couldn't see. Relieved, I dropped onto a bench, leaning back against the cool wall, glad to be in a shaded area that was at least a few degrees cooler than the general warmth of the day. I stared up through the tree canopies at the overcast sky. No rain, though it certainly looked as though it should be. Considering the time of year, it should have been snowing.

Just getting myself out to this place had exhausted me and I closed my eyes for several minutes, allowing my aching body to rest. Pulling up my sleeve, I stared in angry disgust at the symbols crawling across my skin. I didn't know how much time I had today before someone found me. It was getting harder and harder to slip off, away from watchful eyes. Suspicion and concern seemed to have everyone around me on their guard. And I was sure that I was being watched by the Council. It might have just been paranoia, but I was positive that I was being shadowed nearly everywhere I chose to venture. Practice time was becoming a commodity.

With a dejected sigh, I reached out and latched on to the Dark, wrestling it into my control. Though nowhere near the wrenching sensation it had been at the start, I still winced slightly at the uncomfortable change-over as one energy was replaced by the other. Just as quickly though, blessed relief coursed through my body as the trickle of Dark energy temporarily drove away the pain and exhaustion. Holding out my hand, fingers splayed, I played with a crackling pulse of energy, watching it dance across my fingertips, before mentally snuffing it out. As I did at the start of every practice session, I tried to summon my wings. By this point, I didn't expect anything to happen, yet I kept trying, kept hoping. I'd been trying for weeks with the same result. I didn't know if a Seri's wings, mine especially, were such an inherent part of the Source that it was simply impossible or if there was some other blockage. The outcome was the same regardless. Grimacing in frustration, I moved on: forging weapons and going through stances, playing with the raw energy. Attempting, as always, to use the Dark no differently than I would the Source. And, for better or worse, I was starting to get good at it.

In the beginning, doing anything, other than channeling the energy, had proven almost impossible. The Dark was wild, chaotic. The wavering flame in my mind flickered and shifted, dancing around any binds I tried to instill. I'd eventually learned that, quite unlike the Source, the Dark required a much firmer hand and tightly enforced control.

Morphing a short sword into my favorite glaive, I couldn't help but gape at the now noticeable physical difference in the weapon, the haft dark and glittering in my shaded seclusion. Shimmering strands of blue and silver threaded through the marbled weapon and the blade had a strange patina that reflected oddly in the dappled light of the folly.

The snap of a nearby twig had me suddenly on my guard. Quickly releasing the energy, I let the Source flood back into my system, bringing the entropy with it. Snagging a book from my bag, I folded myself onto the bench, only just in time as a figure moved past the doorway. The blue and gold of an officer's uniform. An unusual elevation in status compared to my normal tails. I felt my brows knit together in consternation as I peered over the book, leaning forward slightly as I tried to see who it might be, but they seemed to be gone. Settling back, I felt my anxiety rising. If I'd been seen...

"What are you doing here?"

I jumped in shock at the soft voice behind me, jerking around to find Sendaryn standing, arms folded, scowling at me from the back of the folly, where the wall ended. My surprise was quickly replaced by anger and I felt heat rising in my face as I glared back at him.

"Up until you interrupted, I was enjoying a peaceful moment by myself. And, last I checked, I haven't yet been forbidden to go where I please."

I snapped my mouth shut, my brain abruptly catching up and berating me for my stupidity. Much as I hated him, Sendaryn was still an officer who could make life difficult and, more importantly, we were alone together in an out-of-the-way garden.

For a moment he didn't say anything, didn't move, but the creases around his eyes tightened in anger. Snapping my book shut, I grabbed my bag and started to move off, suddenly wanting to put as much space between us as possible. With lightning speed, he darted forward and grabbed my arm, stopping me in my tracks. My eyes widened, my entire body stiffening in revulsion at his touch.

"I didn't give you permission to leave," he hissed. "Nephael has been far too lenient and you've forgotten your place. Now, something is going on and I want some answers."

As his fingers latched on to the sleeve covering the mark, I wrenched out of his grip, quickly backing out of the folly, not wanting to be in an enclosed space with him. He unhurriedly followed after me.

Gripping my bag tightly, I continued to back away, trying to remain calm, keep my voice steady. "I don't need your permission to come and go, Sendaryn. Talk to the Council if you have a problem with that."

Shaken, I finally turned and hurried off in the direction of the main complex, casting a final glance over my shoulder as I exited the garden. Sendaryn hadn't moved, had made no move to follow, simply stood in the folly's entrance watching me.

Private Thoughts

"What are you drawing?"

The odd edge to Neph's voice, a sort of fascinated horror, brought me out of the foggy daze I'd been in. The pencil dropped from my numb fingers, rolled across the table and teetered on the edge before clattering to the floor. Neph picked up the sketchpad. After a moment of staring at the current piece, he began to leaf backwards, his face contorting the further he went.

"There are dozens of these," he whispered. "Going back weeks. They're…horrible."

With shaking hands, I snatched back the book.

Dragging a chair up next to me, Neph sat down, his eyes still glued to the paper.

"That's all that's in there," he said. "Why?"

There were a lot of individual questions packed into that singular one. And I couldn't answer any of them. My fingers clamped down on the sketchbook, full of pictures of the Depths. Monstrous creatures and places, rendered in disturbing detail. Some were things I'd seen, many of them not. It was all I'd been able to draw lately, all that came out when I picked up a pencil. Most of the time I wasn't even aware of what I'd drawn until I was finished. It had quickly become one of the more upsetting side effects of what I'd done.

I became aware of Neph's penetrating stare, now centered on me

340

rather than the grotesque drawings. I shook my head slightly and closed the cover.

"I - I don't know," I managed to stammer, swiftly pushing back and getting to my feet. "It just happens."

A violent quake struck and I collapsed back in the chair, unable to keep my feet in my weakened state. The Watch shuddered. The lights snapped out with an audible pop. From outside, the eerie light of the ley lines could be seen, now routine players in the outside drama. But they didn't seem to be fading out like they usually did.

Neph fought his way to the kitchen window as the quake continued, rattling furniture and threatening to knock artwork off the walls. His knuckles whitened as he gripped the counter. Lightning streaked across the dark, green-tinged sky.

"What's going on out there," I said, trying and failing to keep the tension out of my voice. I could feel something shift, a change in the energy. It was more Dark than Source and it was pulsing, flowing, moving towards some unknown point, sucking the life out of the surface as it moved.

"The lines," Neph said, audible fear in his voice. "They're black. They're everywhere."

As the quake finally subsided and the lights flickered back on, I staggered over to stand next to him, drawing in a sharp breath as I looked outside at the spider web of scrawling energy that crisscrossed the land, looking for all the world like an insane artist had scribbled across the landscape in black ink. One of the Source-powered lamps behind us gave an audible hiss and crackle and I turned towards the sound. The light had taken on a distinctly odd color, the soft blueish tinge of the Source replaced with an ugly purple-black.

I shuddered, feeling sick and exhausted, the Source ever further out of reach. Moving silently towards the bedroom, I left Neph to watch the ley lines. Ducking through the doorway, I grabbed at the Dark, tapping in like an addict. The shock of replacing energies was almost nonexistent at this point. I sighed in relief as the Dark flooded my system, rushing in to push out the sickness. I let it go just as quickly, knowing it would only hold me for a few short hours. Sitting on the edge of the bed, I scrubbed a hand across my dark-rimmed eyes, wondering when I'd last had a decent night's sleep that wasn't interrupted by dark dreams or physical pain.

After a few moments, I began to notice a creeping sensation moving up my spine. I looked up. Neph stood in the doorway, watching me, his face inscrutable.

I tried to smile, failed. His expression softened. Sitting down beside me, he took my hands, fingers twining through mine.

"Is there anything I can do? Anything I can get you?"

"No. I just need some rest."

He nodded slowly. "Piri, are you sure you don't want to talk?"

I pulled my hand away. "You keep asking that and I keep telling you no. My answer hasn't changed. There's nothing to discuss." Gods, that question was starting to bother me. I felt like it was a constant, nagging mantra ringing in the back of my mind as he tried to wear me down.

"You and I both know that isn't true."

I moved to the window, not particularly wanting to look outside at the disturbed world, but it was better than meeting Neph's slightly accusing eyes. The blackened ley lines still spiderwebbed across the terrain and I somehow knew they wouldn't be going away this time. The mountain range looked dead, the land itself sick. Shadowy creatures scampered across the open ground before vanishing into the murk and dying trees. The once lush greenery of the Karthwyst range seemed to have faded and vanished when I wasn't paying attention; the carefully tended Seri gardens of The Watch, so close to a Source spring, the last remnants of what once was.

Even without an active connection, I could feel the energy coalescing somewhere farther than I could see, farther than I'd flown. Did it look like this everywhere? Was it worse closer to the buildup? And what about the human territories? They were surely dealing with the same decay and ruin, the same shadowy creatures stalking their lands. Yet they sided with the Brotherhood and moved against us, even as their world died alongside ours.

I leaned forward, resting my head against the cool glass, lost in my own world, feeling more isolated than ever. As awful as it had been, I'd always been at the center of things at Skycrest, as part of the original ENF. Down time had been a rarity, something I'd had to go out of my way to create. And now...now I was cut off from everything. Even Neph had stopped filling me in on the daily happenings. I had no idea what was going on outside of my own shrinking world. The only thing I knew for certain was the energy I could feel. The infection that was spreading through the world, building and coming to a head as it replaced the Source and drained the springs.

Everything since coming to The Watch had been different. So... normal. I'd done my best, but normal was something I still hadn't entirely come to terms with. I glanced over at Neph, still sitting on the bed, head in hands, lost in his own private thoughts. My stomach twisted. Neph had made me believe that normal was possible, made me realize that there was life beyond the world I'd been trapped in. He'd changed everything. And what good had come of it?

I gritted my teeth as I glared at the horizon, Vharga-covered fingers clenching into a fist, anger coursing through me. I didn't know exactly where or when it would happen, and I could only fantasize about how it would play out, but the revenge I was waiting for was coming and no amount of orders from the Council was going to stop me from getting it. The only person who could possibly stop me, break my will, was Neph. And I couldn't...*wouldn't* let that happen.

When the Source died, so would everything that made the Seri what they were. He couldn't come with me and if he asked me to stay, I wouldn't be able to leave. No, I had to do this alone. Just like I'd always done.

The Fight

Sitting on the secluded ledge, I leaned back against the statue's plinth and stared off into the distance. My gloomy mood was perfectly complimented by the perpetually dark clouds hanging down over the battered mountains. I rubbed at my shoulders, trying to ease the aching pain out of my exhausted muscles. I'd let go of the Dark some twenty minutes previous, after a rather short practice with it, and I could already feel the entropy settling in. I pushed down a spike of terror at what was happening to me. I didn't want to think about it. I just needed to focus on what was coming. I closed my eyes, once again running through various scenarios, as I'd done now for days.

A thump next to me brought me back from my fantasies. I glared at Neph, his officer's uniform crisp and vibrant against the darkness.

"What, so now *you're* following me around too," I snapped, instantly regretting my anger at the hurt look in his eyes.

Pulling an apple and a pastry out of his bag, he sat them on the smooth stone between us.

"I thought you might be hungry," he said quietly. "It was just a good guess that I found you here." He hesitated. "Do you want me to leave?"

I stared at the snack he'd brought, hating myself. Hating myself for hurting him.

"No," I whispered, picking at the pastry. "I'm sorry."

We sat in silence for a while. I couldn't help but remember when

345

we'd sat here together what seemed like ages ago, gazing out at a much different landscape. Sliding a tentative hand across the gap, I latched on to his fingers and felt him respond with a light squeeze.

"I have to get back," he said, leaning across to kiss the side of my head. "Sendaryn's got his hounds out trying to find you. You won't be alone here for much longer."

"Thanks," I muttered. "I'll head home shortly."

"Piri?" It was the briefest whisper. "You awake?"

I felt the bed compress slightly beside me and cracked my eyes open. Neph was finally back for the night. I was still awake, despite the late hour. It's not like I really slept anymore; an hour here, an hour there, afraid of what sleep brought. My dreams were so haunted by the Dark, consumed by the energy that I had opened myself up to. The dark bruise-like marks beneath my eyes were a testament to my perpetual exhaustion; an exhaustion kept at bay by the same thing that was causing it. When I wasn't tapping the Dark, my body was slowly dying. When I was - it was a different sort of death, just as slow and inevitable. My body was no longer my own; it felt like a stranger, a shell that I had borrowed.

An arm draped over my side, a warm body pressed into my back. I felt a twinge of guilt over earlier as I leaned into him, savoring his warmth and comfort, the only bright spot left to me.

"We'll get through this." I could feel his breath on the back of my neck as he whispered what had recently become his evening mantra over the past few weeks. It was more for him than it had ever been for me and I was fairly certain he'd have changed 'we' to 'I' if he'd really thought about it.

I rolled over and buried my face in his chest. It wouldn't be long before this would end. I didn't know when, but I'd know the sign when it came. With every day that passed, the energy grew stronger. By tapping into the Dark, I'd made myself more acutely aware of the changing world around me. By now I didn't need to look out the window to see what was going on. I could feel it in every fiber of my being: the springs nearly drained, the world falling into decay as its lifeblood vanished, the strange building of energy.

"So…are you ready to tell me what you've been hiding?"

I stiffened. My breathing froze. I forced myself to relax. He didn't know what I'd done. He couldn't know.

"I'm not hiding anything," I forced out. "How many times do I have to tell you that?"

"Until I believe you. And you're a terrible liar, you know that?"

"So I've been told," I said, somewhat sourly.

"I wish you'd tell me," he said with a sigh, pulling back and putting a hand under my chin. He tilted my head back, looked me in the eye. "I know there's more to what's happening than just that mark. Something changed that day you collapsed."

The sadness in his voice was almost unbearable and I nearly broke. But this wasn't something I could share. That was one wall that I couldn't let him inside. The end, for me, would be the same, but how it played out would change. I needed that strength of will. I couldn't lose that.

I looked away, no longer able to meet his gaze. If I looked any longer, I felt like those piercing blue eyes would see through me, rip out my secret.

"You just have to trust me," I said quietly. "Please. That's all I can ask, all I can tell you."

Neph pulled away. "I...do trust you. But you're making it hard."

I struggled to sit up and face him. Sat there for a moment, unhappily staring at him. He gazed back from under hooded eyes, lips drawn in a tight, angry frown. Lowering my head I finally whispered, "There - there is one thing. But knowing it isn't going to help anything."

He crossed his arms, didn't say anything, only continued looking at me expectantly. A harsh tremor shook The Watch and the lights briefly flickered as the energy of the Source spring was disrupted. Something crashed to the floor and shattered in the other room. I glanced out the window at the darkened sky, its low, black clouds shifting restlessly as they sped across the sky. In the far distance, lightning flashed, splitting the night. Out beyond the horizon, the monstrous energy gained in power even as the life energy of the surface world faded and died. I repressed a shudder.

"The end is coming, faster than anyone realizes. And you can't stop it," I said quietly. It was the truth. If only partial.

The silence dragged on as Neph narrowed his eyes. The quake increased in intensity for a moment and a sudden wash of nausea and weakness swept through me. I leaned forward, head bowed down to my knees, breathing heavily. Reaching out, I connected to the Dark ever so briefly, just the barest touch to try to soothe the symptoms. I did it almost unconsciously, immediately cursing myself for doing it in front of Neph. I felt the mark respond. Felt it jerk, the characters crawling slightly more erratically. Saw the faintest flash of light. Hard fingers curled around my wrist, jerking my arm forward as Neph grabbed me and pulled me up, his face coming close to mine.

"What in the hell is that supposed to mean?"

Fear streaked through me at his voice, at his grip. I didn't know if he was referring to what I had said or the mark. It didn't matter. I struggled to pull back, but he didn't let go, only loosened his fingers so they were no longer digging into my skin.

"Piri, I'm not going to lie," he said in a harsh voice. "I'm afraid, terrified. We all are. And you're right. We can't stop whatever is happening. We don't even understand it enough to pretend we could stop it. I can't stop what's happening to you anymore than I can what's happening outside of this room. But what scares me more than that is the fact that you know something, are somehow a part of this. You're asking me to trust you, but you won't talk to me. Won't trust me enough to tell me what's going on. I *want* to trust you. But sometimes I feel like half my job anymore is defending you and -," he pulled my arm up and his voice rose an octave, "THIS to everyone. Trying to convince everyone else when I haven't even convinced myself. I want to believe you when you say that you're not hiding anything. You have no idea how much it tears me apart. But you are and I *can't*." He let go, voice cracking. Refusing to look at me, he glared at the wall.

I reached out, fingers tentatively brushing against his hand. I was too terrified to say anything. He jerked his hand away.

Without another word, he swung his legs over the edge of the bed and stalked out of the room. I heard the soft swish of the main door sliding open, closing. I stared in stunned silence. For several moments I felt nothing, only numbness as the emptiness of the apartment closed in on me. Stumbling from the bedroom, I came to a halt in the living room, catching myself on the side of the couch as my legs started to give way. I grabbed at the Dark again, feeling strength course back through my system. Tears were beginning to form as I stared at the closed door, felt something inside myself starting to crack. I sank down on the couch, head bowed, fingers clutching at my hair.

The mark, which burned brightly on initial contact, settled into a faint luminescence as I held onto the energy, letting it simply trickle through my system. I'd become completely reliant upon it, craving it while at the same time loathing it. I didn't know if that was simply the mark at work or if I'd been speeding the process along with my secret practices. Not that I had much of a choice. I'd known when I'd made the decision to channel it that I'd crossed the point of no return. Loathing for the mark, for Merythalis, for myself nearly overwhelmed me as I sat hunched over on the couch.

I could never tell Neph that I'd done this, never tell anyone. And it wouldn't matter in the end anyway. I began to wander aimlessly about the apartment, not having any idea what to do with myself, desperately wondering where Neph had gone and what was going to happen when he came back. I found myself in the bathroom, in front of the mirror, staring at my haggard reflection, eyes brimming, hating what I was seeing. Gritting my teeth, I tried to summon my wings again, straining on the Dark, flooding my system as I channeled all my anger and grief into the effort. And, finally, they burst forth, the energy breaking through some internal barrier. I gasped, grabbing at the edge of the sink to steady myself as I looked in abject horror at the unfamiliar person now staring back at me. My once white wings were stained with black. The narrow area of energy where they connected near the shoulder blades was warped shadow. It looked like someone had injected the feathers with black ink that had soaked into the shafts and begun to spread outward. Patches of white could still be seen, some of the primaries still untouched, but the disease was spreading. I let go of the energy, wishing I'd left well enough alone as I sank down to the floor and they faded from sight.

I awoke cramped and aching, still sitting curled up on the bathroom floor, eyes nearly crusted shut from crying myself to sleep. Late morning light lanced through the windows, throwing pools of luminescence across the main living area. An area shrouded in silence. I uncurled, stretching, trying to rub life back into my limbs as I wandered into the bedroom, paused, quickly moved out into the living room. The apartment was empty. Neph was still gone.

A thread of panic. My knuckles whitened as I gripped the counter, staring out the window at the patchy sky. A brief tremor made me wander back across the room, searching for the source of the previous night's crash. I found it readily enough. A small earthenware vase I'd found in the market, its brightly glazed shards now scattered across the floor. I sighed as I picked up the pieces and placed them on the table, gingerly moving them about, wondering if I could somehow glue it back together. The mark caught my attention as its dim light briefly reflected off the glaze on one of the shards. I stared at it, barely registering what I was looking at. It was still lit. I was still connected. Had been all night. I tried to break it off, found that I couldn't. Much like the Source had been for me, it was now a constant undercurrent. I was horrified. I'd never expected to lose control over the tap. And then I realized that, physically, I was feeling, well…not normal, but nearly as strong as ever. It would never last though. I could still feel the underlying decay as the Dark now wore away at me, changed the very core of what I was. A creature of the Source could never survive without it forever. But I'd known that from the start. Resignedly pulling out a chair, I sat down, idly shifting the pieces about.

I heard the soft hiss of the door sliding open. My back was to the entryway and I froze with a shard in my hand, not turning. The sudden physical change wasn't something I could easily explain away. Everyone knew what a bad liar I was. But I certainly knew what it felt like to be sick, knew how to play it up. I didn't know what else I could possibly do.

The door swished shut and I could tell Neph was there, but he didn't say anything. As the silence dragged on, I felt my shoulders hunch forward, my fingers tighten around the broken ceramic, shaking slightly. I didn't, couldn't, turn around, my fears and insecurities keeping my eyes rooted to the table.

He entered the kitchen, made himself a cup of coffee, each movement slow and methodical, and then he came to the table and sat down across from me. For a moment neither of us said anything, did anything. Neph simply stared for a while at my arm. Then he reached out and slowly took the shard from my fingers.

"Shame," he whispered, "I liked that vase."

I pushed back from the table and stood up, suddenly annoyed.

"It's just a vase."

Neph stood up just as quickly, moving faster than I expected and caught my wrist, pulling me close and wrapping his arms around me. There was something about the way he was holding me though that seemed off, a tension in his stance, wound up tight as a spring.

"I spent the night thinking, trying to figure out what's been going on. What happened that day you collapsed." He paused. I didn't like where this was going. "I can really only come to one conclusion. You tapped the Dark."

My hands came up between us and I shoved him away, so hard that he nearly fell as he stumbled back several feet. I stared at him in rising horror as I backed away. With a sigh, he retook his seat at the table and sipped from his mug, running shaking fingers through his disheveled hair.

"So, I'm right. Gods above, Piri. Why didn't you tell me?"

My back hit the wall, stopping me short. "Why didn't I tell you? Are you insane?" I snapped my mouth shut, eyeing him fearfully. My hands were shaking and I clenched them into fists, willing them to stop. "What

352

are you going to do?" I finally whispered.

Neph frowned, looking genuinely confused. "Do? Like what? You think I'm going to turn you over to the Council? I'm not your enemy, Piri. How could you possibly think I'd do anything to hurt you? I might be angry and frustrated, but I think that's justified, considering. All I want right now is to talk, that's all."

I didn't move. "You know what they've done to people in the past. You know what they'll do to me -"

"I have no intention of allowing my partner to be executed," Neph said. "Which is exactly what will happen if someone like Sendaryn finds out." He frowned into the coffee. "Or just about anyone for that matter." He glanced up. "Would you please sit down?"

I was pretty sure he meant in a chair, but my shaking legs had other ideas as they finally gave way and I sank to the floor. How could he possibly just want to talk. Hatred of the Dark was practically an inborn part of the Seri culture. Hadn't we ended a nearly two hundred year long war with its denizens only a few short years past?

Giving up on a civil conversation at the table, Neph came over and settled himself down beside me on the floor, mug still in hand. "Can you control it?" he finally asked.

Control it. "I - I think so. Yes."

"Does it, does it change anything?"

I glanced sideways, alarmed at the odd question, but the pleading, hopeful look in his eyes... He thought I'd done it to save myself. Good. Better that he didn't know.

"No," I whispered. "It's still eating away. Like poison. The Source is still there, but it's a trickle, background noise." I shivered. "The Dark has replaced it and it's changing me. On a fundamental level. Given time, I don't know what it would eventually turn me into, what it would do to me." It didn't matter. I wouldn't live long enough to find out.

He eyed me critically, tentative fingers reaching out to stroke the side of my face. "You seem almost...healthy. You still look sick, but you're holding yourself differently. The illness seems superficial somehow. How are you planning - "

"I'm going to fake it," I interrupted, nervously picking at my sleeve. "What else can I do? As long as I look ill, I just need to keep everyone else convinced that I am. Stay in here as much as possible. If anyone else finds out, it's over." I stared down at my hands, letting a crackle of energy cross my fingers. "This energy is different, Neph. It's wild, chaotic...nearly as powerful as the Source. People were afraid of what I was before...this would terrify them. The Council wouldn't even hesitate to remove me. And...I can't let that happen. Not yet. Not before the end comes." I winced at my own words, shut my mouth.

Neph looked at me quizzically. "And then what?"

"What do you mean?"

He sighed and I could see him struggling to maintain his composure, his already stretched patience wearing thin. "And what happens when the end comes?"

I stayed silent, not knowing what to say.

His fingers reached out in the silence and pulled back the collar of my shirt to reveal the eerily-lit runes. I started to pull away, but stopped myself as he clamped down on the fabric, his eyes narrowing to slits. I slumped in resignation. Grasping his hand, I pried it off my collar.

"You want to see it? Fine."

In one swift motion, I pulled off my shirt, exposing the permanently lit scrawl across my upper body. Leaning my head back against the wall, I closed my eyes. I could hear Neph suck in a sharp breath as he looked at it, spread across my arm, chest, neck. His fingers brushed across my skin.

"What about your wings," he whispered. "Without the Source…"
He trailed off as I shook my head.

"They're gone."

The Atrium

Covered from neck to toe in an Old Kingdom Seri robe that I'd found stashed in the back of the closet, I slunk across an open walk, trying to work my way towards one of the few gardens that still looked vaguely alive. I hadn't been out of the apartment in a good week and I was going stir crazy, desperate for some fresh air. Looking around though, I couldn't say that being outside was helping. The black scrawl weaving its way across the landscape had finally made its way into The Watch, inching across the carefully tended grounds as the power of the spring waned.

I looked up at the stormy sky. It was only mid-morning, yet it could easily have been early evening. The garden lamps, now permanently lit in the perpetual twilight, flickered. Several went out and didn't come back on. Lightning arched across the sky, temporarily re-illuminating the area.

As I passed an atrium of sorts, an arm snaked out and, before I could react, dragged me inside. Reva slammed me up against the wall. Pressing me back, both hands on my chest, she looked me up and down in stony silence.

"Let him go, Reva. He might look terrible, but I'm pretty sure he hasn't turned into some sort of Dark monster."

I glanced over Reva's shoulder as she slowly let me go. Farryn sat on a stone bench on the edge of the shallow pond, shoulders hunched, staring at his reflection in the still water.

"Where have you been," Reva demanded, her voice cracking slightly. "We haven't seen you, haven't heard from you in weeks, not since you collapsed. There were all these awful rumors. And Sendaryn has been out for your blood and we have no idea why."

"I'm fine," I whispered, taking her hands and gently pushing her away. "Why are you here?"

"Why am I here? *Why am I here?!* That's your question? You vanish for weeks, dead for all we know. I tried to visit, but every time I went near your place I was stopped by Sendaryn's men. Then Nephael gets removed from the ENF with no explanation. We were all forbidden from trying to contact either -"

"Wait, what?" I stared at her, stunned.

She paused and took a hesitant step back. I reached out and grabbed her, my voice rising.

"What did you say about Neph?"

Farryn came over, putting an arm out, separating us.

"You didn't know?"

I shook my head. Sank to the ground. Farryn and Reva knelt down beside me, exchanging glances.

"Look, I probably don't have much time." I squeezed my eyes shut and dug my fingers into my hair. "Please just tell me what's going on."

"Piri…" Reva's hand touched my cheek. I batted it away.

"*Tell me, Reva!*"

"Calm down," Farryn said, lowering himself to the ground, leaning up against the wall next to me. "Nephael was removed as our officer about a week after your collapse. We were never told why and no one was willing to talk about it. He's been acting as a standard division officer. I heard he'd been temporarily removed from the Council as well. He didn't tell you any of this?"

"No. He didn't."

"Are you two ok?" Reva asked with no small manner of hesitation in her voice.

"We're fine," I snapped. "What else is going on?"

Reva sighed and dropped down with a thump.

"I suppose you haven't heard then that the army is going to march north after the Brotherhood. One last ditch attempt to stop whatever it is they're planning, wipe them out. Now that they've crossed into our territory." When I didn't respond, she continued, nervously picking at the hem of her uniform. "The human armies are on the move, with the Brotherhood at their head, from what the scouts have reported."

North... I felt my stomach twist. North, towards the energy buildup.

"Do you know where they're going?" I asked as calmly as I could manage.

Farryn shifted uncomfortably. "They're heading towards the great northern plains. Towards the Ancient's Ruins."

"When...?"

"Not long. A few days maybe? We're all just waiting for the Ruling Council to give the order. Piri, it's everyone, the entire army. Special units included. The full force." Reva tugged at her ponytail.

I got to my feet. The Ancient's Ruins. Farryn and Reva scrambled up after me.

Reva touched my sleeve. "Piri, please, you look awful. Tell me what's happened."

I shook my head. "I can't, Reva. I wish I could, but I can't. I need to get back." On a whim, I grabbed her in a swift, awkward hug. "Be careful. Please."

Farryn extended his arm and I took it, squeezing it lightly as we nodded to each other.

"I don't know what you're planning," he said softly, "but take care. I've known you too long and, whatever is coming, I don't think you're going to go quietly."

I felt my throat tighten as I looked at them, knowing it might be the last time I saw them. Realizing that, somewhere along the line, Farryn had somehow, unexpectedly, become my friend.

With a sharp nod, I ducked out of the atrium.

Farewell

I stormed into the apartment in high dudgeon, intent on getting answers from Neph. Somehow convinced that he should have been one hundred percent honest with me when I couldn't be with him. Why keep his transfer a secret from me; what purpose could it have served?

"Why didn't you tell me?" I demanded, slamming my hands down on the table. "About your transfer? About the army?"

Neph looked up, eyes red-rimmed, face hollow. I instantly deflated. Something was definitely off. My stomach sank.

"I didn't want to worry you," he whispered. "Things were bad enough without adding that into the mix."

"I still wish you'd told me," I said, unable to muster even a fraction of my former fury.

"And I wish you'd told me what you'd done. What you're planning. We all make mistakes." He leaned back with a sigh.

Ouch. Feeling incredibly guilty, I sat down.

"Neph…" I reached across the table and touched his hand. "When -"

"Tomorrow. The officers were informed not long after you left this morning."

I sat back, feeling like I'd been shot. Tomorrow. I had one night left with him. I'd thought I had longer, hadn't been expecting such short notice.

"They can't go. You can't let them," I said, voice breaking, grasping. "The Source is dying. If...when it dies, they'll be defenseless."

"They've all been training and outfitted with real steel. The Council has been preparing for the inevitable for quite a while now."

He lapsed back into silence, staring at the table top, absentmindedly rubbing at a smudge in the polish. My eyes began to well up as I watched him. I didn't know what to say, what to do, now that this day had finally come. A small voice in my mind was saying that this made things easier, would eliminate the temptation to throw it all away and spend the end with him. Another voice was fighting desperately against it, crying out for him to stay.

Pushing back from the table, I stood up and began to move fitfully around the apartment, at a loss. I finally found myself in the bedroom where I collapsed heavily on the edge of the bed, head in my hands. It wasn't long before Neph joined me, arms wrapping around my shaking body, pulling me into a crushing embrace.

"There are things I have to do, preparations to be made. Meetings. I'll be back in a few hours. I don't have a choice."

"Please don't." I choked back a sob. "There's too little time."

He squeezed harder. "We'll have tonight. It'll have to be enough."

Curled up against Neph's side, I wistfully ran my fingers over his bare skin, knowing this would be it. He'd be gone come morning.

"You know, I could stay. Forget the army and stay with you. We could wait it out together."

It took me a moment to register his words and, when they finally broke through, they brought a wash of panic with them. He couldn't. If he stayed, I knew now that I would never leave.

"You can't, Neph," I forced out as calmly as I could manage. "You know what will happen afterwards if you don't go. I'll see you soon. When you get back."

"Yeah. Afterwards…" His voice trailed off, laced with uncertainty.

I could hear the unspoken question, bit my lip to keep from crying. Pulling away, Neph sat up. Reaching out, he brushed aside a stray wisp of my hair, his hand pausing ever so briefly before pulling away.

"Piri, swear to me that you've been telling me the truth. About everything: the mark, what's coming, your wings…"

I took his hand, running my fingers across it, tracing it in my mind, every line, every detail.

"I've told you what I can," I said sadly, choosing my words carefully. "And I promise that we'll see each other soon."

He laughed and I could hear the underlying incredulity. "Sticking to your lie right up to the very end. I trust that it's worth it."

I opened my mouth to reply, but, leaning in, he never gave me the opportunity.

I awoke to the fitful light of dawn in a panic, snapping out of a nightmare-laden sleep, terrified that Neph was gone. My fear only intensified as I rolled over and met emptiness beside me. Throwing on a robe, I dashed from the room.

Neph sat at the table, already fully in uniform. He glanced up, face a carefully controlled mask, but I could see cracks forming as he looked at me.

"I have to go soon." He stood up.

Racing over, I slammed into his chest and threw my arms around him, squeezing like my life depended on it. His arms curled around me.

"Please don't do anything stupid," he whispered.

"Only if you promise not to get yourself killed."

Loosening his grip, he pulled out of the embrace, resting his forehead against mine. I closed my eyes, not wanting to see the tear tracing its way down his cheek.

"I love you, Piri. I'm so sorry that things turned out this way. But I want you to know that I wouldn't change a moment with you."

"I love you too," I managed to choke out. "And…I'm sorry. For everything."

"Don't be."

Leaning in, he kissed me, lips lingering until a knock on the door signaled his imminent departure.

I stood staring at the door in heavy silence after he'd gone. A lifetime seemed to pass before I finally broke away, crawled back into bed and broke down.

For nearly two days I wandered the apartment, alone, feeling like I was drowning in the emptiness. The Seri army, the only concentrated Source energy left, was a fiery blaze in my mind's eye as it moved farther north. The Watch felt utterly deserted with only its civilian body remaining and the fear permeated the air.

Feeling like nothing was changing, I was beginning to seriously question my judgment, wondering if I'd been wrong. If I'd misjudged it all. Maybe the Source would just die and take all of us with it. A slow death with no final confrontation.

It was as I was wondering this, for perhaps the thousandth time, that the power died and The Watch went dark. On the edge of my senses, I felt the far-flung energy surge, felt a massive shift. And right then, I knew I'd been right. Knew that the sign I'd been waiting for had finally arrived and that my time to act had come.

The heavy silence around me began to subtly change as the Source-reinforced architecture began to settle under the stress. I prayed it was built well enough to survive without it.

Taking a deep breath, I moved to the kitchen, climbed onto the counter and reached out to the massive window. I closed my eyes, steeling myself as I tried to destabilize the glass. It cracked, shattered.

I stared vacantly at the shards littered around me. Soon it would all come to a head.

It was time to leave.

A Dying Land

I streaked across the landscape, my figure casting a pale shadow across the cracked and blackened earth far below me. How long had it been since I'd been up in the sky? I shivered in apprehension as I cast around, staring in shock at the dead and dying earth. I had felt it happening, my own body mirroring the change on a much smaller scale, but seeing it from above was an entirely different matter. What had once been lush greenery looked like a post-apocalyptic wasteland. The scrawling blackness didn't just crawl across the land. It *was* the land. A poison spreading its inky fingers over the world as it smothered it in a deadly embrace. I stared ahead, my eyes following the line of darkness to where it all converged, paving my path forward like a golden road towards the intense mass of energy looming somewhere beyond the horizon.

I sighed and closed my eyes, trying to lose myself in the feeling of the air rushing across my skin, through my hair and wings. Trying, if only for a moment, to forget what was spread out below me and ahead of me. I reached out, trying to pinpoint the Seri army. Their presence, so much a beacon for the past few days, was now just barely detectable far off in the distance. They still felt like the one last concentrated point of Source energy, lost in a sea of shadow, but it was fading quickly. Soon it would be gone, leaving them stranded and vulnerable. My eyes snapped open as I put on a fresh burst of speed.

I was pushing myself at a dangerously fast pace, with all the Dark force I could muster. As I banked slightly, correcting my course, I chanced a glance at my feathers, wincing at their now pitch black state, looking more like coalesced shadow than anything grounded in reality. It was the final indication that the Source was well and truly beyond my reach. The mark glowed with its eerie, pulsing light, the figures jerking erratically as they crawled across my skin. I held a hand up in front of my face, pulling on the Dark, now as strong in my system as the Source had ever been, and watched as the sinister energy crackled across my fingertips.

The mountainous landscape of my home quickly gave way to low hills and then to rolling countryside, all barren and dying, crisscrossed with the streaking blackness. Seri outposts and holds were dark and silent beneath me, their Source springs shut down, their life-blood drained. Farmer's fields lay in crumbling ruin, terraced farms brown and blackened. Crossing over human-controlled territory, I sped back into Seri, through Ellundara and Khazda lands, all dead or dying. And then I was in no man's land, flying across the great plains of the Ancients, dotted with primordial ruins and crumbling stone. Even I had never been to this place. It was a forgotten land that few visited. Whether out of fear or respect, most were content to let its ghostly city lie in undisturbed ruin. From so far above, with the land falling into darkness, I couldn't help but notice, with a slight shiver, the unsettling similarity to the frozen metropolis in the Depths.

The land before me was suddenly peppered with figures and I felt my eyes widen as the armies were suddenly spread out before me. The Seri, their colorful uniforms in stark contrast to the surroundings, had fought valiantly against a far greater human host. Despite the numbers, the Seri should have been winning, but the dying Source was taking its toll. I felt a brief burst of pride that they had thrown themselves into what they had surely known was a losing battle. Coming out here had been a pointless venture and I liked to believe the Seri had recognized it. They had gone out of desperation, hoping there was something they could do, some final desperate act that would save their world.

The battle seemed to have been temporarily suspended. The two forces were spread across the landscape, neither moving as they faced each other, commanding officers from both sides, in a frozen moment of peace, standing shoulder to shoulder and staring at the anomalous scene before them. Both sides seemed to sense that something major was changing. Whatever hold the Brotherhood had over the human forces seemed to be collapsing under the sudden weight of fear.

My feathers flared as I spread my wings to their fullest and slowed myself, wanting to take everything in, what I was actually flying into.

Ahead, the land suddenly fell away into Ethringar, the great cliff, the endless chasm. It stretched as far as the eye could see, a scar that ended the plains, and crossing the chasm was the great stone bridge of the Ancients. At its terminus, the lone mountain rose from the watery depths; behind and surrounding it, the sea. I could feel the energy pulsing from it, knew that the Source spring within its base, a spring so old and wild that no Seri would dare try to harness it, had been completely corrupted. The scene was otherworldly and strange. Stranger still was the line of hooded figures on the cliff edge. The Brotherhood, a thousand of them, with arms raised, knives glinting dully.

I slowed to a stop, holding myself stable as I gazed out at the mountain. The sky had turned an ugly shade of purple; unnatural and dark. Black clouds roiled over the angry sea, lightning flashing in the distance. This was the epicenter. The blackness that now covered the land in snaking tendrils was a solid mass here, covering everything, leeching away any remaining color and sucking life itself back into the depths of the mountain.

The energy was coalescing, growing and pulsing and I tried to withdraw, pull myself away from the sensation, feeling sickened. Suddenly it calmed, quieted. The throbbing pulse silenced. I glanced around, unease growing inside of me. And then without warning, in the brief stillness that followed, I felt the Source die. I gasped in shock, despair washing over me as the last vestige of energy vanished. Below me, human soldiers staggered, dropped to their knees as even they felt the life force of their world vanish. The pain and panic from the Seri, such an intimate part of it, was nearly tangible as their weapons dematerialized and their wings faded. Their cries could be heard even from my height. .

The ground began to quake and the pulsing of the Dark resumed, audible now as a resounding shriek that cut to the bone, and my attention was drawn back to the mountain. Dark cracks began to trace their way up the mountain's surface. Massive chunks of rock breaking away to tumble crashing down into the swirling waters. A single figure stepped away from the others lining the cliff. I screamed out a warning, but it was too late. The leader of the Brotherhood raised a hand, called out in the language of the Dark, a single word that his followers bellowed in unison with him as their knives flashed down and, as a single unit, they collapsed to the earth, blood pooling beneath them. Once again, all sound momentarily died. Only the harsh, insane laughter of the Brotherhood's leader, the only survivor, filled the void. As his laughter reached a crescendo, a shock wave exploded from the mountain, radiating outward, and knocking many off their feet as a creature burst forth from the dark entrance leading down to the spring. It was a hellish, monstrous nightmare of energy, curling itself around the stone, encompassing the mountain as it rose upward and filled the sky. My heart nearly stopped as Merythalis rose above the land, summoned to the surface world, its body a writhing, swirling mass of dark energy. Behind it, the ocean churned into a vortex and the physical world began to waver as the shifting, swirling maelstrom of the Depths became visible. Its dark form crackled as lighting streaked down and was sucked into the depths. My breath caught in my throat and I put my hands to my ears, trying to drive out the roaring shriek of the whirlpool that now filled the air.

Screams erupted below me. I looked on in horror as a giant clawed hand reached out, slammed down among the human armies on the cliff edge, which were now breaking, those still able fleeing in terror. Seri commanders were desperately trying to keep the lines even as they motioned a retreat, soldiers madly unsheathing metal weapons. Even as they tried to flee, shadowy creatures rose from the ground, hemming in both sides. Claws and teeth flashed as they drove into the

368

crush, lashing out indiscriminately at anything in their path. Screams erupted, intensified. The battle suddenly became a fight for the lives of humans and Seri alike. Fear shot through my system as I looked on. Neph was down there, somewhere in that chaos. I had to stop this.

Like a dark arrow, I shot across the remaining distance, aiming for the bridge, where I would make my last stand. Soldiers below

stopped, gaping upward as I passed over them. I sped out over the cliffs where the land fell away, dropping down into a distant abyss with the sea itself cresting over the edge into endless, roaring falls. Dropping out of the sky, I slammed down on the ancient stone, wings spread, feathers flared wide. I rose and stared up at the creature before me.

Interludes: On The Brink

Reva pushed her way through the Seri army, elbowing past openly terrified soldiers. Those not fighting the shadow creatures were staring in unconcealed terror at the figure now dominating the skyline. They were deprived of both power and flight, and struggling to maintain their composure. She had to find Nephael. If only she could fly, finding him in the crowd would have been a moment's task. But he would be with the other commanders and she generally knew where they were located. And so she kept pushing forward, forcefully moving people out of her way, faster now that she had sighted a familiar shock of blond hair.

"Sir...I think you're going to want to see this." Reva's hand grabbed his shoulder as she moved up beside him, not stopping, but simply pulling him back towards where she had started. Shouldering her way through the final group of soldiers blocking her path, all staring aghast at the behemoth that filled the sky, she suddenly stopped, bringing him to a halt with her. Neph frowned, peering over her shoulder, but having no idea what she could possibly want to show him or why she had suddenly come to a halt before they had even reached the cliff edge. What was there to see? The form of Merythalis was visible from anywhere you stood. The maelstrom of the Wild Dark

stretching out behind it, merging with the above-ground world, which was now slowly dying as it took over, the Source shut down. It was a living nightmare. Reva's face twitched slightly and she looked away, wrestling with some inner emotion. Neph squared his shoulders.

"*Trevanys.*" The name was a barked command and she instantly straightened, looking him in the eye. What he saw there wasn't something he wanted to see. The pain was visible as she stared back at him and he suddenly went cold.

"He's down there," she said quietly.

"Piri…" he whispered, dread suddenly coursing through his body. Swallowing hard, Reva grabbed his arm and pulled him to the edge of the cliff. The rest of the ENForcers lined the rim, at the head of the military, all staring in mute silence at the ruins far in front and below them. Throwing out her arm in the direction of the bridge, Reva jerked her head. She didn't need to say anything else. There he was, a tiny figure in the distance, standing at the head of the massive bridge, black wings shining with the light of the Dark, feathers spread wide. Numbness crept through Neph's body as his hand reached up, fingers tightly clenching the front of his uniform.

"He lied to me, right up to the end. And I knew it," he said, his voice catching in his throat. "And now there's nothing that I can do. Except stand here and watch."

A glaive flared to life in the dark figure's hand, the flash drawing their attention back to the scene, the weapon as black as the wings. The tip of the blade dipped, touching the stone of the bridge. Merythalis's eyes, mountain-high, suddenly snapped to the small form, its attention instantly drawn to its challenger.

Final Confrontation

Merythalis waited. Across the bridge, towering, monolithic. It wrapped around the mountain itself and perched on the edge of the vortex. I took a deep breath, glancing back. I tried to imagine that I could just barely pick out a tiny figure standing at the edge of the cliff in the distance, the army spread out behind him. Panicking. I shut my eyes, trying not to think about Neph. Trying not to think about what I was about to do. Trying not to think. Because I knew, if I did, that I would turn back and let the world come to ruin if I could only spend one last moment with the person I loved. I didn't know what was going to happen. I wasn't sure if I would survive; I didn't know how I possibly could. But this was what I had been waiting for. Merythalis had branded me and, in doing so, I was sure that I had also been given the only means to defeat it.

I reached out in one last attempt to find what I knew wasn't there. But I kept pushing my senses, trying in vain to find some indication of the Source. I wanted to feel it one last time, but I knew it was gone. The energy of the Dark coursed through my system as I pushed harder, stretching further, to the limits of my abilities. There was nothing. Nothing but the void and the Darkness that was coursing in to fill the vast emptiness.

The mark pulsed as I spread my wings, feathers dark as the void. I'd worn my uniform, the pure white shining in stark contrast to my midnight wings and the crawling mark on my bare arm, now glowing fiercely. Let the creature see what it had given me; the curse that was slowly killing me, the gift that would be both my revenge and its downfall.

The shock of energy I sent out as I dropped my blade wasn't large, but it was enough to get the creature's attention. The full focus of Merythalis shifted to me, eyes narrowing to slits, the mouth sliding open into a silent snarl, revealing its sharp teeth. My anger flared, resolve hardening as I stared upwards, all thought of what was behind me suddenly driven away as hatred coursed through my veins. The mark flared violently as energy crackled around me.

In the background, the raging maelstrom jerked and writhed, its interior shifting and changing. A window into the Depths. Glimpses of the ruined city could be seen through the vortex, the eerie, glowing eyes of its residents shining through. And they weren't the only eyes that could be seen. As the barrier between the two worlds thinned, the Masters began to appear, drawn like moths to a flame. Monstrous dark, horned figures reached upwards, eyes shining in anticipation.

Ignoring everything else, focused entirely on me, Merythalis's mood shifted like quicksilver and the corners of its mouth suddenly snapped up as it began to laugh, the sound deafening in such close proximity. I didn't care, let it laugh. I was more interested in the gleaming blue veins running throughout its form. Merythalis was no longer purely a creature of the Dark. That was Source energy, stolen and incorporated into its very being. It had been warped and corrupted, bent to the whim of the Dark, but, at its core, it was still the Source. And I was going to take it back.

Launching myself at breakneck speed, I slammed my glaive into the creature's side, sending an explosion of crackling energy cascading outwards. Its previous amusement evaporated in an instant. One massive hand swung towards me at incredible speed, outstretched claws swatting ineffectually as I wove between its swings, dodging out of its reach, burning through energy as I desperately avoided a swift death. Soaring high, wings pumping furiously, I reached a peak, flipped over and pushed myself into a steep dive, driving the Dark down through my weapon in a furious burst as I once again crashed into Merythalis, the impact numbing my hands. Howling in rage, but, to my dismay, seemingly unaffected, Merythalis turned its attention back towards the cliffs.

Lightning streaked down from the sky and crashed into the ground, scattering soldiers and sowing panic. Reaching out, Merythalis ground its clawed fingers into the earth. The ground shuddered, quaked, and the black inky scrawl covering the land writhed. Like a ghostly afterimage, the city of the Depths began to waver in and out of existence, overlaying the Ancient's Ruins, casting a pall over the area. Time seemed to slow. I cast a fearful glance over my shoulder as the maelstrom's shriek rose to an ear-shattering pitch, the creatures within clawing and struggling to tear free.

I could feel real fear beginning to rip at my insides. This wasn't working. Throwing my polearm to the open air, letting it dissolve away, I grabbed at the Dark with all the force of panic to drive it. Energy began to crackle across my skin as I pulled on the energy, shaping and bending it, forming it into something I could use. Cracks flared on my hands as the energy coalesced and I gritted my teeth against the pain, feeling the blood begin to run down my fingers. Burning under my skin. Sucking in a sharp breath, I let it go.

The searing globe of concentrated energy smashed into the

nightmarish apparition before me. I was rewarded with a genuine bellow of pain, though my triumph faded quickly. Pulling its claws free, raking up the earth and tearing through the armies, Merythalis rounded on me with a deafening snarl. I pulled back, quailing under the fury of its gaze.

Monstrous arms gripped the mountain, muscles bulging beneath morphed shadow skin. Pushing itself up, Merythalis seemed to grow even larger, filling my vision as it loomed over me, unwinding its sinewy, serpentine form. With a speed I never imagined possible, it launched itself towards me, mouth stretching wide, monolithic wings of smoke and shadow unfolding from its back. I tried to push myself backwards, unable to keep the brief scream of terror from escaping my lips as it rushed towards me, the worst of my nightmares. I barely had time to register the hand that hurtled forward, striking me with the force of a mountain. Something cracked, tore. Pain shot through my body as I hurtled out across the maelstrom, vision blurred, black around the edges. Gasping for air against the pain in my side, chest.

The wind whistled through my wings, limp feathers trailing upwards in my downward fall, the swirling arms of the vortex visible through them as I wavered on the edge of consciousness and they began to lose their form. My mind screamed, panic tearing through every fiber as I swept below the outer rim of the whirlpool, gaining speed as I plummeted. I grabbed desperately for the Dark, pulled on it with everything I had, felt it burn through my system as my wings flared back to life, snapped out. I nearly screamed at the tearing sensation that ripped through my body as I pulled out of my fall, banking to the side and speeding out over the void. The creatures below me clawed at the barrier, straining towards me as I rushed over them. The crash of thunder overhead, the shriek of the whirlpool below, Merythalis's roar from behind as it pursued me. I pushed harder, picking up speed, feeling blood streaming down my side, every muscle screaming in pain.

Pulling around in a sharp turn, ignoring my injuries, I went back after Merythalis. Claws raked my arm, my face as I got too close, releasing a pulse of devastating energy that caused it to reel back. Calling back my glaive, I struck out, launching it through the air, watching it connect with an explosion of electricity. But it wasn't doing any lasting damage. Nothing was.

My anger from earlier, my craving for revenge, had dissolved into blind panic. Circling back over the mountain, I dropped to a craggy outcrop, my breath coming in ragged sobs. My fingers, torn and bleeding and still crackling with raw energy, grasped the edge of the rocky precipice. Hunching down, I squeezed my eyes shut, despair washing over me. I had played out a thousand different scenarios in my mind and none of them had prepared me for failure. I wasn't strong enough, couldn't drag enough power forward to win this fight. The Source, stolen and corrupted as it was, was still stronger than the Dark. And it belonged to Merythalis. Infused within every fiber of its being.

Merythalis's manic laughter broke through into my mind, a rising crescendo that echoed across the plains. I gritted my teeth, hands clenching at my head as I tried to shut it out. It rose in intensity, a physical pain that blocked out the rest of the world.

"You have lost, Little Seri."

I shook my head, could feel hot tears slip down my cheeks as the pain became almost unbearable.

"I told you in the beginning that it would end this way. You would submit or die."

I looked up, vision blurred around the edges, the world tinged red. Merythalis, a nightmare vision, hung before me, filling the sky. Blazing blue energy crackled and writhed within its massive frame. Beneath it, the great maelstrom roared as it circled, great arms swirling across the visible ocean. The dark forms within it jerked and twisted, ever struggling upwards, now truly visible in the chill air as the barrier broke down and they began to claw their way to the surface.

"Look around you. This world is over and this is your last chance. You have already given in to the energy, forsaken what you were. You can save yourself, destroy everything that hurt you. You are unique, powerful, the likes of which have not been seen in your culture in many thousands of years. Would you throw that away, waste that power?"

No.

I locked eyes with the creature before me. Its mouth widened into a sickly grin, sharp teeth flashing in the eldritch light.

"Give in. You are more than this. Take the power. Use it."

My lips pulled back, matching Merythalis's. It was right.

I staggered to my feet, one hand clutching at an open wound across my chest, ignoring a hundred other bleeding lesions. The ground beneath me was stained red where I'd crouched.

Spreading my wings, I launched myself skyward, black wings glistening as the lightning broke the sky. I brought myself level with the giant gleaming eyes. They narrowed as the smile widened.

"Join me, Little Seri. You could become one of the Masters. Join your kin and unleash your true power."

Yes.

My eyes widened. That was the way forward.

I slowly turned my head, glancing back at the cliff, the plains stretching away to the horizon. Minuscule figures scrambled about, fighting for their lives against the creatures of shadow, struggling back from Ethringar as the claws of the Masters grasped for the cliff edge. Some, those closest to the precipice, stood frozen as they watched our performance play out. Regret and sorrow coursed through me as I viewed the scene. I crushed it. Merythalis laughed again as it watched me.

"Come, be more than you are. I understand you, little one. Take the power."

I exhaled slowly and turned back, glaring.

"Maybe you're right," I whispered. "But you don't understand me as well as you think."

Spreading my arms wide, I opened myself up to the mass of energy around me, pushing out into the void as the Dark swept the land and let the flame, already burning so brightly inside, consume me. I screamed as the energy raged through me, transformed me.

I could feel the Vharga awaken, felt them pulse and clamber across the rest of my body as they exploded outward. The raging whirlpool surged upwards, the smoke and shadow twisting and curling as it reached towards me. I drew in the power, laughing bitterly through the pain as it filled me. The air around me began to shimmer and glow, electricity sizzling across my skin.

Merythalis's smile faltered. The veins of pure Source that coursed through its body flared brightly, expanding and coalescing into a vibrant vortex at its center.

"What is this," the voice snarled.

The air around me crackled with violent energy. I could feel it reaching out, pulling on the Source. Could feel the Source pulling back, suddenly reacting to this new threat. The space between us began to warp and twist.

379

What was it that I had told Reva a lifetime ago?

The Source will always reassert itself.

"You stole everything from me," I hissed. With a monumental burst of energy, I plunged towards the figure.

I briefly registered Merythalis jerk backwards in surprise and shock as my outstretched fingers connected, split its skin, sank into the shadow. And touched the Source. With a wrenching that felt like it would tear me apart, the Dark rushed through my body, now nothing more than a conduit, spreading outward and merging with the Source. For a brief instant, there was nothing. Silence. Reality distorted, time slowed. And then the world around me exploded.

Alive

The mountain was gone, its shattered remains crumbling into the turbid, raging sea. Pieces of the monolithic bridge fell into the chasm, crashing through the waterfalls. The cliffs themselves threatened to collapse as the ground quaked. The ancient spring beneath the remains of the mountain roiled, bubbling to the surface, exposed to the open air for the first time ever. A beam of steely blue light pulsed in the depths before erupting upwards into the atmosphere in an explosion of thunderous noise.

Neph hit the crumbling remnants of the bridge hard, dropping from the sky to land in a stumbling run as he made his way towards the prone figure he'd sighted from the air, half buried in rubble and ruin. Still. Bloodied.

Coming to a skidding halt, he dropped to his knees, hands reaching forward and stopping mere inches from the limp, sodden bundle. He could feel tears starting to etch their way through the blood and grime that coated his face. He wanted nothing more than to reach out, grab the body, hold it close. But he hesitated, knowing that once he did, the physicality of the situation would make it all too real.

His trembling hand finally settled on Piri's head, fingers running through blood-soaked hair. Neph bowed his head, gritted his teeth.

He could feel his control slipping, breaking. He barely noticed Larkyn drop down next to him, hardly registered the shocked intake of breath as he knelt down, fingers splayed outward, already feeling for what no one else would have been skilled enough to find. It was only when Larkyn forcefully pushed his way in, shoving Neph sideways and placing his hands upon Piri's chest that Neph finally looked up, grief-stricken, eyes widening.

"This isn't possible," Larkyn feverishly muttered to himself. "Impossible. There shouldn't even have been a body after that." He closed his eyes.

Neph could feel the shock-wave surge of energy as Larkyn pushed with everything he had, flooding the still form. With a ragged gasp, Piri's body arched upwards, painfully dragging in air, coughing, bloody bubbles bursting at the corners of his mouth, before once again settling, looking just as broken as before. But breathing. Alive.

Larkyn was still mumbling to himself as he probed the extent of the damage, eyes darting frantically back and forth, gaze turned inward, seeking some inner source. Suddenly snapping back to the present, he turned to Neph.

"Can you carry him? We need to move fast."

Visibly shaking, tear tracks etched down his cheeks, Neph simply stared at Piri, hardly daring to believe what he was seeing.

"*Nephael!*"

Neph shook his head ever so slightly, reaching out with trembling fingers to touch the body. Alive. Larkyn roughly grabbed him around the forearms and violently shook him.

"Listen to me, you can fall apart later. Right now, he's alive, but just barely. And he's not going to be if we don't get him back and get a team working. I can only stabilize that sort of damage by myself for a short time. Can you carry him or not?"

"I -...yes."

382

Without another word, they began to hastily clear away the rubble, uncovering the rest of the body. As gently as he could manage, Neph wrapped his arms around Piri's upper body and under his legs, lifting him clear of the debris. As they stood, the remains of the bridge rumbled beneath their feet.

"This thing isn't going to last much longer," Larkyn said, nervously eyeing the ground. "Come on. As fast as we can. Whatever city is closest and still has healers. Forget the army."

I opened my eyes, the merest fraction. Closed them just as quickly as the full light of day assaulted my senses. I opened them again, slowly. For a moment I couldn't register who I was or where I'd woken up. I moved my fingers, grasping at the cool sheets covering my body, rubbing my thumb over light, cotton pants. I could barely move, but I was alive. My mind had difficultly registering the notion and, for a brief moment, rejected it altogether. There had been Merythalis and the light. And then…nothing. Nothing?

There was a shift in weight beside me, warmth against my side. I struggled to turn my head, vision blurring, head swimming at the movement. As if that shift had somehow flipped a switch, my brain suddenly decided to register that the rest of my body existed. And it appeared to be intact. Searing pain raced through my system. Every muscle, every nerve seemed to be on fire. The old scar on my back throbbed. I felt broken, destroyed.

I couldn't help the whimper that escaped my lips. And in that instant, I realized that it was Neph beside me, wedged up against me like he was trying to become a part of my anatomy. Neph throwing down the book he'd been reading, suddenly on his knees, hands cupping my face, tears openly streaming down his cheeks as he began to laugh in overwhelming joy and relief.

I closed my eyes again, gritting my teeth against the pain raging through my body. Sharper sensations stood out in the agony: Neph's fingers against my skin as he brushed the hair from my forehead, his thumb moving across my cheek, a hand coming to rest on my chest. Every time he touched my broken body, a shock would streak through that area, lighting it up. But I didn't care. I relished the touch. I was alive.

Epilogue: Dissension

Arafel leaned around the door frame and rapped hesitantly on the wood.

"Hey Nephael...can we talk?"

Neph raised his head from his hand, pushing the paperwork in front of him to the side. He'd been staring at it without actually seeing it for the better part of an hour. It had been six weeks since Piri's confrontation with Merythalis, one week since he had awoken from the coma-like state he had been found in following the battle. He was sleeping at the moment, peacefully thanks to Larkyn. And Neph felt more exhausted than he ever had. He'd barely rested the entire time Piri had been unconscious, afraid that something might happen while he slept, terrified that he would lose him. And now that he was awake, out of the danger zone, Neph was realizing just how much the stress had worn him down. With the flood of relief and the release of all the emotion he'd pent up for over two months, he was burnt out. And he could just tell by the tone of Arafel's request that whatever this talk was, it wasn't going to help his mental state.

He leaned back, glaring at the figure filling the doorway. Arafel quietly crossed the room and slid into the chair across from him, not meeting his eyes. They sat in silence for several minutes.

"Well? What do you want?" Neph couldn't help the words coming out with a curt snap.

Arafel's eyes briefly darted towards the closed door leading to the bedroom.

"How is he?"

"Alive," Neph said in an angry whisper. "Time will tell past that."

Silence fell once more, Arafel becoming more agitated as the seconds dragged by. He began picking at a corner of Neph's paperwork, still refusing to look at him. Neph finally reached across the table and snatched the paper out of his fingers.

"Araf, don't take this the wrong way, but you're starting to piss me off. I'm absolutely exhausted and my temper is wearing thin. And I'm guessing that whatever you want to tell me isn't going to improve my mood. So spit it out."

"I - fine. I wanted to talk to you about Enpirion. I've got some… concerns."

"Concerns," Neph snorted. "You made your 'concerns' known ages ago."

Arafel pushed his chair back slightly, putting a bit more distance between himself and Nephael.

"Look, I've kept mostly quiet about this. As you well know, I can't say I've supported this relationship, but I've tried to keep my views to myself. This isn't personal."

"Like hell it isn't," Neph angrily interrupted. "You can't be serious."

Arafel took a deep breath and continued. "Look, I know that you love him, but you're absolutely blinded to the situation because of it and someone needs to open your eyes. I think it's time that you took a serious look at what Enpirion really is."

He plowed on before Neph could interrupt again, pushing his chair even farther back at the dangerous light that was beginning to gleam in Neph's eyes. He held up his hands defensively.

"I know he's being lauded as a hero right now, but what happens

when that wears off? Have you actually thought about what took place with Merythalis? The power he manipulated? The fact that he survived something that, by all rights, not only should have killed him, but probably shouldn't have left any remains for us to even identify? You're as aware as I am of what the ENForcers were originally. He was a living weapon, Nephael. An unstable, living weapon. Have you actually read his file? He's supposed to be your subordinate, so I can only assume that you have."

"What is your point exactly?" Neph's voice was quiet, flat, emotionless. Arafel knew he was on the border of pushing him over the edge, but he took another deep breath and continued.

"My point is that he has a fairly lavish history of unstable behavior. Insubordination, depression, recklessness." He pulled a file out from under his robes and slid out a heavily redacted sheet. "And have you seen any of the classified stuff from during the Uprisings? Read about some of the missions he carried out, the atrocities he committed in the name of war? And forgetting all of that, I know there's something in there that you haven't seen because I only recently managed to get my hands on it. It's some of his childhood case file. There's a reason the military nabbed him so early. He was barely five years old when they started training him. He had already gained total control of the Source earlier than that."

"Where did you get this?" Neph interrupted, trying and failing to snatch the file from Arafel's fingers.

"It - it doesn't matter." Arafel guiltily looked away, once again refusing to make eye contact. "What matters is that the group in charge of the ENForcers knew from the start that he was abnormal, even for a living Spring. They took him, conditioned him, trained him. He's not normal, Nephael, not even close. And don't think for a minute that Sendaryn isn't already planting the seeds among his closest followers about how dangerous Enpirion is. None of us are stupid. We've all figured out what he managed to do. Nephael, he harnessed the *Dark*. Channeled it and used it as a Source replacement. And, on top of it, he lied to you, to everyone about it."

"Can you really blame him?" The pain in Neph's voice was audible. "The mark was killing him, Araf. If he hadn't done what he did, none of us would be alive. We wouldn't even have a world to worry about being part of."

"Look, there's...there's also a disturbing precedent for his powers."

"Oh come off it, Arafel," Neph said in exasperation. "Are you really so desperate to prove your case that you're grasping at children's stories now? Please don't tell me you're actually putting stock in ridiculous mythology. I know that you're on edge about what happened, but don't be an idiot."

"I'm not just talking about old mythology. I'm a scholar. I understand that histories need to be taken with more than a grain of salt. But there are innumerable accounts in not only our history, but other races as well. The humans and Ellundara both have old stories detailing the power of the ancient Seri. Power that nearly destroyed our race, culminated in our civilization being knocked down a peg. The power corrupted those strong enough to wield it, turned them into...something else."

Neph rolled his eyes. "So, what? You think that Piri is wired like one of our mythological ancestors and that he's going to go crazy and destroy the world? I'm pretty sure we just established that he recently did the exact opposite of that. And as far as Sendaryn goes, the man is an asshole and always has been. I'm not afraid of Sendaryn."

Arafel stood up. "Just please think about this and keep an eye on him, will you? He's not wired like the rest of us. And after what happened, who knows how he might have changed. He merged with the Dark, Nephael. We don't know what sort of lasting effects there might be from using that sort of power, especially on, well, him."

Neph stood up as well, matching Arafel's faltering gaze. "Get out."

"Neph -"

"I said *get out.*"

With a nod, Arafel turned on his heel and strode to the door. He paused in the doorway and turned back, eyes narrowed. "You may not be afraid of Sendaryn, but you should be." Neph watched his retreating form as it slipped out the door and vanished.

"He might be right you know."

It was barely a whisper, but Neph nearly jumped out of his skin. Piri was standing in the bedroom door, having come out, silent as a wraith. He certainly looked like one. His pale skin was covered in slowly healing wounds and deep bruises wound up his arms and legs. The black and blue mark that ran down the right side of his face only served to highlight the healing gash across his eye and the slightly skewed bandage wound around his head covered a wound beneath his hair line. Neph couldn't help but flinch at the sight, despite how much better he looked than even just a week before. The scrawl of Vharga had thankfully vanished with Merythalis.

"You shouldn't be out of bed…"

Piri ignored him and limped his way over to the couch, collapsing onto it, wincing. "I've been in bed for…-" he paused.

"Months," Neph weakly filled in for him.

"Thank you. Descriptive. I'm tired of being in bed." His lips thinned, twitching into a humorless smile. "Though, to be fair, I suppose I wasn't awake for most of it."

Neph sat down beside him. "I wish you hadn't heard that. And Sendaryn is the least of my concerns -"

"I wasn't talking about Sendaryn. I meant what he said about me."

He lapsed into silence, his hands folded in his lap, tightly clasped together to keep them from shaking.

"Piri?"

Drawing a deep breath, he looked up. Neph was slightly taken aback at the fear he could clearly see there.

"I need to show you something. And…I'm scared, Neph. I don't know what it means. It might not mean anything, but…"

He shakily stood and summoned his wings, slowly spreading them wide. Neph's breath caught in this throat as he stared at them. They were shimmering midnight and shone with an eerie light, the same as they had been on the bridge. 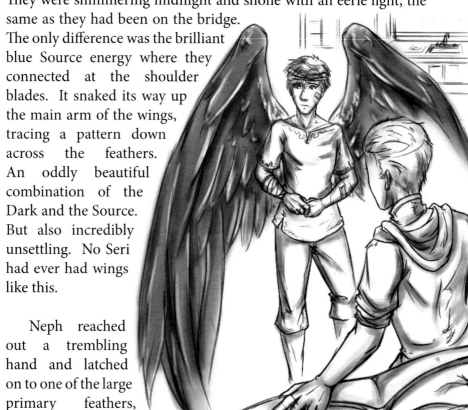 The only difference was the brilliant blue Source energy where they connected at the shoulder blades. It snaked its way up the main arm of the wings, tracing a pattern down across the feathers. An oddly beautiful combination of the Dark and the Source. But also incredibly unsettling. No Seri had ever had wings like this.

Neph reached out a trembling hand and latched on to one of the large primary feathers, running his fingers down the barb. He could actually feel the hum of energy running through it. A shiver ran through the feather at his touch and it quickly vanished, dissolving in his fingers. Piri sat back down, arms wrapped around himself, looking as if he was going to be sick. Neph's heart nearly broke looking at him sitting there; weak, shaking, injured and terrified of himself. He wrapped his arms around him, pulling him across his chest as he pushed himself into the corner of the couch. Piri was still shaking, his breathing slightly ragged as he fought to keep himself in control. Neph buried his face in his hair and closed his eyes, holding him tightly.

"I love you, and no matter what happens, I'm here. And I'll always be here. I don't care what anyone else says. I'm not going to love you any less because you channel energy differently from the rest of us or because you have a strange history. That's part of what makes you who you are. One of the reasons I love you is *because* you're different from everyone else. If life winds up being you and me versus the world, at least we'll fight it together. And to be honest, the wings are kind of beautiful. They suit you."

"You know we need to talk," Piri said, voice trembling slightly. "There's…a lot."

"I know. But it can wait."

He could feel Piri's fingers plucking at his shirt and he smiled slightly. It was a nervous tick, something he often did when he was thinking. Neither said anything for several minutes.

Piri's hand finally stilled. "Did you really mean that? About the wings?"

"I wouldn't have said it if I hadn't meant it." Neph paused. "Reva's going to be jealous you know. I caught her trying to dye her feathers one day, trying to match her hair I suspect. Obviously, it didn't work. I'm not entirely sure why she thought it would."

Piri laughed weakly, but Neph could tell he was on the verge of sleep again. He shifted slightly, sliding down a bit on the couch. He could feel the rhythm of Piri's breathing changing against his chest.

He pushed a stray bit of hair from his forehead and settled in.

The Small Council sat around the large, circular table. Nephael's seat was noticeably vacant. Many of the members looked frayed and frustrated. The discussion, more of an argument, had been going in circles.

"He needs to be taken care of," Sendaryn snarled, angrily leaning forward in his seat, brows knitted.

"Let it be, Sendaryn. Enpirion isn't a threat anymore. And Nephael can be a dangerous enemy when pushed too far. He already dislikes you, try not to piss him off any further."

Sendaryn forced a mocking laugh and stood up, moving to the window. He stared out at the mountainous vista beyond the meeting room, hands clasped behind his back. "Are you all blind? You know what he did and you all know I was right. You're sorely mistaken if you think he's no longer a threat. He's more a threat now than he's ever been. I know what he's capable of and now he wields a power far greater than any Seri in centuries." He turned to face the group, face contorting in anger as he slammed his hands down on the table. "Just because Nephael has taken him for a pet doesn't mean that he's been tamed."

Bayn rolled his eyes, "Charming as always, Sen. You do realize that those two are practically inseparable. Especially since the incident. Get a grip on yourself and stop acting like Nephael's adopted some sort of dangerous creature he found wandering out of the Veil."

"Bayn's right, Sendaryn. Whatever Enpirion was, he isn't anymore. Let's be honest, Nephael was the best thing that ever happened to that kid, both for him personally and for the rest of us. I suggest you let this thing drop. And I'm fairly certain that the rest of the Council agrees with me." Evari glanced around the table meaningfully.

Merrant had remained quiet through the entire discussion and he finally placed his hands flat on the table and cleared his throat. "I agree that the discussion should be put to rest for the time being. Nephael is a highly valued officer and member of this council and Enpirion is an excellent soldier. I feel very strongly that it should not even need to be stated that he is an intelligent Seri who should not be idly discussed as though he is some brutish, dumb beast. I'm also sure," he looked pointedly at Sendaryn, "that I needn't remind anyone that Enpirion has put his life on the line several times in defense of The Watch and, more recently, nearly sacrificed his life to save all of us. It was happy circumstance that he survived the incident."

Sendaryn snorted. Several members of the Council nodded in agreement, though just as many looked away uncomfortably.

"That being said, you are all aware that the Ruling Council does not necessarily agree with me on this. But for us, I believe that we have wasted enough time on this matter and I would hope that it does not come up again unless there is significant reason."

Standing up from the table he began to move towards the door, hands clasped before him, a strained smile on his calm face that did not extend to the angry, cold eyes above it. With general nods of agreement, the other Council members began to rise and silently move towards the door. Only Sendaryn lagged behind, staring out the window, past the mountains, at a distant point on the horizon.

Piri's Sketchbook: Excerpts

About the Author

    I was formerly a fashion designer and graphic designer, creating everything from footwear and apparel to tradeshow booths and marketing materials. From the time I've been young, I've held an intimate love for both art and writing. This project has allowed me to merge those together and create something special.

    While I work in pencils, acrylics and oils, my true love and the medium I most commonly work with is digital. I spend most of my time in Photoshop CS6 on my trusty 13" Cintiq.

    I have 10 years of experience in the fashion industry and over 15 in art and graphic design. Trained for the game industry at DigiPen Institute of Technology, I currently freelance to the industry as well as doing private commissions and contract graphic design work.

piriproject.com